GW00467953

PRAISE FOR *

'It was not until I finished it ~~that I realised how many~~ ~~~~
*and turns the book had taken me on, because they were
subtle and clever.'*

Helen Jennings, Amazon.co.uk

*'...the edgy dance between a glossy cover model and more than
one mad, bad and dangerous-to-know Broadmoor inhabitant
was completely gripping.'*

Amazon Customer, Amazon.co.uk

'...gripping from the very first page.'

Jill Burkinshaw, Amazon.co.uk

PRAISE FOR **HEARTBREAKER**

*'Nick Louth somehow transforms the stuff you half-hear on the
breakfast news to an utterly believable and multi-layered narrative.'*

Amazon Customer, Amazon.co.uk

*'I loved this book from start to finish. A gripping page-turning
thriller with plenty of twists and clever turns. The author
obviously delves into his own experiences to portray with
panache the complex and confusing Middle East conflict.'*

Estuary, Amazon.co.uk

PRAISE FOR **BITE**

'*Fast, smart and terrifyingly plausible. Bite is a thoroughly assured thriller with an unusual and alarming setting – it sinks its hooks into the reader from the first chapter and does not let go.*'
Jon Henley, *Guardian* journalist

'*A fast-paced thrill-ride, a book that I couldn't put down and that took me on a journey of fear.*'
Linda Mather, author of *Gut Instinct*

'*The depth of the author's research is staggering. His story, and the accompanying sub-plots, are entirely convincing and held my attention from beginning to end. A thriller in every sense of the word.*'
John Leach, Amazon.co.uk

Nick Louth is a best-selling thriller writer, award-winning financial journalist and an investment commentator. He has been a regular contributor to the *Financial Times*, *Investors Chronicle* and *Money Observer*, and has published seven other books. Nick Louth is married and lives in Lincolnshire.

www.nicklouth.com

Mirror Mirror

NICK LOUTH

To Ruth,

with best wishes

Nick Louth

LUDENSIAN BOOKS

Oct 2016

First published in Great Britain in 2016
by Ludensian Books

www.ludensianbooks.co.uk
www.nicklouth.com

Copyright © Nick Louth 2016

The right of Nick Louth to be identified as the Author has been asserted in
accordance with the Copyright, Design and Patents Act 1988.

eBook ISBN: 9780955493959
Paperback ISBN: 9780955493966

British Library Cataloguing in Publication Data
A CIP catalogue record for this book can be obtained
from the British Library

*This is a work of fiction. Any resemblance between the characters herein and
real persons living or otherwise is purely coincidental.*

For Louise

Chapter One

It was the night of her twenty-third birthday. Surely she should be granted a wish? A desperate little prayer to save her life? That now, nearly midnight on a wild and rainswept January Saturday, someone should drive along the B6478 in Lancashire's Forest of Bowland, near the village of Thewick. That on this lonely rural road they would notice Lowe Mill Barn, a converted stone farmhouse, isolated on the shoulder of Easington Fell. They would see her trapped in the first floor bathroom, the only light for miles, banging frantically on the window. They would hear her screaming for help and the repeated booms of the locked door which was being kicked down by a man intent on killing her. And they would rescue her.

She needed a prayer. She was bruised, bleeding and defenceless. No phone, no money, no shoes. Just pyjamas, and a grey hooded jogging top grabbed from the bedroom when she fled. All she wanted was someone to hear her screams, someone to fetch help, someone to save her. Someone. Anyone. Anyone at all.

For five desperate minutes there had been no one. No car, van or truck. No pedestrians, no late-night dog walkers. Only the scudding clouds, the lashing rain, and the howling wind. And an empty, narrow, winding road.

Everything now depended on her own decisions. Her tactics, her determination, her survival skills. Her only ally was the solid oak bathroom door, with its good iron bolt and mortice lock, plus the heavy antique linen box she had wedged against it. Each kick still made the door shudder. She had to get out, before he got in. But how? The old sash window over the washbasin was tight, and would only slide up eighteen inches. Then it was a fifteen foot drop onto a gravel drive. She threw some towels out, to cushion her fall but the wind whipped them away. She climbed onto the basin, and began to squeeze out, feet first, face down, holding onto the taps. Her cut lip spattered the porcelain crimson as she wriggled out into the freezing cold and driving rain, until finally her arms were fully extended. She listened, trying to screen out the pounding on the door.

She dropped. The pain of landing made her cry out, but she had to move. Fast. That bathroom door would be broken down in a moment, and he would be after her. She hobbled down the short drive to the road, her feet stinging. There she had a choice. Going right led into the village four or so miles downhill, normally an easy jogging distance. But not barefoot. She knew too that if she followed it she would be found and murdered, because this was the logical way to run. For safety, for survival. And he would follow. Going left, she might escape him, but at what cost? It would take her high into the moors. No houses, nothing, for many miles. She could quickly die of exposure waiting for a car-borne saviour.

As she dithered she heard behind her Lawrence's bellow of fury as he finally burst into the bathroom. Still there was no car. The next one now would be his black Range Rover, pursuing her. In this rage he would run her down, the same way he had knocked down and then reversed over the cyclist in Manchester.

Cross-country was the safest way, through the garden and out into the rough pastures and the myriad stone-walled fields. A slower and colder way down to the village, but safer. She ran back up the drive, and ducked under the arched hedge. The damp turf felt freezing under her feet as she edged along to the stile, beyond the light from the bathroom, a light which was now her enemy. Her bruised feet welcomed the numbing cold. She had walked this footpath only yesterday, enjoying the cream stone byres and gurgling brooks, the rustic gates, and the memories it had brought back. But now, effectively blind, under the soughing and groaning branches, and chilled by rain-laden gusts, it was alive with danger. Rough stones from tumbled walls on which to stub her tender toes, windblown sticks, brambles and nettles, all cloaked by darkness. Far to the south, way beyond Thewick, the clouds held the faint reflected orange glow of the lights of Clitheroe, a town she had once called home. One of many fleeting childhood homes in the north of England, from a time when flight and fear had been a way of life. Against the glow she could see dripping jagged branches of blackthorn, dotted with shrivelled sloes, swaying in the gale. The slimy wooden plank stile, edged with barbed wire, was next to it. She tore the leg of her pyjamas getting over, and at the bottom put her foot in something soft, that squeezed between her toes. The sound of the Range Rover, and the sweep of headlights made her duck. The far end of the field, two hundred yards ahead, was briefly illuminated, showing a wooden ladder stile over a high stone wall. She made for that point, running close to the left hand wall which bordered the road. The rough stone construction was a man's height and reassuringly solid, enough to shield her from the road and from some of the freezing rain. The Range Rover shot past towards the village, the gunned engine indicating that his fury had not subsided.

Relaxing just a little as the engine faded into the distance she smashed her foot on something metal and fell in agony. It was an abandoned rusty harrow, almost swallowed by encroaching grassy tussocks. Her left foot bleeding and throbbing, she hobbled carefully down the length of the field, her eyes gradually becoming more accustomed to the darkness. She climbed the ladder stile, into another long and hummocky field, and then stumbled down to another stile at the end. She climbed and looked over the top into a farm track, like a dark canal between high stone walls. Opposite was another high ladder stile. She climbed down into the puddled lane and listened carefully, considering whether to turn right. This lane she recalled led eventually to the rear grounds of Hooksworth Hall, a crumbling manor house now being renovated by the National Trust. Partially roofless, shrouded in scaffolding and uninhabited, there was perhaps refuge there from the weather, but nothing more.

She had just started to edge right along the lane when she heard ahead of her a ticking sound, as of cooling metal, and saw the faintest of reflections from a chrome trim a few dozen yards further on. Dazzling lights flicked on, and an engine gunned into life. She threw herself forward towards the stile, leaping up to the top rung just in time. The Range Rover shot past, the wing mirror smacking her trailing ankle as she threw herself over the wall. Landing in a heap on the other side, she rolled onto her back as she heard the car door open and heavy footsteps ascend the ladder.

'I know where you are, you slippery bitch.' The voice was slurred. Drunk.

She crawled into the lee of the wall, trying to insinuate herself into the hewn fabric of rough but comforting stone, the soaking pads of lichen and moss; petrified, that's exactly what she was. She smeared mud on her face and her hood, and sank her feet into the freezing ooze between a bank of thistles and a hawthorn bush. Lawrence had a torch, and was cursing her as he climbed the stile. She held her breath. She was never going to escape. Lawrence Wall was a world-class athlete, adored by millions, a man who had built a career from speed, strength and intimidation on the pitch, whose name was a chant that rang round the stadium before the start of every match.

'The Wall, the Wall don't never cross the Wall, no way, no way, not any fucking day.'

The rhyme rang in her head as she tried to still her panicky, ragged breathing. The torch light shone down, sliding over the lumps and bumps of misplaced stones and the straggly rosehips that sprouted through the craggy fissures in the wall. The beam crossed her mud-caked feet not once but twice. Now she was a piece of landscape, as fluid as mud, as cold as stone. The light then swung out into the field, left and right. It picked out the reflective eyes of a score of cattle only a dozen yards away, brooding and implacable, clouds of vapour rising from their cud-sodden mouths.

The vision triggered a groan from her pursuer. This was a chance. Lawrence was a city boy. Even getting him here for a supposedly romantic weekend two months into their relationship had been a trial. He preferred terraced streets to hills, motorways to lanes, and manicured stadium turf to its real country cousin. Countryside was as much a mystery to him as the moons of Neptune. He'd never admit to being afraid of cattle, or afraid of anything. But actions speak louder. He wouldn't follow her there. Five freezing rain-sodden minutes passed, and she heard him get back into the Range Rover and roar off.

* * *

Mick Tasker rarely got to bed before one-thirty on a Saturday night, otherwise he might have missed it. He and Mary had been the licensees of The Hare at Thewick for only a few weeks, and balancing the till, clearing the bars and correctly loading the idiosyncratic dishwasher still took time. The locals were always reluctant to head off home before midnight, especially on a night like tonight. Squally rain had been forecast, and at seven that evening it had swept in from the Irish Sea and across the hills and vales of Lancashire. Mick had stoked the fireplaces in the two lounges and the snug while rain dripped from the moss-blocked gutters and pattered on the metal tables still stacked outside from the long-forgotten summer. The pub's rusting metal sign squeaked in the wind, and the weed-strewn hanging baskets twisted on their chains. With all that racket they might have been at sea. It would certainly have been easy to miss the frantic knocking at the kitchen door. Mary was already in bed, and the bar staff had long gone home. Wiping his hands on a tea towel Mick walked through the still-lit kitchen, and saw a tallish figure in a filthy grey hooded top banging on the window.

'We're long closed, mate. Go home to bed,' he said in his most authoritative tone. He didn't know all the locals yet, but there were some he'd seen already who didn't know when enough was enough.

'Please, I need the police. My boyfriend attacked me. Please, I'm freezing.' A woman's voice, educated. Not a local accent. There was blood and dirt on the pane where she'd pressed her face and filthy hands against the glass.

'Don't you have a mobile?'

'He's got it, and my purse, everything. Please. Please. Please.'

'Alright, alright.' With a heavy sigh, Mick undid the lock, and opened the door a crack. He saw a flash of pleading green eyes under the soaking hood. Rain-darkened hair framed a muddy face, and a top lip crusted with blood. Thin, soaked pyjama

7

bottoms, spattered with blood, bruised and swollen feet. She was shivering.

'You had better come in, love. Christ, you are in a state,' he said. 'I'll get you a towel.'

'Thank you so much.'

She flipped down the hood, and despite the mud, the bruises and the matted hair, Mick absorbed the slender neck, the curves, the poise, the class. He realised with a jolt that she wasn't wearing any underwear.

Mary had come downstairs and was framed in the doorway in a bathrobe, watching the girl wiping mud off her face and legs with the hand towel Mick had given her. 'What's happened?'

'Beaten up by the boyfriend,' Mick said, indicating the woman with his thumb, as if it happened every day. 'Wants us to phone the bobbies.'

'They'll not come out all the way from Clitheroe, duck. Not this late. Not for a domestic. What we've got to do is get you out of those wet clothes, before you die of cold. What's your name?'

'Call me Lydia.' She flashed a quick but dazzling smile, shyly pulling a hank of hair across the swelling bruise below her eye.

'Earth calling Mick,' Mary said, prodding him in the back. 'Stop gawping and get her a brandy, while I find her something to wear. She'll need ice for that eye.'

When he returned from the bar, Mick found the woman in the snug, on a wooden chair close to the fire wearing his bathrobe and holding an ice pack to her eye. He gave her the drink. 'On the house on this occasion, but please don't tell the locals.'

'Thank you so much.'

'You're welcome.' Realising he was staring again, he then set to at the fire where the dying embers were receptive to some judicious poking.

Mary arrived with the cordless phone. 'Is there anyone who can come pick you up?'

'I'm sorry, I don't know anyone in the area. Do you mind if I make an international call?'

Mick heard his own sharp intake of breath. 'Of course,' he heard himself say, surprised at his largesse.

'I'll be quite quick and I'll pay you back.' That smile again. 'Thank you very much.'

Mary guided Mick away, telling him to organise a hot bath, turn on the electric blanket in the spare room, and get some fluffy socks warmed on the radiator. She went to look for bandages, scissors and antiseptic. A little later Mick found himself outside the bathroom door, listening to Lydia sobbing in the bath. The face he had glimpsed seemed somehow familiar, not a person he knew as such, but one that reminded him of some glamorous TV actress, though he couldn't think who might be about in this neck of the woods. Through the frosted glass the girl's long back was a slender pink blancmange topped by a dark swirl of hair. He tapped on the glass and asked her if she needed a cup of tea. She sniffed, thanked him and said yes please, but did not turn around as he had hoped.

'I'll get it,' Mary said, manhandling Mick away from the door.

'Did you see her feet?' he said. 'They are in a terrible state. They really need bandaging.'

'Well, don't you even think of offering to do it. First aid certificate, or no first aid certificate, Michael Philip Tasker. I'll do it.' She wagged a warning finger at him.

The mood of suspicion lasted until Mary had taken care of the girl, shown her into one of the guest rooms and had come to join him in bed. As she slipped under the covers, Mary tossed him the copy of *Marie Claire* magazine from her bedside table. He picked it up and gasped at the cover. ' "Mira Roskova: The new face of beauty"? Never heard of her.'

'Now there's a surprise. Advertises posh shampoo, lovely Swiss chocolates, designer handbags, Asprey's jewellery. Pretty much everything I never get bought,' Mary said, flicking absent-mindedly through a copy of *Cosmopolitan*.

'But she said she was Lydia.'

'Oh get a grip, Mick. Really.'

* * *

Mira lay very still in a bed she had never wanted to return to, watching an unwelcome Sunday morning slide in through Lowe Mill Barn's pale yellow curtains. The clock showed ten forty-five. Lawrence was out of it, rumbling away; a dormant cider-drenched volcano. In the half light he was a brutalist monument: giant concrete shoulder, a blue-green python of an arm sleeved in tattoos and a craggy crop-haired boulder of a head, with that scorpion tattoo on the scalp that she had never liked.

They had made up, after a fashion. Diane had been right. Mira was so glad she had managed to get through from the pub phone to her agent in New York. Even from the sidelines of some glitzy Manhattan soirée, Diane Glassman had all the answers: keep calm. Do not get the police involved. Consider your image. Don't blow it, not now. There will be better moments to ease yourself gracefully away from this animal. Wait until he's sober. Ring him. Pout, play vulnerable but whatever you do do not attempt to rehash the row. You can get even later, I promise. We'll figure it out.

Mira had rung Lawrence at eight in the morning from the pub. On the third attempt he'd woken to take the call. She used her 'little girl lost' voice, and he immediately apologised. Didn't know what came over him. It was the booze. And he had said he loved her. It was the first time he'd ever said that. If that's love, she thought, I don't want to see hate. But she'd agreed to let him drive over and get her, reluctantly, if only because everything she needed – money, phone, flat keys – were all there with him at Lowe Mill Barn. She was dog-tired, and so had agreed to stay for a few hours. If only sleep had been possible next to a man of whom she was now terrified.

She had been an idiot. Fooled from the first by his energy and zest. Initially it was attractive, sexy, irresistible, a flame of spontaneity. Flying to Barcelona for the afternoon, Monaco just for lunch. Lawrence buying her a soft-top Porsche because she had casually admired one. Pleading for her to cancel a shoot to come see him in an FA Cup tie. Even unzipping himself and demanding her mouth while they were stuck in a traffic jam on the M25. Passion, energy, impatience. She had convinced herself that this heady cocktail was only a manifestation of a mayfly soccer career. Catapulted to stardom at sixteen and peaking within a decade. No time to lose, ever. As he described it ninety minutes was often enough for an affair, with a fifteen minute break before swapping ends. If so, she now realised, seven and a bit weeks was nearly a marriage.

Later she had begun to see him for the monstrous child he was, indulged by riches and fortified by impunity; physical, financial and even legal. Every photograph of him, jaw set, dripping with sweat and saliva, bellowing, pointing, demanding. A huge arm enforced the singular physicality of him. A hard man. An alpha male on steroids. A man infamous for his massive tackle. A man who believed in God but not foreplay. A man who always got his way, who chopped down opponents on their way to his penalty box. Lawrence Wall didn't just believe rules were made to be broken. Rules were made to be annihilated.

Ten hours ago Lawrence had punched her in the face because she foolishly revealed a secret she had long kept. The enormity of that secret passed him by, but not the fact that it was about another man. A man whom she had adored. Lawrence, once married and even then a serial adulterer, could tolerate no other male in his women's lives, not even in their past. Lawrence was a man jealous even of memories.

From what she had seen last night, Lawrence Wall was easily capable of killing. He'd told her so. He had picked up the entire sofa on which she was sitting. She only just jumped off in time before he hurled it through Lowe Mill Barn's bay window. 'I come from a mad family,' he had shouted through the bathroom door. 'Fucking mental. Did you know that? So don't you ever cross Lawrence Wall. Or you'll end up dead.'

Then this morning, in a torrent of apologies, he had begged her to promise she would never leave him. And for the sake of peace, she had made the promise. Now, cleverly, and with all her considerable guile, she had to break that promise. She had to break off their stormy relationship and live to tell the tale. And she had to hope against hope that he would never realise the danger in that terrible secret she had revealed. Silently, she slipped out of bed, dressed quietly, gathered up keys, purse and phone. Then fled to her car.

Chapter Two

Sunday

Thad Cobalt, chief talent architect at Stardust Brands, took the call from Mira's agent Diane Glassman at breakfast time on Sunday. As director of Mira's brand, Thad orchestrated her product endorsements, personal couture and style signifiers, and most importantly, tried to protect her from reputational damage.

Lawrence Wall looked like being some serious reputational damage.

By lunchtime he had convened an emergency meeting of Team Mira in the breakfast room of his Pimlico home, with Portia Casals, senior creative and curator of Mira's online presence, and Jonesy Tolling, PR consultant.

'I spoke with Mira this morning about the attack,' Thad said in his soft transatlantic drawl. 'She is really upset and now completely terrified of Lawrence Wall. He really knocked her about.'

'Oh poor thing!' said Portia. A former JWT advertising copywriter, Portia wrote Mira's fashion, fitness and lifestyle blogs, authored her tweets and directed the external agency which ran her various websites and fanzines. 'Is she injured?'

'It's serious enough: a big black eye, facial and neck bruises and lots of scratches from running barefoot through fields to get away from him,' said Thad.

'That's Monday's effing Dolce & Gabbana shoot in Milan kiboshed,' said Jonesy, swigging the remains of his gin and tonic. 'Four weeks graft down the khazi. Diane will not be happy.' Jonesy was an ex-Sunday Mirror celeb journalist, a no-nonsense down-to-earth south Londoner with a gift for PR, and a retro taste in big boozy lunches which showed in his expanding waistline and grotesque expenses bill.

'Where is Mira now?' Portia asked.

'In a private medical clinic in Manchester,' Thad said. 'After treatment, I've arranged her a private flight to a spa retreat in Ireland with orders not to go out in public for a few days, at least until the bruises can be covered by make-up and sunglasses. From there she'll fly off for ten days at Paulsen Edelweiss's private Caribbean island.'

'Always nice to have a spare billionaire knocking about when you need one,' murmured Portia.

'More important is that she will be out of reach of the paparazzi,' Thad said. 'Edelweiss won't be there, he's in Vegas apparently, but his people say he is happy to let her have the run of the place. He's offered to reserve all the mainland helicopters so the photographers can't go snooping overhead.'

'That's very thoughtful,' Jonesy said, with an expression that conveyed other motives.

'Now, I have already explained to Mira that we have to strategise this from a branding and PR point of view,' Thad said. 'She mustn't answer any calls or do anything vis-à-vis Lawrence Wall without discussing it with us.'

'But what about the police?' Portia said. 'News is bound to get out.'

'They haven't been told,' Thad said. 'Diane told Mira to hold off, and I agree…'

'What? Are you mad?' exclaimed Portia.

'The publicity would be a disaster, of course, given the delicate stage of talks with Suressence.' They all knew that a tie-up with the French skincare group, under negotiation now for months, was vital. Potentially worth ten million over five years, it would treble the value of all Mira's deals to date, and finally bring her into the endorsement big league, within sight of Gisele Bündchen, Beyoncé and Maria Sharapova.

'Portia,' said Jonesy, 'it's my job to assess the PR. If we go public, I guarantee you our beautiful green-eyed brand asset would be left lying in the gutter like a piece of effing roadkill.' His job was not only to place Mira in the public eye, but to do so in a way that burnished her brand, adding value to her endorsement deals and the products of the firms which underwrote them. Rumour had it that he was unbearably bad-tempered when sober, a rumour that few ever had the chance to test. No one meeting him for the first time would guess that his real name was Lionel Jones-Tolling, that his father was an Appeal Court judge and that he'd been to prep school, Winchester and Oxford. Jonesy's most audacious piece of PR reinvention was himself, as the working class kid made good.

'But people will really, really sympathise with her,' Portia insisted. 'It could help.'

'They sympathised with Nigella Lawson too,' Thad said gently. 'She was the victim of a public attack by her partner, but then someone dug up details of her drug habit. You know, once things go public, everyone gets damaged. Nigella's celebrity chef brand is robust and well-established. Domestic goddesses may get second chances, Mira may not. So we can't risk it. Especially not right now.'

'It was a criminal assault,' Portia shrilled, her bangles jangling as she smacked the table for emphasis. 'We can't let this animal get away with it,' she said.

'Oh, but he will,' Jonesy said, shaking his head at the inevitability of it. 'Lawrence Wall is an irreplaceable footballing asset with a global following, worth thirty million in the transfer market, and at least ten million a year in endorsements. The club can't afford to let him go to jail. *Ergo*, top barrister, bottomless funds. Even if he was convicted, his lawyers would dig up enough dirt to make Mira look like a spoiled gold digger with the morals of a skunk.'

'Your approach is morally *wrong*.' Portia's fleshy face was burning with righteous indignation as she stared at her male colleagues.

'That's a relief. Principle always gets in the way of profit,' Jonesy chuckled, turning his pen over and over between his fat fingers. 'Going public on this now is a classic Preventable Fuck-Up, and I have said time and again, our main job as brand managers is to head off all PFUs.'

'This is more important than her bloody brand, it's about her dignity,' Portia insisted.

'Listen. In 2011, Lawrence Wall stood trial for running down and killing a cyclist in Manchester, remember that?' Jonesy said.

'I think so, yes. Didn't he reverse over the chap?' Portia said.

'Very good. Yes, "allegedly",' Jonesy said, rabbit-earing his fingers. 'He was originally charged with voluntary manslaughter for driving while texting. But his legal team not only got the judge to defer the case for six weeks so he could train for England's match against Brazil, they then destroyed the character and reliability of the only witness. In the end Wall pleaded guilty to the lesser charge of driving without due care and attention. Six points on his licence and sixty hours community service. A nothing sentence, and even that was cut to twenty hours on appeal.'

'That's disgusting!'

Jonesy shrugged. 'Portia, I deal in the world as it is. Money talks.'

Thad raise his hands. 'Look, Portia, we'll take better care of Mira by preserving her career than by playing Russian roulette in the courts. We've got to play a cool game. Diane suggested a four-stage strategy. First, no police complaint. Second, we keep her hidden from the press for a while. Third, we take control of the narrative if the story of the assault does emerge into the public domain. Fourth, she works with us to distance herself from Lawrence Wall gracefully over the longer term. Does everyone agree?'

Portia's shoulders slumped as she assented.

'So, onto points two and three of our strategy. What are the chances of this assault on her getting into the tabloids, Jonesy?' Thad asked.

'Depends if someone snapped a pic of her with bruises,' Jonesy said. 'If they did, we're stuffed. Without it, the story's deniable. The signs are pretty good. I've already spoken to the couple at the pub, who are the only sources who could back it up,' Jonesy said. 'We're offering them five grand for their help and hospitality to Mira, so long as they sign the non-disclosure form. If anything appears in the press our lawyers will eviscerate them.'

'Okay,' Thad said, steepling his hands. 'Portia, get Kelly to scour social media for any hint of this news, and let Jonesy know straightaway. Jonesy, I want our version of events ready for publication if needed. Mira's vulnerability, her innocence. Christ, I mean on this occasion the truth should actually do the job. We don't need to make anything up.'

'On point four, what about a bodyguard?' Portia said.

'That's already in hand,' Thad said. 'This time we're getting someone good and experienced, who'll be up to the job. He made a name for himself fighting the Taliban. Should be good enough to handle even Lawrence Wall.'

Chapter Three

'*Incoming. Get **down** you idiot.*' The first giant bang woke Virgil Bliss immediately, his hand scrabbling for his Glock 17 even before his eyes had opened. He could not find it, and as his panic rose the dream receded to the grind and clang of a Southwark Council bin lorry twelve floors below. A huge exhalation. He turned over and felt the springs of his mum's worn-out couch jab his ribs with the reminder: here there is no Glock, no Helmand, no grots, no boot polishing, no rig-cleaning. No IEDs neither. No fear, no pain. No-one to call him a fucking wog. Yeah, no Sergeant Davies. Just good old south east London on a damp January morning. The clock showed a quarter to seven. O-six forty-five hours, as he used to know it. He yawned extravagantly, listening to the huge communal bins still undergoing their square bashing. He'd been settee surfing for months now, wearing out his welcome in the spare bedrooms of mates, and finally ending up back here on the Walworth Road, in Mum's two-bed flat on the Castlemead Estate. Virgil's caramel-coloured feet poked out over one worn

Paisley-pattern arm, his nut-brown shaven head propped by a lumpy pillow on the other. It ain't Helmand, this life, but it ain't perfect. No job, no woman, no money and another twelve days till the benefit payment.

Virgil got up and made a brew in the pokey kitchen, with its lemon yellow walls and 1960s glass-fronted cupboards. On them were cling film wrapped postcards from extended family in Lagos and Abuja, Mum's little fragments of girlhood heat and colour that still inspired her soul, but left his cold. London was his home, both real and imagined. This flat was even smaller than the grots in Helmand, but his long-suffering mum had managed fine in it for thirty years. Without a reliable man, with hardly any money, she had brought up both of them, while getting up at silly-o'clock every morning to clean endless washbasins and khazis at King's College Hospital. His younger brother, Troy, had done well. A trainee ophthalmologist. At least he had work and his own flat.

Virgil rubbed his aching neck. At twenty-eight years old what did he have to show for his life? Nine GCSEs, four A levels and one term at Leeds University, to study psychology of all things. Dropped out, joined up. Royal Green Jackets, F Coy, 2 Rifles. Two tours of Helmand, and lucky with it. Only one minor injury, completed four years. Still, the things he'd seen. Terrible. Then back in Blighty. Couldn't stand the dull routine back in Catterick. Resigned to take up a bit of close protection work for a South African businessman in Nigeria. That's where the smattering of Yoruba and Hausa he'd learned from his grandmother gave him a leg up. That was only for a month. But

21

while he was in Lagos, he hooked up with a Paris-based outfit doing close protection work for diplomats and NGOs across West Africa. While still on probation, he'd been given a junior role for a hush-hush UNHCR diplomatic fact-finding mission to Chad. He and a dozen others, half of them ex Foreign Legion weirdos with wolfish eyes and bad breath, spent two days boiling their arses off at a dusty airport in Njadamena waiting for the big cheese who would lead the mission. It was fifty degrees of short-temper, taunted by the shimmering mirage of Lake Chad in the northerly distance. The rumour was that it would be Tony Blair, or Hillary Clinton. But when the private jet arrived, there was a tiny little old guy, a former president of Botswana who nobody had heard of. This guy only stayed half an hour while the jet refuelled, politely shook each of their hands, then headed off to Cairo. This was much to the irritation of the legionnaires, who muttered to each other about some *petit noir bâtard* wasting their time, until Virgil verballed that he himself was a *grande* black bastard, who also spoke French. That shut them up, but he never got any more work from them. The Paris outfit allegedly folded for some reason a month later and he never got his full pay.

The final job was the weirdest. A skincare entrepreneur had been threatened by UK-based animal rights extremists. Based in LA, he was well protected himself, but was worried about his London-based ex-wife and their seven-year-old daughter. For the first week Virgil's job seemed to involve being an overpaid childminder, until one cold November day when he arrived to pick up the girl from her private school, he found her emerging from the gates struggling to remove a wrapper from a Magnum ice cream. She was defensive about where she'd got it, but eventually said the mother of a new girl at the school had just given it to her. Virgil helped take the wrapper off, but noticed a tiny hole in the chocolate coating. He rushed the girl home, with the ice cream sealed in a bag of frozen peas to stop it melting. Chemical analysis confirmed that the ice cream had been injected with strychnine. The ex and her daughter were whisked abroad the next day. Virgil got huge thanks and a hefty payoff, most of it deferred for a year on condition he didn't speak to the press. There was ten months still to run, and he no longer had the job.

Today's dilemma was simpler. He was torn between going to the Job Centre to embroider a story of looking for work to please the Benefits Agency, or a quick bacon sandwich down at the greasy spoon to please himself. The sizzle at Tucker's Tuckstop was definitely ahead. Virgil took a quick glance at the leaden skies and the damp pavements, then pulled on his red hoodie, jogging trousers and a pair of trainers.

It was then his phone rang. Not a number on his contact list, so he answered it cautiously. Probably his payday lender again, pound to a penny, just like their rate of interest.

'Lance Corporal Virgil Bliss, Royal Green Jackets,' came a crisp authoritative Scottish burr. It wasn't phrased as a question, more a command.

'Yes,' he replied sibilantly, a reflex 'Sir' shaped on his lips, unvoiced at the last moment.

'Glad I've caught you, Bliss. Colonel Alasdair Forsyth, retired. I oversaw your MI interviews at Chicksands.'

'I remember.' Virgil had thought it would be worth getting into military intelligence, and had been put through his paces at the unit's Bedfordshire HQ. He recalled the colonel as a stick thin sandy-haired type, so crisply attired it looked like he'd ironed everything bar his bushy eyebrows.

'I was actually sorry we couldn't recruit you for my MI unit, Bliss. In fact, having seen your scores you would have been perfect for data analysis at Camp Bastion.'

'Thank you.'

Virgil knew he'd done fine on the interview: general knowledge, always good, well read, French and German to a good standard. They said they wanted him for MI. But that was just before HMG's latest cuts to the armed forces, deferring new recruitment. It was either take up the existing offer from the Royal Green Jackets or sling your hook.

The Green Jackets still appreciated him when they saw the MI interview scores. That raised a few eyebrows. But nothing compared to the intelligence test result. On day one in basic training at Catterick, Sergeant Davies had whispered to him during kit inspection: 'So you're the coon with the IQ of a hundred and forty-three. I should fucking cocoa. Think you can find the fucking boot polish, Einstein?'

But they had all expected him to be well hard. Black geezer from sarf London? Comes with the territory, dunnit? Sergeant Davies stuck him into the boxing ring and found he was quite tasty as a heavyweight. After a bit of a diet one year he got down to cruiserweight and made the regimental semis. Still, the British Army's assumptions hadn't changed in two centuries:

black recruits have brawn not brains.

'How did you get my mobile number, Sir?' The vocative slipped out.

'From Chacewater Associates. They've hired me for some urgent recruitment.' Virgil had registered with Chacewater months ago, and was disappointed not to have been offered anything since the childminding gig. It was a Swiss-based agency, more low-key than the big American firms, but with a good reputation.

'So Bliss, we need a close protection officer to start immediately for a very high-profile principal. As well as the usual CPO requirements, they are looking for social and diplomatic skills, and an unusual analytical role. Right up your street, Bliss, I would have thought. Interested?'

'Very much.'

'Good. Chacewater already has your full background check, but we still need a notional CV, by e-mail if you'd oblige. Can't quote details, but I think you'll find the compensation package is very good. By the way, you got an extraordinary glowing reference from one of their clients. Saved his daughter's life, apparently. Is that true?'

'Contractually, I can't comment.'

'You have good instincts, Bliss. Meet me at this address at O-nine forty-five hours tomorrow. Stardust Brands Ltd, reporting to a Mr Thad Cobalt. Interesting name, yes? I haven't met him myself yet.'

Virgil wrote down the central London location Colonel Forsyth gave him, and the e-mail address.

'And Bliss? Client's female, by the way. Young, attractive, famous. Remember which way your eyes should face.'

'Thank you, I will,' Virgil said, but the colonel had already hung up.

* * *

That night, Virgil dreamed he was back in Helmand. As so often it started with the IED blast that got Kev. He crawled over to the burning Spartan troop carrier, a track blown off, the commander dead in his turret. There were cries of pain from those inside, and frantic banging. Virgil tried to release the rear door, but it was too hot to touch. The smoke grabbed his throat, a mixture of acrid plastic and seared flesh. Then the door blew open from inside, and he stared within. He couldn't describe what he saw, but it filled him with horror. Then he was running, running for cover. He found reed beds, thick and welcoming, and soft earth. He crawled towards a darkened river, its coolness inviting. Reeds swayed, and eddies tugged at the stems. A solitary crow cracked the dusk with its cry. Tendrils of weed parted and a pale woman, swathed in white, floated slowly into view. Water lapped at her ears, her eyelids closed but still fluttering. Then suddenly, he was floating above her, close to her face. Full lips, bluish with cold and trembling, as if in silent prayer. Her hands picked at the white, richly embroidered shift which flapped slowly around her, clinging to her youthful body as she slipped down the languid watercourse. A twig cracked, and her eyes opened. Huge pale green eyes, beauty laced with fear. A shadow passed over her as the river became a calming stream. The girl looked asleep, relaxed and easy. Finally, she lifted her head from the water, smiled and opened her eyes. The eyes were horribly changed. Solid black orbs, each weeping three inky streams down her face and into the stream.

Virgil awoke gasping. He'd had the Helmand dream so many times, but this was different. The dream had morphed into a river sequence with that girl from some TV series. He'd seen it on Kev's DVDs when he was out there, just the last few minutes of the final episode. Kev had explained it to him A beautiful girl, the last surviving child of a family in a town under siege by zombies, was consigned to the water. 'These zombies, with the white faces and black tear stains, are called Qaeggan. They can't stand running water. It's the only place she's safe. So that's why she has to float down the river to get help.'

He couldn't remember the girl's name, but she was a great hit amongst the lads. Kev had a picture of her taped inside his locker. Virgil remembered that because he'd wondered whether or not to include it in Kev's personal effects to send back to his parents. 'One day, I'm gonna marry a woman like that,' Kev had said. They were the last words he'd ever said to Virgil. He was nineteen.

Chapter Four

Virgil had squeezed himself into his best dark suit and forced his way onto a packed Bakerloo Line underground train from Elephant & Castle to Piccadilly. He found MacMillan House easily enough, an anonymous 1930s frontage just off lower Regent Street. Stardust Brands was on the fourth floor, and he emerged from the lift into what looked like an advertising agency. Pop art replicas and magazine front page blow-ups lined the curved pastel-hued walls right up to the ceiling. A very tall and almost jet black receptionist with green lipstick to match her stilettos pointed him to the low tubular chairs in reception. He reclined there uncomfortably for ten minutes looking between his knees at leggy young women carrying artwork and bearded young men in T-shirts with eyebrow rings, gravity-defying quiffs and trendy beards, while sweaty package-laden cycle messengers clattered back and forth to the lift.

Colonel Forsyth arrived looking just as Virgil had remembered him, with perhaps a bit more white among the sparse sandy hair. He'd obviously tried to dress casually, but his country-tweed jacket, regimental tie, carefully pressed charcoal grey trousers and mirror-shined black brogues made him look like a relic. Thank God he hadn't worn a cravat.

They had barely time to exchange greetings before the receptionist took them through to what she called the 'brand narrative hub', a large glass-walled oval space. Creative types were just streaming out after a meeting, arms full of glossy documents. One tall man in his thirties stood unmoving at the epicentre of this activity. He had trendy horn-rimmed glasses, a pepper-and-salt goatee beard, a sky-blue jacket and extensively ripped jeans. 'Sorry to keep you guys waiting. I'm Thad Cobalt.' As he pumped the colonel's hand, his other gripped Forsyth's bicep. Virgil saw Forsyth stiffen. 'And Virgil Bliss.' The American had a firm shake. 'So Virgil, I'm pleased to say we were very impressed by your credentials,' Cobalt said, signalling they should all sit in more of the absurdly low chairs.

'I'm delighted you found me,' Virgil said.

'That was down to the colonel,' Thad laughed. 'You can't advertise a job like this.'

Virgil couldn't help noticing how the colonel's eyes were drawn repeatedly to the torn knees of Thad's jeans. There was something like disbelief etched onto his face, as if the world was flat after all.

Thad turned to Virgil. 'The person you are protecting, the principal, is someone I'm sure you've heard of. She's on her way to the Caribbean at the moment, but she's looking forward to meeting you of course.' Thad took a remote and clicked. The venetian blinds closed, casting the room into semi-darkness, and a wall-sized screen at the far end burst into life: a shimmering unfocused background, the sound of a woman's heels clicking down a street, each click echoed in a flamenco soundtrack. Then a darkened female outline emerged, with flowing chestnut hair silhouetted against a dazzling white door. The clicking continued as she walked towards the screen.

'This is the start of the Silky commercial, I love it,' breathed Thad. The woman's face was caught in a searchlight: huge green eyes, dark, almost commanding eyebrows, and a wide and infectious smile. Virgil had dreamed about her. And now he remembered the name: Mira Roskova. The girl that poor Kev had wanted to marry. Right now, the most talked-about face on the planet.

Thad smirked to see the expression paralysed on Virgil's face. 'Surprised?'

'Yeah.' He shook his head. 'Astounded.'

Thad beamed. 'You might like this just as much.' He passed across a letter of appointment, which included a payscale at least twice what he had expected. Virgil thought he'd have to pinch himself.

'The serious pay comes with a serious responsibility, Virgil. Mira is not just a person, she is a multi-million dollar brand. That brand image embodies connotations not only of beauty, but of innocence, of purity. That's a lot rarer than beauty alone. I can't emphasise that enough. Her edge over her many modelling competitors is down to being pristine. Men desire her, women aspire to be like her. Advertisers pay top-dollar to have their products associated with that stardust. Shampoo, make-up, skin cream, jewellery, you name it.'

'Yeah, I've seen some of the adverts.'

'Well, Virgil here's the thing. It takes a lot of work to build a woman like Mira into a brand. It takes more than beauty, it's an aura, a mystique and of course her huge online following. And it has to be carefully managed. There's a risk asymmetry here too, like tightrope walking. Thousands of hours of concentration and patience to build, but one slip and in a heartbeat it's gone.'

'Like snorting coke or leaked nude photographs?'

'Yeah, or sometimes even a single ill-judged tweet. We help all we can, but ultimately it's down to her. Don't underestimate your role. Your discretion, social intelligence and empathy in steering her public appearances will be as important to preserving our investment as your ability to disarm an attacker. That's why you got the job. The moment Colonel Forsyth showed us your profile and experience, we knew you'd be right for us, and right for Mira.'

'That's very flattering.'

Thad passed him a heavy envelope. 'Virgil, read it carefully before you sign. I want to underline that you will owe a duty of total confidentiality to Miss Roskova at all times. The fact that you are working for her is confidential, where she lives, any personal habits that you observe, anyone she spends time with, these are all absolutely confidential. The contract is explicit that this prohibition will endure beyond any termination of the service. Any attempt to sell, give or pass on any non-public information, in any medium, and in any jurisdiction unless explicitly pre-approved by Stardust Brands, will incur exceptional financial penalties which our rather savage legal team will pursue from you until Hell freezes over.'

'Got it,' Virgil said. 'No boasting to me mates.'

'Spot on,' the colonel said. 'So Bliss, we require a lot from you in other ways. You will be on duty as personal protection when Mira's travelling in public, at public events, parties, news conferences and so on both here and eventually abroad. Mostly you will work alone but sometimes you will be part of a team. You will often double as her driver, but you may also be required to protect her at her own home. We don't generally envisage you will need a firearm, but my colleagues at Chacewater will file applications on your behalf for all relevant jurisdictions. You'll need to update your target practice too. We've got you down for defensive and evasive driving courses, and to brush up your medical and triage qualifications. Your job is to be at hand, within reach, but not obtrusive.'

Virgil flicked through the documents, stopping to gaze at one of Mira's publicity pics.

Thad continued. 'There is more. Up until now, an intern here at Stardust has been logging and assessing all the online commentary about Mira. She's not qualified to assess threats, so it really isn't satisfactory. She'll continue to collate the material and copy it to you. We want you to do the analysis, and produce reports. We want prevention as well as protection. She needs to *feel* safe as well as be safe.'

'Has Mira had personal security before?'

'Of course,' said the colonel. 'Mainly on an ad hoc basis, for public events. It wasn't truly professional, so we were brought in to tighten things up. Things have to be very different now. Chacewater's risk analysis report is in your folder here.' He tapped a thick binder lying on the desk. 'Your job is to execute the strategy laid out in that report.'

'Right,' Virgil said. 'I assume that you wouldn't be recruiting me in such a hurry if she wasn't in imminent danger.'

Colonel Forsyth turned to Thad, who answered. 'Absolutely, Virgil. Do you read the gossip columns?'

'No, not normally.'

'Well, that might change,' Thad said. 'Developing a celebrity and PR antenna will make your work easier. Mira has been dating Lawrence Wall. I'm sure you've heard of him.'

'The England defender? Of course. Lucky guy.'

'Not any more. They will be breaking up. Not quite yet, but soon. It's a sad story, and it's theirs alone, but we don't expect Mr Wall to take it very well.'

Virgil laughed. 'Are you guys running her love life too?'

'I wish.' Thad smiled. 'It would make life a lot simpler.'

The colonel opened his briefcase, and offered Virgil a thick envelope. Inside was a heavy sheaf of documents. 'In here is all you need to know about Mr Wall. But it's basically this. Lawrence Wall doesn't understand the word "No". He may try to get at Mira in some way, either online or in person. He knows where she lives, and where to find her. They have friends in common. He has the resources to make her life extremely difficult if he so chooses. We are taking precautions, but she cannot be hidden completely away from him. She is a public person too. Your job is to stop him. Preferably diplomatically, preferably gently, but above all effectively. Starting tomorrow.'

'Okay. Are we just talking harassment, or is her life in danger?'

'Up until a few days ago, Virgil, we would have said harassment,' said Thad. 'Then Mira showed us this.' He passed across a sealed envelope. 'This may be the most valuable thing you will ever hold in your hands. And the most dangerous in the wrong hands. Open it.'

Virgil did so. Inside was a five-by-seven photograph. It was a selfie, the face of a slim young woman with one eye so swollen it was almost shut. She also had a bloated lip crusted with blood, and grazes to her shoulders and arms. But most horrifying were the purple finger marks on her slender throat, squeezed by a single strong hand. It was hardly recognisable as Mira Roskova, but it was her.

'That's terrible,' Virgil said.

Thad reached across the table and took the photo back. 'Lawrence Wall did this. And he threatened to kill her.'

'What do the cops say?'

'They will never know.'

'Are you kidding? Look at the fingermarks on her neck. That's attempted murder!'

'Virgil,' Thad said firmly, 'we've all made this decision, including Mira herself. If this comes out, her career is over, image smashed, carefully-built brand destroyed. Gone. Finito.'

'So this will stay a secret?'

'Most definitely. Virgil, I'm afraid that stopping Lawrence Wall is down to you, and you alone.'

Chapter Five

Mira Roskova: The new face of beauty?

To see Mira Roskova in the flesh, the thing that strikes you isn't just her beauty, though she has, let's admit it, a face that most of us would die for. It's a vulnerability, a kind of projection of innocence. It seems so personal that I'm reluctant to remark upon it, until I realise that this is exactly what has made her the most talked about celebrity of 2014. But how can you define what makes someone unique? The look that made the young Brigitte Bardot, Elizabeth Taylor, Nastassja Kinski. While I mull how to tackle this delicate subject, and conscious that her publicist is sitting there reminding me we only have half an hour, I try to tease out some details of this rags-to-riches story.

MC: So Mira, first of all your name seems to indicate Russian extraction. Tell us a little about that.

MR: My father was from St Petersburg and my mother is half Italian and half Georgian, so you could say I am a bit of a mongrel. My full name is Lydia Mira Nikolayevna Roskova, which is a bit of a mouthful. They were in London when I was born, so I have British citizenship as well as Russian, though I have never actually visited Russia. They divorced when I was five.

MC: I know you were an only child, but were you a happy one?

MR: Well, my childhood was unusual (laughs). After my dad went back to Moscow, my mother – who was a classical musician, a violinist – at first worked at the Royal Academy of Music in London, but then we lived in lots of different towns, mostly across the north of England, wherever she managed to get teaching work.

MC: Your big break was the BBC series *Village of the Dead*, just eighteen months ago wasn't it?

MR: Yes, it completely changed my life. It was just a bit part, honestly, five minutes at the very end of the series. I was the third choice, picked out of the agency book at literally an hour's notice. Then I was given this amazing dress, and filmed in the tank, floating down the river like Ophelia, to escape the zombies, Qaeggan they were called, and suddenly... I don't know, the last scene turned up on YouTube, and went viral, I mean ...

MC: And some of your fans dress up as Qaeggan, is that right?

MR: (Laughs) Yes, wherever I go there is someone with a curly wig, white face, those horrible black eyes, with three black tear stains under each eye. It's really huge in Japan, where there is a manga magazine and, I'm now hearing, an anime cartoon based on it. It's all a bit overwhelming actually.

MC: But it's not all good, is it? Tell me about that incident in Copenhagen.

MR: Ah, that. (Smiles wistfully) Back in February, I was in Denmark for a product launch. Someone managed to get into my hotel room when I wasn't there and waited for me. I didn't get back until nearly midnight, exhausted and he waited until I was getting ready for bed. I opened the closet door, in my underwear, and there was this zombie, he even had the black contact lenses...

MC: Oh my god! That sounds awful...

MR: I screamed the place down. I'd never been so terrified in my life. Fortunately, the guy was basically harmless. He rolled up in a ball when I started throwing things at him. Hotel security was quickly on the scene.

MC: How do you feel about zombies now?

MR: Look, I appreciate that most of my fans originally saw me because of *Village*, and the clips on YouTube, and of course Instagram which is where I have the most fans. I really enjoy knowing that there are lots of enthusiasts who like to dress as Qaeggan, and if it wasn't for them and their support I wouldn't be where I am now. But obviously (long pause)...

MC: Nobody wants to open a wardrobe door and see a six-foot zombie there, right?

MR: Exactly. Of course, I now have to employ people like Portia here to look after this whole online and fan thing for me. (Turns to PR woman)

MC: So your first modelling calls followed the TV show?

MR: Not my first. I was scouted as a model when I was sixteen in a shopping centre in Manchester, and did a few shoots in London and New York, but basically I'm only five nine, not quite tall enough for the catwalk, and with the preference for size zero models coming on I wasn't getting much work...'

MC: And then came *Village of the Dead*...

MR: Yes, it changed my life. I've got all this work, and I get sent more clothing, bags, couture, you name it, than I could ever use. Life has become much busier, but of course that doesn't mean it's always easy. Things are challenging when you are in demand, just in a different way from when you're not. But my god, I have to be careful of everything I say and do!

MC: I know you don't like to discuss your private life, but I have to ask you about the footballer rumours. You have been photographed with Lawrence Wall. Is there something significant in your life you would like to share?

MR: Well, it's hard to have anything private, isn't it? (Laughs) Lawrence and I have had a few dates, that's all I can say.

He's great fun and has a kind of energy about him, which I think many women find very attractive.

MC: Sergei, our photographer, was very excited about the shoot you did for us. He said 'I've never seen a model who gives so much to the camera, especially close up. This woman gives you her soul. No wonder all the greats want to shoot her.'

MR: (Laughs) I never know how to react to compliments! I'm very flattered, of course, but I can only be me. I don't know how to be anyone else.

MC: I think the shots we've published for this issue of *Marie Claire* bear out your promise. Thank you.

MR: Thank you too!

(Marie Claire magazine – September 2014)

* * *

Virgil had never read so many women's magazines. In close protection, getting to know the client is essential, and you can't do that without understanding the world they operate in. There he was, sitting in his mum's lounge, flicking through *Cosmopolitan*, *Vanity Fair*, *Vogue*, *Harpers* and a load of others he'd been given by Thad. They included the copy of *GQ* in which Mira had been voted the world's most desirable woman. His mum, set up for the evening with *The Jeremy Kyle Show* and *You've Been Framed* had laughed at him when he dropped the magazines on the coffee table.

'You're not hiding *Mayfair* in there are you?'

'God, Mum, I'm not fifteen. This is work.'

She looked over his shoulder at the magazine. ' "Teach your guy to find the G-spot" –what kind of work is this, Virgil?' she asked.

'It's close protection work, Mum.'

'Sounds a bit too close to me.'

'I'm researching my client,' he said, flicking away from the article she'd seen.

'You guarding a model then?'

He looked up and shrugged. 'Maybe.'

She roared with laughter. 'What are you guarding her against, son? Name calling, tittle-tattle, all nail scratching and hair-pulling?'

He sighed. 'It's a bit more serious than that, Mum. And it's secret, right?'

'My big soldier son, bodyguard for a girl. I never did...' she laughed.

'Alright, Mum. Look, the other news is that now I'm getting some money I should be able to move out.'

'You don't have to, Virgil. It's been lovely to have you here, just like when you was a boy.' She rubbed his shoulder, her bony fingers, calloused by years of scrubbing washbasins, gripping him with surprising strength.

'I need a bit of space, Mum, and so do you. Shan't go far, promise. I'll still call round.' He looked up and risked a quick smile.

'Okay, you go your own way.' Her eyes were moist.

Virgil, feeling the full weight of guilt that she had intended, retreated into the hall, and balanced his laptop on the tiny rickety telephone table. It was the only place he could get online, by piggybacking on next-door's wi-fi signal. Internet access was something he'd have to have at his new place.

It was midnight by the time Virgil had finished reading the Lawrence Wall background report. Chacewater Associates had obviously been on the hurry-up, because it was to Virgil's eye a botch job. Most of the material they had e-mailed was culled from Wikipedia or the tabloids.

Born in a working class neighbourhood in Bury, Greater Manchester, Lawrence Leonard Wall was the oldest child in a family of five kids. His mother was a care worker at a nursing home, who had brought up Lawrence alone for the first three years of his life before marrying a pipe fitter. An online fan magazine covered uneventful school days in Manchester's industrial relic of Dukinfield, skating over what seemed to be a poor academic record, and an expulsion from one school for fighting. The trajectory of his footballing career was there in great depth, the clubs, the goals, and everything that a fan might want, but not much help on Lawrence Wall the man. The many fights, on the pitch, and in pubs and nightclubs, were enthusiastically covered in the tabloids. Only at the time of his divorce, a couple of years ago, did his personal life get a scandalised airing. A drunken hellraiser, he was brilliant on the pitch, but wild outside it. *The Sun* had termed him the 'Dukinfield Dreadnought.' The tabloids seemed to praise his serial adultery, cheerfully showing two women photographed in lingerie who'd claimed he was a demon in bed, and "unbelievably well-endowed". Flicking past the salacious verbiage, Virgil looked for the finer details, some of which came out after the failed manslaughter prosecution over the cyclist incident in 2011.

The Guardian had a long story which documented fans' harassment of the witness who had claimed to see Wall reverse over the cyclist. Mostly these attacks were vented online by trolls, but paint had been thrown on the witness's car, and a brick hurled through the window of his home. After the trial, it was disclosed that Lawrence Wall had previous convictions for drunk and disorderly, affray and common assault. There were no details of the sentences.

Virgil went online to learn more. Lawrence Wall. Six-one, two hundred and five pounds, a man who at twenty-seven could still run a hundred metres in eleven and a half seconds. His three million pound home was in the posh Manchester satellite village of Wilmslow, where he lived with a Rhodesian ridgeback called Kipper. He had a three-year-old daughter named Danielle from his short marriage to Michelle Canavan, but she lived with the mother.

YouTube clips showed Wall in only a few 'best goals' collections, and many more vignettes of the passing and tackling skill which made his reputation. But the faraway winner was 'Stopped by the Wall' with 12.6 million views. This was a collection of sixteen fouls over the last seven years in which the majority of victims were stretchered off the pitch. There was a rap soundtrack, and enthusiastic captions which gave the medical outcomes, from strained hamstring to a broken femur. The final one, repeated over and over, was a brutal and gory headbutt on a non-league goalkeeper who'd had the temerity to snatch the ball away from Wall's head during an early round cup-tie. For all the fact that it was a pretty slickly produced video, put together by 'TheWallBoys', Virgil found the glorification unsettling.

Nevertheless, it was one thing to see the ferocious creature that Lawrence Wall was on the pitch, and quite another to extrapolate that behaviour to his private life. What was he really capable of? What was he thinking now? Only Mira herself could tell him that, and he had yet to meet her.

* * *

It was almost midnight when Virgil turned to the password he'd been e-mailed by Stardust Brands to the online Mira fan mail database. It allowed access to the raw feed of messages about her culled by specialist software from the most popular social media websites, and a separate file of potentially threatening messages collated over the last year by intern Kelly Hopkins.

For Virgil, who had rarely used social media, a dip into the raw feed was a revelation. Under the popular Twitter hashtag #Miramostbeautiful one fan had pleaded for guidance on becoming an underwear model. Yet the photo seemed to show a girl who was barely twelve. This was just one among hundreds just in the last month, all wannabe teenage models. Men used the same hashtag to speculate on the size of Mira's breasts, whether she shaved her pubic hair, and musings on intimate sexual preferences. And these people were her *fans*. Her detractors, scores of them active on Facebook, casually ran down everything about her, criticised her choice of clothing, her body, her weight and impugned her morals. Protected by relative anonymity, they felt free to treat her as a public product, no different from a second-hand appliance traded on eBay. Mira's fans, and some of those self-styled as #QaeggenBoys, replied in kind.

He switched to the threats file. There, pasted on various Word documents were threads of Twitter or Facebook conversations where containing quite explicit threats against Mira. Most of these were sexual, and some stomach-turning. Kelly had marked those that had been referred to the police with a reference number. Though there were few details, this was clearly something he'd have to chase up.

Virgil was just about ready to turn in when his phone rang. 'Mr Bliss? Sorry to disturb,' a male voice said. 'Battsersea Harbour here.'

'What?'

'Battersea Harbour. I'm the night manager. We're under instructions to call you about any incidents regarding Ms Roskova's apartment during her absence.'

'Oh, right. So has something happened?'

'There was an unauthorised attempt to gain access to her apartment a few minutes ago. A well-known footballer and several male colleagues arrived here…'

'Lawrence Wall?'

'Yes. They were all a little the worse for wear, drink-wise, demanding to see her.'

Virgil silently cursed himself. Wall would obviously have been in London tonight for the away league fixture against

Arsenal. If he hadn't been reading women's mags, he would have watched it on TV.

'They've gone now. They weren't able to get beyond the foyer.'

'Did they cause any trouble?'

'A little damage, nothing serious. A cracked glass door panel, a broken bottle and a chipped mirror. Although Mr Wall did threaten me.'

'I'm sorry to hear that.'

'As per the agreement, I didn't call the police. We'll send Stardust the bill, okay?'

'If that's the arrangement they made, fine. What kind of threat did Mr Wall make?'

'Oh, he threatened to glass me with the champagne bottle he was carrying if I didn't unlock the lift. His colleagues eventually persuaded him to leave, but on his way out he threw the bottle at the foyer mirror. Fortunately it's toughened glass. But what a waste of Krug.'

'Thank you for letting me know,' Virgil said, and hung up. He walked out to the balcony and looked across the sodium-lit streets of South London. Tonight's incident was a warning to him. He'd have to track Wall's movements a lot better when Mira was back.

* * *

For Jonesy Tolling, first thing in the morning was ten-thirty, never earlier. Everyone at the office knew that. So getting a call at home at nine-thirty, before he'd had the day's first Bloody Mary was never popular. Especially when the caller was his old sparring partner Nigel Carr, celebrity editor at *The Sun*.

'Good morning, Jonesy.'

'What's effing good about it, Nigel?' Jonesy croaked. He rubbed his eyes, sat up in bed and looked around in vain for the woman who he'd been sure went to bed with him last night. That at least was what he'd paid her to do.

'We'd like your comment on a juicy story about Mira Roskova.'

'Course you would.' Jonesy eased himself out of bed, tucked the cordless phone into his neck and reached down to the floor for a stained dressing gown. 'You've been trying to dig something up on her ever since she arrived on the scene, haven't you?' He donned the gown then gingerly picked up a moist rubber object from the floor and dropped it into the bin.

'I won't deny it. But we do have something this time,' Carr said. 'We're trying to stand up a report that Lawrence Wall was staying with her in a holiday cottage in the Forest of Bowland last weekend, beat the crap out of her, after which she ran out half naked in search of help.'

'You're barking up the wrong tree, mate.' Jonesy laughed, an oily sound like trying to start an old car with a duff battery. He walked down the stairs, stepping first over a pair of his discarded underpants, then trousers. In the kitchen he finally found his spectacles, and propped them on his nose. 'Are we off the record?'

'Go on, you old sod, just for old times' sake.'

'Right.' He padded to the fridge, unscrewed a nearly empty bottle of vodka and tipped the last of it into last night's dirty glass on the draining board. 'I don't know where Mira was most of last weekend. But I do know that she was in Milan

on Sunday night, and had a big photo shoot there yesterday.'
He slopped in a hefty glug of tomato juice, and a dash of Lea
and Perrins. Finding no cutlery in the drawer, he stirred the
mixture with a pair of nail clippers he'd found in his pocket.

'She could have got there from the nearest airport,' Carr said.

'It's not that, Nige, it's that if she'd just had her lights punched
out as you claim the only photographers interested would be
from *Wifebeater's Weekly*.'

Silence.

'And if he'd hit her, she'd have rung the Old Bill, straightaway.
Then her lawyers. Then me. Except she hasn't.' he swilled the
drink around his mouth. It felt good.

'You're very clever, Jonesy, but you're in denial. It's a strong
story.'

'Who's the source?'

'Oh, come on mate,' Carr chuckled 'I'm not going to disclose
that.'

'Okay, but it's not come from her, has it? It's not from the Old
Bill, and I imagine it's not Lawrence Wall's people either.'

'Sure they denied it. But the denial I got yesterday evening
from Harvey Cohen at Sports Management seemed a little
too well prepared to me. A Monday evening and they weren't
caught by surprise. They've already got a spin on it.'

'Which was?'

'No, no, no, my friend. You'd better call Harvey yourself for
that.'

'With friends like you, Nige, who needs enemas?' Jonesy
chuckled as the heat of the vodka soothed his throat. Fencing

with Nige was one of life's great sources of comradely pleasure. 'Cut to the chase, Nige. This is all waffle. If something happened you better tell me what it is and I'll see if I can get a reaction for you.'

'Okay. The owner of the holiday cottage sent us pictures of the damage. A bathroom door smashed down and a settee hurled out through the french windows downstairs. The cottage was booked in a false name, but the woman recognised them both when they arrived.'

'That doesn't prove that Lawrence Wall hit Mira.'

'No, but what does Mira say?'

'I'll have to ask her.'

'Ah. But you already have, Jonesy. I know for a fact *The Sunday Mirror* called you about it yesterday afternoon. We aren't the first to ask.'

He was right. Jonesy hesitated for just a second too long. Nige would pick that up. 'Nige, I wasn't able to speak to her. She wasn't returning calls.'

'Which is just what would happen, if she didn't want to hear from him after being smacked a big one,' Carr said.

'That's desperate speculation, Nige, and you know it.' They both laughed. 'Alright. Here's what I'll do. We were aware that someone was spreading wild rumours. Not ones any professional journalist would believe, of course. Now if you force me to go on the record, I'll tell you that no such thing happened, and I'll place a detailed denial in *The Daily Star* tomorrow. I'll let them have a picture of her lovely unmarked face, dated yesterday, which won't make you look very clever.' Jonesy picked up a plate of half-eaten food and found a packet of Rothmans underneath. He stuck one in his mouth. 'You can go with it, but it ain't a very good story, is it? Unless you actually have a picture of the alleged bruises.' He lit the fag and inhaled greedily. 'Which you don't, do you? Otherwise you wouldn't be whining around me.'

Silence.

'However, if you are a good little boy and spike this pile of horseshit, I'll be able to offer you something a bit tastier. Exclusive.'

'Like what?'

'We're getting some exclusive Mira stills from an upcoming skincare product launch.'

'I'd prefer lingerie, to be honest. Or topless.'

Jonesy started laughing which turned into a coughing fit of a good half minute. 'For Christ's sake, Nige. This is Mira Roskova, as pure as driven effing snow. Okay, there are a few rather daring stills where she isn't wearing anything, but they are tasteful. Limbs arranged just so.'

'Yeah, so you can't see anything,' Carr muttered.

'Well, you can see that she has breathtaking green eyes, a soft sensuous smile and the longest, smoothest legs on the planet. And you can still put "Mira nude pics exclusive" on the front page banner. Which should be good for a half million extra sales, right?'

'I'd need to see them.'

'They'd have to be run with the product clearly visible. There would have to be a contract about that, I'm afraid. And I can't do it yet.'

'What's the product?'

'Can't say, obviously. But you'd be ahead of the launch, which will be huge, and I mean effing massive. And they would be big advertisers for your pages, very big. That is so long as you don't spoil the show by saying horrible things about her now.'

'The pictures are free?'

'Maybe. So long as you run the video on your website.'

'What video?'

'The commercial. It's an "unapproved" version, without the edits required by the broadcasters, so it's quite sexy. We'd leak in onto YouTube eventually, director's cut kind of thing, or we'd claim it had been stolen, but so long as you buy it from us and keep it prominent on the website you can have the stills for nothing.'

'Hang on a minute, Jonesy, how much…?'

'Fifty thou.'

'Well, I'm not sure. So instead of you paying us for ads, we'd be bloody paying you.'

'Just think though: Mira Roskova, voted world's most beautiful woman, kit off. *Sun* exclusive…'

'Fifty big ones though…,' Carr complained.

'Well, Nige, it's much less than what we quoted *The Sunday Mirror*. Think about it. You've got until six o'clock. Sorry Nige, got a call on the other line. Probably the *Mirror*. Bye.' He hung up, leaned back against the kitchen counter, and inhaled deeply. Victory from the jaws of defeat. Nice. At least now, with a tastier morsel dangled, *The Sun* might not go to the trouble of finding out that Mira never did go to Milan.

Now, Jonesy would just have to make sure that Mira did get that Suressence skincare contract, and then get some photos and a video made to match what he'd promised Nigel Carr. Still, with tabloid publicity like that lined up, something he'd tell them about tomorrow, it was all the more likely to happen.

Jonesy shuffled over and picked up the stack of newspapers from his doormat. As usual, he went straight for the Mirror, his *alma mater*. After a quick scan through for alluring female flesh, and clever headlines, he flipped over to the back page sports section. There was a half page photograph of Lawrence Wall bringing down Everton's Karl Lutis in a cup tie last season. The picture, obviously taken with a telephoto lens, was a savagely foreshortened vision of predator and prey, like a *National Geographic* feature from the Serengeti. No wonder it had won a prize: the brutality of the tackle; the spray of mud frozen in space, like droplets of blood; the pain scribbled on the Everton forward's features; and above all, the bestial snarl on Lawrence Wall's face, level with the throat, as if he was about to bite his victim. Football? No. A matter of life and death.

Jonesy shuddered. He just hoped that this former soldier they'd hired to protect Mira was going to be up to the job. He'd imagine that some bloke who fought the Taliban would think it was a cushy number to guard some slip of a girl. He'd tell him. Beneath the glitz, beauty is as tough an industry as there is. It may be mascara and face cream, but they don't take no effing prisoners.

Chapter Six

Virgil was welcomed into his first Team Mira meeting at noon on Wednesday. As he arrived, Stardust Brands' offices were a hive of activity: corridor conversations, urgent phone calls and presentations in glass-walled meeting rooms. In Helmand, it just seemed like yesterday, he'd been used to hurried tactical meetings conducted at a bellow under a camouflaged tent, with the noise and dust of choppers in the background; gobbling down food on the hurry-up, squeezed out of foil packages into dented mess tins.

Here the walls were decorated with the luminously beautiful models, each the spearhead of a campaign to motivate women to part with serious cash for shampoo or face cream, handbags or clothing, in the hope of looking a little more like a goddess. On the large oval table there were danish pastries and fresh fruit, endless coffee, and a smoked salmon spread to allow them to work right through lunch and into the afternoon.

In Afghanistan his kit was permanently filthy from the dust and grime, his bergen roughly stitched where a fragment from an RPG that would otherwise have severed his spine had shredded and scorched the material. At Stardust Brands, if anything was torn, it was meant to be torn. Dirt was only present by design. The tall Somali receptionist, Adula, was wearing a mauve dress whose strategically placed slits made it look like it had been raked by an AK47. Jarvis McTear, the quiffed and bearded art director, had the limpest handshake he'd ever felt, but his jeans sported shiny ingrained filth as if he'd spent a lifetime mending tractors, something Virgil seriously doubted. Virgil was no Army lifer, but he felt that this world was all dreams and desires, somehow lacking gravity and grit.

Virgil had been talking to Portia, who wanted to know all about Afghanistan. He tried to explain that there was no glamour in lying and bleeding in a wadi, wondering which of your mates was alive, while a couple of Afghan seven-year-olds sat nearby, waiting for you to die so they could steal and sell your kit. The conversation stopped when Thad swept into the room, already dispensing instructions, followed by Jonesy Tolling, and a couple of people he didn't know. Virgil had spent his time on the Stardust Brands website last night in preparation and he had memorised the faces and titles. The gushing tribute to the talents of so-called brand managers and envisioning consultants had made him cringe.

Virgil was here to present a strategy, something that Colonel Forsyth and Chacewater had dreamed up, to protect Mira Roskova not only against Lawrence Wall, but against any of the many threats that can trouble celebrity life.

After welcoming Virgil, Thad detailed what he and Jonesy had done so far to keep the Lawrence Wall issue out of the press. 'Now as for keeping her safe in future, it's up to you Virgil.'

'Well, I'd like to start by assessing the risk from Lawrence Wall. I understand that you're working on how she delicately disengages her life from his.'

'Yeah,' said Jonesy. 'She's got a new phone, and Kelly is monitoring her personal e-mails. Lawrence Wall has e-mailed her numerous times, and for now she's ignoring him. Long term, we've got some thinking to do, which is where you can help.'

'Well, I take it you've all seen the Chacewater security strategy,' Virgil said.

'Perhaps you would summarise it for us,' Thad said.

'Okay. Like any high-profile celebrity, Mira needs her public exposure mapped in advance, to times and places where we can assess and manage the security risks. Press conferences, photo ops, public dinners, galas, charity events and so on, plus the planned transits to and from them. Even this week's unplanned visit by Lawrence Wall to her apartment building. These are all set pieces because we know what the threats are likely to be, and how to protect her against them. UPIs, what we call unplanned public interactions, by contrast create hard-to-manage security situations.'

'What type of thing are you thinking about?' Portia asked.

'Say Mira is driving alone and has a minor accident, and needs help. A guy stops to help, then asks for her phone number, or worse. Or if she is buttonholed in a hotel lift by an overly-persistent fan. Or nips out for a pizza, and is followed.'

'Huh, so basically any moment of spontaneous human activity in the outside world is a UPI,' said Portia.

'In security terms, yes,' Virgil said.

'We've had to deal with all this in the past,' Thad said. 'But the ubiquity of camera phones now means there is a publishable record of every public moment: Mira looking ungainly emerging from a car, on holiday looking anything other than super-slim, eating a burger with ketchup on her face. All potentially damaging.'

'As Diane Glassman so memorably said,' Portia muttered, 'fame has a habit of devouring its most perfect children.'

'And quickly turning them into shit,' added Jonesy, smirking.

'So how well has she adjusted to it, would you say?' Virgil asked.

'Not bad, so far,' Thad said. 'I know she likes to go for a run, and from now on that can't happen without you, Virgil. She likes to meet friends in pubs or restaurants, but worries it might be increasingly difficult.'

'It doesn't have to be,' Virgil said. 'There are quiet times and quiet rooms, if we choose the venues carefully. But we also need genuinely safe places for her when it all becomes too much. Private places she can go to at short notice, with outdoor space, room for friends to come and stay. Not hotels, they cannot really be regarded as private, particularly after the Copenhagen experience. I imagine she's not short of offers from wealthy men inviting her to use their private islands, country estates, grand villas, yachts, whatever.'

'You're right there, Virgil. She's got to be about the most eligible woman on the planet right now,' Portia said.

'But all such offers obviously need careful vetting,' Virgil continued. 'We don't want her to jump out of the public frying pan and into a private fire.'

'True,' said Portia. 'There are emotionally manipulative people out there who may be much cleverer than Lawrence Wall, even if less violent. At least with Wall, he's got a public brand of his own to protect, which should give us some leverage.'

'Nah, nah, not all brands are like the ones we push,' Jonesy said. 'Lawrence Wall is a bad boy image already. No one thinks he sends his birds effing flowers, Portia. He shags 'em from behind over the breakfast table.' Jonesy leaned back, hands behind his head, exposing the dark sweat stains in the armpits of his blue shirt. 'This was the guy, remember, who headbutted a referee at the age of seventeen, who's been sent off countless times, and had endless nightclub punch-ups. Yet no one can so reliably stop an opposing forward. He's always in the right place. That's why despite the injuries and his red cards, he's still an England regular.'

'But he has sponsors, Jonesy, and they get nervous about bad behaviour,' Portia said.

'Some do,' Jonesy said. 'But don't forget Wall's brand is built around being the meanest player on the pitch. After all, it was word-for-word Nike's slogan when it launched its Destroyer range of Lawrence Wall footwear, a deal worth ten million, which may I remind you is more than anything we've yet got for Mira. That's why all these eight-year-olds begged their dads to buy them a pair of eighty-five quid Lawrence Wall red and black football boots with those words on the side. That's why their older brothers shaved the same stripe into their hair as his, with the scorpion tattoo underneath. I mean every bus stop and dole queue is heaving with 'Wallheads'. They *love* him nasty. That's why the camera is always on him. He's media magic. Lawrence Wall is like the pile-ups that stop Formula One being boring.'

'But this is 2015,' Portia persisted. 'Public opinion won't stand for it.'

'In *The Guardian*, no doubt,' Jonesy chuckled. 'But look broader. Lawrence Wall's demographic is all those blokes in white vans with copies of the tabloids stuffed down the dashboards. The people who got left behind in the metrosexual, multicultural, pancetta-nibbling Britain. They're on minimum wage, zero hours contracts, and a bit of cash in hand if they're lucky. They love football, and they idolise Lawrence Wall because he is their dreams made flesh. Look at their faces in the crowd when Wall brings someone down. You must have seen it on telly. Snarling faces, clenched fists and a chorus of "Another one bites the dust". Don't you understand, Portia? He's getting even for them all.'

'Okay people,' Thad said. 'Focus, focus. Suressence is absolute priority one until we close the deal. No budget for anything else. Okay?'

'Shame,' said Virgil. 'We could do with an additional bodyguard, even part-time.'

'I'll think about it,' Thad said. 'But you have to understand that we can't sign any new branding deals for Mira until Suressence finalises all the product rights it wants. In the

57

meantime all other long-term brand associations are on hold. We lost Pond's skincream last month because they won't wait, and the Silky hair products deal has expired. Look, I'm sure you'll do fine.'

'Lawrence Wall has already made one public attempt to get into her flat,' Virgil said. 'The lock to the apartment has only just been changed today, and he still has a key to the lift which they aren't going to change. If he'd gone in through the car park level he'd have got in. We could do with someone there.'

'But Mira's away, right?' Jonesy said. 'She's sunning herself on a private island in the Caribbean until the bruises heal. All you have to do, Virgil, is protect her until Lawrence Wall loses interest. He's bound to have a queue of women, so his interest in her should soon start to wind down.'

'Unless he's fallen in love,' Portia laughed. 'Then you'll have a job for life.'

* * *

Virgil left the meeting before its conclusion in order to meet intern Kelly Hopkins, who monitored all the media comment on Stardust clients, and collected and filed plaudits and threats. He was pointed towards an office marked admin. The door was open and he saw where a slim-but-stacked redhead in a tight white shirt and jeans was hard at work at a screen, surrounded by stacks of files. The office was small and windowless.

'You must be Virgil,' said Kelly, picking up a hefty stack of files. 'Welcome to my hutch. Let's get a coffee and have a chat somewhere with some space.'

She took him to one of the glass meeting rooms, closed the door and leaned back against it to look at him. 'I'm really glad to have you aboard. Never mind about saving Mira's life, you're going to save mine,' she said. 'I am absolutely snowed under. If you are able to take over most of the Mira work, I'll at least be able to do the other fifteen clients.'

'I'm just writing the reports, I think,' Virgil said.

'Mainly yes, but I'm sure you've got a keener eye for the threats than I have. You'd notice things that would pass me by, I'm sure.'

'I've noticed something already. There's a sleeping bag under your desk,' he jerked his thumb back towards her office.

'Well, yes. Last night was a particularly long one. I had to get up to date for today's big meeting. I'm refusing to do any more overnighters until they start paying me.'

'You're not paid?'

'I'm an intern. Doing it for love.' She narrowed her eyes. 'And training of course. But I already know more about the monitoring and record systems than any of them, because I set them up. I could train *them*. But, between you and me, I don't. The idea is that by making myself indispensible they'll have to give me a proper job.'

'In the army you never volunteer for anything,' Virgil said. 'Still, I'm sure it's different here.'

'Not completely. We don't have the Taliban but we do have Portia bloody Casals. She's my boss, earns a big whack, and has outsourced most of her drudge work to me, basically.' She looked at him again. 'So I take it you are being paid?'

'Yes, I'm glad to say I am.' Virgil stared into those questioning blue eyes which demanded: *and how much*? He already felt that he needed Kelly on his side, and she wouldn't be that way for long if he told her. 'It's not that good,' he lied. 'But they've promised me more down the line...'

'Ha. Jam tomorrow. That sounds like the Stardust Brands I know.'

'What about Thad Cobalt?'

'Nice enough, but he lives in cloud-cuckoo land. An academic, basically. Has to get consultants in to zip up his flies for him.' Without looking up she said, 'Being male, there is one piece of advice you won't need.'

'What's that?'

'Never be caught alone in an office with Jonesy Tolling.' She snaked her arms in front of her. 'The drunken octopus. If he wasn't so bloody brilliant at his job they would have sacked him years ago.'

'What's so clever about him?'

'Well, Thad was negotiating this deal for Mira to endorse a Norwegian mineral water called Purity. Jonesy then started schmoozing his well-connected friends to gain her an entrée into becoming a UN ambassador for water conservation. It's not a done deal yet, but it would quadruple what they can charge Purity for her. Clever or what?'

'What about Mira herself?'

'Ah yes, Snow White, the virginal princess.' She grinned at him. 'You're probably expecting me to come out with the standard jealous bitch response aren't you? Stuck-up, uptight, high-maintenance cow etcetera.'

Virgil laughed. 'No, really I'm not.'

'She is demanding, no doubt about that. And she has a heck of a temper. But she's very professional, especially for someone who has just been catapulted from nowhere into this shitstorm of publicity.' She indicated the heaps of papers around her. 'And she can be very kind. She knows I'm not paid, and when she found out we were the same size, she has given me, literally, dozens of pairs of gorgeous shoes. Manolo Blahniks, Jimmy Choos. She gets given so much, and they would just be in her wardrobe gathering dust. I wish I could get down another dress size, and then I could get some of her clothes too. I wish I'd never had the boob job now.'

'Should I ask why?'

'A couple of years ago I did some glamour modelling... mainly lingerie mind, not porn, but they all say the same thing: "You need to add a cup size, love." These blokes, of course, are usually paunchy alcoholic perverts who no woman would give a second glance to, but to them whatever a woman looks like isn't enough. So I got a loan and had an op, for which I'm still in debt incidentally, but then they wanted me to do collagen injections for my lips and I thought, no way. It's bad enough to know that thousands of spotty fourteen-year- old boys are wanking off over your picture without having to change the shape of your face as well.' She made a cross-eyed pout.

'That's a very graphic image,' Virgil laughed. This was turning out to be an even bigger education than he expected.

Kelly sat down and leafed through the file in front of her. 'This is Mira's post, just for today. There's far more online of course, but these are more interesting. Gifts, pictures and other weird items.'

'Hello. Another one of these.' She held up a large manila envelope. It had been franked by the West London Mental Health Trust. She opened it and slid out two items. One was a form to fill in and return, in case the post was either unwanted or deemed offensive to the recipient. The second was a thick greeting card envelope. It was stamped with an intimidating warning in red:

Broadmoor Psychiatric Hospital: Section 134 of the Mental Health Act 1983 (amended 2007) provides authority for the inspection and withholding of detained patients' outgoing and incoming mail. Contents may have been censored.

Kelly opened it carefully, and slid out a thick handmade card. The front cover was an extraordinary pen and ink drawing, a series of angels and cherubs depicted in the classical style, trailing up a watercoloured banner in the palest rose pink bearing Mira's full name. Inside the card was a message written in copperplate, in a foreign language.

Felix natalis Lydia. Annos sustinui te desideravi tu tibi viderat. Usquequo exspecto ad redemptionem ab hoc inferno quod traditos?

'Isn't it beautiful?' she said.
'No doubt, but what's it say?' Virgil said.

'Let's see.' Kelly led Virgil back to her office, opened the browser on her PC and typed it into Google translate.

Happy Birthday, Lydia. For years I have waited for you, longed for you, dreamed about you. For how long must I wait for the redemption from this hell to which I have been consigned?

'God, it's in Latin. How lovely! My useless boyfriend can't even write me a birthday card in proper English.'

'But he does have one advantage. He's not in Broadmoor. At least I presume not.'

Kelly laughed. 'Good point. But he might as well be for the amount of time he spends at his office.' She looked at the card again. 'Well, she certainly attracts some lunatics.'

'Artistically gifted Latin-speaking lunatics, though,' Virgil added.

'I'm sure she'd like to see this. What do you reckon, mister security guy, what is the risk assessment? Should I add it to the post for her to see?'

'Why not?' said Virgil. 'It's the crazy people who aren't locked up that I'm supposed to worry about.'

Chapter Seven

There is not an adult in the United Kingdom who does not know the name Broadmoor. The country's most high profile secure psychiatric hospital is notorious because of the roll call of the evil and the insane it has at various times contained. Men like Yorkshire Ripper Peter Sutcliffe, East End gangster Ronnie Kray, Son of God killer Robert Torto and Stockwell Strangler Kenneth Erskine.

Dawn Evans worked at Broadmoor. She'd worked for West London Mental Health Trust for six years and two years ago had been offered a pay rise to be assigned to Broadmoor as a psychiatric nursing assistant. Her job varied while she trained, but was mainly in the low-risk Boxhill Ward. Tonight, because of staff shortages, she had been asked to cover a night shift, her first ever, in Cavendish Ward. That was an unsettling place, where new patients were assessed and the most difficult remained. The shift turned out to be a nightmare she would never forget.

She had been taking a coffee break when at 2.18 am she had been told she would have to take part in an SMU, a six man unlock, the most terrifyingly confrontational procedure in the secure psychiatric system. That was frightening enough. When she had been told the name of the patient involved she spilled her drink.

Lucy.

Leonard Lucifer Smith. Britain's most violent prisoner, now Broadmoor's most awkward patient. Six-foot-ten inches and three hundred pounds of paranoid schizophrenic. Lucifer Smith was legendary. He'd been the subject of articles, biographies and TV documentaries. Without ever having seen the Internet himself, he had spawned numerous online copycats and fans. His shaven scarred head and huge black beard were all intimidating enough. But then there were the tattoos. Years ago, when he was the enforcer for a Manchester crime gang, he had had the entire text of chapter twenty of the Book of Revelation inked across his enormous torso, limbs and head. Even his eyeballs. Injections of black pigment under the conjunctiva of each eye had permanently turned the whites jet black.

The screaming from Lunatic Lucy's room had to be heard to be believed. The cries of anguish, and the roar of oaths and threats carried all the way down the ward's east corridor through two reinforced steel security doors and into the security muster station where Dawn Evans and five other members of staff were assembling their riot gear: helmet with shatterproof visor, stab-proof vest, reinforced trousers, steel-toe-capped boots. Dawn had only ever kitted up for SMU in training. Now, as then, she could hardly find any of it small enough to fit her five-foot-four frame. Packed into the muster station with her was the reassuring presence of Geoff Featherstone, a six-foot slab of Geordie and a former Royal Marine. He was Broadmoor's head of security. With him was Tyrone Mgonwe, an athletic Ghanaian with a wonderful smile, and two of the night duty security men, Karl Sullivan and Trevor Cooke. Hope Trenchtown was the only other woman. Hope was incredibly patient, experienced, and empathic. She looked like a solidly-built West Indian dinner lady. No one would guess that the laughing woman with the purple lipstick could benchpress two hundred pounds and had a black belt in karate. But Dawn could see that even Hope's hands were shaking as she buckled up her stab vest.

The six man unlock is designed to bring down even the worst and most disturbed patients. Once the cell door is open, four staffers each immobilise a limb, another the head. The head was Hope's speciality. She had been head-butted, bitten, and showered with bodily fluids more times than she cared to remember but she had a quick and effective headlock technique: the patient's head would be pressed hard to the floor, squeezed between her knees, using only enough force to do the job without compressing his airway. Brutal, but necessary.

Dawn's job as sixth "man" was supposed to be easier, and only began once the patient was face down on the cell floor. She was to pull down his trousers, and administer an injection into the buttock of Clopixol Acuphase, a potent anti-psychotic drug. There was no finesse to this. The training had made that clear. The syringe was huge, like something designed to knock out a horse, because you could not risk a needle break. Likewise, no gentle easing in of the liquid over the course of a few seconds. This was more like a stabbing, and from the roars of pain from the patient, felt just like one. Hope had smiled at her when Dawn had screwed it up during training. 'You'll be fine. It always seems frightening the first time.'

But that was before they knew they were going to tackle Lucy.

First banged up in Wakefield Prison in 2007, Lucy became a one-man riot. On day one in solitary he head-butted the steel door so hard that he dented it. The next day he picked up a sixteen stone warder by the throat with one hand, and held him in midair for half a minute as he struggled to breathe. Wakefield's governor soon learned the lesson. Room was quickly made in the new Supermax high security unit in the prison's basement, where Lucy's cell had bulletproof glass walls, a metal toilet and sink bolted to the floor, a concrete bed and cardboard furniture. His only contact was twice a day when pre-cut food was posted through a slot in the door on a cardboard tray.

In 2010 Lucifer Smith was finally assigned to Broadmoor. His arrival was part of staff folklore. Dozens assembled to watch a ten-tonne Serco prison van rocking in the secure parking bay as Smith threw himself from side to side within it, despite being handcuffed, and despite the efforts of half a dozen accompanying security staff to restrain him. On that day, and every day for six months at Broadmoor, he was confined twenty-four hours a day to a maximum security seclusion room in Cavendish. No exercise. A six-man unlock every day just to give him his medication. Sometimes he still had the energy to kick at the reinforced door for half an hour afterwards, the deafening crash echoing like a tolling bell, before the anti-psychosis drugs finally overcame his resistance. This battle of wills went on week after week. Dozens of nurses were hurt or injured, staff went off sick to avoid being on control and restraint duty. A few resigned.

Then, finally, a change of behaviour. A quieter and more manageable Lucy had slowly emerged over the last six months. Richard Lamb, Broadmoor's clinical director, had even allowed Lucy a little associative time in the day with other patients recently. It had all gone swimmingly.

Until tonight. Now, six frightened staff had to take on Lucy again, and in a hurry. They were all kitted up, but there had been no time for a proper team talk. This was not a time of their choosing. Featherstone, who had seen action in the Falklands War of 1982, flipped up his visor and turned to them. 'Everyone okay? Ready for this?'

They all nodded, then touched their gloved knuckles together for good luck, just like boxers at the start of a bout. Dawn's heart was fluttering in her throat, pulse pounding in her ears, breath fogging up her visor. She'd forgotten to rub the inside with a cut onion, an old motorcyclist's trick that Featherstone had told her during training. They marched down the corridor and Featherstone unlocked each door in turn until they got to the seclusion unit. The roaring was deafening now, like a caged bull. The door to Lucy's cell was booming every few seconds, and she could see it vibrate. Ahead of her, Karl Sullivan, who had been shaking worse than anyone, stepped out of formation. He flipped up his visor and bent over, an arm braced on the corridor wall. As the retching sounds began, Dawn turned away, anxious in case he set her off.

'Dawn!' Featherstone yelled into her helmet, trying to make himself heard over the racket. 'You are going to be fine. Okay, pet? Stand well back until you're ready to give it to him. Don't get kicked. If you stick yourself, you'll be a zombie for a fortnight.'

She nodded.

Lucifer Smith, now aware of their presence, bellowed Featherstone's name and then roared: 'I'm going to chew your fucking *heart* out!'

Featherstone managed half a smile, as if to say: *What a scamp you are, Lucy*. He turned back to Dawn. 'How much Acuphase you got in that syringe?'

'A hundred and fifty milligrams,' she shouted. 'I thought I'd go for the maximum safe intramuscular dose.'

Featherstone shook his head. 'That's the maximum for humans, pet. But that's Lucy we've got in there.' He winked and grinned. 'Make it two fifty, that's the dose for monsters.'

Dawn took out the half-full bottle of oily yellowish liquid and looked at it. 'But Geoff, what if I hit a vein?'

Her question was lost in the noise as Featherstone turned to the cell and peered through the armoured inspection glass. His jaw hung open at what he saw. 'Jesus Christ almighty,' he said.

'What is it, boss?' asked Tyrone.

'Nothing. Forget it.' Featherstone then pulled himself up to his full height. 'Leonard Lucifer Smith,' he bellowed, 'listen to me. Stand away from the door and then lie face down on the floor, limbs outstretched, with your head towards the door. We're coming in. Do you understand?'

Receiving nothing but obscenities and a body check against the door, Featherstone took out his huge bunch of keys, inserted one in the lock and turned it. With Tyrone Mgonwe to his left, and Trevor to his right, he pushed the door open.

What they saw next none of them would ever forget.

* * *

Richard Lamb had been the clinical director at Broadmoor Hospital for almost twenty years. During decades of experience with psychiatric patients he had seen almost everything that the most dangerous and disturbed were capable of. But some things defied belief. This was one of them.

An urgent call had awoken Lamb at home on Sunday morning at 2.57am. 'I'm afraid it's about Lucy,' said Trevor Cooke, the night duty medical staffer.

Lamb groaned.

'He was going crazy in his cell, and there was blood everywhere. The SMU was a disaster, everyone sliding and slipping, took us half an hour to get the needle in. Looked like *The Texas Chainsaw Massacre* by the time we got him tranquilised. But no serious injuries to staff. He was then taken by ambulance to Frimley Park Hospital.'

'What's wrong with him?'

'Agonising internal pains. That was no act. I thought it might be peritonitis from a ruptured appendix, given the amount of blood he's passed, so I authorised the transfer immediately as an emergency. I hope that's alright?'

'Of course. Broadmoor *is* a hospital. We want people to get better, and this is clearly beyond our resources.' Lamb was normally reluctant to sanction external treatment. Medical outings to the nearest accident and emergency department, either Frimley Park or Wokingham General, were highly prized by patients as antidotes to institutional boredom. Broadmoor's many attention-seekers and self-harmers thirsted to be beyond the high fences, to enjoy the stares of the public in A&E, and to revel in being so dangerous they needed a small accompanying army to restrain them. That was no exaggeration in Lucy's case.

'I'll ring you back, Director, when we know more.'

'Okay, okay. Goodbye.' Lamb hung up and rubbed his eyes, feeling that one of his few aspiring success stories was now in danger.

It was nearly 5am and Lamb was just falling back to sleep when the next call came. Dr Prakesh Choudary, Frimley's hospital registrar, was on the line. He wanted high-level consent for the operation that he was proposing. What he described led Lamb to do something he had never done before. To get up at night and go to the hospital to see what a patient had apparently done to himself. What he had just been told did not make sense, because Lucy for all his troubles had not once in four years self-harmed. But there was apparently an X-ray to prove it. He had to see it for himself.

Self-harm is a way of life in secure psychiatric hospitals. The obvious objects which patients could use to hurt themselves like razors, scissors and knives are banned. Prohibition also covered some less obvious ones: small batteries which could be swallowed and cause internal burns; DVDs and CDs which could be snapped and turned into blades; sticky tape, lengths of which could be twisted into almost unbreakable ligatures. But there was always something new.

When Lamb arrived, Featherstone was still there. He said he had sanctioned the full 'royal procession' of eight burly escorts for Lucy, two of them handcuffed to him. Despite by then being in a wheelchair, Lucy's presence and roars of pain had virtually emptied the place. According to Featherstone, the drunken Saturday night girls, tottering on high-heels with semi-conscious friends, the bruised lads recounting the night's post-pub skirmishes, and the winos with their Carlsberg Special all fell silent. Lamb could imagine it. Lucy was the ultimate sobering vision.

A nurse quickly took Lamb through to see the registrar. Lucy himself was under sedation, and his many minders were standing around chuckling to themselves at what had happened to him.

'This is what I wanted to show you,' said Dr Choudary, a short and harried-looking man. The X-ray of Lucy's abdomen showed the pale grey of massive hip bones and the spine right up to the ribs, with dark smoky shadows for kidneys, spleen and intestines. But that wasn't where the eye was drawn. Occupying most of the length of what Choudary identified as the colon was something that at first glance resembled the skeleton of a snake. Yet it was too bright, too hard-edged and alien to be that. Even a layman like Lamb could see it did not belong within the soft vulnerable viscera of any creature.

'I've been a doctor for fifteen years,' Choudary said. 'I've seen all sorts of things inside patients. But this,' he pointed, 'I have never seen. It could not be swallowed, and if it had been inserted anally there would be even more extensive trauma and blood loss at the point of entry and beyond. But there isn't. The bleeding is coming from its present location, from intestinal spasms. Somehow I've got to get it out without killing him.'

Lamb felt his testicles contract in sympathy with Lucy's pain. 'Is it really what it appear to be?'

'I'm afraid so. He has eighteen inches of razor wire inside him.'

* * *

Back in Broadmoor Hospital, another patient had by Sunday morning heard the news of Smith's injury. William Mordant was lying on his bed in his cell in the low-security Boxhill Ward with the door open. His blond wavy hair had just been carefully cut, he was meticulously clean shaven and he had an even tan that brought out the perfection of his large whitened teeth. Mordant had acquired the tan from hours spent catching every ray outside the ward, either painting, sketching or working in Broadmoor's vegetable garden. He was listening on headphones to Stravinsky's *The Rite of Spring* on BBC Radio Three, and smiling to himself. Boxhill Ward houses the assertive rehabilitation unit, where patients who are both cooperative and making progress towards normality have some privileges. Key amongst them are unlocked cell doors during daylight hours and monitored times of free association with fellow patients. There was carefully-censored cable TV and a large collection of programmes held on the hospital's hard drive. But Mordant had even more privileges than this. They had been granted in recognition of his unique standing, unprecedented in the history of British secure psychiatric care. These privileges, and indeed every aspect of his incarceration, were secret. The British public would be outraged, particularly given the horrific nature of his crimes. But then the British public didn't know about his crimes. Powerful forces within the Home Office had made sure of that.

Mordant stared up at the pictures and sketches which had been carefully fixed to almost every square inch of his cell walls and ceiling. Most of the photos had been cut from magazines. This was not the pornographic fare which besmirched the cells of the prison system. These were mostly photographs from glossy fashion magazines, *Elle*, *Vogue*, *Vanity Fair*, and the weekend magazines of the British press. Every one of those pictures, covering a period of eighteen months, was of the same person. Some were shampoo advertisements that made much of her luxuriant chestnut hair, some were for cosmetics, while one in *Vanity Fair* showed an emerald pendant to match those astonishing viridian eyes. Among the later issues was one in *Hello!* of her in a green silk dress on a red carpet for some event. The *Elle* picture was a front cover just a month old. The headline was 'Destined for stardom: Meet Mira Roskova'.

Mordant pulled out his sketchpad and a soft 3b pencil, and once again tried to capture the ethereal beauty of this young woman who so occupied his thoughts. Twenty minutes later he set the pad down. He'd certainly drawn a face of beauty, recognisable as the subject. Most art students would have been more than happy with the result. But Mordant was quite unlike most art students, and was far from satisfied. Very far. Mordant was a seeker after perfection. And this young woman was *absolute* perfection. Ultimate beauty in a tarnished world. She was the one subject he regarded as beyond his artistic ability, the one who despite repeated effort he only perfectly captured in the cavernous halls of his imagination.

Mira Roskova was William Mordant's obsession. And no-one does obsession quite like those within the walls of Broadmoor. Mordant had been diagnosed with a severe personality disorder, exhibiting manipulative and highly intelligent narcissistic psychopathy. A man for whom taking a life is no more troubling than clipping his nails. But one eminent former professor of psychiatry, who himself suffered a nervous breakdown after his very first session with Mordant, had a different view. It was expressed in a clinical assessment unusually free of psychiatric jargon: 'William Mordant may appear perfectly normal and well-adjusted. But underneath he is a cauldron of simmering, concentrated evil.'

That was Professor Shapiro's view, though Mordant had heard it before from others. But it was merely that in his pursuit of beauty Mordant detested anything unsightly. Of course the ugly and the repulsive, the twisted or the crippled sullied his life in this place. To be immersed so unjustly in such a place was of course a test, and a superlative one, of his aspiration for the flawless and the sublime. It was one to which he was equal. Disciplining his mind to filter out the dirt, tuning out the dissonance left him free to wander as the god of his own ethereal and immaculate world.

Almost always.

Just two weeks ago, Leonard Lucifer Smith was being escorted by two male nurses from the visits centre through Boxhill Ward, when he should have gone the direct route to Cavendish. Smith and Mordant had history and were considered incompatible. They were not supposed to run into each other. But when Mordant looked up in Boxhill's refectory, he saw Smith shambling towards him, ignoring the calls from the two male nurses. Smith looked at the copy of *Cosmopolitan* on whose cover Mira was quite demurely displayed. He bent over Mordant and said: 'I know who's shagging her. And I hear she's a dirty little bitch.'

Chapter Eight

Across the prosperous and leafy suburbs of Berkshire sirens began to wail, drowning out conversation over fifty square miles. While these aged sirens evoke a half-remembered dread of air raids among those old enough to recall World War II, they now have a more practical purpose. They are Broadmoor escape alarms, tested every Monday morning at ten o'clock precisely. They are a reminder that while this secure psychiatric hospital is no longer listed as a home for the criminally insane, that is still a very good working definition for its most dangerous patients. Especially those minded to escape.

As the two-minute all clear sounded, Richard Lamb called the Serious Incident Review meeting to order. With him was Clive Harrington, Smith's primary nurse. Harrington's relaxed manner belied the huge experience that the gangly British-born Jamaican had. If anyone understood Lunatic Lucy, Harrington did. Also around the table were Lucy's forensic psychiatrist Dr Miguel Kasovas, police liaison officer Sergeant Deborah Crooke, and head of security Geoff Featherstone.

'Down to business, then,' Lamb said. 'As you know, yesterday Smith had a partial colectomy in Frimley Park Hospital in which a length of razor wire was removed from his large intestine.' He looked around. Even though everyone had heard what had happened, there were cringes around the table. 'He may just avoid having to use a colostomy bag for the rest of his life.'

Harrington grinned. 'I don't think SMUs and colostomy bags would mix very well.'

'How on earth did razor wire get inside him?' Crooke asked. 'If he couldn't have done it to himself, then someone did it to him. And then we have a crime.'

'Let's not be too hasty,' Lamb said, mindful of the burdensome regulatory oversight that registering a crime would incur. 'Can you remind us what Smith himself said about it, Geoff?'

Featherstone responded, 'Not too much. When he was asked if he had hurt himself, he replied, and I quote: "Not me. It was GCHQ. I won't listen to the messages they beam into my head, so now they want me fucking dead." Unquote. He wasn't very coherent, but claimed no memory of anything after watching TV in the afternoon. He thought he'd been hypnotised by GCHQ while watching.'

'That sounds significant,' said Kasovas, a small and balding figure, sucking ruminatively on the arm of his spectacles. 'Could he have been sedated by someone else?'

'I have to confess it's hard to see how anyone else but him could have done it,' Featherstone said.

'His blood tests will be through in a day or two,' Lamb said.

'If we can untangle his own extensive medication regime from something he should not have been given.'

'There's nothing on the CCTV record,' Featherstone said. 'No one went to his room. It corresponds with the duty log. Smith had been seen watching TV in the afternoon. He was absent for the evening meal. His room was checked about half an hour afterwards, and he was inside, apparently asleep. There was no reply when the Cavendish ward night duty nurse called to him.'

'Which nurse?' Crooke asked.

'Dawn Evans,' Harrington said.

Featherstone continued. 'There was no further contact until 10.48pm. The duty nurse on the east corridor checked to see Smith was inside, which he was, apparently asleep, and locked the door. Then the corridor locks were set at 11pm, which I checked personally.' Featherstone flicked over the page and then continued. 'It was 2.08am when the duty medic was called.'

'When did Smith first complain of being unwell?' Dr Kasovas asked.

'He started shouting at about one, one-thirty,' Featherstone said, scanning his notes.

'That sounds a bit vague. Who was on duty for his corridor?' Lamb asked.

'Tyrone Mgonwe. When I spoke to him he said that he ignored it for a while, knowing what Smith is like.'

'But he was in pain, Geoffrey,' said Kasovas.

'To be fair, Mgonwe couldn't know that. Obviously, we've had no end of shenanigans from Smith over the years, yelling, and shouting and getting attention. I can well understand why he took a while to register that it wasn't the usual nonsense.'

Lamb leaned forward, hands steepled before him. 'The fact remains, Geoff, that Smith was in pain for an hour or so before help was called.'

'Yes, but that's hindsight. We've had times in the past when we would have needed an extra nurse just to check up on him every time he made a racket.'

'This is a *hospital*. It's not a prison. We're here to make people better,' Lamb said gently. 'Look at it through an inspector's eyes. They won't care if Smith cries wolf a dozen times a day. It will go down as a lapse in clinical care.'

'Clive and I had a look in Smith's room yesterday,' said Crooke, pushing her fringe of grey hair aside. 'No one's to go in there, in case it is declared a crime scene. I can't remember ever seeing so much blood.'

'If you think that was bad, you should have seen how much was on him,' Featherstone said. 'He'd smeared it all over himself. After the SMU we all looked like him.'

'I want to see all the CCTV again, for the twelve hours leading up to the intervention,' said Lamb. 'By Thursday morning I want to be able to answer the following questions: One, did he do it himself? Two, was it another patient…'

'Or a member of staff with a grudge,' Crooke interjected. 'We can't rule that out.'

'Yes, indeed,' Lamb conceded. 'And three, how was razor wire and whatever else was required, procured within Britain's allegedly most secure psychiatric hospital.'

* * *

It was gone eleven on a Wednesday evening. Lamb sat next to the bulky figure of security chief Geoff Featherstone in the Broadmoor CCTV control centre. They had polished off three packets of crisps, two Mars Bars and a Twix in the last four hours as they screened the most boring re-runs in television history: Broadmoor doors, corridors and fences. Lamb thought wistfully of the leftover *boeuf bourguignon* that his wife would have waiting for him at their home in Crowthorne when he finally finished.

Though there were a hundred and twenty-six CCTV cameras in Broadmoor, they did not give total coverage. The architectural peculiarities of the Grade II listed Victorian building provided dozens of blind spots and hidden corners well known to patients. Those corners had over the years been used for pre-arranged fights and the settling of scores, for gambling, for drug-taking and, inevitably, for sex. The only bedrooms covered by CCTV were those for patients in seclusion, where self-harm or suicide were a clear risk. The control room could only display twenty-seven camera views at a time on its monitors, three rows of nine. Those were watched by two security staff, sometimes only one at night. All the camera files were recorded and automatically downloaded every hour to a huge sixty-terabyte database. Even so, the huge data demands of even this low definition video meant that each file was overwritten after thirty days to free up space. That wasn't a problem because with the staffing levels at Broadmoor, five for every patient, incidents always came to light pretty quickly.

Featherstone had narrowed down the search on the system. The folder for Saturday 24 January broke down into folders by ward, then by time of day and finally by camera. Eight cameras covered the patient-accessible areas of Cavendish Ward, including one on the east corridor which led to Lucifer Smith's room. Lamb and Featherstone split the files between them, and fast-forwarded through eight hours of footage per camera to track Lucy's movements. At four times normal speed, the tattooed giant was frenetic. On Saturday afternoon Smith watched TV, got up, sprinted around, gobbled food, sprinted about, watched more TV, sat around, dozed off, woke up, watched more TV, gobbled more food, and then sprinted off to his room. No-one came to visit him in his room. Indeed, nobody seemed to talk to him much at all. When he walked into a room, other patients and even staff just parted like water beneath the prow of a ship. That presumably was the effect Leonard Lucifer Smith had in mind when he decided to get tattooed to look like the devil incarnate.

'This just doesn't make sense,' Lamb said. 'We've seen all the recordings. There is literally nothing to see. No social contact. No one else has been to his room, except staff checking on him.'

'Let's look at the recreation room again,' Featherstone said. He clicked on the icon and the video began. Lucy was sitting in his usual place, in front of the big TV holding the remote control, which was supposed to be at the nurse's station. One of the enduring issues with Lucy was about consideration and sharing. He consistently monopolised the big TV. Many patients shared Smith's obsession with football so didn't mind.

Those who did mind were too intimidated to contest it or to complain to the staff. Instead they just returned to their rooms where they had their own smaller TV sets. However, it wasn't sport showing that day, but a children's cartoon. Lamb recognised the animated features of Princess Fiona.

'Hang on a minute,' Lamb said. 'Freeze that a minute.' He turned to the computer and searched online for the TV listings. 'That's *Shrek II* on ITV, yes?'

'That's right,' Featherstone chuckled. 'I bought my grandson the DVD. He loves it.'

'Geoff,' Lamb said, 'ITV *didn't* show *Shrek II* on 24 January. The listings say they showed it on the seventeenth. But we've got it here on the recording for the twenty-fourth.'

'What are you saying?'

'That these aren't the files for the twenty-fourth. Someone's overwritten them with files from a week earlier.'

Featherstone frowned. 'No that can't be.'

'What else could it be?'

'Okay. There's one way to check.' He opened the corresponding camera file for 17 January and ran it side by side with that from 24 January. They were identical.

'Fuck.' Featherstone leaned back and ran his hands through his cropped greying hair.

'Has this ever happened before?' Lamb asked.

'It could happen by accident. The overwrites are done manually on a Sunday night. I did them myself yesterday. But 24 January files shouldn't be overwritten until February. Let me see who edited them.' He clicked through to a different log.

The long silence made Lamb look up 'Who was it?'

'It says I did it. My initials. Someone logged in as me.'

'How is that possible?'

'It shouldn't be. It's password protected.' He sat down, head in his hands. 'I can't explain this.'

'Geoff, get me a list of all the staff who were on control room duty from Saturday night until nine this morning,' Lamb said. 'Do we have a camera that covers this room?'

'The control room? No, we don't spy on staff.'

'Perhaps we should,' Lamb said.

'Okay,' said Featherstone. He then checked the other seven camera folders on the ward, running corresponding video files side by side for 24 January and 17 January, and for 25 January and 18 January. They were all identical. He checked the deleted file bin, and the data sticks. There was nothing there marked as 24 or 17 January.

At midnight they had to admit it. 'We have no record of what happened anywhere in Cavendish Ward from noon on Saturday until 5am on Sunday,' Featherstone said.

'The first file that hasn't been overwritten on Sunday was the 6am, so the overwriting must have happened just before that while most of us were at the hospital. Whoever did it needed to hide their tracks for the previous eighteen hours,' Lamb said.

'Dawn Evans was on duty here alone until 7am after the SMU,' Featherstone said. 'But it can't be her. She's only been in the control room once before, and only has a training password which gives no access to file editing. And frankly she couldn't even find her way round the 'read-only' screens on the training session I ran.'

'So why was she allowed to be here on her own?' Lamb asked.

'Because, Richard, we were desperate. I needed everyone else to either escort Lucy or calm the other patients who'd heard him ranting and screaming. We literally had no one else available.'

Lamb sighed. He understood the difficulty. It was always difficult to recruit and retain the best staff, and even fewer were happy to work night shifts.

'Ah, but we can check exactly when the files were altered,' Featherstone said, suddenly enthused. 'There's a system activity user log, which should give us a time stamp for each type of operation.'

He called up the file, and then stared in amazement. 'The clock has been zeroed.' He cursored down the screen and blew a huge sigh. 'Everything for both those days happened at 00:00. Christ, I don't even know how to do that myself. I'd have to look at the manual.' He reached across and pulled the system manual down from the shelf behind his desk.

Lamb was silent, stroking his face thoughtfully. 'Geoff, whoever did this knows more about the system than you. Is that a fair assessment?'

Featherstone shrugged. 'I suppose so. It must be staff. I can't see even our cleverest psychopaths getting in here to do this, Richard.'

'Not without help, that's for sure.' Lamb shuddered. 'Okay, let's call it a day. Go home. We'll think more clearly tomorrow.'

Fifteen minutes later Lamb was walking across the car park, fretting about the report he was going to have to write about this terrible lapse in security. He pressed his key fob and the Volvo flashed its orange welcome. He stowed his briefcase in the boot, then turned around and surveyed Broadmoor's grim gothic silhouette, the backdrop to his working life. He recalled again the words of the departing clinical director, Gerald Templeman, on Lamb's first day in post all those years ago. 'Never forget, Richard that some of these people are more intelligent than any of us. They have motive, they have ability, and they certainly have lots and lots of time. They are untroubled by moral doubt. Never, ever underestimate them.'

Chapter Nine

William Mordant was unique within Broadmoor because he was allowed to set his daily regime. While staff and patients followed the dreary institutional timetable, he had been able to negotiate his own, within limits. He would awaken at 6am, do a brisk thirty minutes of Canadian Air Force exercises in his room, usually while listening to Wagner on cordless headphones, finishing off with a dozen one-armed press-ups, alternating arms, executed to *The Flying Dutchman*. His door would be unlocked at 6.30am, half an hour earlier than anyone else's, and he was first in the refectory for a breakfast of fruit and low-sugar muesli before heading for the studio adjoining Boxhill Ward, to which he was allowed a key. The studio was pretty much his personal property every Monday, Wednesday and Friday morning, which he considered right and proper seeing as it was the sales of his art that had raised most of the one and a quarter million pounds it had cost to build. The vaulted space, designed *pro bono* by Norman Foster, was only four months old and still had the aromatic sappy smell of new wood. The curved beams underneath the glass-roofed atrium gave it a wonderful lightness. Many of the other patients, uglies and simpletons without an ounce of artistic sentiment or skill, would still come to sit in the studio, simply to feel the wonder of it. He would always shoo them out when he wanted to work.

These early morning sessions were artistically very important to him. His unfettered mind roamed the ether at night and the wisps and shreds of ideas that he retained from these voyages were the inspiration for his art. But there were more practical reasons for the timing too. He had been nurturing Dawn Evans for almost two years now, and the first half hour of his studio days were the only chance for them to make their assignations with privacy. Few other patients were yet free from their rooms, other staff were busy with breakfast and could anyway be heard approaching. There was in this new annexe only one CCTV camera, and it covered only the area around the doors.

Dawn was setting up his easel when he arrived on Wednesday. She had been off rota for two days, but now she set out the paints and brushes, and his sketchpad. He knew these were just the small tasks to still her beating heart.

She was twenty-seven years old, decidedly plain and a little pudgy, with shoulder-length mousy hair. Her shy little grin entertained him. For all the fact that she had a BSc in clinical psychology from some dull suburban former polytechnic, she was an innocent. Better still, in the nervous twisting of her St. Christopher and her subtly submissive posture, she radiated loneliness and insecurity. How charitable of West London Mental Health Trust to cast this succulent and innocent morsel to the consummate predators of Broadmoor. Mordant had first noticed her at a clinical reassessment meeting in 2012 when he was first being considered for moving to Boxhill Ward from the more onerous restrictions of Cavendish Ward. Did the shrinks not realise? At every meeting when they were looking at and trying to understand him, he too was effortlessly logging and understanding them. He assessed their strengths and limitations, their nervous tics and irritabilities, their vulnerabilities and phobias. He could see them all.

He had seen Dawn across the table that first time. Like most of those present she avoided eye contact with him. Only Harrington and Lamb had ever managed to return his level gaze for more than a few seconds. Dawn had constantly changed the position of her legs, which were crossed, with the higher knee in a tight position which indicated her foot, though hidden from his sight by the table, was tucked behind her calf. Beyond the rustling of papers he had detected too, the slight tapping of a narrow heel, a feminine shoe, nervously thrumming against the chrome of her metal chair leg. Knotted legs, oscillating foot: uptight, nervous, maybe frightened too. She would presumably never have been allowed to read his confidential file, the one that Mr Justice Kirby had ruled should never be put into the public record. But she may have seen the redacted summary that Lamb probably had. His own barrister had shown it to him after the trial. That alone would terrify anyone.

The clincher was Dawn's lack of professional assertiveness. During the meeting she had been sucking her pen, and was making intermittent notes on a copy of the senior shrink's assessment report on him. Although Mordant couldn't read what she was writing, he could see that her notes were made on the corners of each page, at a slant, as if they were somehow a supplicant's addendum, not worthy of inclusion in the conventionally-written level text. Mordant's vulnerability radar latched onto it immediately. He had decided to watch Dawn Evans and wait for his moment.

That moment arrived a few weeks later when Dawn took her turn on the Tuesday afternoon group art sessions. Mordant was irritated that these sessions were largely time-killing exercises for the uglies. Those patients that appeared receptive were filtered off for small group art therapy sessions, led by Professor Ronald Shapiro, a consultant shrink from Reading University who instructed them in how to let art open up their childhood problems. Mordant had no intention of discussing his early life with some nosy academic. But by refusing to take part he was left in the company of a rump of the most troublesome, paranoid and delusional patients, and with poorer art equipment. Back then it had meant cheap watercolours, thin non-absorbent paper, and artificial fibre brushes that failed to retain their shape. They were not even allowed sharpeners for their ridiculously blunt pencils, for fear someone would unscrew the tiny blade and make a weapon.

They were supposed to be either drawing or painting a pair of colliery boots, crumpled and stained and full of character, which Dawn had placed on a stool in the centre of the class. While he quickly sketched them out in charcoal and chalk,

Mordant had noticed that Dawn's gaze kept skating over him. It wasn't surprising, it happened a lot. Not just the female staff either. He was fit, tanned and healthy, wearing a fresh tight white T-shirt every day, pressed chinos and, despite the irritating ban on shoelaces, polished brown brogues. He had used some of his meagre allowance to get the hospital hairdresser to put highlights in his blond wavy hair. No wonder Dawn's eyes were drawn to him, when the alternative visions were of shuffling overweight wrecks with straggly beards and halitosis, oversized acrylic sports shirts, food-stained jogging bottoms and scuffed trainers.

She had walked over to see what he was drawing. She complimented him on the charcoal drawing and picked it up. As he'd intended, a pencil sketch beneath slid to the floor. He picked it up quickly, but made sure she had seen it. It was a sketch of her, a little slimmer, a bit more upright and with a tad stronger cheekbones. Flattering but not false. Mordant had never mentioned to anyone in Broadmoor that in a previous life, and under his original name, he had briefly attended Goldsmiths College of Art. Anyone who had access to the confidential files would know that his long-dead father, Sir Anthony Hooksworth, was a famous society portraitist. Only a handful of people knew the truth.

He and Dawn fell into conversation about art, and she professed an interest in the Pre-Raphaelites and Impressionists. He stressed that it was impossible to paint properly without the right materials. He particularly pleaded for acid-free, buffered paper with a high rag content. 'Or even just a single size four sable-hair brush. If

I don't get a proper brush, I think I'll go insane…Oh.' He put a hand over his mouth in mock horror at his joke.

She laughed, but said nothing.

The next week she slipped onto his easel a slim tissue-wrapped object. Inside was a Winsor & Newton sable No. 4. He looked up and gave her his most winning smile. She raised a brief finger to her lips: say nothing. Which of course meant that she hadn't found it in the art therapy cupboard but had bought it herself and smuggled it in. A thin skein of complicity was thus spun between them, a tendril that Mordant would imperceptibly shorten and strengthen in the following months into friendship, conspiracy and finally, dependency.

The following week Mordant noticed that she was wearing a little make-up. Just a touch of eyeshadow and blusher. Subtle but, to him, obvious. Her lipstick, previously a coral-colour was now a little more scarlet, generously applied. Her teeth were a little pink where the colour had strayed. Did she know the anthropological origin of reddened lips? Perhaps not. Her psychology course wouldn't have covered lipstick's promised echo of an inviting engorged vulva.

He had all the time in the world to let their friendship blossom, and give her the illusion that he was the more reticent. If she felt in control their collusion could deepen more quickly, unaware that she was merely a transitory and disposable instrument in his long-term strategy. He had so much more experience of seduction than she, it was so easy as to be almost boring. The hardest part of his strategy had been to feign enthusiasm and passion.

Only by gradually revealing his artistry was he determined to be bold. While she had in the early days been unable to get him better quality paper, she had at least got him larger sheets, A1 cartridge paper almost a metre wide, perfect for drawing. With a larger easel, borrowed from art therapy, he was able to do something to show his gratitude. The drawing he came up with was a huge pair of hands four times life-size, cupping a grimy almost medieval key. They were the hands of an old labouring man, thick knobbly knuckles, liver-spotted, massive worn fingers with chipped nails, calloused tips and ingrained dirt. He made use of the full tonal range of the pencils, from the solid black shadow beneath the key, to the highlights caught on its time-burnished bow and shank.

He tormented Dawn by covering the drawing whenever she came near. That didn't stop him calling her over every few minutes so that he could use the pencil sharpener that was connected to the key chain at her belt. At those moments they were very close, and as he sat on the stool turning a pencil that he could so easily have stabbed her with, he could feel her cool breath on the top of his head.

The drawing took several weeks, but when it was finished, the key had a power that demanded the viewer reach out and grab it. For once, he was fully satisfied. When he finally unveiled the drawing, named *Proffered Freedom*, Dawn was astounded. Not least because he had drawn it entirely from imagination. The drawing was then framed, shown to the great and the good, the visiting consultants, the shrinks and the director. Everyone wanted to be his friend. How nice. The consultant psychiatrist from Reading had even asked to see him, one-to-one. Here, after all, was a chance to make art therapy snag a big prize. To redeem the irredeemable. Mordant recognised Professor Shapiro's professional hunger, and played with him, deferring the meeting time and again, eventually demanding to see him at the obtusely inconvenient time of nine on a Sunday bank holiday evening.

That meeting was to Mordant, hilarious. This eager man, stiff with paper qualifications and thwarted ambition, sat opposite him at a table with the drawing between them. But the professor could not sit still. Despite the presence of two beefy male nurses at the door of the interview room, he sweated a pungent fear. Mordant instinctively felt that this man had been allowed to glimpse his detailed records.

'So William,' Shapiro had said, failing to make any eye contact. 'You can go a long way with your art. In the future it can be sold, for the benefit of the psychiatric hospital system and to raise awareness of the talent that would otherwise lie rotting away...'

'I don't regard myself as rotting, do you?' Mordant said, staring at the professor.

'No, of course, I don't mean actually...,' Shapiro said, staring down at his notes. 'Erm, more like, um...'

'I would suggest latent, or inchoate. Not rotting.' Mordant touched his fingertips to the tabletop. 'Why are your legs trembling, Professor?'

'It's nervous energy, when I'm concentrating.'

'Something in common with the patients, then. They are a frequent symptom among those nurturing a psychosis. Medication can help, you know.'

'But about your artwork…'

There was a knock at the door. Trevor let in a young female nurse whom Mordant had never seen before. 'I've got a message for Professor Shapiro,' she said, and passed it straight to Mordant.

'Umm, I'm Professor Shapiro, actually,' Shapiro said sharply, snatching the message and waving his lanyard.

'Oh, sorry, I just thought…' Mordant watched the nurse's glance flick from him, upright and poised in his sharp grey jacket and brilliant white open-neck shirt, across to Shapiro who slouched in a baggy worn-out suit, with his straggly moustache and greasy spectacles.

'That's perfectly alright,' Mordant oozed, holding her gaze. 'It's an easy mistake to make. He's been consorting with nutcases for an awfully long time. Don't worry about it.' The nurse grinned at him as she turned away.

Despite offending the professor, Mordant found that concessions began to be seen. He was granted his own easel and paper supply in his room. His own pencils and, after six months and an intervention from Dawn, oil paints so long as he painted in the art room. Linseed oil for mixing colours, alas, was forbidden as was white spirit. Flammable solvents were a step too far. This meant that poor Dawn had to clean his brushes. Soon after the Künzler Trust sold his first two drawings, *Proffered Freedom* and *Remembrance of Seaside*, a portrait of his own bare feet resting in a bowl of bowl of water, for eight hundred pounds. Realising where this could take him, Mordant found a rush of artistic energy. Director Richard

Lamb agreed that a portion of the cash from sales could go to providing art equipment throughout Boxhill Ward. Mordant's colourful portrait of Clive Harrington, his first oil painting on proper stretched canvas, was snapped up before the trust could even display it.

That was when the Bishop of Uxbridge first came to see him, with news that a foreign buyer was interested in commissioning work from him, a large oil painting. Though the bishop said he couldn't betray confidences, he had been told that this was one of the world's most savvy collectors, who already owned paintings by Holbein, Delacroix, Titian and Van Gogh.

'He said you exhibited the craft of an old master, which is now so very rare. But he would like to know what type of paintings you would be prepared to create.'

On a whim Mordant said, 'I'm inspired to make a devotional work.'

'Really?' the bishop had said, all soft brown eyes, Hush Puppies and forgiveness. 'Have you been feeling a connection with the Lord?'

Mordant adopted a pained expression and hesitated. 'You know, I was reticent. For many years I drifted in a moral wilderness, not listening to what my soul was telling me.' He opened his eyes wide and stared intently at the bishop. 'Do you know, there was a time when I could extinguish a human life with less regret than a half-burned cigarette?' He crushed an imaginary butt on the table. 'Can you believe that?' Mordant watched the bishop's throat contract. Yes, he could.

'I understand you were originally imprisoned for murder,' the bishop said. Mordant had rarely heard a more naked attempt to elicit information.

'Yes,' Mordant whispered, shaking his head. 'Horrible murders, unforgiveable.'

'There is always forgiveness in the Lord,' the bishop said gently. 'If you truly repent. There is always hope.'

'I saw a vision, you know. In my room. A few weeks ago. I saw the cross, and the suffering of Christ. I saw him die to save me, there in my own room. And I heard a voice.'

The bishop reached out for his hand, stroking it. 'What did this voice say?'

Mordant hesitated, closing his eyes and raising his head, whispered: 'It said, "there is mercy in the Lord". It was then that I knew I had to paint, for my own spiritual salvation.'

All that had gone very well indeed. Mordant had established a track record of impeccable behaviour, and he had insinuated himself into the soul of a bishop who he now knew would champion his moral rehabilitation through art. He had also been able to get Dawn to do extraordinary things for him, to get to the next stage of his plan.

Today, though, he was going to have to be very careful. As soon as he saw Dawn, he could tell that she was upset with him. He knew exactly why. There had been a different atmosphere in the ward for the last few days after Lucy's 'accident.' There was a stiff formality in the staff, and he wanted to find out if his expectations were correct.

The moment he arrived, with smouldering eyes, she turned her back to him. 'Dawn,' he whispered. 'My muse, I've been dreaming about you.' He took her arm gently and pulled her into the corner of the studio, where no one passing the reinforced glass door could see them.

'You had better leave me alone,' she said. 'I am in so much trouble, Will, because of you.' She bit her lip. 'I should never have let you come with me to the security room on Sunday.'

'But kitten, what an opportunity! All the night security staff were with Lunatic Lucy at hospital, and just you to mind the screens for a couple of hours. It is the only room without CCTV coverage. How else are we to tryst, my darling, without being observed?' He put his bare arms around her, and felt her soften a little. 'Was it not wonderful?' A small smile played on her lips and she looked up cheekily. It was, he knew that. Mordant instinctively knew that she had never had a lover who spent time to give her pleasure, after pleasure, after pleasure.

'But Dr Lamb's on the warpath. Did you muck about with the computers when I was in the loo?'

Mordant kissed her neck and whispered into her ear. 'I did tell you that I would have to overwrite the video that showed me walking in.'

'I don't remember you saying that.'

'Of course. That's why you photocopied the CCTV manual for me. It was only to protect you. You could lose your job, and then I couldn't see you anymore. You do understand that, don't you?'

'Mmm,' Dawn sighed, putting her arms around him. 'But Will, they rang me up on Monday and asked about the database overwrites. I told them the truth. I've never been trained how to do the overwrites. I only know how to use the monitoring console. I don't even know the password.'

'If you don't know the password, then it couldn't have been you, could it, Puss?'

'They did accept what I said. They've also interviewed Tyrone Mgonwe and Nigel Robb. They both were trained in the system. But now there's a formal investigation and I'm really worried.'

'You've done nothing to the computer so you have nothing to worry about.'

Mordant himself had had no trouble cracking the six-digit password. Geoff Featherstone was a man of no imagination, and his untidy workstation at the back of the security room was a pastiche of family pictures, including the dog-eared christening invitation for a grandson, Daniel, born 17 April 2008. The date was underlined in felt tip. Mordant had typed in 170408, and got straight in. Had it failed, Featherstone had left plenty of other clues. Featherstone's P60 was in his unlocked desk, giving his date of birth, national insurance number and his address in Crowthorne. His office diary had a reminder for his wedding anniversary. Lots of dates to go on. He memorised them all just in case he ever needed to get out in a hurry, or trade information for something even more precious. Perhaps the most valuable nugget, gleaned from a local newspaper cutting on the pinboard, was that little Daniel went to Abbotsmead Primary School in Wokingham. Perfect if he ever needed to exert a little pressure on Featherstone. He had friends outside who could help.

'Will, I'm worried. Sometimes I think that we're on a runaway

99

train, and I don't know where it's going to end.' Dawn pressed her face into the warmth of his chest.

'Dawn, the moment I first saw your sweet innocent face, it was like the first opening of a rosebud, bejewelled in dew on a spring morning. You're precious to me and I'll keep you safe,' Mordant said. 'Because I love you.'

Dawn kissed him tenderly. 'Will, no one has ever said such things to me before. I've never loved anyone, Will, like I love you.'

It was true. Mordant had received dozens of little notes from her over the months. Sweet little cards with pussycats and puppies and hearts, all in her careful neat well-brought up handwriting in which she pledged her undying love, and her determination to right the miscarriage of justice which had brought him to this place, for crimes which he had never committed. She had even, in her innocent and amateurish way, tried to please him by writing her own sexual suggestions. For him she was trying to break her own boundaries, but to Mordant they were kitchen sink vignettes, fifty shades of gravy. While he knew every word of John Donne's and Shakespeare's love sonnets, she could manage only *The Owl and the Pussycat*. Nevertheless, Mordant had carefully preserved each and every note, nails in her professional coffin should he ever really need to apply some pressure.

'We have to wait, my sweet one,' Mordant murmured, stroking her hair and nuzzling her ears. 'There will be more time on Friday, and the shifts make it safer. We mustn't compromise your career. Sometimes, you know, I have to think for both of us.'

'I'd throw it all away for you,' she said, and he knew she meant it. In the end, whether she wanted to or not, she would.

As they embraced, Mordant looked over Dawn's trembling shoulder at a magazine picture of Mira Roskova he had stuck on the wall. *Soon, my dear, I will be with you. Just be patient.*

* * *

Mordant was surprised how long it took for the director to call him to interview about Lucy's injuries. With the director were Mordant's own psychiatrist, the wonderfully malleable Dr Miguel Kasovas, and a stone-faced police liaison officer, Sergeant Deborah Crooke. *Not an ally, I fear.* Richard Lamb began by describing the events of that night, and Mordant feigned ignorance of much of the detail. 'So what exactly were the nature of those injuries?' Mordant asked. 'I'd assumed it was self-inflicted.'

He absorbed a very hard glare from the grey helmet-haired sergeant. 'No it wasn't. A sharp object was inserted inside him, causing serious injury.'

'Inserted? Ouch.' Mordant pouted sympathetic pain. 'It would be a brave man to tackle him, surely.'

'Smith was clearly drugged,' Sergeant Crooke said.

'So it must have been a member of staff,' Mordant said. *Ah, the word 'clearly' meaning you don't actually know. Of course not. Rohypnol is very quickly metabolised.*

The director leaned forward, his hands steepled in front of him. 'William, you and Smith have a bit of history, don't you?'

Oh, here we go. 'Our paths crossed at Wakefield.'

'I'd put it more strongly than that, William,' Lamb said, looking down at a document in front of him. 'The report from HMP Wakefield mentions two incidents, one of which involved boiling water being poured over him from the landing above, causing second degree burns to his head, neck and shoulders.'

'That wasn't me. And the report doesn't say so either.' *You forgot to mention all the sugar I had dissolved in the saucepan so it would really stick and burn.*

Lamb sighed. 'You were among those identified as being present, and having a motive...'

'Dr Lamb, please. Lucy generates motives in almost everyone. Can I ask how many members of your staff he's hurt? How many have gone off sick, resigned from having to deal with him? They all have motives as good if not better than mine for revenge. But I, alone, spend almost all my time in a separate ward with a security-coded door between us. Surely your CCTV would show exactly who was able to do this.'

It was with the greatest satisfaction that Mordant noticed not one of them had anything left to say.

Chapter Ten

Two weeks after the assault on Mira

Dear Lawrence,

As you know things have been very difficult between us in the past few weeks. I feel hurt and frightened and saw a side of you that I did not know was there. I have thought long and hard about our relationship, and given the intensity of both of our lives at the moment, feel that it would be best for both of us if we took time away. I still have feelings for you, and I know you have about me. I will do everything to protect the privacy of this news, and of the time we spent together, and I'm sure you will too.

With affection

Mira XX

'Nice one,' Jonesy said, passing the photocopy back to Thad. 'Like it.'

'What do you think, Virgil?' Portia asked.

He read it twice and nodded. 'I've never been dumped this gracefully.'

'It's perfect,' Thad said. 'Gentle tone, and hints at the possibility of a reconciliation, so long as he behaves.'

'Thank you,' said Portia. 'Diane and I worked through several drafts, all of which we copied to Mira. This is the one she chose, and copied onto a card. She's already prepared the ground by cancelling a couple of dates they had planned. He's getting the hint, I think.'

'So we've got the letter. What we need to figure out is the right time to send it,' Jonesy said.

'Actually, he's already received it,' said Portia.

'What!' shrieked Jonesy. 'Why didn't anyone check with me?'

'Read your e-mails. The card was Fedexed to arrive yesterday morning,' Portia said. 'Kelly's spent the last day setting up Mira's new contact numbers to coincide with the letter. We couldn't do it beforehand or he might get the hint. But it works well because Mira said he was due to fly abroad in the evening.'

'Yes, I know, to effing Croatia!' Jonesy said.

'It's good timing for us, Jonesy,' Portia insisted. 'She's still in the Caribbean for the next couple of days. So even if it leaks the UK press won't be able to get hold of her easily.'

'Jesus, another bloody PFU! Didn't you stop to consider the England game tonight?' Jonesy wailed.

'What England game?' Portia asked.

Jonesy took his spectacles off and rubbed his face. 'Christ, Portia, the reason he's abroad is for the European Championship qualifier against Croatia. You've let Mira dump England's crucial defender just before this vital match. We've got to win or we're out. A draw won't do it.'

'Who cares, Jonesy?' Portia said, hands up in despair. 'He's over. He's history.'

'Nah, nah, you don't understand,' Jonesy wailed. 'Lawrence Wall will think the timing is deliberate. If he's pissed off, plays badly and we lose, he'll be tempted to leak the news. It'll deflect the spotlight from him. Then there will be an absolute shit storm in the papers, on Facebook and on Twitter. Mira will get death threats. I mean it. If England are eliminated, some of these guys may actually try to kill her.'

Portia looked stunned.

'He could be right, unfortunately,' Virgil added.

Thad turned to the others and said, 'I guess we better hope England win.'

* * *

At Jonesy's suggestion, Virgil joined him that Friday evening at his local, the White Hart in Richmond, West London, to watch the England game. The pub's quaint low-beamed ceilings and cosy nooks didn't quite fit the big screen sports bar image, but already squashed into a corner with Jonesy an hour before the match, he had to concede that the punters didn't care. The bar was already four deep with big men wearing replica England shirts, rapidly sinking pints. Virgil watched fascinated at

Jonesy's dextrous betting by smartphone, and the never-ending witty patter he kept up with a neighbouring drinker, their club rivalries buried for an evening for a greater cause: England. All conversation ceased for the kick-off.

Within half a minute Lawrence Wall was in trouble. He thudded into a Croatian striker a good two seconds after the ball had been passed, knocking him to the ground where he writhed in pain. A bellowing chorus followed in the pub about how no-one could get past 'The Wall,' which ended with vigorous rhythmic clapping. The referee gave Wall a yellow card, but a close-up of the centre-half's pugnacious face thrust within two inches of the referee's made it look like the face-off at the start of a boxing match.

'He's taken the Mira news well, then,' Virgil shouted into Jonesy's ear.

Jonesy shook his head, speechless for once. The pub quietened down into a restless ill-temper as the game deteriorated into a series of niggling tackles, injuries and confrontations, with Lawrence Wall never far from the trouble. Finally, a minute before half-time, Wall burst through a knot of Croatian defenders and laid the ball off to Wayne Rooney who fed him back a quick looping return on the edge of Croatia's eighteen-yard area. Wall sprinted past the last defender, but was felled by a high tackle. A deafening cry of 'penalty!' chorused across the pub. Almost everyone jumped to their feet, yelling. But the referee, a short, balding fellow, didn't award a penalty and was immediately surrounded by remonstrating England players.

First among them was Lawrence Wall, who after pointing angrily at the penalty spot, bellowed into the referee's face. A couple of England players tried to steer Wall away from this dangerous confrontation, but he pushed them away angrily.

'Oh no,' Virgil muttered, seeing Wall move further forward. 'Don't, don't do it. Oh God. No.'

The push wasn't hard but the referee stumbled nonetheless. He lifted a red card from his pocket and held it aloft. Curse-laden groans of disappointment washed round the pub, and one obese man in a Lawrence Wall replica shirt fell to his knees and held his head, groaning the word 'idiot' time and again.

Virgil and Jonesy exchanged a glance of exasperation and turned back to the screen, to see the push and the stumble repeated again and again from every camera angle.

'Well, at least it wasn't a head-butt,' Jonesy said.

A low-angled camera tracked Lawrence Wall stalking angrily off the pitch. He turned to the camera and spat, the viscous fluid spattering the lens. Virgil shook his head.

The game ended nil-nil, so England failed to get through to the next round. The post-match analysis focused on blaming Lawrence Wall's lack of self-discipline. Then the camera switched. In the tunnel leading to the changing room, an intrepid Sky TV reporter buttonholed Wall as he was walking out for the team press conference. 'Not one of your best days today, Lawrence. What happened?'

Wall muttered for a while, looking at the floor, before turning to the reporter and saying: 'Ah, well, you know how it is. I was in a bit of bad mood, with this and that at home, y'know?'

'Ah, the forthcoming home tie against Arsenal?'

'Nah,' muttered Wall. 'Just girlfriend stuff an' that.'

'Yes, the lovely Mira Roskova,' the reporter said, helpfully filling in the details. 'Well, I'm sure she's watching you right now. Is there anything you'd like to say to her, exclusively on Sky, Lawrence?'

The player stared at the camera and then the reporter before his forehead creased angrily. 'Yeah, actually there is.' His face closed right in on the camera. 'Mira, thank you *very much*, right? And don't worry, love, you can keep the Porsche, the jewellery and the fur coats.' He blew a kiss, and as he stalked away he could be heard muttering one word: 'Bitch.'

'Jesus Christ,' Jonesy muttered. 'Now we're really screwed.'

* * *

Portia Casals usually tried to avoid going into the office at the weekend. When it was her turn to be Stardust Brands' out-of-hours spokesperson, she could normally manage from home by getting up early on Saturday to skim through the papers while her husband George was still asleep, then getting Tamsin and Columbine their muesli and waiting for the *au pair* to arrive. A normal weekend would be no more than half a dozen calls about clients, most of which could be dealt with as a proforma 'no comment'.

Today was going to be different, she realised, when she got the first call at 6.15am, waking George, who thought it must be about his ailing mother. Instead it was some chirpy producer from a London radio station asking for someone to go on their

8am breakfast show to talk about Mira in the light of what happened at the England game last night. She declined that offer but knew that things were going to be bad. The papers arrived at 7am, an enormous bundle that took the paper girl a full minute so shove through her letterbox. The moment she saw the headlines she immediately regretted not having bothered to watch the late sports bulletin last night. She looked at her mobile and saw three missed messages from Jonesy warning her about the news.

The *Daily Mirror* headline was: 'England fiasco: Wall blames Mira'. The verdict of the *Daily Mail*, across two inside pages, was 'Mira, Mira on the Wall: I just don't want you, not at all'. Underneath was a centrespread of a suntanned Mira looking sultry in a white bikini, with seven small inset pictures all around her of Wall's face during many footballing disappointments: glum, petulant and furious, like seven dwarves, all of them grumpy. Very clever, she conceded. *The Sun* had somehow managed to get hold of a copy of the letter she had written for Mira, and there it was printed on page five superimposed on a picture of Mira and Lawrence Wall hand-in-hand at some formal event the previous month. By 9am, with twenty-three calls logged, Portia realised she would have to go in.

It was a beautiful sunny morning, and being a Saturday an easier bus ride than usual, but when she arrived at the office she knew that the craziness had already started. Right across the glass doors and the imposing white stonework of MacMillan House someone had spray painted in two-foot high letters 'England hate Mira' and 'Kill the slag'.

Inside, the duty security guard apologised to Portia and explained that he had tried to get the paint off with white spirit. 'You need nail varnish remover,' Portia said. 'I'm sure we have some upstairs. Make sure we have the CCTV checked and the footage saved, call maintenance and get someone to remove or cover up the damaged stonework.'

For the next eight hours she never quite caught up. Jonesy and Thad each called with their advice on how to handle the press calls, the maintenance company wouldn't come until Monday except for lift emergencies, the lunchtime Sky news bulletin had footage of the graffiti-damaged building, and there were already roundtable discussions being advertised for the evening schedule with leading psychologists, feminist writers, footballing pundits and God-knows-who to give their opinion on how ending a relationship can damage your self-esteem.

By the time it got dark shortly before four, Portia had had enough. She scooped up her notes into her bag, set the answering machine to night mode, turned off the lights and decided that she need a big coffee before going home. She donned her nice warm Peruvian poncho, draped the pashmina around her neck, and headed out. She said goodbye to the security guard, who had finally done a decent job on the doors, and stepped out into the bustle of the West End. The two-minute walk to Regent Street cheered her up as she joined the throng of January shoppers. It was only when she went into Costa Coffee that she got a feeling she was being followed. A group of three shaven-headed twenty-something lads, oblivious to the cold in sleeveless sports shirts and jogging trousers, came in after her. She ordered a skinny latte from the barista and risked a look over her shoulder. They were staring right at her, and making it obvious they were doing so. They looked to her like football fans: coarse, tough, belligerent and completely out of place here. One, with a dagger tattooed on his cheek, had a can of Foster's in his hand. They were muttering to each other and eyeing her.

Portia started to get really nervous. She picked up the coffee and looked around to see if there was a CCTV camera. There was. It might be safe to stay, but she didn't feel safe. The bus stop wasn't far away but she wanted the sanctuary of a taxi. To get to the seating area or to get out she now needed to get past them. And they were blocking her path. She took a deep breath and turned to get past them.

'What the fuck are you looking at?' said dagger tattoo, his pale eyebrows knitted in fury.

'Excuse me, please. I just want to get past.'

'Oooh, I'm so posh! I want to get parrrst!' he waved his hands in an affected manner, to the amusement of his mates.

'Look. I don't know who you are, or what you want…'

'But I know you,' dagger whispered, pointing at her, a nicotine-stained finger with its dirty hard-bitten nail just an inch from her mouth. 'You just tell that Russian slag that she's as good as dead, right?'

He showed no sign of moving out of the way. You could hear a pin drop in the café. Dagger's mates pointed at the other customers, eyebrows raised in a warning which said:

we're looking at you. Suddenly the customers all seemed overly engrossed in their phones, laptops and newspapers. Portia looked towards the barista, a tall student-type fellow who was staring at them, but radiating a fear that even Portia could feel. Following her eyes, dagger looked at the barista and pointed a menacing arm. 'Oi, cunt. Don't you fucking start. Understand? Get me a cider.'

The barista couldn't meet his gaze. 'Um. We've only got apple juice.'

'No fucking cider? What a dump.' With that he threw Portia to the ground, dousing her with scalding coffee. Then leaned over her. 'She's fucking dead, understand?'

* * *

Virgil was watching football at home with his mother when he took the call. Portia was in tears, in the ladies toilet at Costa, and it took a while to get from her what had actually happened. The police were already at the scene, waiting to take her statement.

'Are you hurt?'

'Just a scalded arm. But they ruined my poncho.' She started to cry again. 'And George is out and about somewhere and not answering his phone. Thad and Jonesy's numbers are busy.'

'Don't worry. Stay there. I'll be there in half an hour,' Virgil said.

'Would you? That's very sweet,' Portia said.

'What are you going to tell the police?'

'About Mira? Nothing. Jonesy and Thad would kill me.'

'The bloke who attacked you, how do you think he knew you were working with her?'

'It's not rocket science, Virgil. My bloody picture and CV is on the Stardust website, and she's listed as my client.'

'Alright. I'm meeting Mira at the airport on Monday,' Virgil said. 'We've got to move fast to get her out of the public eye.'

* * *

It had taken half an hour to calm Portia down. Virgil had seen her into a taxi, made her promise that she would ring him once she got home, and asked her to make sure she wasn't alone that evening.

It was nearly six when he arrived at the Stardust Brands office. Most of the lights were off. There were still plenty of shoppers on Regent Street, but fifty yards back there were just a few pedestrians weaving their way among the crush of parked cars. The security man, a Jamaican in his sixties, was still working away on the stonework, but the red paint was hard to shift. His name was Nelson, and he remembered Virgil. 'We're the only two men of colour in the building,' he chuckled. He hadn't seen anyone else hanging around. The police had come around for a quick check of the CCTV, but didn't stay.

Nelson showed Virgil the footage of the graffiti sprayers. There were three of them, and they matched the description Portia had given of her attackers. The foyer camera had caught one of them spraying the glass door, and despite the hoodie, there was a decent image of his face. Good. That meant catching them was something he could now leave to the police.

Virgil had as a fourteen-year-old been pulled off his bike in Lewisham High Street and casually punched by a couple of Millwall supporters, while a dozen others egged them on. Virgil had gradually learned that most football supporters were okay, if boisterous, and with the ever-growing profusion of black talent on the pitch it was only a dwindling minority who retained that reflex racism. But for years it was enough to put him off going to a match. Today's events were a reminder he could have done without.

* * *

Thirty-seven miles to the west, a sleek silver Mercedes slipped into the public car park at Frimley Park Hospital in Surrey. A large and athletic-looking young man in a dark suit and raincoat emerged, wearing sunglasses despite the overcast weather. He made his way directly towards reception, vaulting effortlessly over the three-foot railing that separated the car park from the pavement. Two men smoking outside the door, one wearing a dressing gown and with his foot in a cast-boot, stopped conversation and stared openly, their heads tracking him as he walked rapidly past. He made his way to reception and had a brief conversation. Directed to the colorectal surgery unit, he took the lift to the second floor. A middle-aged female receptionist at the nurses station asked him his business.

'I've come to see Len Smith,' he said, in a strong Mancunian accent. 'It's all been arranged. You've got my name.'

The receptionist nodded and looked down at a list. 'Leonard

Lucifer Smith. Yes, we were notified. You are a family member, Mr Wall, is that right?'

'Yes.' He looked around him, slightly nervously. He had never before disclosed his family connection to the man who was the most famous mental patient in the country.

'As you were probably told, Mr Smith is still under sedation in intensive care. I'm afraid, because of the security issues, I'm also going to need some form of identification.'

The man took out a passport and passed it across. The receptionist looked at the document and then her eyes flashed up to his face, surprised. The man briefly lifted his sunglasses, and smiled, used to the recognition that always came. 'Yes, it is me.'

'Oh.' The woman put her hand to her chest, as if short of breath. 'Well, my son would love to be here. He's a great fan of yours.'

'Okay. But you won't tell him who I've been to see, love, will you?' the man said leaning over the desk, his bulky shoulders spreading, his bull neck extended over her. 'It's personal, right?'

'Naturally Mr Wall,' the woman said, recovering her poise. 'Patient confidentiality is paramount.' She stood up. 'Follow me.'

Five minutes later, after further security checks and a pat-down, Lawrence Wall was allowed to sit by the side of his father's bed, while two large male nurses from West London Mental Health Trust stood by. The big man was asleep, hooked up to a couple of monitors, and snoring loudly.

Lawrence Wall stood up and reached out a hand towards his father, prompting one of the nurses, who looked like a nightclub bouncer, to hold up an arm between them. 'Sorry. Rules, I'm afraid.'

Wall's face darkened. 'What's the fucking problem, pal?'

'It's probably alright, Tony, seeing as he's unconscious,' the other nurse said to his colleague, who shrugged and backed away.

Wall leant over and ran his hand gently over the huge tattooed head, inked in a greenish-black. 'I can't stay long, Dad,' he whispered. 'I've just got back from Croatia. But get better soon, okay? I'll phone you when I can. I've had some bad news of my own.' He placed a get-well card by the bedside, and stood up to walk out. As he walked back down the corridor he briefly removed his sunglasses, and wiped a sleeve across his face. It was wet.

* * *

Monday morning arrived with rain and an early start. Virgil Bliss had never been a commuter, and on the days his presence was required at Stardust Brands first thing, he didn't like it one bit. He'd splashed out on a new suit, raincoat and briefcase, but really couldn't face the umbrella. There he was, on a packed platform at the Elephant, waiting for the next Bakerloo Line tube up to Oxford Street, fifteen minutes of an alternative existence. The jostling for position as the carriage doors opened, and the indignity of the rush for favoured territory. The prizes were elbow space, leg room for those seated, and most of all quality of standing room, all of which was allocated according to factors any baboon would recognise: speed, size and intimidation, laced with the occasional dash of civility and altruism. Finally, as the doors closed, the muting of personality. Denied personal space, travellers became sides of strap-hanging meat, eyes only for the smartphone, the book or the newspaper.

In these rattling, smelly transits, Virgil averted his eyes from the dandruff and the comb-overs and closed his nose to the excessive perfume and the unwashed damp coats. Instead he conjured the open spaces of Afghanistan. The shimmering desiccated mountains, the scoured sandy plains and the keen winter winds that knifed the face, a reminder you were alive. He had never expected to miss that feeling, bound up as it was with the fear that he might die there.

Emerging into mayhem on Britain's premier shopping street, he scoured the headlines at a newsstand. Coverage of Lawrence Wall hadn't abated much, though the focus was now on Wall's uncertain future in the England team, and accorded him the majority of the blame for losing the match. One downmarket tabloid led with an exclusive that Mira was actually not of Russian descent, but Croatian, and had played her part to get her country through.

When Virgil arrived at MacMillan House he saw three young girls hanging around by the entrance. The youngest, a willowy bespectacled twelve-year-old, had a *Village of the Dead* backpack and her face made up like a Qaeggan. The other two looked thirteen or fourteen. One had a white coat with a fringed hood, and high-heeled boots. The other was unseasonably dressed in a miniskirt and high heels with a designer-looking handbag and too much make-up.

The one in the white coat called out to him. 'Excuse me, is Mira in there? The security man didn't know.'

'No. She doesn't spend much time here,' Virgil said. 'Shouldn't you be at school?

'Free period,' they all chorused, a truant line obviously well-prepared.

'I suppose you want autographs or something?'

'I'm going to become a top model,' said miniskirt girl, shaking her long dark hair. 'I wrote to her. Are you an agent?'

'No, I'm not. This isn't the best way to see or contact her.'

'I'd like an autograph,' said the youngest, her head a mass of corkscrew curls framing a pretty face. 'Do you have some pictures?'

Virgil smiled. 'I'm sure I can get you a publicity picture or two. Wait here.'

'Can we come in with you?'

'No, wait in the foyer. I'll tell the guard that it's okay.'

Virgil returned in five minutes with a sheaf of signed photographs.

The girl with the fringed white coat flicked through them. 'Nah, we've both got that one,' she said, starting to hand one back.

'Steff, don't be a dimwit!' said miniskirt. 'We can get a tenner for it on eBay.'

'Oh yeah.'

'So have you got a business card, mister?' asked miniskirt, lifting her shoulders back to display her burgeoning figure.

'No,' said Virgil. 'Not on me.'

'But can you get her to reply to me? I just got directed to a list of FAQs about modelling, but it doesn't answer my questions,' she said.

'I'm sorry, she gets thousands of messages a year, she can't reply to them all.'

'Okay,' said white coat. 'Just tell her that Steff, Kat and Ellie from Erith still think she's cool, despite everything what they are saying about her.'

Virgil grinned. 'And what are they saying about her?'

They all looked heavenward, as if Virgil was an idiot. 'That she's a slag an' that,' miniskirt said.

'Okay, I promise I'll tell her.'

* * *

Virgil's smile only lasted until he emerged from the lift into Stardust Brands' reception. Adula the receptionist was hunched over her PC, her normally rangy posture tight with tension. She barely looked up as Virgil walked past. Thad Cobalt was making some kind of presentation in the Brand Narrative Hub, but the usual conversational hubbub around the office was gone. Jarvis McTeer slid past him in the corridor without even replying to his greeting, and the tiny Chinese-looking woman he knew only as 'Think outside the box' from the framed slogan on the pillar by her workstation, managed only a tiny guarded smile instead of her usual infectious grin. If he'd been at regimental HQ in Helmand he'd have guessed news had just arrived of a fatal IED attack. But here, what could it be?

Virgil was heading past Kelly's office, and noticed the lower panel had been kicked out. The carpet outside was stained with coffee. He walked back to the tiny woman and asked: 'What happened here?'

'Jonesy had a meltdown. It was poor Kelly who got it this time, though I've no idea why. He called her a silicone-filled moron.'

'Where is she now?'

'Still in the loo I expect.'

Virgil thanked her and made his way towards the female toilet, which was identified by a pop-art sign showing a gloved feminine fist bursting through a glass ceiling. From within he heard gentle sobbing. He tapped on the door and gingerly pushed it open. Kelly was standing at a washbasin ringed with cosmetics and balled up tissues. She turned to Virgil, her face distorted in distress.

'Kelly, what happened?

She shook her head slowly, the recognition of an ally allowing her moue of defiance to dissolve. 'Jonesy has been a complete pig to me,' she sobbed.

Virgil pulled her into a brief bear hug, holding her wet face into his shoulder. 'He's a pig to everyone. You just happened to be in the way today.' He propped her back on her feet, nervous in case someone came into the bathroom. 'So what was it about?'

'A French magazine was critical of Mira and I missed it. We don't subscribe, and I didn't see it online in English, but it was a big thing in French social media. Jonesy got some call from *The Times* about it, and was caught off-balance because it had been out a month and hadn't heard abouit it. The journalist made him feel an idiot.'

'You can't read everything,' Virgil said.

'Maybe, but I should have seen this one. It quotes Christophe Ledieu saying about Mira: "she's quite pretty, but obviously not really top-tier material".'

'Is that it?' Virgil asked.

'Well, there were a few other things. But it's about who said it. He's almost ninety, but he's a towering figure in couture. There's this saying that when Christophe the God says something, it stays said. That's what Jonesy told me. And of course, as it was in France, inevitably everyone at Suressence is bound to have read it.'

'You couldn't have done anything about it.'

'That's what I said. But Jonesy has to blame someone. And today it was me.'

'And the door to your hutch?'

'Yes.' A tentative smile flashed across her face, impressed that he remembered what she called it. 'It was so bloody puerile of him to kick it down.'

'Okay. Let me take you out for for a double hot chocolate from Peronelli's, which I hear is the best around…'

'That's so nice, but I've got a huge stack of fan mail that Portia's just dumped on me.'

'I'll split it with you. What we haven't done by five, I'll take home. If you're not paid you shouldn't be doing overtime. I'm also going to have a discreet word with Jonesy.'

'No, Virgil. That will make things worse.'

Finally Virgil led her back to her office, went out to fetch her a top notch hot chocolate fetched her a double helping of coffee, and told her the good news from the girls on the street. Soon Kelly was laughing again.

* * *

Stardust Brands had given Virgil free reign on Tuesday morning for an emergency self-defence talk for staff. He didn't expect a repeat of the attack on Portia, but if there was one he'd feel terrible, even though it wasn't part of his job description to protect the entire firm. He'd cleared the furniture from one of the largest meeting rooms, thrown some exercise mats on the floor, and in the first of three sessions now had the attention of half a dozen female employees in gym gear.

Virgil had never been a personal trainer, but he'd had been trained in self-defence. While most of the women he saw before him were young and clearly fit in every sense of the word, there were two, including Portia, who were somewhat overweight and physically hesitant.

'You can encapsulate public self-defence in two sentences,' he said. 'One, radiate confidence and capability, it will put a potential attacker off. Second, understand that any woman, however small, can with determination see off a large attacker, even if he's as big as me.' No one said anything, but they exchanged sceptical glances with each other.

'Okay,' he said, turning down the lights and clicking on a screen. 'I'm going to show you what happened to me at Chacewater's close combat training session. I'm six-two, and a former regimental welterweight semi-finalist. My opponent here is five-three and less than a hundred pounds.'

The video showed Virgil and a tiny woman, each wearing knuckle gloves and helmets, warily circling one another. The woman came in for a quick couple of jabs, and just managed to duck a couple of hefty punches Virgil sent her way. Suddenly she turned her back, whipped her left leg high and around, catching Virgil on the right ear with her heel. She then kicked at his left knee, causing him to stumble and then drove her foot hard into his solar plexus. Virgil tumbled to the floor, and although he was up in a few seconds, someone stepped in to separate them.

There was laughter in the room. 'Okay, this woman is a mixed-martial arts expert, and her timing is perfect. But she is also fifty-two years old. It was her self-confidence that was key, as much as her technique.'

Virgil asked for a volunteer. Kelly, in T-shirt and shorts stepped forward. 'Right,' she said, playing to the girls, waving her fists. 'Prepare for a thrashing!'

He gently took her arms, placed her feet closer to him, and said. 'If you are assaulted in a public place, your first tactic is surprisingly simple, and comes naturally: scream like hell, and keep screaming. The next may not be natural, but it shows you are going to fight back. Make him believe you can win, and, yes, you really can. Men have vulnerable points just like you do: eyes for gouging, ears for biting or twisting, a throat for punching, fingers for bending, and toes for those high heels to stamp on. But they also have one huge vulnerability that women do not… Testicles.'

There was some laughing, and Virgil noticed Kelly, her faced screwed up into a parody of brutality, miming squeezing something with both hands. 'Whoa, wait a minute tiger,' he laughed. 'Now, the testicles are like a kill button on any man. It's hard to get right, but if you do, you are going to immobilise him, no question.'

Over the next half an hour Virgil gently took them through a series of moves: how to break an attacker's grip, how to unbalance him; how to put a thumb in an eye, a heel of the hand hard into the nose. Virgil used a football to mimic a man's head, and got them to feel what it was like to strike with a fist, or the heel of the hand, how to free the punching shoulder, and roll in with weight as if driving right through the target. On the third attempt Portia managed to knock the ball from his hands, to a huge cheer. The lesson finished with the women bubbling with enthusiasm.

'Aw. When do we get to squeeze your nuts?' Kelly said, to general giggling.

'A ballbreaker like you? Never, I hope.'

The later lessons were less-well attended. Thad and Jonesy didn't show up at all. But that was fine. He had offered. Tomorrow morning he had to meet the woman who he really was there to protect. And he was already nervous. It was the same gut-churning feeling he'd had the day before his first ever patrol in Helmand.

Chapter Eleven

It was seven in the morning on a dismal freezing Thursday when the British Airways overnight flight from Antigua nosed up to the stand at London's Gatwick Airport. Virgil Bliss watched from the gate as baggage trucks arrived, and ground crew in high-vis jackets started the unloading process. He was there with editorial assistant Kelly Hopkins, and the airport's VIP greeter, who would whisk Mira away to a private lounge while the formalities were conducted.

To fool the paparazzi, PR chief Jonesy Tolling had mocked up an e-mail ostensibly to Kelly about greeting Mira's arrival at Heathrow on the 7.45am flight, and had his PA 'accidentally' copy it to the Press Association newsdesk, where he knew it would be fired out to hundreds of publications and freelancers. With luck, most of the photographers would now be going to the wrong airport. Virgil had taken a quick walk to arrivals to see if the plan was working, but was dismayed to see half a dozen photographers gathered there. He asked them who they were waiting for, and was told that it was the foreign secretary, coming back from a UN meeting on climate change. Perhaps they could sneak Mira past them, with sunglasses and a headscarf.

'This football stuff isn't the first trouble she's had you know,' Kelly said.

'I read about the Qaeggan guy in Denmark.'

'Well there was also the first security guy we recruited too. An American called Curtis Hyde who made a pass at her. We had to sack him. He still sends her pervy e-mails and stuff.'

'Is that in the legal action file?'

'Yes. The lawyers are sending copies of everything. Sorry we didn't already have it.'

The aircraft door opened, and Mira was the first passenger to emerge. Now blonde, wearing large dark sunglasses and dressed in a navy blue two-piece she oozed casual glamour. The stewardesses alongside, both attractive women, seemed dowdy by comparison. As she strode up the sloping aerobridge, even Virgil could see from the set of her mouth that she wasn't happy. Kelly ran down to meet her halfway, at which point Mira let go of her wheeled silver case, and otherwise ignored her.

'This is Virgil, I told you about him,' Kelly said, wheeling the heavy case behind Mira.

'Delighted to meet you, Miss Roskova,' Virgil said.

'Likewise, Mr Bliss,' Mira said, without slowing down or looking at him. A uniformed greeter from the airline unlocked a door marked private and led them down to the tarmac where a Mercedes saloon and chauffeur were waiting. In five minutes they were in an almost deserted luxury lounge. As the greeter departed to oversee the luggage formalities, Mira took off her sunglasses. The clarity of her green eyes took Virgil's breath away. She looked flawless, almost too dazzling to look at. How could anyone punch such a face?

'So Virgil, are you going to be able to protect me?' It was almost as if she'd been reading his mind.

'I'll do my very best,' Virgil said.

She looked him over, taking her time. 'I hear you were in Afghanistan. How was that?'

'Not like it's portrayed. Long, long periods of heat, dust and boredom punctuated by a few mad minutes of terror. In my unit, almost everyone who was killed or injured was hit by booby traps. Firefights were rare. Didn't often see anyone that you could say he's Taliban or he's not. It made you feel like a sitting duck sometimes.'

'I know how you feel,' she smiled. 'I'm a sitting duck too. Apparently responsible for England's sporting misery.'

'Well, I shouldn't take it personally,' Virgil said.

'Really? When someone tweeted to me that I should be anally raped for considering myself too good for Lawrence Wall? That's just one I happened to see. I'm sure there are others, right Kelly?'

Kelly nodded. 'Dozens, I'm afraid. I'll spare you the details.'

Virgil muttered his apologies and shut up. In his head he imagined the voice of Sergeant Davies whispering in his ear: *Top marks for diplomacy? I should fucking cocoa.*

Half an hour later, they were all on their way to London in Stardust Brands' own Mercedes. Virgil sat in the front with the chauffeur while Kelly and Mira sat behind. Kelly asked her if she wanted to see the papers.

'No, I saw as much as I could bear online.' Mira got her phone out and prodded the screen a couple of times. She held it to her ear and launched into a south London twang. 'Jonesy old son, I thought this couldn't happen, mate.' Virgil turned and caught her eye. She responded with a conspiratorial grin. 'No, Jonesy. I needed to Fedex the letter straightaway. I wanted him to get it before he left for Croatia. Sorry, I do not dump boyfriends by text. I'm considerate and kind. It's not just your brand image, sunshine, it's really who I am.'

There was then a long and heated discussion about the week's newspapers. Mira was really in her stride now. 'Jonesy, do you think that Lawrence leaked my letter to the *Sun*? No, neither do I. It shows how gentle I am, so why would he? So how did they get it? Yes, Jonesy, it is an effing disaster. I dedicate it to you, my friend. Sort it out. Kiss kiss.' She hung up. Virgil caught that little grin again. She clearly knew how to handle him.

'Can I cheer you up with some of the last week's fan mail,' Kelly asked.

'Go on then,' Mira said.

'It's only a selection. You've a hundred and twenty-eight thousand more Twitter followers, which makes over fourteen million, and nearly eleven thousand direct messages in the last three days. Best of all, you've added half a million on Instagram. There were about twenty thousand posts on your Facebook page. Here are a selection of the best.' She handed across a sheaf of print-outs.

'How many proposals of marriage in the last week?' Mira asked, putting them aside and inspecting her nails in a faux arrogant way. Virgil suddenly realised she was showing off, possibly for him. Somehow that cheered him up.

'A hundred and sixty-three, most of them since they heard you had dumped Mr Wall. You got some poems, and a few video greetings. Lots of donations to the orphans.'

'Nice. And what's the willy count?'

Kelly laughed. 'Only twelve last week, all disgusting.'

Mira caught Virgil's glance over his shoulder. 'Yes, Virgil,' she said. 'One of the great privileges of being a public face is that pasty, overweight plumbers from Arbroath, hairy van drivers from Northampton and skinny students from Coventry imagine that I will be impressed by photos of their genitalia. Can you protect me from that? No you can't. But Kelly does. She's an angel. She's the one who sees them. I prefer not to.'

'We've had an e-mail from Norris Dolan about you appearing in the video for a song on his new solo album,' Kelly said. 'Thad's advice is to decline.'

'Who on earth is Norris Dolan?' Mira asked Virgil. He shrugged.

'I had to look him up,' Kelly said. 'He's the drummer from 1970s metal band Hot Rivet.'

'Ah, I have heard of them,' Virgil said. 'They were big once.'

'Norris Dolan is seventy-two,' said Kelly. 'He has financial problems from his divorces, they say.'

Mira laughed and held up her hand with thumb pointing downwards. 'Next, please. Tell me about Mr Kulchuk.'

'Ulan Kulchuk is a Kazakh-born hedge fund manager and art collector, known as the Magpie, for his unrivalled collection of old masters. He is seen as being very close to the Russian leadership. He has homes in London, New York, Monaco, São Paolo and a few other places. He has a yacht with its own helipad.' Kelly looked up meaningfully.

'Hmmm,' said Mira, rolling her eyes and smiling.

'He's quite old, of course. Fifty-eight. Bald and fat.'

Mira laughed. 'Okay, okay, why am I having lunch with him today?'

'The lead came from Diane Glassman. There's an art event he wants to hire you for. He's hinted at product endorsement possibilities too. He's on the board of lots of different companies, including Suressence. Thad had originally planned to meet him alone, but Kulchuk asked that you be there.'

Mira got out her phone and started texting. 'Anything else today?'

Kelly grinned. 'Here's today's clever clogs award.' She handed across a card which seemed to be written by a very young child in multi-coloured crayon. Mira read it, laughed and handed it forward to Virgil. 'Take a look at this,' she said.

Virgil took it. 'Dear Miss Beautiful. My daddy's very unhappy since Mummy left two years ago. He's a very nice man, and quite handsome but since I got leukaemia last year, he hasn't smiled once in months. If you would come out for dinner with him, I'm sure he would be happy again. With love. Ben xxx.' There was a photograph of Ben, a beautiful little boy of perhaps five, clipped to the card.

'Shameless,' said Virgil. 'But clever.'

'Trouble is I can't ignore them,' Mira said. 'Jonesy is quite right about that. It could be a tabloid put-up job, ready-made for the headline: "Stuck-up Mira ignores cancer boy's dying wish." So now Portia has to check if the boy exists, if he's really ill, and to craft a nice reply without committing me to anything.'

'I see what you mean,' Virgil said.

Mira looked out of the window at the motorway traffic and muttered: 'Sometimes I wish I wasn't branded as some Little Miss Perfect. They've left me so far to fall I feel bloody giddy.'

'Look at that,' the driver interrupted. They were approaching an articulated lorry, on whose rear doors was emblazoned a giant picture of Lawrence Wall in overalls, arms across his chest with a paint brush in one hand, and a roller in the other. The slogan was: 'Dulux Wallguard: No moisture gets past, period.'

'Overtake please, John, I'm feeling a little car sick,' Mira said. She stole a glance at Virgil and muttered. 'He made over a million from that deal.'

Virgil said nothing.

'Here's one to cheer you up,' Kelly said, passing across the white Broadmoor envelope. 'The translation is on a card inside.'

Mira examined the card, and her hand strayed to her mouth.

'So do you know who this is from?' Virgil asked.

'Sorry, what was that?'

Virgil repeated the question.

'How could I possibly know that? It isn't signed.'

'He writes like he knows you.'

'Virgil, they *all* think they know me. And they don't. What they know is the Mira created by Stardust Brands. Not the real Mira, thank God.'

* * *

The car dropped Kelly off at a tube station, and then headed to Mira's new south London apartment in Battersea. 'I spent two and a half million on this bloody place, and have only spent ten nights there,' Mira told Virgil.

The chauffeur took the car down into a huge basement garage, passing a card over a sensor to lift the barrier. Mira took off her sunglasses as they drove slowly around the cavernous floor and scanned the gleaming rows of Audis, BMWs and Mercedes. 'I guessed as much. Typical!'

'What's the matter?' Virgil said.

'Lawrence has taken my Porsche back. It was parked right here.'

'Wasn't it a gift?'

'It was, but knowing Lawrence it will have been financed on the never-never and in his name.'

'What petulant behaviour,' Virgil observed, shaking his head.

Mira glared at him. 'Actually, if I want your assessment, I'll ask for it.'

'Understood. My apologies.'

'Granted, Corporal Bliss.'

He looked behind. She was grinning, playing with him again. The chauffeur took the car up to the doors of the residents' secure lift. Virgil stepped out, checked the coast was clear and used Mira's access card to open the lift doors. He then retrieved her three heavy suitcases from the boot, and opened the car door for Mira. He followed her into the lift. She seemed completely unaware of him, checking her phone and muttering to herself, while he tried not to stare. At the penthouse floor, eleven, he stepped out first, and checked the short corridor, which led to only two doors. She approached the door to her flat while he brought the luggage.

'Would you like me to go in first?' Virgil asked.

'No, Virgil, you stay out here and check your mascara while I go in and karate the burglars and rapists myself.' She looked at him, deadpan.

'Look, I only asked because it's your private…Okay, okay,' Virgil grinned at the wind-up, and slipped through the door. It was a dark-walled two-bedroom apartment with an enormous lounge. Beyond was a giant patio giving views over the Thames from Westminster to Hammersmith. Looking far right he could see the Houses of Parliament and the London Eye. On the dining table and on the kitchen counter were at least ten vases of red roses. Virgil walked up to the table and saw a huge white envelope with Mira's name written untidily on it. He cursorily checked each room before returning to her.

'He's been here. Must have been before the locks were changed, and before that drunken escapade I told you about.' Virgil led her in.

'Oh wow.' Mira surveyed the roses, smelling them, and rearranging them before picking up and opening the card. 'So he's very, very sorry.'

Virgil decided it would be best to say nothing.

'Yet I just got a text from his solicitors confirming that they took my Porsche back because it was supposedly only on loan. Now Lawrence is filling the place with roses and saying he wants me back. That's a pretty mixed message, isn't it?'

'It certainly is,' Virgil ventured. 'But in my opinion the roses have been here quite a few days. There are a lot of dropped petals, and there's not much water left in the vases. So my guess would be that they were put here when you first went abroad, well before he received your letter.'

'Yes,' Mira said absent-mindedly. 'That's quite possible.'

'In which case he may be doubly angry because you apparently ignored his floral efforts at reconciliation, and then finished the relationship. If he's the kind of bloke who has trouble saying sorry, it could really be humiliating to him.'

Mira looked candidly at him. 'Well, Mr Bliss, surprises come in all shapes, sizes and colours, don't they? If I ever sack you, you could always get a job as an agony aunt in a women's magazine.'

Virgil laughed. 'Really? I failed my first year psychology exams at uni.'

'Well, never mind. I think I like you. Perhaps you can keep yourself busy while I get changed.'

'Understood.' He used the time to assess the flat. The apartment block was laid out like a cruise liner, with each floor set back half a dozen metres from the one beneath, to give each residence a big patio. Climbing up from the floor below would require standing on the patio balustrade, in full view of several adjacent apartment blocks. The patio door locks were good, five lever deadlocks, but not beyond the wit of a professional. The apartment door's electronic locks were more secure.

Mira emerged dressed in a white Lycra sports bra and jogging trousers, which revealed a tanned flat tummy and beautifully sun-burnished shoulders. 'I'm feeling fat and frumpy after all that time on the plane, so I'm going for a run.'

'At a gym I hope?' Virgil was alarmed.

'No, Battersea Park. I need fresh air.'

'I have to come with you, but I don't have any running gear with me.' He looked down. Dark suit, white shirt and best dark shoes. 'I'd look like the presidential secret service.'

She laughed. 'Really, you don't have to come.'

'There's not much point in being a bodyguard if I don't, is there? I can go home and be back in forty minutes, if that's alright?'

'Virgil. Listen. I have a lunch in just over two hours, so not a huge amount of time. I do need exercise.' She stared at him, up and down. 'Okay, let's have a look.' She wandered into the spare room, and opened a big cardboard box. 'This is a load of stuff from my old place that I've never had chance to unpack.' She tossed a pair of stretch jogging bottoms at him. 'Try those. They were Johnny's.'

'Johnny?'

'A boyfriend and personal trainer, a while back. They have been washed. I'd been meaning to send them to Oxfam.' Next she found a selection of T-shirts. 'These are men's, one's bound to fit.' She tossed them at him. 'Aha!' She reached down and hauled up a box. Inside was a pair of enormous, very expensive and almost new Nike trainers. 'Try these. Size thirteen.'

'They'll be a bit big,' Virgil said. 'Who's are they?'

'Who's do you think?'

Mira found him some socks and then let him use the bathroom to change. He emerged a bit sheepishly. 'The trackies are a bit tight,' he said. In fact they were almost indecent, and the legs ended mid-calf.

Mira's gaze flicked down to his groin, and raised one slow eyebrow. 'So, that's where you keep your concealed weapon.'

'I don't know what you mean,' he said, thinking: *Careful, Virgil. You're being tested.*

They began with stretches in her lounge, in which the benefits of Mira's many sessions with Pilates guru Cassandra Ko came to the fore. She had the straight-backed posture of a ballet dancer, could stand holding one leg vertically above, and do the splits. Virgil, by no means as supple, tried not to stare while he went through his own more aerobic warm-up regime.

Once out on the street, Virgil felt like a scarecrow. It wouldn't have been so bad wearing giant trainers and overly-tight trackies if it wasn't for Mira's casual film star look: the unseasonable tan in London's winter, the body-hugging Lycra, pink trainers, Fitbit, iPod, wrap-around amber-tinted sunglasses and a casually gorgeous plait of silky blonde hair. It was lunchtime, and as they jogged down Parkgate Road in the watery sunshine, they passed the Prince Albert, a great old gin palace of a pub, now refurbished. A dozen trendily dressed young men were standing outside, grasping pints and smoking.

As Mira floated effortlessly past, they turned as one and stared. A pace or two ahead of Virgil, she ignored the red pedestrian lights, gliding across Albert Bridge Road through a gap in the traffic. That left Virgil to take his life in his hands with a white van, much to the amusement of the pub goers behind him. Mira was already in the park beyond, but the beacon of her perfect white-clad bottom, flexing thirty yards ahead dazzled like a rising sun. She never once looked behind as he caught up, wondering why she had upped the pace.

'Trying to get away?' Virgil said as he drew level.

'I'm not,' she replied. 'This is my usual speed and route.'

'I'd say it was time to start varying your routines,' Virgil said. 'Different times of day, different routes. I can drive you out to different parks each time. Otherwise you are vulnerable.'

'Look, Virgil, I know this is what Thad and Jonesy want you to do, but I'm not going to live my life in a bunker just because Lawrence Wall is upset over being dumped.'

They ran on hard for another three miles doing laps around the formal riverside park, before finally finishing at the pagoda. Virgil was aware that he was breathing far more heavily than she was. Fit, certainly. As they sat on a bench, Virgil said: 'My job isn't just about Lawrence Wall. It's about the threats you might not be aware of. Overly intrusive fans and hidden enemies, annoying Qaeggan, and plain old kidnappers and muggers.'

She turned to look at him, her eyes narrowed in scrutiny. 'I've always had enemies,' she said. 'But I learned long ago to look after myself.' She looked down and examined her hands, as if she was unsure if they belonged to her or not.

Virgil wanted to ask more, but got the vibe that he shouldn't. Not on his first day of knowing her. 'Look, I will always disappear if you want. I won't cramp your style, your independence, or your freedom. But keep me in the loop, so I can always be there in an emergency. Is that a deal?'

She nodded. When they got back to the flat and finished their warm-down exercises Mira thanked Virgil for being there. 'I really don't want to seem ungrateful, not to Stardust nor to you. But I've got to have space. I've got to be able to breathe. You do understand?'

'Of course,' Virgil said.

Mira offered him the guest bathroom, while she went off to her own. The granite-tiled cubicle was as big as Virgil's mother's kitchen, and he took a good ten minutes under the powerful hot water, letting the refreshing soap course down his sweaty body. He towelled himself dry quickly, his Helmand hurry-up still second nature. Twenty minutes passed and Mira still hadn't emerged, so he passed the time by looking through her DVD collection. Mainly mainstream rom-coms, but also a few surprising horror vids. *Hostel*, *Ichi the Killer* and *Martyrs* were ones he had heard of, because some of his oppos in Camp Bastion were fans, but there were half a dozen others he didn't know. Maybe this was Lawrence Wall's personal selection. He shrugged and then flicked through a big pile of women's magazines stacked on the kitchen counter. He dislodged a newspaper cutting. It was from the opinion section of the *Daily Telegraph* back in 2013.

The Invisible Monster Who Murdered Several Young Women

Protected against justice by Britain's legal system. Kept in luxury at taxpayers' expense.

Mr A, as he is referred to in court papers, is one of Britain's worst murderers. His crimes, so awful as to beggar belief, involve the agonising deaths of several young women. You won't have heard his name because his trial in 2005 was held entirely in camera, behind closed doors, in front of a judge alone. No jury has seen his face, nor assessed the evidence against him. Not even the families of his victims have been allowed to see him, nor read that evidence in full. The names of his victims cannot be published, nor the dates of their deaths, nor their number. You are not allowed to know what he looks like, to have his appearance described, or to know his name. Indeed, Lord Justice Kirby ruled at the end of the trial that nothing that may identify him can ever be published in a British newspaper. As far as the British public is concerned, he is completely invisible.

All we can tell you is that he has been in a top-security mental institution for the last five years, is aged 46, and was born in Staffordshire. Mr A is not officially in isolation, but according to documents obtained by the Daily Telegraph under the Freedom of Information Act, he has been granted separate facilities from all other patients. He has his own personal recreation area, his own en-suite, and listens to his own music collection on expensive cordless headphones. He receives £86.18 per week in various state benefits, even though almost all his day-to-day expenses are found. A hairdresser comes to him once a week, he has a regular manicure, and his shirts are pressed daily. His is a form of luxury isolation sanctioned by a British court, the only person in British legal history to benefit from a gagging order of unlimited duration on the British press.

In May last year this newspaper made a High Court application to have Mr A's anonymity removed in the public interest. A separate request for Judicial Review of Mr Justice Kirby's 2005 ruling was also refused later in the same year. This paper continues to believe that the British people deserve justice to be seen to be done and will continue to press for the removal of this order.

Hearing Mira's footsteps, Virgil quickly replaced the cutting. Looking at his watch, he now realised that they were supposed to be in central London in less than half an hour, but he had to remind himself that Mira's punctuality was none of his business. Mira then went back to her bedroom, and finally emerged with a quarter of an hour to spare. He must have stared because she asked: 'How do I look?'

'Not bad,' Virgil said.

'Not bad!' she laughed, in mock outrage. 'I'm meeting a billionaire!'

'I'm sure he'll be impressed.'

In the lift on the way down she described how the entire ensemble had cost less than twenty pounds: 'Astrakhan hat from a Camberwell jumble sale, three pounds; 1940s style overcoat with sable collar, Paris flea market, seven Euros; high-collared maroon tunic, Oxfam, fifty pence; black embroidered Turkish trousers, from Istanbul, around a pound. Oh yes, well, the mauve Jimmy Choos were expensive.'

'Can I ask you something?' Virgil asked, as they settled themselves in the limousine that had been waiting for her. 'That Broadmoor card seemed to shock you. Is there an issue there you'd like me to deal with?'

Mira checked her make-up in the mirror and didn't answer for a long time. 'No, it's alright, Virgil. The warning on the envelope sort of knocks you back, doesn't it? A reminder who these people are. It's like any fan mail. You have no idea what people are capable of.'

'Well, that's why I'm here. To do any worrying for you.'

'Thank you Virgil. That's nice to know. But I'm not worried.'

Virgil saw her face narrow. She was lying. And the article she had clipped proved it.

* * *

Caspian was an Azerbaijani restaurant in Knightsbridge famous for its caviar and quail. The reservation had been for noon, with the idea that there would be few other patrons around. However, as Mira was forty-five minutes late, there were already quite a few diners there. This was the first opportunity for Virgil to see how the general public reacted to seeing her, and walking behind he noticed how conversation stopped, how forks were suspended in mid-air. They were shown to the far end of the basement dining room, all black marble and engraved mirrors. Thad was already there, sitting in a circular booth with Ulan Kulchuk and his PA, a slender Chinese-looking woman. As they arrived, they each stood. The billionaire stood and took Mira's hand in both of his as Thad made the introductions.

'I am delighted you could make it, my dear,' he said in a thick Russian accent. He looked up at her through thick blue-tinted lenses, his face so speckled with moles it looked like a weathered currant bun.

'I'm very happy to be here, Mr Kulchuk.' Mira sat between them at the back of the booth. Virgil was seated at a small table opposite, about fifteen feet away, where he could only just hear their conversation but could see the door.

This certainly didn't look like the kind of place that Lawrence Wall would feel comfortable in, but Virgil wasn't taking any chances. Close protection in a restaurant is all about subtlety and preparation, though he'd had no time for the latter. He checked for alternative exits (one, through the kitchen), checked both male and female bathrooms (no one hiding), and assessed the other diners. Satisfied that there was no one suspicious, he ordered a sandwich and a Perrier, nothing that would get in the way of a fast reaction time should it be required. From the conversation opposite it was clear that under Kulchuk's guidance Mira and Thad were being offered the works. Champagne arrived, the cork popped with great aplomb by the waiter.

At this point the waiter appeared at Virgil's table with a glass of Georgian champagne, a basket of toast and a small dish of caviar. 'With Mr Kulchuk's compliment's Sir. As he says it is a shame for any visitor to this restaurant to leave without sampling our country's most famous produce.'

Virgil declined the champagne, and attempted to catch Kulchuk's eye to thank him. However, the Kazakh was in full flow.

'Now, Mira, you may be aware of next month's Art with Conviction auction at Christies,' Virgil heard Kulchuk say. 'As you may know I'm the honorary president of the Art in Philanthropy Association. It does great work, and I know you are yourself involved in charitable work for access to water.'

'Mira's been a prime mover in ThirstyPlanet,' Thad replied. Caviar arrived, and Virgil watched as Mira tucked in while Thad and Kulchuk did most of the talking. But the Kazakh's eye's rarely left her face, something that Virgil assumed she was already used to.

'So what I'd really like to get your agreement to, Mira, is to introduce the auction, and then stay for a couple of hours to talk to the clients.' Their voices softened as the subject of fees came up, but their expressions seemed to indicate a deal had been agreed.

As soon as he got home, Virgil followed up on the cutting he had found at her flat. There were numerous articles online about the legal implications of the ruling, but nothing on who the murderer actually was. However, one piece in the *Independent* had a little more detail, indicating that the accused had been transferred in secrecy from a prison abroad where he had been serving a long sentence. Virgil could glean no reason why Mira might be interested in such a case. Unless it was somehow connected to the birthday card she had just received from Broadmoor. But then the article was presumably clipped more than a year ago, long before that card arrived. Something else must have been the trigger. But what?

Chapter Twelve

Mira was away for a week in New York, with back-to-back photoshoots for Tiffanys, Saks Fifth Avenue and some top-secret new conditioner for Procter & Gamble. Virgil had wanted to know why he wasn't going.

'We don't have the budget to send you,' Thad had said. 'But she'll be safe. She's being provided with a chi-chi service apartment just off Central Park, with its own doorman and security, door-to-door car service, and in the evening she can order in from any restaurant in town.'

Virgil's expression must have spoken volumes because Thad then said: 'Yes, I know she'll hate it. It's a gilded cage. But she's got friends over there, models, you name it. She'll still have a blast. I know I keep saying this, but when the Suressence deal comes in, things will be different. I guess we may even be able to sanction the expense of having you fly first class with her. I know you'd like that.'

Virgil met Mira on her return to Heathrow on the overnight flight. This time he was ready when she said she'd like to go for a run, with his gear already in the car. They agreed on Wandsworth Common, a few minutes' drive south of her apartment.

'I see you've finally got some proper gear,' Mira said, as they set off, having parked opposite the County Arms pub.

'I already had it,' he said. 'You just never gave me the chance to get it.'

'Ah, but you see I'm royalty,' Mira said with a sly smile. 'Your job is to anticipate my every whim.'

At Virgil's request, Mira had dressed incognito this time. A New York Yankees baseball cap with a ponytail poked through the back, sunglasses, loose jogging trousers and a plain blue T-shirt. They ran hard for forty minutes, along the edge of the railway embankment, and then across the bridge up Nightingale Lane. When the rain began they took shelter under a tree by a duck pond. Virgil knew they couldn't stay too long, because Mira had a lunch engagement in less than two hours.

By the time they got back to the apartment they were both drenched. As before, she offered him the guest bathroom, and this time he showered and dried himself at speed, guessing that he would be a good half hour ahead of her. The newspaper cutting had intrigued him, and he wanted to do a little illicit snooping. He emerged, in a guest bathrobe, intending to have a look in her bedroom. But then he heard a text tone. Mira's iPhone was on the kitchen counter. He glanced at it. The text was some routine reminder from Portia. But once he had the phone in his hand, Virgil couldn't resist a quick flick through. Hearing Mira's power shower still going, he used his own phone to take pictures of her contacts, messages and browsing history. If she had been following up on the cutting recently, there should be some evidence of it.

* * *

It was a while before he got a chance to look the photos. A cosmetics photoshoot had been arranged for 2pm at a studio in Islington, but first Mira had Virgil drive her to the Berners Street head office of Top Shop, for whom she was designing a range of handbags. An hour later they diverted to a couture workshop in surprisingly run-down looking facilities above a dry-cleaners in Jermyn Street to see how the work on the mock-ups was progressing. In each case, Virgil was told to wait either in reception or close to the car because he wasn't cleared to have sight of the new product range. He found the secrecy laughable, as if he'd even know who to tell about a new line of bags or purses. What he soon began to understand, though, was how the most elastic fabric in the world of beauty was time. Punctuality was iron in the army, here it was like gossamer.

They arrived at the studio just after three. A washed-out skinny girl of perhaps eighteen was waiting for Mira outside the converted Victorian warehouse, fag in hand, hopping from one foot to another and anxiously scanning the traffic. On seeing the car, her rigid face almost collapsed in relief. 'Oh thank Christ,' she said as Mira emerged. 'Richard is in meltdown. He's looking for someone to kill.'

'Well, it shouldn't be you, Miranda' Mira observed. 'Let me apologise to him.'

Virgil followed them up a scruffy staircase into a cavernous loft-type space, lined with white paper and stuffed with lighting equipment. The photographer, a pony-tailed leather-jacketed Cockney in his sixties called Richard Day, was leaning against the far wall, bellowing over the phone to someone and pounding the wall with his fist for emphasis. 'But where is she *now*, Kelly? I've had two make-up girls and the fucking hairdresser here since half one, you useless cretinous asinine dimwit. Just get her here, for Christ's sake.' He hung up and muttered to himself. 'Fucking Stardust, couldn't organise a drug rave in Keith Richards' kitchen.'

Day's assistant coughed nervously. He turned angrily to her, and then swivelled his eyes to Mira. The truculent thug persona evaporated instantly, replaced by a broad grin, as he spread his arms in delight. 'Ah, Mira, my one true love. Anoint me with your grace, darling!'

'Richard, nice to see you. So sorry for the delay,' she replied.

'Oh, don't worry about that.' He flicked the suggestion aside like an irritating fly. They air-kissed, and he held her arms. 'God, you look so delicious I could eat you with a spoon.' He turned his head aside. 'Miranda, tell Yvonne she's here and get us all a nice cup of Lapsang souchong.' Mira was shown into a side room packed with a now frenetic bevy of young women, and did not emerge for almost an hour. Virgil sat on a chair in the corner of the studio with his phone out, examining the photographs of Mira's browsing history. There was plenty of it, and he'd need a larger screen to check it in detail, but nothing stood out as alarming.

When Mira emerged, her hair was shorter and wavy, her eyes highlighted by huge amounts of green and purple eyeshadow. The photographer arranged her on a white leather settee, and keeping up a continued monologue of breathy encouragement, took hundreds of close-up photos.

'Pout for me, love.' Click, click. 'Marvellous.' Click, click, click. 'Okay. Now eyes left and high, you've seen something you adore on a high shelf.' Click, click, click. 'Fantastic. Brilliant. Now reach for it, extend that lovely neck.' Click, click. 'Gorgeous. Just gorgeous.' Click, click. 'And again. Lovely.'

Virgil blocked out the racket as best he could. He'd found a website that from her browsing history Mira seemed to look at every day. It was entirely blank and white except for a single heading above a large picture of an antique clock.

ONE HUNDRED AND SEVEN DAYS

In the centre of the clock was a digital counter labelled with days, hours and minutes shown in red. As he watched the counter the minutes dropped by one.

107:05:16

What on earth could this mean to Mira? He had no idea, and couldn't ask without revealing that he had been spying on her.

* * *

Virgil spent most of the evening squeezed into the lounge at his mum's flat, poring over the legal files from Stardust's solicitors. These covered the most serious threats to Mira. The TV was on in the background as he munched his way through a packet of jaffa cakes. There was nowhere near enough space for all the paperwork, so he had it stacked around on the carpet, and on the seat next to him. Only a week until he'd have a place of his own, a one-bedroom flat in Balham, newly-decorated with a skylight in the bedroom. Until then he'd have to be careful about all his stuff, which was monopolising all the high cupboards in the hall.

So far he'd come across three cases which were with the police for specific violent or sexual threats made through social media. Two were ongoing cases less than six weeks old but one, the most persistent, had been identified as a fifteen-year-old boy from Colchester. He had e-mailed and Facebooked Mira with suggestive comments, culminating in sending her a Snapchat video showing himself masturbating. The police had not disclosed his name, but he had served a short sentence in a young offenders' institution. Virgil realised that while the boy was only doing what many thousands of others of his age probably did when fantasising about Mira, only today's technology made it possible for them to let the world, and the victim, know all about it.

The fattest files were over allegations of defamation. Bloggers who had claimed Mira had undergone cosmetic surgery, online columnists who suggested she had taken illegal drugs, and one middle-aged woman from the Orkneys who persistently posted that Mira was sleeping with her husband. They were each sent firm and formal letters about the legal risks they were running. About half seemed to go quiet, though not Eileen from the Islands.

Japan seemed to be the source of some of the most over-enthusiastic fans, some of whom wrote asking for her discarded underwear. One it seemed had cut out the middleman by actually trying to steal some from her hand luggage on an overnight flight from Osaka to London. The man had lost his job at a major Japanese airline. The manga cartoon books had generated literally millions of tweets, Facebook posts and other comments on online forums. The lawyers had blithely advised that there was very little if anything that could be done to monitor yet alone influence this, except where messages were personally directed to Mira.

Foreign trouble was generally ignored, there being little possibility of pursuing anything that wasn't clearly criminal. The former bodyguard, Curtis Hyde, was an exception. A case against him in New York was pending. Likewise, an American multiple rapist, serving a 248-year term, had been able to make lurid threats against her via Facebook. The California Department of Corrections and Rehabilitation breezily confirmed that they would now remove his Internet access. Virgil was amazed he was ever allowed it.

There were no files mentioning the man in Broadmoor who had sent her the card. Yet something about such a man had alarmed her enough to track down a cutting. But who was this mysterious man, and what had he done?

Finally, Virgil got round to examining the countdown website. Based on the domain name, it was called Lovely Dia. Virgil was baffled. There were no links visible. Maybe there was something hidden. He moved the mouse around, trying to see if the white arrow would turn into the pointing finger that denoted a hyperlink. Nothing. Then he defined and copied the entire page to a Word document, and set the font colour to black. No text became visible. All he had to go on was the website address *www.lovelydia.xyz*. Virgil knew that 'day' in Spanish was 'dia'. In a few other languages perhaps. But what was the point in a website called lovely day? Then he realised that it wasn't lovely dia. It was love Lydia, Mira's real name. And what would happen once it had counted off the days to zero? Virgil decided to monitor it daily.

Chapter Thirteen

ONE HUNDRED AND TWO DAYS

The Right Reverend Harry Fielding, Bishop of Uxbridge and passionate prison reformer, was in civvies today to lead a personal preview of the *Reform Through Art* exhibition at Halifax Town Hall for Baroness Earl of West Bromwich. He excused his chinos, grey fleece and what might be termed urban walking gear, as he was heading off for an outdoor weekend in the Yorkshire Dales as soon as he'd finished, and because he knew from long acquaintance that the baroness wouldn't mind. The Künzler Trust, of which he was a trustee, had invited her to make the train journey up from London because she was opposition spokesman on prisons, but Harry admitted that like many members of the Lords, it was a pleasure just to be in the company of a woman of such energy, passion and intellect, not to mention her rather shapely legs. To see her there in the grand entrance to the hall, in a russet knee-length coat which matched her copper hair, black tights and high-heeled boots it was hard to believe she was at forty-seven a life peer, and chair of the cross-party Parliamentary Committee on Prison Reform. A Labour MP since 2005, she had in the previous government briefly been Under Secretary of State, Minister for Prisons, Probation and Rehabilitation, an appointment brought to an end by the 2010 election. However, she was elevated to the Lords the following year as a working peer. For years before she had been a pioneering immigration barrister in Birmingham, specialising in political asylum and extraordinary rendition cases. She had many admirers and a few enemies. Some in Parliament, having seen her devastating debating skills firsthand, were both.

After greeting her with a peck on both cheeks, Harry led her up the stairs towards the galleries.

'You're going to see a bit of everything today, Suzy, the good the bad and the very ugly. The point of it is whether the art helps the offender, rather than whether it is good art *per se*,' Harry said. 'Though one could suppose there are exceptions in both directions.'

As he had conceded, much of what was on show was mediocre: puerile erotica, badly-drawn figures, garishly coloured canvases, and sometimes the over-detailed imagination of some startlingly disturbed psychiatric patients.

'This I think you will enjoy,' Harry said, stopping by a rather fine ink and charcoal study from an offender at HMP Lincoln. Entitled simply *Cellmate*, it was of a heavily tattooed prisoner, whose gaunt frame and flat vacant eyes conveyed volumes about the endless futility of incarceration. The orange sticker on the frame indicated that it had been sold. He next pointed out the prolific work of a patient at Rampton. They were a series of photographically precise portraits of children, winsomely and deftly executed in acrylic paints.

'Very sad case. She drowned her own babies, and now imagines them still growing up. Lots and lots of catharsis required,' Fielding muttered. 'But I hear she has stopped self-harming, finally.'

Harry led her over to the giant double doors of the Victoria Hall. 'Now this is really what I wanted you to see. I'm rather keeping it under wraps until the *Art with Conviction* auction in three months.'

He eased open the doors into the huge hall, reaching up to a mansard roof. There in the centre under three spotlights was an enormous oil painting, fifteen feet wide by nine high. Or more precisely it was three paintings, because the rectangular form was split from bottom corners to top middle into three separately framed triangular canvases.

'My God,' Suzannah said. 'It is astonishing.'

'A work of genius, without a doubt,' said Harry.

Dominating the central panel of the triptych was the Crucifixion, angled from below against a star-emblazoned ultramarine night sky. Christ was immense, handsome, well-muscled and nude, handcuffed to a cross in the form of a living oak tree. He was being embraced by a viridian-cloaked female centurion, gracefully depicted with an arm cupping his head while her sword simultaneously pierced him low on the abdomen. Sweeping low flying behind the tree, laying a cerulean cloak across the breadth of the piece was the figure of God. He was bearded, majestic and tattooed, His arms out in support of his son. So powerful was the projection of those mighty hands that they seemed to leap from the canvas, three times life-size, and superbly executed. The crown of thorns, cruelly depicted as razor wire, was framed into a halo that itself wrapped the setting sun. The left panel took its point of view from Christ, looking down on the disciples, depicted as prisoners, heads bent in supplication. Only one, a young woman right in the foreground, looked up, offering a cup of water. The darker right-hand panel, was dominated by a raven-haired Madonna, eyes heavenward, wearing a violet cloak and offering up a steaming bowl of some kind.

'Who on earth painted this?' she whispered.

'He signs himself as Wôdan, and he's in Broadmoor.'

'But who is he, really?'

'Ah yes, well that's an issue. They are very ticklish about the privacy of patients, I think you are aware of that.'

'I presume this was the same man who painted a version of Botticelli's *Birth of Venus*? I saw it in the *Guardian* a few months ago.'

'Yes. That sold for over a million dollars at Sotheby's in New York in October, a record sum for a piece of work by a psychiatric patient. But this is in my view worth more.'

'Has he produced much other work?'

'Enough for several exhibitions. Last year we were lucky enough to secure the use of a Bond Street gallery, and sold a portrait of a prison officer for thirty thousand pounds.'

'I think I recall seeing that. Wasn't it called '*Screw. You*' or something like that?'

'Indeed it was. The trust has been talking for months to a foreign buyer who is interested in buying more, not surprisingly, so with a developing *oeuvre* of this maturity, I believe Mr Wōdan could help bring the cause of art and indeed art therapy centre stage for the benefit of the entire secure psychiatric system.'

'What are the financial arrangements?'

'With Künzler sales, a quarter of all the money goes straight to victim support. Where it is possible to identify actual victims, a direct payment can also be offered. In the prison service, the arrangement is that prisoners can have some limited cash as a reward, with any larger amounts reserved by the director. In mental health institutions it is always at the discretion of the director. But in this case, the artist has said that half of all the money raised can go to funding art in psychiatric hospitals, so long as any sale is free of gallery commission.'

'Someone in secure psychiatric dictating terms!'

Harry gave her a slightly patronising look. 'Oh yes, he's very assertive. Two galleries have agreed to waive commission, so long as there is widespread publicity for their generosity.'

'Have you met him?'

The bishop paused. 'Yes, I have met him.' She noticed his Adam's apple bob at the memory. His features were not quite controlled.

'And you do know his real name?'

The bishop looked down at his watch. 'Well, he changed his name by deed poll several years ago. I know what he is called *now*, but not what his real name is, or was.'

'What did he do?'

The bishop didn't answer immediately.

'Come on, Harry. I do need to know.'

He stroked his chin. 'Well, obviously, he has committed some really quite questionable acts. But his behaviour these days is quite impeccable.'

'Was it murder?'

'Good heavens, yes. Several, I believe.'

'You will undoubtedly appreciate that I can't possibly begin to mass the kind of political oomph required to get more support for art in psychiatric hospitals without having the full details of what we're dealing with. If he's changed his name, if we can't find out what his real name is, then obviously he's done something quite horrible.'

'I actually don't know the details. Richard Lamb wouldn't tell me.'

'It's an important aspect. I mean you've got to think tabloid, Harry. I'm a reformer, you're a reformer, but we can't risk headlines like "Labour offers art therapy for mass-murderers".'

'Well, these people are sick, Suzy. But they can be cured, they can make a contribution to society to atone for their errors of judgment.'

'There are many, many people out there who believe we cannot take the chance,' she said. 'And they all have a vote.'

Bishop Fielding didn't reply, but instead turned to the central panel of the triptych. 'Without going all *Thought for the Day* on you, Suzy, just take a look at this. God made us all with free will, yes? Every day every single one of us could, possibly, choose to murder. The weapons are just to hand. To stab a partner, a child or a stranger. Most of us never do, because we have a functioning moral compass. The choices we have, the immense power whether to stab or to talk to those who are troubling us, is what makes us human. To err is human, but so is to forgive. Redemption, in the sight of God, is what the Crucifixion is all about. This is what Wōdan has so brilliantly personalised.'

'I won't deny his brilliance. But what about his mind?'

'He really has showed enormous remorse. In our conversations, which have gone on now for two years, he has gradually come to embrace God. Indeed, it is only since he has done so that he has produced this quality of art. There is perhaps a divine pathway being illuminated here.'

'What might that be?'

'Well, it's undoubtedly a controversial view, but, if he continues to make progress like this, I think he should be released.'

* * *

ONE HUNDRED DAYS

Dawn Evans and her best friend Sue were getting their breath back in the changing rooms after their usual Thursday evening Badminton session. 'You were on killer form today,' Sue said. 'I couldn't get close to some of those shots.'

Dawn smiled. 'I'm feeling quite good about myself at the moment. I've lost some weight too.'

'I thought so. Do I detect the presence of a man in your life?' Sue enquired.

Dawn grinned, and grasped Sue's arm. 'Yes. Three years since Simon and I've finally got someone!'

'Wow, Dawn! I want to hear all about it,' Sue said. 'How long has it…?'

'For a few months. It started slowly, but it's got more…serious recently.'

'A few months! And you only just told me! C'mon, what's he like?' Sue's eyes were almost popping out.

'He's very romantic, and very clever. He gives me poetry, oh, and he's a great artist.' She opened her bag and took out a carefully rolled piece of paper. 'He did a drawing of me.'

Sue unrolled the drawing and stared in amazement. 'Bloody hell, Dawn. This is like Leonardo! You're beautiful. Omigod. Are you in love?'

Dawn's smile was more wistful than ecstatic. 'I am, but…it's complicated.'

'He's married isn't he?' Sue said.

'No, but he is someone from work. He's a fair bit older.'

Sue put her hands on her hips and said with mock offence: 'Now, Dawn Christine Evans, are you sleeping with the boss?'

Dawn laughed and shook her head. 'It's worse than that.' Sue continued to pepper her with questions, but Dawn knew she had already said too much. Like many staff at Broadmoor she had never told family or friends exactly where she worked.

'When can I meet him?'

Dawn gave a wan smile. 'I really don't know.'

* * *

160

Broadmoor director Richard Lamb had got nowhere trying to prove who had injured Leonard Lucifer Smith, nor indeed how. The mental health trust had requested his report, but at this stage it didn't look like being the comprehensive one they would expect. He knew that he couldn't avoid declaring that a crime had been committed, which would mean he would lose control of the investigation. Whatever report emerged would be bound to blame him. It would certainly damage his career.

So what did he have so far? Blood tests had shown that Smith had been drugged with the date-rape drug Rohypnol, but he was no further along in identifying which members of staff could have been complicit. Everyone had plausible denials. While he was prepared to believe that a patient would have had as strong a motive as any member of staff to hurt Lucy, they would have needed help to nobble the CCTV system. But Dawn Evans, the staffer who radiated the most guilt, didn't even know how to use the system that was interfered with. Any attempt to link her with Smith's half dozen known enemies among the patients, including William Mordant, foundered on that irrefutable fact.

It was early afternoon by the time Lamb got around to opening his post. Right on top was a Jiffy bag he'd just been sent by Dr Choudary of Frimley Park Hospital. Security had already opened it, and he soon discovered why. There inside a plastic bag, folded, cleaned and sterilised, was the section of razor wire recovered from inside Lucy. The doctor's accompanying letter was fascinating. Since the operation on Smith, Choudary had obviously scoured the literature for similar cases, because he'd dug up an article from the Italian *Journal of Medicine* back in 1962, and enclosed a photocopy.

A gastro-intestinal specialist working in Naples had in a ten-hour operation removed a length of barbed wire from a middle-aged male patient. The process involved lubricating a piece of sterilised garden hose and carefully pushing it into the patient to envelop the wire. The wire of course had to be carefully stabilised to prevent it moving. Once the hose was fully in, the entire assembly could be drawn out. The surgeon noted that it was merely the reversing of the process by which the wire was inserted. Having read the article, Lamb was still baffled as to why anyone would want to do something so horrible. Then he noticed a footnote:

* The forcible anal insertion of barbed wire is occasionally recorded as a punishment by the Camorra, the Naples-based mafia, for breaking the code of silence known as Omerta.

Lamb looked at the final paragraph of Choudary's letter, which referred to something having been engraved onto the blades of the wire. He held it up to a desk light, where he could see some neatly-wrought scratches. They were too small for him to discern. He took out a magnifying glass, only bought last week to examine details on CCTV stills. Leaning forward and using his lamp he could just make out the words, beautifully and professionally engraved on both sides of the blades. Once he'd read them he recoiled as if struck.

And I saw when the Lamb opened one of the seals, and I heard,
as it were the noise of thunder, one of the four beasts saying,
Come and see! (Revelations 6, v1)

* * *

Richard Lamb was a scientist, a realist and a man of rational disposition. But only now did he realise that he was up against an intelligence of extraordinary malice, one that named him, and aimed to destroy him. The only 'seal' that made sense, that he in any sense controlled, was the gate out of Broadmoor. Of the more than two hundred patients under his management, half would do anything to get out. Of those there were probably fewer than five, all dangerous psychopaths, who would have the patience, the cunning and the resources to engineer this attack. Because this wasn't just an attack on Lunatic Lucy, it was an attack on him, and a warning to the entire secure psychiatric system.

Of those five, perhaps only three had the educational background and the technical skills to have engraved those words so neatly into the blades of the razor wire. There was no proof of course, because of the absence of CCTV footage, and the perplexing lack of witnesses to Lunatic Lucy's departure from the recreation lounge. But if Lamb had to choose a culprit, it was William Mordant. The man remained an enigma, perpetuated by officialdom.

Just last week, Lamb had run into the Home Office consultant psychiatrist who came to visit Mordant twice a year, quite often with one or two equally enigmatic associates. Godfrey Allen looked like a rotund bank manager, in an expensive suit, with slip-on shoes and a hefty briefcase, and always arrived at very short notice. He resembled no shrink that Lamb had ever met, and was evasive about his *alma mater* in the brief conversation they shared. Yet his letter granting him privileges of client confidentiality and excusing him from the security search was signed by the Home Secretary herself. Lamb had made inquiries through his various professional memberships and LinkedIn, and though there were plenty of people of that name, none seemed to be quite appropriate for the job that Godfrey Allen appeared to be doing.

So what was it about William Mordant that the Home Office was still so interested in almost a decade after he was sectioned? And why was it so important that it was kept absolutely secret?

Chapter Fourteen

EIGHTY-EIGHT DAYS

Virgil couldn't believe they were doing this. If anyone at Stardust Brands got even a whisper of the risks they were running he could be fired, but Mira was insistent that this was the best way to discover the truth about the Qaeggan zombie cult that had grown up around *Village of the Dead*. 'You said you wanted to find out firsthand what this whole scene is about, and to do that you have to feel it, dive into it, immerse yourself. Tapping into social media messages will only get you so far,' she had said.

So now, at seven o'clock on a Saturday evening, Virgil, Mira and her old school friend Natasha, were stuffed into a packed Metropolitan Line tube train on their way to hear the biggest names in Qaegrock playing at Wembley Arena. There would be tens of thousands there, followers of the TV show, fans of zombie house music, and many of them besotted with Mira. He and Mira could have taken VIP tickets, arrived by chauffeured car, been escorted in safely and then watched the show from on high, safe from the press of the kids who 'lived the nightmare,' as Dr Swampheart's lead singer Trudge had memorably termed it. But now at Mira's insistence they were right there with them.

'I'm not sure this is good idea,' Virgil had said, when Mira first mentioned going by public transport. 'Someone is bound to recognise you.'

'No they won't. If I'm qaegged up they won't have a clue,' Mira said. 'Look. If you don't want to come, then don't.'

'You know full well that if you're in public, I have to be there. But it's also my job to point out to you when you are putting yourself in danger.'

'In danger of being able to feel a bit of freedom? Yes, well, you've told me. And I'm still going to go. Tasha is coming too.'

The saving grace was the costume. A good half of those on the train were in full Qaeggan gear. Mira was wearing a cheap black curly wig, white face paint with the three black tear stains under each eye, and a black body suit, suitably tattered as if by claws. Her final additions were the crucial ones: ugly plastic dentures to give her snaggly brown teeth, and the black full iris contact lenses instead of her usual ones. So she could actually see, she had spectacles too. When Virgil came to meet her, she had jumped out at him the moment the lift doors opened on her floor.

'Jesus, you almost gave me a heart attack!' he said.

'So much for my tough bodyguard,' she murmured, her voice muffled by the teeth. It had succeeded in making her ugly. But for a monster, she still had a wonderful body. Virgil had been more troubled by the disguise she had procured for him. The baggy patched dungarees with a single shoulder strap was okay, but the curly wig and make-up made him feel like a refugee from the *Black and White Minstrel Show*. Natasha was wearing a ripped yellow vest, torn hot pants and black tights painted with bones. She had in a pair of cats eye contact lenses. Now they were squeezed into a corner of a carriage, hemmed in by a group of six bewigged Geordies, with open beer cans, singing their hearts out. All hefty lads, they cannoned into them with each sway and buck of the train as it roared and squealed its way under north London. Ticket touts worked their way up and down the carriage, followed by hawkers offering the very same cheap Mira merchandise that Jonesy Tolling had railed against.

Virgil had spent a few hours on YouTube researching Qaegrock, or Q-wave as it was sometimes known, which turned out to be a combination of eighties style electronic house music with *Dr Who* theme tune overtones, plus a heavy drum beat which was the incidental music for zombie arrival on *Village of the Dead*. Half a dozen bands seemed prominent, including Dr Swampheart, Qaegattack, and The Death Tears. However, most of the innovation seemed to take place through DJ mixes, which allowed uninterrupted zombie dances of up to an hour, stiff-shouldered hip gyrations, plus plenty of head lolling. To Virgil's viewpoint it was a perfect encapsulation of the zombie idea. Deathly dull, repetitive entropy.

The thumping drumbeats of Qaeggan sound hit them hard as soon as they got into the huge arena. In the distance the first band was already on stage. Lasers played across the crowd and dry ice drifted out of a huge brown inflatable mushroom on stage. They queued for half an hour for bottles of water, and watched hundreds of zombies gyrating in strobe lights. Virgil noted that there were far more men than women, and that quite a few were taking tablets. Mira wanted to wade up towards the stage, but before they had a chance to move, someone came up and asked Mira to dance. She waved him away, and instead grabbed Virgil and Tasha and went as a threesome to the dance floor. Virgil adopted the stumbling gait of most of the male zombies. Tasha kept her body still, but swung her head side-to-side, a Qaeggan move copied from the TV show and now a *bona fide* dance move. Mira though, despite claiming not to be able to dance, swung her shoulders and hips in an extraordinarily alluring way, nothing like a true Qaeggan dance. Virgil nudged her shoulder and bellowed into her ear that she shouldn't be drawing such attention to herself. 'Don't nanny me, Virgil. Do you realise how long it is since I've been able to dance in public? I'm sick of having to hide away.'

Virgil shrugged. He could see her point, but there was going to be trouble, he knew it.

Soon the inevitable happened. A tall zombie with full black eyes manhandled his way into the group and seized Mira's hand. 'You can't have them both,' he yelled to Virgil. Virgil looked to Mira, who mouthed 'It's okay.'

Virgil and Tasha danced for a while, but Virgil always propelled her to a place where he was close to Mira. The tall guy seemed to be angling for what was the nearest to zombie close dancing, but Mira kept him at a distance. Virgil noticed that Mira no longer had her zombie teeth in. Tasha, meanwhile, was dancing with a couple of youthful zombies, one male, one female. She too seemed to be having fun. Three big guys pushed past with drinks, and Virgil lost sight of Mira. It was a couple of minutes before he saw her again, further away, dancing with a different partner, a beefy-looking shaven-headed guy wearing almost no zombie gear. Virgil began to push his way through the crowd towards her. He saw the guy swallow a couple of tablets. He offered some to Mira, and she shook her head. Few could keep up with her dance energy, and Virgil noticed a little knot of zombies just standing watching her, looking her up and down. The way they were talking to each other, arms folded, while ogling her gave him a bad feeling. He strode up and put his hand on her shoulder, the better to whisper to her. The beefy guy shoved Virgil's arm away, putting his own arm around Mira's shoulder. Virgil didn't need his lip-reading skills to know he was being told to fuck off. This is *exactly* what I knew would happen, Virgil thought. I bloody knew it. I'm probably going to have to deck someone to keep her safe. While he considered how much of a scene to make, Mira said something that made the guy turn towards her. She rested an arm on the man's shoulder, held up her other hand, and pointed towards Virgil. The other guy released his hold on her, and she turned, walked up to Virgil, seized his face in both hands and kissed him hard, for five long seconds. The shock of her mouth on his: hot, soft and delicious, took his breath away.

'I told him you were my boyfriend,' she shouted into his ear. 'I apologise for abusing you. I needed to do this to back up the story.'

Virgil tried to stop the grin splitting his head open. He had just been kissed by the most beautiful and desirable woman in the world, and she was apologising for it. 'It's okay. Certainly preferable to me having to smack him one.'

Mira nodded. 'I hope you are keeping an eye on Tasha too.'

'I am, but that's in my spare time. I'm paid to look after you. So can we go now?'

'Oh, stop being such a wuss,' Mira said. 'The best bit is just about to happen.' She grabbed Tasha and led them both towards the biggest stage where Dr Swampheart were just getting ready to play their session. The lead singer, an enormously tall and pale man known as Trudge with a passing resemblance to Herman Munster, grabbed hold of the mic, and yelled a hello to Wembley. As he did so, more and more people began to converge at the stage. Zombies of all kinds were moving over, swigging from cans, some holding poles with skulls mounted on them, others swaddled in hooded capes. As Mira led Virgil and Tasha down to the front it got more and more crowded. The drummer started a series of explosive beats, and the feedback of guitars wailed and soared in the background. A giant screen at the back of the stage flickered into life, with a countdown from twenty.

'So Wembley,' Trudge bellowed as the drums thundered faster and faster. 'Do you know what you want?'

The crowd roared back.

'I can't fucking hear you,' Trudge said, hand to his ear. The countdown had got to twelve. Around Mira, the press of bodies got tighter and tighter.

'Mira! We want Mira!' they roared.

Virgil suddenly felt very anxious. The crowd, the press of bodies, the screaming and the roaring drums. He stood right behind Mira, ready to protect her, but she seemed elated, as if unaware of the gathering danger she was in. The roars for Mira got even louder, and Mira herself joined in at the top of her voice.'

'Well, lucky you,' roared Trudge. 'Because we have Mira, RIGHT HERE TONIGHT.'

'We're going NOW,' Virgil bellowed in Mira's ear. 'This is going to get very bad.'

'No,' Mira said, 'wait,' but already Virgil had taken hold of her arm, and was trying to carve a way through the press behind her. As far as he could see in every direction there were dark, writhing bodies, zombie dancing. The countdown was down to three, and Virgil was expecting that at any moment some searchlight would find them, and the woman he was employed to protect would be torn to pieces by her fans.

The drumming reached a crescendo then Trudge bellowed: 'Ladies and gentleman, zombies and Qaeggan, tonight, live from LA, I give you, Mira!'

Virgil turned his head as the screen burst into life, and there twenty feet high, was Mira. She was dressed in a white gauzy dress, its fabric billowing around her in the breeze. In the background, silhouettes of gnarled trees emerged from clouds of dry ice. She was barefoot, as she had been in the *Village of the Dead*, but her eyes looked huge and bewitchingly green.

'Hello Wembley!' the screen Mira said. 'How are you all?'

The crowd went absolutely berserk, screaming her name. All around him the fans were sticking out their tongues and undulating them in a vaguely obscene fashion, which Virgil had learned was the Qaeggan reaction to the smell of human flesh.

'We're just great, Mira,' yelled Trudge.

'It's fantastic to see so many of you there at Qaegfest,' screen Mira said. 'Show me a light, so I know you are there.'

Almost immediately, thousands of torches, coloured lanterns and various other forms of illumination appeared. Virgil was amazed. A chant of Mira's name grew louder and louder.

'Now come closer, reach out and touch me!' screen Mira called.

At that moment Virgil, Tasha and Mira were picked up and carried forward by an ocean wave of humanity that squeezed the breath out of them. Everyone was stretching out an arm, most of them with talons glued on their fingers, desperate to reach the screen. To Virgil's left a whole group of youths fell over, and those behind started to climb over the writhing press of bodies.

'Okay everybody!' Trudge shouted. 'We'll say goodbye to Mira now, and get on with the show.'

'Love to you all,' screen Mira said and blew a kiss. The crowd went wild. The screen faded to black and Dr Swampheart started its signature track "Hunger for the flesh". The human wave rebounded a little, and using his greater height Virgil was able to make sure that neither Mira nor Tasha were knocked over. Gradually they were able to cut back through the crowd until they could walk easily.

'So how did you manage that?' asked Virgil.

'It was recorded in a studio round the corner three days ago,' Mira said. 'I'd been invited to Qaegfest months ago. Thad didn't want me to attend, but it was Jonesy's idea to mock up the video as a live link. As long as the script is simple, it's not hard.'

'A little unethical.'

'You think so?' she looked at him curiously. He realised she had taken her Qaeggan contact lenses out, and was no longer wearing her glasses.

'Sure. You deceived your fans.'

She laughed and patted him on the shoulder. 'Yes, I'm not as perfect as they say.'

Virgil was now itching to leave, but Mira and Tasha had joined a huge queue for the toilets, which snaked through a well-lit corridor.

'I need to get you away from here,' he hissed into her ear. 'And put your teeth back in. They'll recognise you.'

'I lost them. And I'm boiling in this thing.' Mira took off her wig, and shook out her hair, which cascaded down her shoulders. Most of the disguise was now gone, though the face paint still made it hard to be sure who she was.

Virgil noticed a few people staring at them. One woman just behind them in the queue had nudged her friend and said: 'It is her. I told you it was.'

Her friend replied: 'Can't be. She's in America. Just seen her, haven't we?'

'Hey, Mira!' a man further down the line shouted. 'Gissa kiss!'

Virgil seized Mira's arm, and started pulling her from the queue. 'Time to go. Don't argue.'

Mira reacted fiercely, and pulled her arm away. 'Don't touch me, you bloody oaf. I'm quite capable of walking.'

'Hey, you really look like her,' yelled a man with a Liverpool accent. Now everyone was staring at them. Hundreds of people choking the corridor, half of them in Qaeggan gear, many brandishing phone cameras. 'Mira, for Christ's sake! You're just making a scene,' Natasha hissed.

Virgil looked heavenwards. *Thank you Tasha for using her name.* People started to call out to Mira, and the message that she was amongst the crowd started to generate hysteria. Two large male zombies lurched over, demanding she be in a selfie, until Virgil firmly blocked their path. But there were dozens more behind, crowding round. Virgil shepherded Mira and Natasha towards the exit, but was soon blocked in. More and more fans were crowding round, everyone trying to take pictures. A few press photographers popped up from nowhere, adding to the crush. Mira hid her face against Virgil's back as he tried to cut through to the turnstiles. A few security staff hurried up, but the mass of arriving Qaeggan fans chanting Mira's name was now so great that they were powerless. Virgil, Mira and Natasha were swept aside, and cornered in a side hall of the ticketing concourse, away from the turnstiles. The nearest emergency exit was an impossible twenty yards away.

The crowd now seemed to have a life of its own, sweeping people along like a river. A few zombies climbed onto a stanchion to get above the crush, holding arms down to help others. Virgil still had Mira's face buried against him, and was finally squeezed against a glass door to an internal office. Inside, through part-open blinds, he saw a woman, on the phone. He pounded on the glass. 'Let us in, we're being crushed to death here.' The woman looked up, face frozen in panic, staring. Others began to kick at the glass, and he could feel the heat of Mira's stifled breath moist against his chest. Somehow he managed to press his security credentials against the glass. 'It's an emergency!' he bellowed.

The woman released the catch on the door and stepped away as he, Mira and a gaggle of dishevelled fans tumbled in and to the floor. Virgil couldn't see Natasha among them. If she was out there alone, she might suffocate among all those painted faces, and taloned hands squeezed against the glass. More people tumbled into the office. Mira had the woman by the shoulders: 'Get us out of here!' she screamed.

'What about Natasha? We can't leave her,' Virgil shouted.

The woman led them though another office, down an emergency staircase and onto a concrete concourse. Three girls, who had been screaming when they first fell into the office with them, had now recovered enough poise to get their cameras out, and ask Mira for an autograph. They looked about sixteen. Virgil thought it was safe enough to leave Mira with them while he raced round the side of the building and back up the stairs to the ticket foyer. He found Natasha there, lying on the floor being treated by St John's Ambulance along with a dozen others who had been in the crush.

* * *

The next morning's Stardust Brands meeting was supposed to be about the Suressence deal, but there was little new to say. Instead it turned into a debrief over the previous night's Qaegfest coverage.

'This,' Jonesy said, pointing to the newspapers, 'is exactly what terrifies sponsors. We could have closed with Ultimate Jewellery this week without this. Quarter of a million quid. Now they're dithering over the contract because they really can't handle the zombie association. Gothic pallor, severed arms and plastic gore. It's the opposite of the youth and innocence we're trying to promote, ain't it? Especially, when something like this happens.'

Almost every front page had the same picture, capturing Mira sheltering behind Virgil's back. The green of her eyes had been caught in the flash, her arms splayed wide and her luxuriant blonde hair thrown out wildly as she turned her head. All the facepaint had done was to give her beauty an untamed edge. 'You might think you are a goddess, Mira, but please don't ever try the omnipresence trick again,' Jonesy said. 'Just be in one place at a time.'

'It was your idea,' Mira retorted.

'Not to go to the gig, it wasn't. It was a completely preventable fuck-up. No more PFUs, understand?'

Mira shrugged and stood up ready to head off to a photoshoot in Paris, but Kelly walked in. 'Got a few bits of fan mail for you to read on the plane,' she said. 'As you seemed to enjoy the previous one, I've included the latest from Broadmoor. More Latin, I'm afraid.'

She passed the sheaf to Mira who started to put them into her huge Louis Vuitton bag.

'Can I see them first?' Virgil asked.

Mira looked heavenwards, and passed them on. Virgil leafed through the post until he reached the Broadmoor envelope, which had been opened. Again there was a handmade card, a beautiful watercolour of a pair of doves in flight. Inside was written:

Tantum id dierum nonaginta dare! Memini me eloquium tuum.

'Did you translate this?' Virgil asked Kelly.

'No, I just assumed that it was more of the same,' Kelly said. 'I do have a lot to do, you know? There are other clients; they all get post.'

Virgil quickly typed it into Google translate.

Only ninety days! Do not forget your promise to me.

He read it out and looked at Mira. 'What promise? Does this mean anything to you?'

'Nothing at all,' she said impassively, holding her hand out for the letter which she added to the sheaf and put in her bag. 'The car's here now, so I've got to go.' She headed out towards the lift.

'It sounded vaguely threatening to me,' said Virgil, looking to Kelly and Jonesy for support.

'What do you expect from Broadmoor?' Jonesy said. 'Effing sanity?' He took a look at the envelope. 'Virgil, it invites us to notify them if the letter is unwanted or offensive. Why don't you fill out and return this form? We've got proper problems here without worrying about this crap. Honestly, Virgil, if we could cut this zombie connection once and for all we'd get more brand money upfront and could fund a back-up for you.'

'But it's the fans of *Village of the Dead* who got her to where she is now.'

'Okay, but our job is to build from here. And right now, most of the dosh she earns is conditional; back-end loaded or dependent on sales uplift a year or more out. She ain't a hypermodel yet, not by a long chalk.'

After that downbeat assessment, Virgil didn't want to bring up the website, for fear of revealing he'd been spying on Mira's Internet usage. But the countdown on the site must tally with these cards. There could be no other explanation. Virgil worked forwards from the postmark on the card and the website counter. The deadline day was Saturday 25 April. He checked for anniversaries, birthdays, famous moments in recent British history and could find nothing that seemed relevant. This day must be personal, notable only to two people who really should not know each other. And what was the promise she had made?

* * *

Virgil had wanted the following day off to equip his new flat, but it wasn't to be. Mira returned from Paris and had decided to visit her mother, who was in a private care home in Swindon. In the past she had driven there alone, but Jonesy was insistent that she be accompanied.

'We've already had a report that the press have tracked her mother down,' he told Virgil. 'Any half decent tabloid reporter will have greased the palm of someone on staff to tip the wink if Mira is there. So she'll just turn up unannounced for a quick visit which should keep PFUs to a minimum.'

What Jonesy hadn't told Virgil was that Mira was determined to drive herself. He had barely finished his breakfast when he heard someone leaning on the horn outside. He looked out to see a midnight blue S-type Jaguar parked all over the pavement outside, amid a crowd of wheelie bins. Mira emerged from the car, dressed in quilted afghan coat, white Beatles-style breton cap, sunglasses and flared jeans, as if she had just escaped from the seventies. He bolted the last of his toast, and grabbed his coat and phone. The moment he got down there she was revving to go, and he only had a moment to slide into the passenger seat before Mira gunned the engine and pulled a fast U-turn into traffic. She had already taken two turns before Virgil had managed to find and fasten his seat belt.

'Are we late?' he asked, as Mira overtook a van in the face of oncoming traffic.

'Not really. But I reckon the sooner we get there the less chance of any reporters snooping around.'

As Mira tore through the Sunday morning traffic Virgil found he was unconsciously pressing his non-existent brake pedal and sucking in hissed breaths. After one particularly deadly manoeuvre in which Mira mounted the pavement and scattered pedestrians to get round a vehicle indicating right, she looked at him and laughed.

'You're scared, aren't you?'

'Bloody terrified, actually. Since you asked.'

She stared at him in amazement. 'But you've served in Afghanistan, under fire, seen friends die, haven't you? This is nothing compared to any of that, surely?'

'Look out for the cyclist,' he squealed, as Mira barely glanced ahead while squeezing through a non-existent gap. 'Mira, I am allowed to be scared. I'm not immune just because I've seen bad things. It makes you more careful, not less.'

'Really?' She turned to look again as they stopped in a queue to get onto the South Circular.

'Of course. Some of my oppos came back and can't cross the road. When you see death, it tears away the kind of protective skin that protects us from our imagination. We can no longer take risks without fully imagining the consequences. It's a kind of accelerated ageing process.'

Mira shrugged and then asked: 'Have you ever killed anyone?'

Virgil sighed and looked at her. 'The best answer I can say is: probably, yes.'

'You don't know?' She gave a short disbelieving laugh. 'How can you not know?'

'Easily. I've shot in the direction of incoming fire, through a window of a building half a mile away. Then it's stopped and I'm not sure why. I've directed air strikes onto a transport depot from which we were taking Taliban fire. After it was blown up, there were no more shots. If you can find and identify the bodies, you can be fairly certain, but not always.'

'Civilians?'

'I always hope not. The Taliban uses civilian areas for cover, knowing it inhibits us returning fire. I've seen dead women and children, lots. If you had the time, you could probably work out who killed them, the enemy or us. But it's not like we can call in forensics. We're too busy trying to stay alive. All I can say is that the rules of engagement are right. We never knowingly target areas where civilians may be present, but knowing that for sure and guessing are different things.'

Virgil's mind was drawn to the first dead civilian he saw, on his first week in Helmand. His unit had worked its way under fire laboriously through a series of apricot orchards, and when the shooting finally stopped heard a child crying. They found a little boy, less than two, frantically pulling on the arm of a dead young woman, under the base of a tree. The back of her skull had been blown off, her brains lying grey and bloodied in a mound. But the kid still thought he could wake her up.

'If you see death when you are young, and can't talk about it, it must mess you up,' Mira said. 'I think it would screw you up completely.'

Virgil noticed that she had moderated her speed. 'It's not even a matter of being young. We're human. Of course it does. Though not everyone. It all depends. I've got no end of friends with PTSD, post-traumatic stress disorder. It's what they use to call shell shock. They are quiet and withdrawn, and then they get furious at the smallest thing. Most of them are now divorced. They are permanently in a different world.'

'What's the worst thing you saw?'

Virgil sighed. 'It's not easy to talk about.' He looked at her, and saw the hunger in her expression, the huge green eyes. This to her was more than a curiosity.

'Sorry,' she said, 'you don't have to. I'm probably being insensitive.'

For five minutes there was no word spoken between them. Mira drove through the congested streets of Wandsworth. Finally Virgil scratched his head and then said: 'In Helmand, five of my best mates burned alive when an IED blew up a personnel carrier. I had been in there with them just thirty seconds before. I turned back to open the door, but it was too hot. When it did open...when I did.' He paused. 'I cannot describe it. I see it every day, and I dream it most nights, but I cannot describe what I saw in there.'

Mira said nothing for a while, then said: 'I'm sorry I asked.' Virgil doubted it.

She then switched to small talk about fashion, and Virgil tuned it out, stuck in his own dark world. They were on the elevated section of the M4, heading west out of London, before Mira asked him another question.

'Some of my friends say that the army should never have been in Afghanistan. That professional soldiers are just guns for hire, paid to kill.'

'It's a point of view,' Virgil responded. 'Particularly now the Taliban seem to be gaining ground since the moment we left. And I don't want to discuss it because I might get annoyed, on behalf of those who never came back.'

'So could you ever kill, just for money?'

He turned and stared at the side of her face: That exquisite profile, the fine cheekbones. She looked so youthful, so innocent. But what a question.

'Are you serious?'

She laughed. 'Hypothetically, I mean.'

Virgil shrugged. 'No. I don't think so. Not in cold blood. I need to have skin in the game. To kill to protect someone I love, someone who couldn't protect themselves, that kind of thing. Then maybe. Why, did you have anyone in mind?'

She didn't answer for a while. The reply when it came was quiet. 'No.'

* * *

They arrived at the care home before 10am. It was a dull two-storey building in tan brick at the end of a tired parade of suburban shops. The car park was almost empty. When Mira walked in, the elderly Asian man on reception clearly didn't recognise her. Mira signed in as Lydia Nikolayevna, then led Virgil along a beige, potpourri-scented corridor.

'I try to come every week. I think the idea that I'm her niece doesn't fool some of the staff.'

Mira knocked on a door and went in. Virgil stood back while Mira and her mother embraced. Svetlana Roskova was a handsome woman, quite tall and fine featured with her hair in a dark bob. Virgil had somehow imagined Mira's mother would be old, bent and grey. In fact she was just fifty-seven. But the stroke she had suffered two years ago had robbed her of coherent speech and stifled her movement and balance. Mira had to interpret her words.

'She's very glad that someone is looking after me,' Mira said, after Svetlana had snuffled her way through some noises and touched Virgil's arm. She still had a wonderful smile, and eyes that sparkled. Virgil looked around at the spacious, comfortable room, with only an orthopaedic bed and the walking frame betraying that this wasn't just ordinary sheltered housing. On one wall was an extraordinary framed drawing of Mira as a teenager, sitting on a stool. Just a few careful lines, it showed the child but hinted at the adult she was to become.

'Who did the drawing?' Virgil asked.

'Good isn't it?' At that moment Svetlana said something, and Mira translated. 'Virgil, she says that someone from a newspaper did come to see her. When they discovered they couldn't understand what she said, they asked her to write down the answers to their questions. She agreed, but chose to write with her left hand, so it was illegible. They went after about five minutes.'

Svetlana laughed uproariously, the sound a shock because it sounded utterly normal. After a few minutes Virgil slipped out to the corridor. A young woman with tufted pink hair and square glasses and wearing a staff lanyard was huddled by the snack vending machine, whispering on a mobile phone. When she saw him, she sidled away into an office looking a bit guilty. 'Yes, she is. Here. Right now,' was the only phrase that Virgil caught. His suspicions raised, he slipped quietly back into Svetlana's room, where Mira pointed out that the tea she had made for him was getting cold. Virgil considered trying to hurry Mira away, but seeing how animated they were together, he shrugged it off. If the press has been called, it could only be a local photographer. Fleet Street wouldn't be able to react this quickly.

An hour later when Mira was ready to leave, Virgil went ahead to reconnoitre the corridor and exit to the car park. A mileage-soiled estate car laden with silver camera cases and black bags was parked by the entrance, with someone sitting inside, eating a pasty, long lens camera on the seat beside him. There was no one else. Virgil went up and tapped on the window. It slid down.

'Local or national press?' Virgil asked.

'Whoever pays,' said the man, a greasy fifty-something with a ponytail and flecks of pastry in his moustache. 'You the bodyguard?'

'Yeah. So let's be civilised,' Virgil said. 'Show us your card.'

The man flashed a press card which identified him as Bob Newsome, freelance.

'Okay Bob, it's your exclusive, so you'll have ten seconds to get a posed pic or two of her by the door, right?'

'Suits me.'

'But if you ever photograph her mother, or try to follow us, or do anything sneaky, you have to remember that I never forget a face.'

Newsome smiled nervously.

'I'm serious,' Virgil said, pointing a warning finger. 'So is that a deal?'

'Fine by me,' Newsome said.

Virgil thought he was on top of media worries until he got back inside and heard shouting coming from down the corridor. Mira was demanding that the young female care assistant Virgil had seen earlier should hand over her phone. 'Don't you dare sneak pictures of me with my mum!' Mira shouted. 'Is nothing private?'

'I didn't take a picture,' the woman said. 'Honest.'

'Don't lie to me,' Mira said, reaching for the phone.

Virgil ran to her side, and rested an arm carefully on Mira's shoulder. 'Cool it,' he whispered. A middle-aged tank of a woman was approaching from the far end of the corridor, with a thunderous look on her face. 'Sandra Clarke, what IS going on here?' she bellowed.

'Shit! Mrs Delaney,' said Sandra.

'Simple solution, Sandra,' Virgil said, bending down to speak into Sandra's ear. 'Give me the phone, I'll delete the picture, and we'll say we were mistaken. Then we don't have to complain, and you don't get sacked. Okay?'

'Yeah, s'pose.' Sandra complied, scowling at Mira as she walked haughtily past. Virgil edited the phone and handed it back, then as agreed smoothed the way with the manageress.

Five minutes later they were on the road, with Mira breaking every speed limit by a factor of two. He kept his counsel until they roared past a nursery school at sixty-five.

'Squash a school kid and you can say goodbye to your career,' Virgil muttered.

'When I want your opinion, I'll give it to you,' she growled, dropping the Jag down into second to overtake a fuel tanker on the brow of a hill. 'You're just an old woman.'

'If that means I'm paid to lie awake at night and worry about your safety, I agree. Right now you've got a two-for-one bonus: I'm worried about my own safety too.'

Mira let out an involuntary chuckle and braked hard. 'Look,' she said, banging the steering wheel. 'Let me tell you something. Every time I see my mother it reminds me why she's in here. That stroke didn't just happen. She was beaten up by a loan shark. It caused a clot on her brain and three years later, bang. A stroke destroys her ability to speak.'

'That's awful, when was she beaten up?'

'June 2007. She had borrowed two grand and a few months later they reckoned she owed twenty. We moved house, from Dewsbury to Bradford, which is what we usually did when debts got out of hand, but they found us.'

'Were you there when it happened?'

'No. I'd seen the enforcer before, a really huge tattooed guy, black eyes, like a monster really, who had banged on the door one evening and scared us all to death. But the guy who beat her up was a smaller bloke. He bent her left wrist back so far she it dislocated some tendons, and now she can't get up to third position on the violin. But the stroke was caused when he knocked her about and she fell and banged her head.'

'Did they catch the guy?'

'No. She was too scared to report it. He was from some Manchester crime family, and we knew they would take it out on us. So we fled and used another version of Mum's name.'

'I had no idea. I assumed a well-thought-of classical musician wouldn't have money problems …'

'Yes, well, you've been reading too much of Jonesy's PR,' Mira said, flicking her hair, and running fingers through imaginary tangles. 'My mother is a gifted violinist, but after the divorce she got into debt. We had to leave London when we lost the house, and couldn't afford another. So we moved around from one town to another, first Birmingham, then Leeds and Bradford, then into Lancashire.'

'I had no idea.'

'Why would you? She started doing private tuition but she still got into debt. She just wasn't used to making do without lovely clothes. She rented homes that were beyond our means because she wouldn't live in squalor. She still gave plenty of violin and piano tuition, but once she borrowed from loan sharks, she soon realised there was only one way to earn the money she needed to make the repayments.' She turned to Virgil, her eyes flashing angrily, daring him to reproach the choice.

'That must have been difficult for you, as a teenager.'

'Not normally. My mother worked hard to keep it all away from me. I was generally at school during the day, when she had her gentlemen callers. Those I met at evenings and weekends were mostly genuine music students. The neighbours didn't suspect, because there was always classical music playing. But still, I could always read in her face what kind of day she had endured. She developed a kind of melancholy expression in repose, even though she could still occasionally manage the gaiety which I remembered. Then the stroke came, just as my modelling career began. I was in New York, and came back to look after her. It was only when I started to make some money that I could afford to get her proper care. But the first thing I did was to pay off her debts.'

Virgil took a deep breath and slid out the question he had been dying to ask. 'Mira, I realise this sounds intrusive, but it is only because I need to do my job fully. I want you to be straight with me about these letters from Broadmoor. Do you know who this guy is?'

'No Virgil, I have no idea. I've told you before, there are thousands of people who think they know me because my face is familiar. They project their own fantasies, destiny, desires and dreams onto me, that's all it is.'

'Okay, well I hope you don't mind if I try to get to the bottom of it. I've already asked Broadmoor to stop the letters.'

'Whatever you want, Virgil. But I'd really prefer if you concentrated on protecting me from Lawrence Wall. That really is your job.'

'I can do both, I assure you.' Virgil had already made a start. Kelly had let slip that there had been previous cards from Broadmoor, months ago, though she couldn't recall how many.

Only the birthday card and today's dove card had ever been forwarded to Mira. The rest, Kelly said, would have been sent off to the East London warehouse where fan mail and gifts were archived. That might shed more light on what the connection was between a dangerous mental patient and Mira.

Chapter Fifteen

EIGHTY-THREE DAYS

It was pouring with rain when Kelly and Virgil got off the Central Line tube at East Ham. The warehouse was a few minutes' walk away, but despite running they were soaked by the time they arrived. Shaking the water off their clothes, they were shown into the hangar-like building. The middle-aged Asian woman managing the facility gave them coffee, and explained the set-up for Virgil's benefit. Stardust Brands had leased half the space in the building, and Mira's fan mail alone was nearly three quarters of that. A team of three dealt with indexing each sack of mail that was sent to her dedicated PO Box. It was opened, senders listed on a database, and signed photos or other merchandise sent out as required. Letters were dumped in cardboard boxes, sorted by date of receipt and cross-referenced by sender, while gifts – which included everything from shoes and clothing to bicycles and stuffed animals – were inventoried and after a period of six months sold for charity.

Every few months Mira would be photographed standing in front of an assortment of newer gifts, and copies would be posted on Instagram and sent to directly to donors, to prove that she cared about her fans. Every day, a random selection of letters were forwarded directly to Kelly.

The manager reckoned they had more than fifteen million items of mail for Mira in the last eighteen months. 'And here as requested are the letters sent from Broadmoor Hospital over that period,' she said. 'Just two of them.'

Virgil picked up the identical West London Mental Health Trust envelopes and opened them. Like the previous ones they were beautiful cards, hand painted, inscribed in Latin and addressed to Mira by her real name. The first one was sent more than a year ago. Kelly used her iPad to translate the message:

> *Congratulations, Lydia. The world has only now discovered what I always knew was there. But as you reach for the stars, I do hope you haven't forgotten me, or our pact. Only 442 days to go!*

The second, a few months later, was shorter and harsher.

> *Lydia, I am bitterly disappointed you have ignored me. I will not be denied. In 298 days, remember, I will have what is mine.*

'I'm not sure,' said Kelly, biting her lip. 'It could still just be a lunatic. I've seen so much of this stuff from others. It may be more artistic but is it more real?'

Only then did Virgil mention the cutting he had seen at Mira's apartment. 'She may be denying being anxious over this, but whether she knows the guy or not, she still went to the trouble of getting this clipping. If she can connect him to this court case, she definitely knows something we don't.'

'Maybe you're right.' Kelly shrugged and looked out at the pouring rain. 'I'm really not enthusiastic about going out in that again.'

'Then let me buy you some food,' said Virgil. There was a pub across the road whose rain-soaked blackboard board boasted chicken and ham pie, mash and mushy peas for less than a tenner. 'That sounds good to me,' he said.

'I just hope they've got the fire lit,' Kelly said, wrapping her coat tightly around her.

While they were still thinking about the rain, the manager called them back. 'There is this, as well. I don't know whether it counts.' She had in her arms a large white box, and laid it down on the counter. It had a London designer's label and had been hand-delivered. Virgil lifted the lid off. Inside was a pure white dress.

'Whoa,' said Kelly, picking it out of the box. 'Look at that!' She held it against her and did a little twirl, and then inspected the label. 'An A-line natural-waisted chiffon wedding dress with lace-up bodice and train. Simple and elegant.'

'This surely can't have come from Broadmoor,' said Virgil.

The manager handed him the card from in the box. There, in exactly the same handwriting they had seen before, was a greeting.

Can't wait to see you wear it! It was designed specially for Hooksworth.

'Well, now I know what the countdown is for,' said Virgil.

'A wedding? You must be joking,' Kelly said. 'He might be convinced he's going to marry her, but I doubt she'll see it that way!'

'I wonder what Hooksworth is?' she said. 'It's not a couture house I've heard of. There's nothing on the label. I'd like to take it to the office and look it up.'

They packed the dress back up in its box then braved the elements. Virgil hooked his coat over Kelly's head while they waited for the pedestrian lights. Finally, soaked by splashes from passing traffic, they squelched into the pub, where they found a quiet corner by the fireplace. Kelly ordered a white wine, and Virgil a half of Guinness, which for some reason Kelly found hilarious.

'Are you topping up your pigment then?'

Virgil grinned. 'Let's hope that's not how it works, or you'll have jaundice.' He clinked her glass. She slipped off her jacket and put it to dry by the fire, leaving her white blouse, clinging and translucent from the rain. There was plenty to see, but Virgil tried his best not to look. Instead he told her what the West London Mental Health Trust had said in response to his e-mail.

'They said that because the letter was being sent to a fan mail address the recipient was therefore "not cited under section 134 of the 2003 Health and Social Care Act", and they didn't need to vet the contents. However they did cite patient confidentiality for refusing to disclose who the sender was. They would only disclose that if the actual intended recipient made a formal request, which would have to be Mira herself.'

'Well, I'm sure she won't,' Kelly said.

'Fine. But they have agreed to remove Stardust Brands from the list of allowed destinations for this patient's letters. We'll certainly hear no more from this guy.'

The food came quickly, the homemade pies crammed with white chicken, sauce and a mound of flaky pastry on top. The mushy peas filled a crater within a fluffy volcano of mash. It was delicious.

Virgil hadn't had the chance to update Kelly on the Qaegfest visit or the trip to see Mira's mother, and they both giggled at the craziness that seemed to get worse the whole time.

'You know,' said Virgil. 'I told a couple of mates that I was going to be working in the beauty industry, and they killed themselves laughing. They thought it was so soft. But of course they were jealous too.'

Kelly gave a small smile, and looked out of the window. 'Everyone wants to work with a beauty like Mira, right?'

'She's not the only gorgeous woman I work with.'

Kelly turned her gaze on him. Deep blue eyes assessed him. 'Thank you.'

'Oh I didn't mean you,' he laughed. 'I was referring to Portia.'

She dipped her fingers in his drink and flicked it in his face, laughing. 'Bit of a comedian aren't you?'

'Not really,' he said, wiping the droplets from his forehead with a napkin. 'So, do you like Shakespeare?'

Kelly suddenly started giggling. 'Do I like Shakespeare? Never met him, who does he play for?'

Virgil was bemused, unsure what to say. Kelly was still giggling, and pulled in her chin, adopted a mock-serious expression and imitated Virgil's deep voice: ' "Do you like Shakespeare, my dear? My father went to school with him you know. A fine fellow, actually"'.

'You like to make things easy, don't you?' Virgil shrugged. 'They are showing *Othello* at the National next week. I was wondering if you'd like to come along.'

'On a date, you mean? Knowing that I already have a boyfriend?' She batted her long eyelashes at him.

'Yes, particularly because I know you have a boyfriend.'

Kelly stretched her face up to Virgil's ear and whispered. 'Then, I'd better not tell him I'm going, had I?'

'Probably not,' said Virgil, trying not to crack the huge grin that was bursting out inside him.

* * *

EIGHTY DAYS

Being seen in the right places with the right people was seen as vital to consolidate Mira's celebrity brand. Portia always looked over the invitations and guest lists to decide which parties were essential. Mira didn't require Virgil's presence at the smaller and more intimate soirées, but the big industry bashes were something else. Several times a month he found himself in some high-end hotel, nightclub or palatial apartment, watching the beautiful people pretending to adore each other.

The Golob Advertising mid-winter bash was one never to be missed. The guest list boasted a dozen of the world's top models, plus the Clooneys, Brad and Angelina, and various luminaries of TV and sport, though in practice only a small proportion of the big names ever showed up. It took over the main hall at the Science Museum, and included roller-skating white-clad waiters, artificial snow, jugglers, and acrobats descending from the roof on streamers. Virgil squired Mira from one knot of small talk to another, watching the air-kissing and the glad-handing and trying to sense from her body language where and with whom she was comfortable. One dull bald businessman made a beeline for her. Virgil didn't catch his name, but he was something stratospheric in banking technology and liked the sound of his own voice. Mira and Virgil had cooked up a code – hooking her hair behind her right ear – which triggered a subtle intervention. Always beginning with 'excuse me' he would say 'Mr Kleinfeld has asked to speak to you', and offer her his phone. While Mira escaped to speak to the mythical Kleinfeld, Virgil would comfort the disappointed interlocutor with the whisper 'Hollywood producer,' and tap his nose knowingly.

Until tonight, nothing more interventionist had been required. But after the main party broke up, Mira and thirty others were invited back to the private apartments of Josh Golob, owner of the eponymous company. His place was on Holland Park, a wedding-cake palace with twenty-foot-ceilings, and was already full of champagne-drenched guests who no one at Stardust had vetted. To protect themselves from packs of what Virgil guessed were Golob's clients, Mira teamed up with a couple of models she knew, an androgynous stick insect called Izz Blockley, and a Sudanese beauty called Zoula whose dress seemed to be held up by willpower alone. Virgil clocked Izz for a cokehead immediately, based on her radiant expression each time she emerged from a bathroom trip. Zoula was more down-to-earth and savvy. The daughter of refugees, she'd worked in nail bars, massage parlours and call centres before her big break, and had witty tales of each. It was this distraction that meant Virgil missed Mira being cornered on her own way back from the bathroom. The culprit was a squat fifty-something with luxuriant white hair to match his tuxedo. Virgil abandoned Zoula to make his way over. As he did so, mop-head tried to kiss Mira on the cheek. She squirmed away, and Virgil grabbed his shoulder. The man, a foot shorter than Virgil, turned to him. 'Can I help you, young man?' His public school voice projected authority and confidence.

'You're making Ms Roskova uncomfortable, Sir,' Virgil said. 'Now, please, give her some space.'

'Piffle. It's you who is making us all uncomfortable,' he brayed.

Virgil leaned a little closer: 'I suspect you have had a little more to drink than you realise. Leave it now, and you won't have anything to be embarrassed about tomorrow, will you?'

The man harrumphed, saw someone else he knew, bellowed a greeting and waddled off.

'He had his bloody hand on my arse!' Mira hissed.

'I'm sorry, I didn't see that.'

'Well what are you going to do about it?'

'He's dealt with. If I mention it, he'll only deny it.'

Mira looked at him angrily. She looked less than sober, but grabbed another champagne flute as the tray came past.

Virgil assumed the issue was over, but at 2am when they were finally leaving the party, they saw the same man outside, swaying gently by a rather nice 1970s Rover and trying to get his key into the lock.

'Hey you,' Mira called, walking up to him. 'You should keep your hands to yourself.'

'What *are* you talking about? Dim Soviet hag,' he slurred.

'Mira, I don't think this is a good…' Virgil said. He saw her punch coming, and restrained her arm. He pulled her away. 'Don't!'

'Only wanted a peck on the cheek, don't go all Chernobyl about it.' The man was still struggling with the keys.

She turned to Virgil. 'Hit him. Beat him up,' she hissed. 'It's your job.'

'It is not my job to flatten harmless old drunks,' he whispered. 'And it's bad PR too.'

'Fuck the PR. Would you prefer to be fired? I mean it.'

Virgil sighed. He strode over to the man, who turned and raised his fists, and started to shuffle his feet about. 'I'm warning you, my uncle was an SAS colonel,' he said.

Virgil hit him once in the solar plexus, not too hard, and he folded neatly like a deckchair. Virgil opened the car door, bundled the groaning lump in, and tossed him his car keys. 'Sorry about that. Do get someone to drive you home.'

A minute later the Rover engine roared, and it crept out darkly onto the road. 'Lights!' yelled Virgil, to no effect. Once it was gone, Virgil turned to Mira. 'Don't you ever ask me to do that again,' he said.

'Maybe next time I'll do it myself. At least it would be done properly.'

Virgil glanced sideways at her as he guided her to their car. The huge green eyes, unfathomable but magnetic. The slight but infectious smile. She caught his look and shot him a cheeky grin. 'Poor Virgil, always struggling to do the right thing.' She kissed the tip of her slender fingers and touched them to the end of his nose. That tiny benediction gave him a little magic zing, and he heard himself laughing with her, his face seemingly hers to command. But a protective part of him, the charred component that crawled through wadis, survived IEDs and RPGs, was warning him: *She'll get you killed one day.*

* * *

SEVENTY-SEVEN DAYS

Virgil had never heard of lawyers being involved to negotiate a dinner date. But here he was, sitting in a Stardust Brands meeting room, while Thad, Jonesy and a specialist celebrity lawyer called Brinsley Coad had a conference call with an equivalent team at Lawrence Wall's agents at Sports Management Ltd. The only subject on the agenda was exactly when, where and how Mira Roskova and Lawrence Wall would meet. Mira wanted her personal property, clothing and keys returned to her, including the Porsche. Wall wanted some time alone with her, to explain his feelings, according to his agent Steve Gilpin. He then introduced Sports Management's PR man, Harvey Cohen, and their lawyer, an American called Clayton Ferrall, whose voice sounded like a quarry truck unloading.

'People, I just want to be clear that for the duration of this meeting, any accusation of violence against my client will result in today's contract for return of property being voided,' Ferrall rumbled.

'This allegation stands,' said Brinsley Coad. 'We reserve the right in the future to initiate legal action over it, or publicise it. However, we agree that it is not the subject of this meeting.'

Once the terms of conduct were agreed, Thad opened the door and called Mira in. She was in ripped jeans and a tight white T-shirt bearing the slogan *End violence against women*. She draped herself over a typist's chair at the back, legs over the arm. Thad quietly briefed her on what had been said so far. She didn't look happy. 'I've already said I will have a quick drink with him. I don't want a meal,' she whispered.

Thad conveyed that message to the other side. It brought a quick response.

'Hi. Steve Gilpin here. We understand Ms Roskova's wishes. But Mr Wall would like the privacy and the seclusion that comes with a meal. He's got a lot to say to her, and I think it might be advantageous for her to hear it.'

'I think I've heard it all,' murmured Mira, too softly to be heard on the speakerphone, as she swung her chair left and right, swinging her legs out, examining the crimson varnish on her perfect toes.

'Thad here, Steve. Look, I think we might be able to find a middle way. What about tapas?' He raised his eyebrows towards Mira, who looked heavenwards and swung her chair in a complete circle. After a full minute of an entire room full of mostly-suited men watching a young woman spin on a chair, she finally gave a nod.

'People, we've got a yes to tapas,' Thad said.

'I think Mr Wall would be okay with that too,' Steve said. 'Now, location. We sent you a list earlier of venues, though I guess few do tapas.'

'Steve, it's Jonesy Tolling. To avoid publicity, we want to strike out all the London and Manchester venues. They are too easy for paparazzi. We ideally want a private room in a mid-sized country hotel with a secure rear entrance, as per the list we sent you.'

Virgil could hear some conferring taking place at the other end.

'Okay, Jonesy. That's fine. Now about this bodyguard of hers. Mr Wall's not happy about it,' Gilpin said. Clayton Ferrall could be heard rumbling in assent in the background.

Brinsley Coad leaned over to the speaker and re-introduced himself. 'Can I draw your attention to the original memorandum. Ms Roskova will not go without her close protection officer.'

The point was batted back and forth for some time. Virgil was slightly uncomfortable that the biggest argument was about him. Stardust was adamant that Virgil had to be in the room with Mira, while Wall's people were firm that it would be demeaning to their client. The allegation about Wall's brutal assault on Mira lay unspoken between them.

'He doesn't feel the need to be accompanied,' Steve Gilpin said. 'This is an entirely private meeting.'

Jonesy stifled a sarcastic laugh.

Virgil caught Thad's eye, and was given the go-ahead to speak. 'I'm Virgil Bliss, Mira's close protection officer. Perhaps I can make a suggestion. I am happy to be out of the room and of earshot, so long as I have line of sight. It will be clear to me when I might need to intervene. There are a number of restaurants here with private rooms which have glass doors, and I'm happy to be on the other side, so long as I have a clear route in.'

The other side finally agreed to that, and after ninety minutes, the meeting broke up. Thad, Mira, Virgil and Jonesy stepped out, leaving the lawyers to finish off, detailing exactly what would be returned, and when.

* * *

SEVENTY-THREE DAYS

Virgil was nervous. This was the biggest test so far, against the man who was the biggest proven threat to Mira. He had picked Mira up from her home in a big rented Vauxhall with darkened windows and drove her to the Warwickshire hotel they had finally settled on, halfway between Mira's London base and Wall's place in Cheshire. The booking had been made in Thad's name, and the manager had agreed to open an hour early to maximise their privacy.

The place was an ivy-covered Georgian inn, not much more than an upmarket pub, in an obscure but prosperous village. The car park was almost empty, and there was no sign of Lawrence Wall. Virgil took ten minutes to fully check the place out before bringing Mira in from the car. She was classically dressed: Burberry raincoat, conservatively-cut trouser suit, court shoes, royal-blue designer bag and big sunglasses. She had affected a look of generic beauty. She could have passed for the trophy wife of any lucky millionaire.

Mira was seated in the private room, with a glass of wine to calm her nerves. The agreed time came and went. Wall hadn't arrived. Virgil rang Stardust to ask them to chase the other side. When he still hadn't arrived after forty minutes, Mira stood up. 'He's got five minutes, then we go. He's just trying to make an infantile point,' she told Virgil.

The roar of a high performance engine startled them. A black glossy Lamborghini swung onto the gravel drive at high speed, and screeched to a halt. Two minutes later Lawrence Wall, dressed in wide-cut grey suit with purple tie and aviator shades, walked nonchalantly into the hotel. He was carrying a large bunch of red roses. As the manager greeted him, Wall tossed him the flowers to deal with, and was led along the corridor towards the dining room. Virgil stood aside, a good ten feet out of the way, to let Mira handle the greeting.

Wall pushed open the door glass. 'Hello Lawrence,' she said.

'Hiya.' Wall reached out to embrace her, but she held up her arms to stop him.

'Lawrence, don't.' For a second or two there was confrontation, and Wall's face narrowed. Virgil cleared his throat. Mira's eyes flicked sideways, and Wall's face turned to follow, his jaw clenching, his thick neck corded above the shirt collar. 'Ah, Mira's personal army. Let's have a look.' Wall let her arms go, and strode towards Virgil, only stopping when they were a foot apart, locked eye to eye.

'Good afternoon, Mr Wall.' Virgil, arms crossed in front of him, offered a thin smile. They were exactly the same height and a similar build. Nothing, it seemed, had changed in Lawrence Wall's belligerence toolbox since playground days.

'Lawrence…' Mira said plaintively.

'I want you out of here, pal,' Wall said to Virgil, flexing his shoulders for the denial he expected. Wall's open mouth gusted spearmint, the gum visible as the jaw worked.

'You know the deal.' Virgil stood his ground. After thirty uncomfortable seconds, Wall finally turned away, and stalked back towards Mira. He took a final glance over his shoulder, as if to say: I'm watching you.

Virgil was itching to call him out, to challenge those proprietorial hands, but to make it smooth for Mira he had to bite his lip. That was his job. He knew the line, and so did Wall. Step over it, he'd intervene in a shot. Stop short, he'd just smile sweetly.

The waiter arrived, and led the couple to their seats. Virgil stood behind the glass door, exactly opposite the doors into the kitchen, with Mira and Wall halfway between, perhaps ten metres away, at a large table. On Virgil's instruction, the restaurant had cleared all the other tables away giving him a clean approach if required. He couldn't hear what they were saying, but the body language was clear. Mira was nervous and frightened and Wall had taken charge. The waiter was summoned, and brought a vase of Wall's roses to present to Mira. Wall then pointed to the menu. A discussion ensued, and Mira's face had become small and tight in suppressed disagreement. Virgil presumed that the tapas had fallen victim to the force of nature that was Lawrence Wall. He realised he was watching here a fast-forwarded domestic tableau played out in a million troubled relationships: intimidation, submission, acceptance and fear. If it could happen to Mira, it could happen to any woman. A pale pint arrived for Wall, another glass of wine for Mira. Wall leant forward, monopolising the shared space, full of animation. She leaned back, a fork in one hand, the other moving in emphasis, but also to disrupt the connected space between them.

Food arrived. A steak for him, something with lettuce and red cabbage for her. Virgil took a call from Thad, who asked how it was going. 'Mira will be glad when she can get away,' Virgil said. He was still on the call when Mira got up, handbag in hand. Lawrence Wall grabbed her arm, tight. Virgil opened the door in a second, and took a single stride towards the table.

'...and if you try to, I'm warning you...' Wall looked up, then released her arm.

'I'm the one who's going to be doing the warning, Sir.' Virgil looked pointedly at Wall's fists, still clawed in frustration.

Mira stood, and finally free to do so, walked behind Virgil to find the ladies' toilet. As she did so, she drew a finger along his back, shoulder to shoulder. *Naughty.* Lawrence Wall's eyes flamed, and his chest inflated. Wall seems to have trouble enough distinguishing between a bodyguard and a rival without Mira muddying the waters. But how else could she get back at him?

Once Mira returned, and Virgil resumed his position behind the glass door, things quietened down for a while, Wall looking down at the table. Virgil then realised Mira was showing Wall the picture of the injuries he'd inflicted. He looked up, and his features were squeezed tight, as if in pain. He lifted a napkin to his eyes, briefly wiped then held out his arms to her, fingers open. She did not take them. She was doing the talking, angrily by the look of it.

Virgil saw Wall feel for something in his jacket pocket. He slowly brought it out. Virgil suddenly stood straight up, his hand ready on the door. Wall gave her a small blue jewellery box. Mira's face was shocked as Wall opened it. The diamond on the ring was big enough for Virgil to see from the door. For the first time in the encounter, Mira leaned forward to Wall, but Virgil could still read her lips: 'You haven't listened to a single word have you? This isn't just about what the great Lawrence Wall wants. It's about what I want, and Lawrence, I promise you, I'd rather die than marry you.'

Don't give him ideas. Maybe she had received Virgil's thought telepathically, because she glanced to Virgil anxiously and nodded. Virgil entered the room, and she stood up to leave.

Lawrence Wall seemed to have shrunk, his shoulders sagged, face closed, eyes focused on some middle distance. The ring was still in its box on the table, the footballer's big hands clenched around it, guarding a precious but fragile dream.

As Virgil led Mira to the car, he realised that Portia had been right, Lawrence Wall really was smitten. And he wouldn't give up.

* * *

Mira spent the entire return journey venting about Lawrence Wall over the phone to friends. Virgil gleaned that Wall had grudgingly returned the small bag of Mira's clothing and jewellery, the spare keys to her flat and the documents and key for the Porsche. But he had done his damnedest to try to persuade her to stay with him. Finally, she hung up on the last call as they were coming into north London.

'I hate him, Virgil', she said. 'He's a brute who does not understand the word "no".'

Virgil now knew that it wasn't his job to offer insight, but offered some mild support. 'He doesn't seem to treat you very well.'

'He even tried to make me jealous by telling me that he's seeing some Victoria's Secret underwear model. As if I care!' She punched the seat in frustration.

'You know I'm supposed to be teaching you some self-defence techniques,' Virgil said.

'Yeah, I know,' Mira said, head on hand. 'I'm sorry for the no-shows. I suppose I really should do it.' Mira looked out of the window. She then breathed on the glass, and absent-mindedly doodled in the condensation. 'So who will rid me of this troublesome pest?' she murmured.

Virgil laughed, and she looked up. 'I don't see Lawrence Wall as Thomas à Becket,' he said.

'No, neither do I. But sometimes I still think I'd like to kill him.'

Chapter Sixteen

The Right Reverend Harry Fielding regarded himself as a persuasive fellow, but even he would have his work cut out with this one. He shook his head when he considered the sheer outrageousness of the idea dreamed up by Suzannah Earl, and the reaction it was likely to get from Broadmoor's dour and rather conservative Richard Lamb. Still, as he picked up the phone, he thought it would be worth a try.

'Richard, I've got a rather curious but engaging idea to run up the flagpole.'

'Yes, Harry?'

'Suzannah would like to pose for Mordant, for a painting to promote the excellent therapeutic art work being done in secure institutions.'

'I don't see why that would be a problem. We can arrange…'

'The ticklish bit is this. She has in mind a nude.'

Lamb's coughing fit was so severe that Fielding feared they would have to resume the conversation later. However the director managed to squeak out the word 'preposterous' before glugging a glass of water.

'The thinking, Richard, is very sound…'

'You must be out of your mind!' Lamb spluttered.

'Well, you're the expert on sanity, of course. But just tell me. Which is the most vocal constituency which insists that those held in secure institutions like yours are wicked murderers, rapists and paedophiles, with no redeeming features?'

'The press, of course.'

'Specifically, the tabloids. What chance, do you imagine, would there be of *The Sun* or the *Daily Star* covering the finer points of prison reform? However successful it were to be? If you wanted to take the idea of the redemptive power of the psychiatric system into the mainstream of the British public, you have to take head-on those whose opinions were forged by tabloid headlines. So the thousand female mental patients who have been saved from self-harm or suicide by art therapy would never make it beyond the pages of the *Mental Health Review Journal*. However, the evidence of the rehabilitation of a single mass murderer would be incontrovertible.'

'And you think Page Three would display the naked body of a member of the House of Lords?'

The bishop chuckled. 'Actually, I'm sure they would. I take it you haven't seen Suzannah Earl.'

'Not *au natural*, Harry. Have you?'

Fielding roared with laughter. He had known the Broadmoor director for more than forty years. They had both gone up to Oxford in 1973, Fielding to study Greats at Jesus, Lamb to pore over chemistry at Keble. They had crossed swords early on, when they each discovered they had slept with the same woman, and on the same day. There had been no hard feelings from Harry's point of view. He had met Geraldine Curtis when gatecrashing some otherwise boring Keble cheese and wine party, unaware that Lamb considered her his girlfriend. Fielding was something of a rake in those days, and Geraldine was just the first foothill in a dozen peaks he conquered before his disastrous K2 moment: Katherine Keane's unplanned pregnancy and suicide during her finals. From that avalanche of grief emerged his own rediscovery of the Lord.

Lamb had taken the Geraldine matter more to heart. He snubbed Fielding every time they met at the Gilbert & Sullivan Society before marrying Geraldine in 1980. It was only in the last ten years that the bishop and Lamb had begun professional dealings: Fielding as an advocate of prison and mental health reform, and Lamb as Broadmoor's director. The bishop would never dare say it to him, but once again, it seemed, they were in bed with the same crazy people.

'My word, Harry. It is an extraordinary suggestion. The shrinks will have a fit. Besides, Mordant's crimes are so appalling and repugnant, that if word ever got out...'

'You've managed to protect his anonymity so far, haven't you?'

'Yes, Harry. But this would be a great deal more press scrutiny.'

'I can assure you that the Künzler Trust will continue to refuse to identify which institution the artist comes from. That makes it very hard for the press.'

'I'm still not sure, Harry.'

'But just imagine it, Richard. Those who believe in throwing away the key will be forced to admit that those in secure mental institutions have redeeming features. And once they admit that these benighted souls have something to contribute, the conversation about finding a way back into society can begin.'

There was a long pause before Lamb answered. 'Well, there will be significant practical difficulties…'

The moment Bishop Harry Fielding heard those words, he knew he had won the argument. One of Britain's worst killers would paint Baroness Earl. In the nude.

* * *

SEVENTY-ONE DAYS

Britain's most notorious psychiatric hospital was looking at its most forbidding, when Baroness Earl of West Bromwich parked her BMW in the car park. The cawing of rooks and the leaden sky cast a gothic pall over the Victorian towers and crenulations. The high double fence of razor wire, and the many temporary buildings, extensions and Portakabins beyond were a testament to the difficulties Britain had found in accommodating the growing number of patients who required the sort of round-the-clock and secure care that only a handful of establishments could offer. Broadmoor was one of them.

The baroness walked into the main reception area, where her credentials and appointment were double-checked by a uniformed receptionist. She was then shown through to an airport-style security area with an X-ray machine. Following the instructions of a female guard wearing latex gloves, she emptied her bag of keys, coins, and phone into a plastic tray. She was then asked to remove all jewellery, including her earrings, and to remove her shoes because of the metallic buckles. She passed through the security gate, and an alarm went off. The Baroness was guided into a small booth, where the guard then searched her very thoroughly. In the pocket of her jacket was discovered a spare button still in its tiny plastic bag. This was removed and put with her other items, and she was asked for a second time to step through the metal gate. The alarm still sounded. In the end it was discovered that her underwired bra had set off the sensor. The female guard, apologising for having to do it, asked her to unbutton her blouse and then ran her fingers carefully around and beneath the underwiring.

'One visitor tried to smuggle in razor blades taped under the wire in her bra, so we can't take any chances,' she said. 'We're getting a seat scanner soon, to stop the stuff that still gets in internally.' Kneeling down she proceeded to do a similarly exhaustive check of legs and hips. Unlike at airport security, the only items returned to her were her shoes. She was told she could pick everything else up when she left.

Finally she was escorted along a blue corridor through two elaborately locked doors and up two flights of stairs into the office of the director. Richard Lamb showed her to a seat opposite his desk. After providing her with coffee, biscuits and some small talk he sat down heavily and sighed. 'Suzannah, let's be frank. I really appreciate what you are trying to do with this... project. I'm a great admirer of your energy and commitment to the cause of reform and rehabilitation. However, I've agreed to this with some reluctance, as you know,' he said. 'The patient's name is William Mordant. While I would neither dispute the artistic ability nor the improvement in his behaviour, I would be failing in my duty if I did not remind you that the man you are about to see is potentially one of the most dangerous of our clients. He has an acutely antisocial personality.

'Such euphemisms, Richard. To most people antisocial behaviour means groups of lads revving their motorbikes outside the youth centre or spray-painting their tags on railway bridges. I find it slightly disconcerting that pathological killers are hidden under such relatively benign labels.'

Lamb took off his spectacles and folded them on his desk, before looking out of the window. 'You're right of course. Mental health professionals use words to insulate themselves against the public view that we are wasting our time, that secure psychiatric institutions merely exist to contain patients rather than treat them. From my perspective, however, we have to believe that we can make progress. If nothing else we need it in order to motivate and retain the best staff. I'm afraid the debate goes to the heart of society's view of rehabilitation versus punishment.'

'So what about William Mordant? Do you believe he can be rehabilitated? Or do you believe he is merely manipulating us all to obtain easier conditions for himself?'

'The short answer is: I don't know. Our professional staff have a variety of opinions. But only he *really* knows. We do know that he is a highly intelligent, highly manipulative individual who has from his record shown no compunction whatever in killing when it suited his needs. Having said that, his behaviour here is, or seems to have been, nothing short of impeccable.'

'What was his actual crime?'

Lamb sighed and levelled his gaze at her. 'The privacy of our patients is very important. We are really not allowed to discuss their medical history, which in most cases would also include their interactions with the criminal justice system. Details of Mordant's case are, uniquely, not in the public domain, unlike those of most of our more notorious clients. Indeed, in his case even I am not privy to the full details. However, seeing as you are about to meet him, I think it would only be fair to let you know exactly what you are dealing with before you decide to go ahead with this project.'

Lamb stood, walked over to his office door and locked it, then knelt by a small safe. He fiddled with the combination lock, opened the steel door, and brought out a thin A4 envelope.

'None of my staff have seen this. I will deny that I have ever shown it to you, and can only permit you a brief glimpse.' He passed it across to her. She opened the envelope, which was unsealed. Inside was a poor quality photocopy of a court document, stamped *Ministry of Justice: restricted* and countersigned by an official in 2007. Whole sections of the original seemed to have been blacked out by marker pen. Shorter redactions seemed, from their context, to be names, addresses, ages and descriptions. Anything that might identify those involved.

'It doesn't look like you are supposed to have this,' she said.

'Normally I get full details. But in this case I got a fairly useless summary. I absolutely wasn't having that, and had to go right to the top of the department before the MOJ would reveal even this. They still won't tell me why. As you will see, it's still well short of the full story.'

The baroness flicked through until she saw a section highlighted in the margin, part of the judge's summing up. Then she began to read. As she did so, an icy chill slid down the back of her head and neck. Her hand went to her mouth involuntarily as she absorbed the sparse but grisly details, a horrifying nightmare of crimes committed by this man. In the end she pushed it away. 'I've never in my life read anything like this.'

'Neither had I. And believe me, I have seen most things.'

Lamb took back the sheet and returned it in the envelope to the safe. 'Do you still want to go ahead?'

There was a long silence. 'Yes, I do.'

'Alright, just a few more things. I take it that security have all your personal belongings and so forth? It is very important, particularly with this patient, that you don't discuss any personal information: where you live, your phone number, names or locations of relatives, or anything that could be used to track you down or put you or them at risk. Do not show him any document or image you wouldn't be happy for him to keep.'

'He won't try to take…'

'No, I mean he has an eidetic memory. He can visualise and retain anything you show him, to an almost photographic degree.'

'Good grief.'

'You will recall some of the drawings he has done, purely from memory or imagination. This capability has only recently come to our attention, and we can't be sure he hasn't already used it to memorise security keypad sequences, that kind of thing.'

'Do you think he would try to escape?'

'Well, on balance I doubt it, but it's not that simple. He could sell or barter information with patients who *would* like to escape, and there are plenty of those.' Lamb rubbed his face as if he was very tired. 'Right, now I've scared you silly, perhaps you would like to meet him?'

* * *

Lamb guided Suzannah downstairs where he introduced her to Clive Harrington and two very large and capable-looking black female nurses, who introduced themselves as Serena and Hope. All three then led her through seemingly endless security doors, some of which they opened with keys from a very large bunch, others by using keypads. Finally, they arrived at a door with a glass panel. Through it she could see a man sitting at a table, seemingly deep in thought.

He looked up as they walked in, smiled and stood. She was shocked at how handsome he was, a gymnast's physique, high forehead and strong jaw. Most of all the cold power in those blue, blue eyes. 'Lady Earl, I'm delighted to make your acquaintance.' He put out his hand, and the nurses parted to let her reach forward and shake it. His handshake was cool, firm and utterly businesslike. She was impressed too by his knowledge of the traditional term for addressing a baroness.

'Nice to finally meet you William,' she said, for all the world as if she were dealing with a newly appointed junior minister, rather than a psychopathic murderer.

'I would have preferred to receive you in my studio where most of my work is, but alas…,' he shrugged to indicate that his hands were metaphorically if not literally tied.

'I've seen plenty of your art, William. I really believe that we might have come up with an exciting project which could help the public understand a little more about the important work that goes on here.'

He nodded appreciatively. 'You are, it seems, a very courageous woman. I admire that very much.' He made eye contact with her and conveyed much more than admiration.

Oh, my.

'Here's my business card,' Mordant said, passing it across. 'It's actually just the new Wōdan art sales website that I've had set up with some of the money raised through the Künzler sales. Of course, I've never seen it myself. We aren't allowed the Internet in Broadmoor.' He shrugged.

'I can't give you mine,' Suzannah said, looking at the nurses. 'They kept my bag at security.'

'Oh that's alright,' Mordant said. 'I know where to find you, if I need you.'

Something lurched inside her stomach. She tried to get a grip. *He only means the House of Lords, you fool.* But it seemed more than that.

* * *

SIXTY-FOUR DAYS

It was a week later when Baroness Earl of West Bromwich shrugged off a thin and rather worn bathrobe which had *Broadmoor* stitched on the collar and sat entirely naked on a metal-framed blue plastic chair between two fan heaters. 'How would you like me?' she whispered hoarsely. At her insistence, the only other person in the room was the Jamaican nurse Hope Trenchtown, with an attack alarm, a walkie-talkie and as Lamb had reminded her, a black-belt in karate. The director was taking no chances.

At first Mordant said nothing, his brows lowered and a slight pout as his eyes surveyed her body. It was like being X-rayed. He slowly walked around her, like a leopard assessing its prey. She had been a life model before, years ago. She had enjoyed the frisson of exhibitionism, having a roomful of students artistically explore her skin, which made her aware of every part of herself. But this was more intense. Mordant walked up to her and arranged one arm over the back of the chair, and lifted one leg so that she was more exposed. His hands were cool, comfortable and businesslike. His eyes were not. He looked up and cupped her chin in one hand. Those narrowed, almost indigo, eyes were so powerful she could hardly meet the gaze. He stood a few feet away, and with a sketchbook made some rapid strokes across the paper. The comforting sound of the pencil and the buzz of the heaters was all that could be heard apart from her own quite fast and shallow breathing.

'Now, Lady Earl, I'd like you to sit like this,' he said, indicating that she should reverse so the back of the chair was between her thighs.

'What you might call the *Cabaret* pose,' she said, moving the chair. Mordant looked quizzically at her, to the point where she felt compelled to explain herself. 'You know, from the film with Liza Minnelli and the famous erotic chair dance?'

Mordant nodded ambiguously, and kneeled in front of her, with the chair back between them. He gently opened her knees a little wider. He then gently grasped her hips and encouraged her to slide forward so that the tops of her thighs were tight against the two chrome uprights. Just two feet away, his captivating eyes slid down from her face to dwell on her dark pubic hair, framed in the gap between the seat and the plastic back support. Something about the brief touch and this focused exposure had given her an acute sense of arousal. A moist, hot hunger pulsed within, matching her ragged breathing.

For the next fifteen minutes Mordant sat on a stool three feet away rapidly sketching her, mixing sharp confident strokes with light crosshatching movements. Her skin tingled in the breath of warm air, and her growing excitement. Finally finished, he flipped over to a fresh sheet, and something inside her clenched hard, yearning.

'Lady Earl, do you do yoga?' Mordant asked.

'Years ago, yes.'

'Please stand up.' She did so. He took away the chair and unrolled an exercise mat. 'Sit down, arms braced behind you. Feet facing me slightly apart. No, a little more.'

She adopted the position he described.

'Now I'd like you to perform the crab.'

She looked at him, giving him time to admit that this was a joke. It clearly wasn't. 'I have to say that this isn't something a peer of the realm is asked to do very often,' she laughed. She got an answering grin from the nurse, but none from Mordant. 'It's a long time since I tried.'

'Lady Earl, you have a wonderfully lithe body, I'm sure you will manage admirably. There is an artistic purpose to it.'

She lifted her hips off the ground until they were in line with hips and shoulders. 'Okay?'

'That I would suggest is a table. I think you can do better. You will recall that you need your hands braced with fingers pointing towards your feet so that you can let your head roll back as you lift your body.'

Once she had turned her hands her hips rose more easily and she was surprised how easily she was able to arch her torso upwards. It was certainly a strain, and her arms started to tremble. 'Okay?'

'Just a little higher. I want to stretch you. Now on tiptoe.'

With a grunt, she lifted her pelvis another inch and let her head hang right back with her hair touching the floor. Slowly, she raised herself onto her toes. She was excitedly aware of how graphically exposed she was. *The sacrifices one makes to the cause of rehabilitation.*

'Superb,' said Mordant. 'It will just take a minute.' The sound of the pencil moving rapidly etched out the unbearable seconds as her frame struggled to hold the pose. Another huge, slow internal clench pushed out from her pelvis.

'I can't hold it any longer.'

'Yes you can. Imagine your body is a truculent member of the government, and master it with your willpower, as you do them.'

Her limbs began to tremble more violently, and a shuddering sensation started in her belly. She fought to suppress a gasp that was building inside her, but failed. Just as she was starting to fall, strong hands caught her and lowered her gently to the floor. Looking up into the face of this prodigious man, she knew then that he was absolutely aware of what had just happened to her. He'd barely laid a finger on her, but had engineered it. A small one, but a real one. Somehow, he instinctively understood her. All that betrayed it was a slight smile. But they both knew that she was his.

* * *

THIRTY-FOUR DAYS

Dawn Evans had never been north of Hemel Hempstead before. Her four-year-old Nissan Micra had done all its mileage in what was cosily termed the Home Counties. Almost everyone she knew was more likely to fly to Majorca or Lanzarote than to travel north to Sheffield or Leeds. The north, now that really was another country. When her friend Sue had been told to go on a training course to Birmingham she had rolled her eyes and moaned about it for days, even though she'd never been before.

Today's journey showed Dawn's own travel confidence was more limited still. Even venturing onto the dreaded M25 had given her butterflies, with the London orbital road's aggressively driven four-by-fours and white vans right on her tail, filling up her rearview mirror, even when she sped up to seventy. Then north on the A1(M), filled with roadworks and speed cameras. She passed Hatfield and Stevenage in heavy showers interspersed with dazzling sunshine, but gradually the weight of traffic diminished and the countryside opened up through the wide arable lands of Cambridgeshire. Glimpses of rolling hills and butter-stoned spires around Stamford were a surprise, and she drove into the town, stopping just outside a newsagent-cum-post office. Her pristine atlas showed she was not much more than halfway to her final destination.

Will had said he owed someone a favour, and he would be forever grateful if she would facilitate it. There was no greater vote of confidence in her than when he had whispered his bank PIN code into her ear. Getting access to his bank card at Broadmoor had been easy. She had gone to see the clerk at patient storage, and signed the Patients' Possessions Register. She had been shown to his locker, found the art book that he had requested and signed it out, but taken the cash card too. This was the card that paid for his clothing, laundry and personal care. It was drawn on the account into which his welfare benefits were paid. This must be some favour. The amount he needed had required her to make three trips to the cash machine on successive days because it exceeded the daily withdrawal limit.

She opened her briefcase and took out the bigger of the two envelopes she had smuggled out of Broadmoor yesterday. William had told her that the thick A3 package was of art samples to help publicise his forthcoming auction. It was addressed to

Stardust Brands, some kind of agency, at an address in central London. Dawn had several times smuggled small items out of Broadmoor for Will, but she'd worried that with two envelopes, one of them large, under her coat yesterday, she was taking a really big risk. Though the main job of security staff was to stop items being smuggled in for patients, there were also spot checks when heading out for staff as well as visitors. But it was just as Will had predicted. At half past one in the afternoon the security staff were too busy searching those coming back in after lunch to detain those heading out.

Once Dawn had posted the package, she wished she'd had the courage to open it and take a peek. She always liked to see what his latest work was, and had taken great pleasure in the way she was sharing in his growing fame. Dawn couldn't stop thinking about Will: wondering what he was working on, the highbrow music he listened to, and that strange boyish obsession with fashion models, women he could never hope to meet. She'd soon wean him off all that. With her love and support she was confident that he would one day win his freedom, especially as he'd now made some friends in high places. Even a bishop, for goodness sake! Then she could have him all to herself. She imagined the home they might share, full of art, music and harmony. Even children. Will had not only been the most important relationship in her life, but could transform her career too. So long as she continued to be careful. Don't dream too much, she warned herself. There was still much to do to persuade the world of his innocence, and right this miscarriage of justice.

Back in the car, feeling as happy as she had in a long while, she stopped to eat the low-fat cream cheese and lettuce sandwich she had carefully wrapped earlier.

Back on the road, she headed north for Newark, traversing endless dual carriageways and roundabouts. After passing Lincoln and Wragby she found herself on A roads that seemed to have less traffic than the Wokingham back lane rat run she used to get to work. Finally, after four hours driving, she saw the dock tower of Grimsby, a place that had vague connotations of fish and poverty. She looked down at her list of directions, wishing she owned a sat-nav. Freeman Street wasn't hard to find, but the Anchor Sports Bar on Bethlehem Terrace was elusive. For forty minutes she traversed grids of depressing terraced housing, lined with dented cars, wheelie bins and satellite dishes. She was too shy to ask for directions. But finally she spotted the Anchor, and pulled up on the pavement as everyone else had. The sign was faded to anonymity, there were grilles on two of the windows and a Staffie with a ripped ear chained up to the A-board outside: 'Sindi – classie gentlemen's entertainment' was promised for Saturday night, a fiver on the door. A filthy grey Ford, engine running, was parked just a little ahead. The shaven-headed driver looked at her in the mirror. He got out, flicked the ember of a roll-up into the gutter, and walked towards her. He was big, about thirty, clearly gym-fit under the T-shirt, jeans and trainers, and exuding a vague menace in the roll of his gait. He opened the passenger door, and slid in beside her with a gust of fag breath.

'Dawn?' he said. 'Karl.' He stuck out a huge hand with bitten nails and a tattoo on each finger. She gripped it briefly. 'Got the money then?' he asked.

She leaned behind, took the briefcase from the backseat. She opened it and handed Karl the letter and the fat envelope of cash. He peeked at the cash and flicked through the notes. Then he opened the sealed letter. Dawn was surprised at the speed his eyes flicked over the text. He turned to her and grinned like a hyena contemplating a dead wildebeest. A ripple of fright ran through her. Of course this was going to be illegal. How could it be anything else?

Karl got out of the car, grabbed a heavy black holdall from the boot of the Ford, and dumped it on the backseat of her car. 'Here's the lock-up to take it, alright?' he showed her a garage-type key, with an address in Stoke Newington, London N16 written on the plastic tag. 'Don't mess with the bag,' he warned her. He got back in his car and drove off.

For Will, she had pushed well outside her comfort zone. For him, she had compromised herself ethically, professionally and sexually. She had even allowed him to use a mobile phone which she had smuggled in, uncomfortably, in a plastic bag inside her body. Now she was almost certainly going to be an accessory to breaking the law in a bigger way. But there was no way back. She had cast in her lot with the devil. And, my God, she had enjoyed every second. After a few minutes thought, she reached into the glove compartment and the blister pack of blue tablets from the sick bay that Will had told her could help, and swallowed two more. Soon she felt confident enough to drive to London.

* * *

Virgil sat at the desk with Kelly and looked at the letter. This time it hadn't been franked by West London Mental Health Trust, nor did it contain the official warning, comment form or pre-paid return envelope. It hadn't been diverted to the warehouse because it wasn't addressed to Mira, only to Stardust Brands. Yet inside the first envelope was a second, A4 size in thick card, addressed to Mira and marked personal.

'If it hadn't been for the posh handwriting I might just have sent it on to Mira unopened,' Kelly said.

The card within was extraordinary. It was a fine ink portrait of Mira in repose, almost photographic in its detail, which showed her sitting on a chair drinking from a cup, and reading *The Times* at a table. The way she gripped the cup in both hands showed she was a little cold, while the detail on the newspaper was astonishing. Kelly was adamant it hadn't been copied from any published photograph of Mira. 'It's not the usual fashion or glamour pic,' she said. 'It could be from a sneaky photo someone took when she was in a hotel or something. It's hard to believe anyone could do this from their imagination.'

'Well, at least it's quite demure,' Virgil said. 'Some of the other Mira fantasy stuff I've seen in the warehouse is anything but.'

'Tell me about it,' Kelly muttered.

The message inside, again in Latin, translated as:

Dear Lydia, I'd like to grant your deepest wish. Only thirty-four days to go!

Kelly read it out, and then turned to Virgil. 'I think it bears out my original opinion. It's really not dangerous or offensive, is it?'

'On the face of it you're right,' Virgil said, scrutinising the outer envelope. 'But he's found some way of circumventing Broadmoor's restrictions on writing to her. The postmark is Peterborough.'

'You don't think this guy has been released, do you?' Kelly asked.

'I doubt it. I could report it to the Trust as a breach of rules. But on the other hand, I think I'd like to keep monitoring this correspondence, to collect more evidence of this guy's intentions, and what it is that is just over a month away.'

'Do you think we should show it to Mira?' Kelly asked. 'She was happy to take the wedding dress, so maybe she'd like this too.'

'Not yet.' Actually, there was nothing Virgil wanted more than to watch Mira open this. Just to read the expression on her face. He was convinced that she knew way more than she was letting on. But why was she keeping it a secret?

* * *

TWENTY-NINE DAYS

Suzannah Earl stood before the full-length mirror and admired her naked form. Full breasts with barely a sag, a curved womanly belly and hips with neither a broken vein nor a hint of cellulite. Not bad for a peer of the realm, or indeed for a mother. She stroked her full dark bush, searching for strays, Ladyshave in hand, and already sensed the moistened beginnings of excitement beneath. No time to do anything about it now. Rummaging through drawers she laid out an array of lacy underwear, underwired bras, a couple of suspender belts and a rather memorable basque, an anniversary gift from poor old Neville a decade ago, but worn mostly during her on-off affair with his business partner Justin. No, the basque wouldn't do today. No reminders of failed marriages or past affairs. She was, after all, supposed to be accompanying one of Britain's most dangerous psychopaths to see his artwork displayed, and there would be at least a couple of security people escorting him as well as the gallery people. She settled for the push-up bra and french knickers, which would at least facilitate the speed they might have to employ. The stockings were the very best, run-resistant, but she would take a spare pair in case. The blouse, white silk, was simple and pulled over the head. The buttons were false, no bodice ripping required, thank God. She had to look decent afterwards. There was a Lords reading of the Punishment of Offenders Bill later this afternoon, and she'd have no time to come home and change. The shoes were the toughest call. She tried on the highest heels, which made her calves bulge and her thighs appear to lengthen. She had to admit she looked utterly sexy. But that would be no good for traipsing round the gallery, or the Lords with its endless staircases. She may look younger than forty-seven but her feet would remind her of the painful truth. Kitten heels, half the height and twice the comfort, were the answer. The one thing she could agree with the Home Secretary about.

This whole thing had been quite extraordinary. She'd sat for William three times in the last month. He'd refused to show her the sketches, but had apparently worked day and night on the paintings, even getting permission to work in his room when lights elsewhere were out. She'd worried that it might be just too explicit, and had reminded him that if it was it would never see the light of day. Broadmoor's director would see to that. Mordant just stared at her and smiled in that arrogant and self-possessed way. Nothing happened for a while, but then she'd been surprised a fortnight ago to get the call on her mobile from Broadmoor hospital. A member of staff had said that William Mordant would like to telephone her, and she would have to be visited first by a social worker before being approved, and even then a member of staff would listen in from time to time.

When Mordant was eventually allowed to speak to her he proved a master of art world small talk for the first half an hour. It was only then, when he said staff were unlikely still to be listening, that he said he wanted to do more than just see her. He wanted to get her to suggest an escorted trip to the National Gallery, as a reward for his cooperative behaviour. He rang several times to establish a pattern of contact normality between them, and she agreed to give him her mobile number. Soon after she received a detailed text from him, presumably from an unapproved mobile, detailing exactly what he had in mind. It required only a brief reconnaissance on her part. She was shocked and excited by this outrageous idea, but couldn't let anyone know, not even her closest friends.

Now, finally, the appointed day had come. In an hour and fifteen minutes she would be there, with him. She could hardly wait.

* * *

The National Gallery had taken Mordant's visit seriously. There at five pm waiting in reception for the baroness was the head of press, Caroline Blakely, and Professor Roberto Zumbado, an expert in renaissance painting. Zumbado said he had seen some photos of Wōdan's work, and had flown from Florence to see the work in the flesh and meet its creator. Behind Suzannah, a familiar voice called out. It was Bishop Harry Fielding. He was fresh off the plane from South Africa where he said he had been promoting what he termed the "Christian imperative of the ordination of women" to a largely unreceptive audience. The baroness was perturbed. She had finessed the date so he would miss it, because the bishop seemed to almost revel in Mordant's company, and could complicate their carefully-planned tryst.

They waited another ten minutes for the Broadmoor entourage to arrive. With William Mordant were a burly but bored-looking male nurse called Nigel Braithwaite, nursing assistant Dawn Evans and the director himself, Richard Lamb, all dressed in smart-casual civvies at Suzannah's request. That was no problem, but she been forced to use her full peer of the realm authority to persuade Lamb not to have William in handcuffs. Instead, he was electronically tagged, a small GPS device in a steel and plastic circlet on his left ankle. Common for trusted prisoners, this was a first for a Broadmoor patient.

Blakely made the introduction, identifying the artist only as 'a psychiatric patient who uses the name Wōdan to protect his privacy.' They then moved down to the sub-basement of the gallery's Sainsbury Wing, where as Blakely explained, Wōdan's entire body of unsold work had been assembled for the first time, in a one-day private view. Lamb would have to approve it before it could be opened to the public.

The doors were thrown open, spotlights turned on. The crucifixion triptych was the centrepiece, flanked by several other Christian-themed redemptive works, include the hand and key drawing *Proffered Freedom*. The baroness turned, eager to see her portrait. She had so far only glimpsed an A3-sized sketch, and hungered to see the finished full-sized work before it was published in tomorrow's papers. It was there, behind her, adjacent to the doors and a full two metres high. The almost photographic precision of it at this distance stunned her. There she was, totally nude, but largely protected by the plastic back of the chair she was sitting on. Her face showed smiling relaxation, and a candid self-confidence in her body. Her hair, slightly dishevelled, fell to one side where she was leaning, one arm and a relaxed hand dangling over the chair back. Apart from the bulge of her right breast and a curve of buttock, nothing was really visible. Even the cut-out in the lower chair back, which might have revealed all, was largely lost in shadow. Yet this was the very centre of the painting, and the vanishing point of what little linear perspective it had. Indeed, close up she saw that William had worked as hard on the props as he had on her. There was an almost hypnotic quality to what was in reality a very ordinary blue plastic chair, caused by a pointillist juxtaposition of tiny dots of purple, ultramarine, orange, chrome yellow and titanium white. Even the chair manufacturer's stamp could be read. The overall effect was staggering. Only then did she see the title: *A peer at the realm*. A bit too witty, she thought.

'Well, your confidence was justified,' the bishop said, standing at her shoulder. 'Quite extraordinary, and decorous. At least this one. However this...' Guided by his arm, she turned around to see a smaller painting, entitled *A long stretch*. Though her face could not be seen, it was her, graphically exposed, when she had made the yoga pose for him. It was perfect, every skin tone, the shape of her thighs, her knees, her vulva. She blushed at the full implications of what she had allowed Mordant to do.

'Very Lucian Freud, don't you think? I'd like to buy it, though I'm sure given how hot an artist he has become I wouldn't be able to afford it,' he said.

Suzannah looked around and saw Lamb and the art professor deep in conversation. William caught her eye, with a slight raising of one eyebrow. She looked at her watch. Yes, it was almost time. She brought out her phone and looked at the screen. 'Excuse me, Harry, I've got an urgent call to take.' She walked out into the corridor, and held the phone to her ear until she was out of view. At this moment William was going to ask for a toilet break, and would go past her to the nearest gents and into a cubicle. He appeared right on cue. As expected, nurse Nigel went with him. The rule as William had explained it was that a male nurse was supposed to wait in the bathroom, but Nigel would see there was no window or escape. Sure enough, the nurse came out, looked at his watch and spotted the fire escape door. His hand slid guiltily into his jacket pocket, and he pulled out a packet of

Lambert & Butler. He caught her watching him, and looked even guiltier.

'Go on,' Suzannah said, lowering the phone from its imaginary call. 'They'll be ages in there looking at the paintings. Take a fag break. I'll give you a shout when he comes out.'

He thanked her, and stepped outside into the cold. She then wandered past his line of sight, knocked the agreed signal on the door to the gents, and disappeared into the disabled bathroom next door to await him. Now her heart was hammering. It was really going to happen.

Chapter Seventeen

Baroness Earl of West Bromwich steadied herself inside the disabled toilet at the National Gallery. William had left one minute earlier. Her bottom was still cold from the cistern and her calves still bore the red imprints of his outstretched hands. She could still feel the furnace heat of him inside her. She had no idea where her underwear had gone. It had been the most delicious five-minute madness, but every nerve ending in her body sang with the pleasure and illicit spiciness of it. Living may not require risks, but feeling alive does. For a peer, being taken in the National Gallery by a convicted murderer is as risky as it gets. Here was a man who never asked, but took. It wasn't that William cared so much for her that made him so desirable. It was because he cared so little. She realised that it was precisely because he was a psychopath, whose desire was not lubricated by love or caring, by sweet words or endearments, that she wanted him so much.

A glance in the mirror showed her the full aftermath. Not only was she still flushed, but still spattered. She carefully wiped her mouth, chin and neck, the top of her chest and eyebrows with wet wipes from the family pack she had brought. To cover their tracks properly she had even had to wipe the floor. God knows how long he'd been saving that lot up for. No erotic outlet in Broadmoor, of course. More than anything, though, she was shocked at the craving he had brought out in her. That it was she, not he, who had asked him to do it. Indeed, she had demanded it, just as she had demanded, in the crudest of unparliamentary language, that other penetration which she had never before permitted anyone.

Waiting for her flush to soften, she reapplied her make-up, knowing that by now the male nurse would have finished his smoking break. Finally done and re-dressed, she unlocked the door, to see a twisted young man waiting patiently in a wheelchair.

'You're not disabled,' he accused.

'No, I'm not. I'm terribly sorry. The ladies is blocked.' As she walked back towards the group she felt that of all the day's many deceits, this was the lowest.

* * *

It was less than ten minutes since she'd left the group, but it felt like an hour. The male nurse was back, now standing next to Mordant in the gallery as Baroness Earl approached. The professor was giving an animated appreciation of Mordant's work in front of the triptych. As she stole up to the back of the group, the young nurse Dawn Evans looked around and stared at her, up and down. There was such coldness and hardness in that appraisal that Suzannah was worried. Had she listened at the bathroom door? Had she put two and two together from her absence overlapping William's? Suzannah gave a small smile and looked away. Around the walls were paintings and drawings of William's that she hadn't noticed before. A portrait of Richard Lamb at his desk, a colour sketch of a group of Broadmoor's male nurses sitting casually, drinking coffee. There was a whole wall of drawings in pencil, chalk on black paper, in ink and wash, that were all of the same person: the model and celebrity Mira Roskova, a long-time friend of her daughter Natasha. Suzannah was certain that Mira had never sat for William, at least not without her hearing about it, but the truth and beauty of the portraits made it hard to believe otherwise.

William hadn't looked at her since she emerged, not even a casual glance over the shoulder to see where she was. She now noticed how close by his side the young nurse was standing. As she watched from behind, Dawn's hand briefly caressed William's fingers. So casual and unconscious was this affectionate gesture that the baroness was surprised by the flame of fury it aroused in her. So much for there being no outlet for him within Broadmoor. A minute later, after peremptory goodbyes, she found herself outside above Trafalgar Square. Briskly descending the steps, she now needed to hide herself in the seclusion of one of London's black cabs. Feeling decidedly soiled and shocked at her own stupidity, she would instead use the brief journey along Whitehall in the dusk to read up her briefing notes for tonight's debate, on a bill which she was determined to oppose. Woe betide any man, Lord or commoner, who crossed swords with her tonight.

* * *

TWENTY-EIGHT DAYS

When the Bishop of Uxbridge rang Richard Lamb next day he found the Broadmoor director nonplussed 'So what did you think of the coverage,' Harry Fielding asked.

'Well, there's no shortage of it,' Lamb conceded. 'There is a nude baroness in *The Times, Guardian, Telegraph, Daily Mail* and even the *Scotsman*.'

'I have *The Sun*, where she is on page three, the *Mirror* which has done a pull-out centrefold and the *Daily Star* where she is actually on the front page with a 'censored' banner across her hips,' Fielding said.

'But there isn't quite the matching depth of coverage on rehabilitation, is there, Harry? While the *Mail* has written about the astonishing quality of art that mental patients are capable of, mostly they are furious that they aren't allowed to know who the artist actually is, and what crimes he has committed. I've had no end of calls, even to my house, from reporters trying to find out who he is.'

'The Künzler Trust has been inundated too,' the bishop said. 'I think the baroness is a little bemused that even in the broadsheets, there are more column inches speculating about her courageously enhanced political appeal and ministerial ambitions than what this may mean to the reform agenda.'

'Yes, it clearly has done her no harm,' Lamb said, gingerly opening the *Daily Mirror* and scrutinising the centrefold through his reading glasses. 'Mordant has burnished her into a beauty. He'd have done well as an eighteenth century society portraitist.'

'So what happens next for Mordant?' the bishop asked.

'Well, funny you should ask. Right on my desk here is his application for a tribunal to reassess his being held under the 1983 Act.'

'Quite a cunning fellow, isn't he?'

'Oh yes, Harry. No doubt whatever about that.'

'What are his chances of being released?'

'Oh, none immediately. He'd have to go a low-security facility to be monitored for a number of months, and the Home Office has a veto. But there would be privileges and freedoms he doesn't have here. From what I can see he has a good chance of being able to secure that.'

'Do you think he's still a danger to society?'

'A month ago I might have said no. But now, the more I think about it, he's been making fools of us all. So I'm going to oppose it.'

* * *

TWENTY-SEVEN DAYS

Virgil had arranged to meet Kelly outside the theatre, and while he waited had picked up a copy of London's free paper, the *Metro*. The main story was about some baroness from the

Lords who had stripped off to let a murderous psychopath paint her. The moment he saw the picture, he knew. This must by the man who had been writing to Mira. Virgil read and re-read the article, but the only identification of the artist was the name Wōdan.

'Hey Virgil!' Kelly bounced up to him, and kissed him on the cheek. 'You look a bit engrossed.' She looked gorgeous, with her corkscrew red hair cascading onto the shoulders of a cornflower blue dress, and matching high heels.

Virgil showed her the newspaper. 'It's the same artist. I'm sure of it.'

'Time to knock-off, Virgil,' Kelly said. 'I spend enough unpaid time working in the day, and I won't let it intrude into Saturday night playtime.' She poked him in the ribs. Virgil apologised, and complimented her on the way she looked.

Throughout the play, Virgil's thoughts were elsewhere. How could he connect Wōdan with the sender of the cards? His complaint to the West London Mental Health Trust had disappeared into some bureaucratic labyrinth, and his calls asking for more information were returned by administrative assistants who, while unfailingly polite, didn't themselves have any information they could share.

During the interval, when they were squashed into a corner of the crowded theatre bar, Kelly suddenly seized his arm. 'Are you not listening to me at all?'

'What? Sorry, I was miles away.'

'I said I've broken up with Mike.' Seeing his mystified expression she looked heavenwards. 'Mike. My boyfriend?

Hello, anyone at home?' She knocked on Virgil's skull with her knuckles.

'Right. Um.' Virgil searched for the right tack to take on this conversational nugget.

'I mean, well try not to get too excited.'

'Excited?'

'It means, dimwit, that I'm fully available for you. Oh God, give me a kiss for Christ's sake.'

Virgil took Kelly in his arms, lifted her off the ground, and pretended to be excited. *What was wrong with him?* This beautiful, lively woman, wanted to be his girlfriend, and all he felt was a hard lump of anxiety in his stomach. Fear of caring, fear of connection, fear of pain. And a premonition. The burning troop carrier, the heat of the doors, the charnel house view within. The images swept through his head, and he inhaled hard, his head buried in Kelly's hair, hoping her scent, her skin, her proximity would drive out the cordite, the smoke and the taint of burning flesh.

The anxiety began to coalesce until he was aware of his phone buzzing in his pocket. With a nod of contrition to Kelly, he answered it.

'Virgil it's me,' Mira breathed. 'There's someone on the roof of my flat. I can hear them moving about. It could be Lawrence.'

'Are you alone?'

'Yes. I had some friends here earlier, but they went an hour ago. I'm frightened.'

Virgil sighed. So much for an evening with Kelly. And the second half of the play. 'Okay. Lock the doors and windows,' he said. 'Keep your phone to hand, make sure some lights are on, but don't move around in a way that could easily be seen from outside. Call the cops. I'll be there in half an hour.'

* * *

Virgil was there long before the police. He arrived at the lobby where the building duty manager was awaiting him. Virgil had already run his mind over the possibilities. Sneaking about didn't seem like Lawrence Wall's style. It was much more likely to be a besotted fan, perhaps some unusually determined Qaeggan. The duty manager, a nervous-looking Eastern European called Stefan Kados, came up with him in the lift, apologising profusely for the disturbance that Mira reported. 'I've had a good look around but I didn't see anyone.'

'So what's on the floor above?'

'Air conditioning and ventilation units, a water tank, lift maintenance points, a telecoms cabinet and mast, a utilities control room, a few metal walkways. They are all accessed from a multi-purpose maintenance chamber.'

'What about her neighbours?'

'There's only one other apartment on her floor, and that is currently unoccupied.'

'Can we get into it?'

'The owner is abroad, but I've already taken a look. There's no one there.'

Virgil buzzed on Mira's door. She opened the door wearing jeans and a T-shirt, with a glass of wine in hand. She led them into the apartment and pointed out where she had been sitting when she heard footsteps on the metal walkway above. 'I think someone's been on my patio too,' she said. 'I had some sunglasses and a sunhat out there in a weatherproof locker which have disappeared.'

Kados led Virgil up the fire escape to the maintenance floor. The concrete lobby had a single door leading to the maintenance chamber, with a security keypad, but it wasn't set. Anyone could get in. 'Why don't you set the code?' Virgil asked.

'We did, originally. But the number of different contractors and companies who needed access made it a nightmare. They never sent the same person twice or remembered to bring the latest code, so in the end we gave up.'

The chamber beyond was a seventy-foot high metallic and glass cap at the centre of the building, and was so crammed with pipes, pumps, crawlways and cable ducts that it resembled a hall in the Science Museum. At the far points were four rumbling air conditioning units, each the size of a van, and next to them glass emergency doors led to walkways which crossed the downward-sloping metallic roof, towards the divots and cradles for external maintenance. The manager led Virgil to a higher walkway, which gave terrific views to the south over nighttime Wandsworth. 'What's this?' Virgil spotted an empty box of jaffa cakes on a broad window ledge between walkway levels.

'Surely no one could get right down there,' Kados said.

'Agreed. And we'd see footprints on that white sill if they had.' He looked at a walkway above. 'I reckon they were up there and chucked the box away when they were finished,' he said.

'If they'd got a whole packet, they would probably be around for a while.' Virgil hauled himself up the hatchway and onto a small platform at the apex of the dome, which had a cabinet labelled 'Vodafone engineer only'. He squatted to examine a piece of fluff that had caught on a bolt shaft, and saw two other things that made him nod.

'So what do you think?' said Kados, who was still below.

'Someone has been sleeping here,' he said. 'There are crumbs, a couple of feathers and some red quilting from a sleeping bag, and a couple of smallish grubby footprints. Plus this,' he said, passing down a long brown hair in front of Kados's eyes. 'I think our intruder is female, and she's really been making herself at home.'

* * *

Broadmoor, Boxhill Ward, 3am. Psychiatric nursing assistant Dawn Evans was alone, naked on her knees in the room of a multiple murderer. She could not breathe, she could not speak, only the unhelpful sound: 'Mnnff.'

'I may be a psychopath, but I'm not going to choke you to death, I promise.' William Mordant, naked too but standing, looked down at her. He had both his hands wound in her hair, pulling her onto him. 'You have to breathe through your nose, Puss, then you can take it past the gag reflex. Yes, that's better.'

She had already come on well since yesterday's visit. It had actually been her idea. She was on night shifts for a whole week on his ward, the first time in four months. The fact she was prepared to risk instant dismissal for the opportunity to spend an uninterrupted half hour with him each of those nights spoke volumes about how far he had brought her on in just a few months. Grooming. The technical term, as if it was as innocent as a treatment in a hairdressing salon.

Perhaps it was the scent of competition? Certainly, Dawn's suspicion of Baroness Earl's interest in him had spurred her on to even greater efforts to please him. So that she could spend more time with him she had applied for a postgraduate art therapy certificate too.

Dawn didn't yet know about his tribunal request. She wasn't his primary nurse, so there would be no reason for her to be officially informed, but there was always gossip. He had telephoned Baroness Earl, who was definitely on his side, and spoken to Bishop Fielding, who was now the lay member on Broadmoor's tribunal panel. Despite this, everything would come down to the reports of the two consultant psychiatrists, and in the end to the director. Dr Kasovas seemed to be quite sanguine about his prognosis. But Dr Erin Pridmore, a sour-faced septuagenarian from London University, was vigorously opposed despite the Bishop of Uxbridge's attempts at persuasion. Lamb himself was the hardest one to call. William knew that if there was one intellect that might match his, Lamb was in possession of it. If he was successful, he knew that Dawn would be heartbroken. But by then she might already have been fired because of her own recklessness. If not, he would make it happen. He was tiring of having to imagine Mira.

He wanted the real thing.

And he was much closer now to getting her.

Chapter Eighteen

TWENTY-ONE DAYS

London's Charing Cross looked at its worst late on a rainy Thursday evening in March. Umbrellaed and raincoat-clad commuters were swarming down into the underpasses towards the station, or along Villiers Street to Embankment. Mira had arranged to meet Tasha at the South Bank Centre at six, but roadworks in the Strand and a broken down bus on Waterloo Bridge had paralysed the traffic, so the taxi driver had dropped her off by the station and suggested she cross Hungerford Bridge on foot. Mira was toasty warm in fur-lined charcoal-grey ankle boots, black leggings and a bottle-green overcoat that she had found in a charity shop and for which she had paid just four pounds. Virgil had exacted concessions from her for a public foray alone: her hair was carefully hidden and dry under an oversize flat tweed cap, another charity shop find, pulled low over her forehead, and she had on her most hideous pair of incognito spectacles. As she climbed the Embankment stairs to bridge level she enjoyed the feeling of being part of an anonymous but purposeful crowd, most of them immersed in a common mission to get to Waterloo Station without mishap or delay. The darkling Thames was laid out before her, its sludgy bulk split by quicksilver wakes where half-empty pleasure boats chuntered their way under the bridge. At the far side the lights of the South Bank twinkled, and the giant Ferris wheel of the London Eye opposite the Houses of Parliament, could be seen gently turning. It was soon lost to view when a squealing and rhythmic thrumming through the entrails of the bridge heralded the departure of a train from Charing Cross station. About halfway across the bridge, a gust caught her red folding umbrella, effortlessly turning it inside out. She stumbled into the path of the man behind her as she fought for control, until his hand shot out and grasped the shaft to steady it.

'Got it,' he shouted over the wind.

'Thank you,' Mira said, eyeing the fragile struts now twisted and trembling in the gust.

'Is it one to keep and mend, or should we let it fly away?' he asked.

'Give it its freedom,' Mira replied. She pushed up her peak to look at the smartly-attired Asian in the herringbone overcoat, whose crisp white cuffs were already getting wet. He let go, and the umbrella soared for a moment, a roiling crimson flag, before cartwheeling down into the treacle-black depths of the Thames.

'Well, that's four ninety-nine wasted,' Mira laughed, starting to walk again.

'So much?' said the man, whose accent was both Indian and

Surrey. He turned to her and smiled broadly. 'Do you think all the lost and broken umbrella souls eventually find their way to some parasol paradise?' The man held his own large umbrella over them both.

She looked up at his face. Deep-set brown eyes, strong jaw, white perfect teeth. Nice. Something profound was called for, surely? But profound wasn't her thing. 'Umbrella heaven must be packed. I've lost five this year.' It was the best she could do for now. She gazed out into the distance, beyond Waterloo Bridge where the City's many new glass skyscrapers thrust themselves like splinters into a bruised sky. 'Hey,' she rested her hand on his arm. 'What if there is one of those multi-armed goddesses there, one for each arm of the brolly?'

'Ganesh, or maybe Kali,' the man said, as they started to descend the steps. 'I like that. Now without my brolly I think you will get wet. Are you going to be able to get somewhere dry soon?'

That was a clever way of finding out where she was going. She didn't mind. 'I'm just off to the Festival Hall. I'm meeting a friend.'

'Oh. A friend.' He smiled a slightly disappointed smile. 'I had been wondering whether I could buy you a coffee some time.'

'Oh. I see.'

'But not now. Unfortunately I have a meeting.' He looked at his watch.

'Always be late for meetings, it makes you seem important,' Mira said. The man's expression showed he didn't approve of that philosophy. 'I'm always late,' she persisted. 'I can be five

minutes late for my friend. It's what she would expect anyway.'
The man's face softened at the word *she*.'

'My name is Ram. What is yours?'

Mira's hesitation seemed to unnerve him 'Am I perhaps being too forward?' he asked.

'Probably,' she laughed, and a tendril of hair whipped across her face. She couldn't risk letting him know her public name. The poor bloke would be terrified. Besides, the sheer purity of this chance encounter was already as precious as a raindrop. 'Call me Lydia.' It was, after all, her real birth name.

'Lydia, it's been a pleasure to meet you and your misbehaving umbrella.' With the slightest of nods, he turned and walked away. Mira was suddenly paralysed. She didn't have his phone number. *He just walked away! Aren't you going to do anything woman? Are you just going to grin like an idiot?* He climbed the steps back towards the overpass towards Waterloo Station. She watched his broad, receding back. Just then he turned to give her a wave. She just waved back, as this charming man walked out of her life.

* * *

Cursing herself as a fool, she walked into the reception area of the Royal Festival Hall, and immediately saw Natasha. 'Blimey you're early!' Tasha exclaimed, flicking her damp blonde hair over the collar of her white raincoat.

'Really?' Mira looked at her watch, puzzled. She was actually five minutes late.

'You're always at least fifteen minutes late, usually half an hour,' Tasha laughed. 'Shite weather innit?' she said, reverting to the broad Brummie accent she had worked so hard to lose. Natasha had come down to London three months ago, to work as a publicity agent for a West End publisher.

'It's reet crap,' Mira answered in her own northern tones, which she too had shed over her chameleon life. 'Tasha, I've done something really stupid,' Mira said. 'I've just bumped into this gorgeous chivalrous man, and I let him walk away without getting his phone number.'

'What?' Tasha pulled a face of imbecilic incomprehension, and then began to laugh uproariously. 'You're the woman on the front page of bloody *Vogue*, and this berk didn't actually beg for your number?'

'He doesn't have a clue who I am under this hat and coat.' Mira recounted the brief conversation on Hungerford Bridge. 'He was quite gallant though, I have to say.'

Tasha's expression initially expressed wonderment, but then hardened to what looked like resentment. 'Mira, that's not fair. You're supposed to meet people at glitzy parties that I'm not invited to. On catwalks and photoshoots, at fancy restaurants that I can't afford. But instead you've just pinched one of the few romantic encounters that poor sods like me can aspire to. Why can't you stay in your own territory? I could have walked across that bridge and met him, or someone like him.' For a moment, she seemed genuinely upset.

'Tasha, don't be like that.'

'It's very romantic and I'm envious, that's all. I need sauvignon blanc and I need it now.' They moved into the bar, took a table and Mira bought two big glasses of New Zealand white. Mira always paid. That was the way now, with all her friends.

'Right. What did you say his name was?' Tasha whipped out her phone, as she always did at the slightest excuse. 'We'll Google him.'

'Ram. I didn't get his second name.'

'Is that it?' Tasha said. She typed it in and hit 'images'. She showed Mira her screen and they both roared with laughter. 'Looks like we got a cross between male goats and microchips. Horny and brainy.'

'There are worse combinations!' Mira retorted.

'What else did you notice about him? Was he carrying a book, a newspaper, anything?'

'An umbrella.'

'Hardly rare, Mira, in the rain. You numpty.' Tasha rested her chin in her hand. 'Well, if you were me, you'd come to the bridge next Friday at the same time and wait until he passed. Then pounce. But I expect you're a bit too grand for that. You'll be hoping that he puts a personal in *Time Out*: "Delightful green-eyed creature met on Hungerford Bridge, please meet me at the Dorchester for tea".'

Mira laughed, then tapped her finger on the table. 'His umbrella had a logo on it. Quotidian something,'

'It might not be where he worked, but let's add it to the search.' They scrolled down the seemingly random collection of pictures.

'Alright, let's try some lateral and perhaps wishful thinking.' Tasha typed in 'Ram + millionaire'. There were plenty of pictures, mostly of a character from the film *Slumdog Millionaire*, but by the second page the pictures were of a wider variety.

'Let's raise our game,' Mira said. 'Type in "Ram + billionaire".'

'For God's sake,' Tasha said, rolling her eyes. 'When's the last time a billionaire walked across Hungerford Bridge in the rain?' She typed it in anyway, and showed Mira the phone. And there he was, on the third page.

'Tasha it's him!' Mira squealed. Ram and another younger-looking man were wearing cricket whites and standing next to a small grey-haired man in a suit. She clicked through to the website and found the caption, from the *Times of India*. It was from 2009.

Shipbreaking billionaire L. K. Dipani and his international cricket star son Adhish, ready to play in the annual Mumbai Homeless charity cricket match. They are joined by Mr Dipani's oldest son Ram, right, who came back from London this week.

'Oldest son, Mira,' Tasha said, grasping her wrist 'Omigod, think of the inheritance!'

'You're wicked, Tasha,' Mira said. 'I need a bigger picture.' She pulled her iPad from her soft leather backpack, typed in 'Ram Dipani' and went straight for the image search. Most of the pictures seemed to centre on Adhish, who had recently married some stunning Bollywood starlet, but there were a few of Ram too. He was thirty-one, and described by the Indian papers as a playboy. A broader search showed the British newspapers only referred to him in connection with a series of City property deals.

'So, what do you reckon?' Mira asked, always happy to mine Tasha's deep reserves of commonsense.

'He's more handsome than his brother. A bit more reserved, perhaps less shallow. I hope playboy just means he's unmarried. The crickety one is a bit naff, shirt buttons undone, hairy chest. Barry White meets George Michael.'

Mira shrugged. 'I actually like chest hair.'

'Yuck,' Tasha said absent-mindedly. Under Tasha's expert direction, they soon found the London address of LKD Property (London) Ltd, where Ram Dipani was a director. There was a phone number. 'So what are you going to do, Mira?'

'Well, I'm officially shot of Lawrence now, so I can have some fun.' She explained about the awkward final meal under Virgil's watchful gaze.

'And where is your hunky bodyguard tonight? I was hoping to get a close look.'

'He's tied up with preparations for the big meeting next week.'

'But you will introduce me to him at some point?'

'Yes, but rumour has it he's seeing Kelly, our intern.'

'Bugger,' said Natasha, with a little pout. 'I'm always pipped at the post.'

'Never mind,' said Mira. 'It's not going to be much fun for her because he's at my beck and call, day and night.' She affected a haughty expression and clicked her fingers in the air. 'And I rather enjoy playing Queen Mira.'

'God,' said Natasha in wonderment. 'You're so spoiled!'

Mira clapped her hands and roared with laughter. 'Yes, I suppose I am.'

* * *

Back at Stardust Brands, Virgil was sitting through an interminable strategy meeting ahead of next week's Suressence presentation. This was the pivotal moment for Mira's entire career, and would take place at the London School of Fashion. Suressence product executives had for months been enthusiastic about working with her, but a presentation to the main board was needed before the contract was finalised. Virgil was tasked to prove to the French company that their precious investment in Mira was safe from external threat.

'Jarvis,' said Thad. 'I believe you have had the Mira presentation video re-edited.'

Art director Jarvis McTear ran his hand through his glossy quiff. 'Yes, it's all ready to go. We had it re-edited to splice together the best skincare shots without the brand overlays.'

'Good. Jonesy, run us through the line we're taking on Lawrence Wall. Just in case Suressence bring it up.'

'Right. Lawrence Wall is a bit of a character, don't we agree, and has been pursuing Mira after their brief relationship broke up. Yes, he's smitten, who wouldn't be, but it's all water under the bridge. If the advertising launch is ready for Easter, then we can promise the tabloids will be in line, because they want a share of the advertising. We need Suressence to fund a director's cut teaser video ahead of the launch, which we can offer as an incentive. We've already got takers.'

'Okay, that sounds fine,' Thad said, looking down at a folder. 'Now here is the meat, why Mira is unique. My presentation focuses not just on her, but the global media-cum- marketing context. A new Puritanism is gathering pace; a gathering groundswell against ever-more flesh being on view, whether it's MTV or *Playboy*. Pornography is out there, but once the Internet matures, regulation means access will be restricted. There is no place for the sexualisation pendulum to go, except back. Post Jimmy Savile, we will not only protect children, but the idea of childhood. We'll cherish chastity again, not deride it. We'll insulate innocence in a snowbank of purity. Any multi-year campaign has to be in harmony with the sociological mood music.'

'We might be a bit ahead of the curve,' Portia said. 'But it's plausible.'

Thad nodded and continued: 'In this new world, Mira is the real article. An unspoilt, impeccably behaved, mature and intelligent role model for millennial women and girls, but who also sells well to the richer generation above them. The new Catherine Deneuve, cool, sensual but reticent. Neither aristocratic nor tarty, demure but not a prude, just a distillation of pure womanhood.'

Jonesy took up the theme. 'Unlike any of the others they might have looked at, it isn't image, it's reality. When other wannabes were experimenting with fags behind the bike sheds, she was practising the clarinet. When girls her age were getting off their faces on cider, she was learning Italian and Russian. She's never taken drugs, period.'

'Well, we only have her word for it,' muttered Portia. 'And she likes a drink.'

Jonesy raised his hand as he continued. 'The bottom line is we're not afraid of disgrace clauses in the contract. By investing in Mira, they can be sure that in two years or even five she will be as unsullied and delightful as she is now. That, plus her huge online following and global recognition, is why she is so very expensive.'

'Have you told her Suressence wants contractual random drugs testing?' Portia asked.

'Not yet. But she's going to love the products,' said Thad. 'Moisturisers, face creams, and this new super-secret product Âdoré.'

'Ah yes, collagen molecule anti-ageing facial serum, twenty quid for half an ounce,' Jonesy chuckled. 'Of course they can only legally advertise it as anti-ageing because of the sunscreen in it. The rest of the ingredients are marketing bollocks.'

'Still, forty million euros of marketing bollocks, globally, some of it ours,' said Thad.

'Speaking of skincare, Jonesy, what about the zombies?' asked Portia. 'Much of her online following came from the TV show. Death, decay, violence, nihilism. Not to mention wounds, pus, acne and halitosis. That's a contradiction of everything she stands for, and everything Surressence aspires to.'

'Don't I know it,' Jonesy said. 'Brand contamination keeps me awake at night. It's really crimped her earning potential. Still, the *Village of the Dead* film premiere is next week, she's not in it, so she'll be eclipsed. The zombies will follow Annemaria Claverhorn instead. And good luck to her.'

Virgil raised his hand. 'I'm not sure that's entirely true.'

They all turned to look at him, as if they had forgotten he was there. 'Sure there will be a lot of new fans of the story, but the original fans, the true Qaeggan, are already complaining that it won't be the same without Mira.'

'Not our problem,' said Jonesy. 'She's been in the shadow of the *Village of the Dead* for too long.'

Just then, Kelly burst into the room, her face wild. 'Someone just tried to murder Lawrence Wall,' she gasped. 'He's on life support.'

'Good grief,' Portia said, tapping on her iPad.

They all crowded round to read the news flash.

* * *

By the six o'clock news there was more detail. The BBC news showed the CCTV footage. It was taken at 2am above a car park near a Manchester nightclub. Lawrence Wall emerges from a door, in a light-coloured jacket with his arm around a blonde woman. He sees a slender youth in a hooded top seemingly vandalising his Lamborghini. He races towards the youth, who can be seen scrambling over the bonnet of another car, and disappearing out of view at the bottom of the picture. As Wall gives chase, two doors on the car parked adjacent to his own are flung open, one smashing him in the leg. Two large individuals get out. One has a baseball bat, the other some kind of blade. The footage was pixelated for the TV as Wall gets kicked and punched and eventually drops to the ground. Right at the end of the scene, the man with the baseball bat has the CCTV camera pointed out to him, and turns round to look at it. His face is made-up like a Qaeggan, white clown paint under a wig, and three tear trails below each dark eye. The last view from the camera is the man clambering on top of a car, and swinging his bat at the lens.

Chapter Nineteen

TWENTY-ONE DAYS

They hadn't even finished the meeting before the first press calls for Mira's reaction started to pile up on Jonesy's voicemail.

'We need to get her somewhere safe, abroad perhaps, to keep the media off her back,' said Portia.

'Nah, nah,' said Jonesy, 'not abroad. That would look like a sign of guilt. The attackers were Qaeggan, remember, Mira's personal effing zombies.'

'For God's sake, I don't think anyone's going to think she did it,' Portia retorted.

'She's got the motive and the money to fund a hit,' Jonesy said. 'Suspicious behaviour like fleeing the country will draw attention to that.'

Thad sat with his head in his hands. 'People, we're going to have to postpone Suressence. There is no way we can go ahead in this atmosphere.'

They all sat glumly staring at the documents they had spent so long working on.

'I suppose she could be off the hook if they find the attackers quickly,' Portia said.

'Or on it again, if the attackers turn out to be vigilantes, who did it to protect her,' Jonesy said.

'I'm sorry to bring you all back to earth,' Virgil said, 'but has anyone rung Mira? She may not know, and if she's caught in public, something could happen. There's nothing on my planner to say where she is until I take her to the Lagerfeld shoot tomorrow afternoon...'

Thad had her on speed dial before Virgil had finished the sentence. The call dropped into voicemail, but Mira called back within five minutes, and Thad put her on speakerphone.

'I just heard,' she breathed, voice ragged.

'Where are you now?' Thad asked.

'I'm in the Festival Hall café with a friend.'

'I could be there in half an hour,' Virgil said. 'If you need me.'

'Well, I'm not sure. We're going for dinner, and then I'm meeting up with some other Pinnacle models at a party,' Mira said.

Virgil shook his head at Thad, who said: 'Mira, we don't advise it, even if Virgil comes along. It depends which way the press coverage breaks. You could be in for some blame, seeing as the attackers were made up like Qaeggan.'

'And you could look callous, photographed carousing while your ex is on life support,' Jonesy said.

'But that's ridiculous,' Mira retorted.

'I know. We're sorry to ruin your evening,' Thad said.

'And Mira,' Jonesy said. 'Are you planning to go home tonight? If so we'll get Virgil to meet you there. The press are bound to be camped outside.'

'Oh, this is so boring!' Mira gave a little screech of frustration. 'I want my life back. Okay, I'll see if I can stay at Tasha's tonight. Hold on.' They waited while Mira had a conversation with her friend. 'Yeah, that's okay.'

'Can I have a word with Tasha?' Virgil asked. 'I need to know it's secure.'

The next few minutes did little to ease Virgil's fears. Natasha's flat was the ground floor of a converted house in Balham, south London. Three male students lived upstairs. The press would get to hear about it in no time.

'This is a one-night only solution,' Virgil said, passing the phone back to Thad. 'We need to get a longer term answer.'

'We've tried to persuade her to take a hotel room, but after what happened in Denmark she is reluctant,' he replied.

'Tasha's had a brilliant idea,' Mira said. 'Her mother has a huge flat in St John's Wood. It's got an entryphone, three big bedrooms, and she only uses one. I could stay there until all this rubbish blows over.'

'That's handy,' said Virgil, taking down the address. When Mira hung up, he turned to Thad. 'Baroness Earl of West Bromwich, apparently.'

'Her? The House of Lords Hellcat,' Jonesy chuckled. 'Mira should be safe enough there,' he said, then scratched his head. They stared at each other. 'I suppose we should send Lawrence

Wall some flowers, from Mira, wishing him a speedy recovery?' Jonesy looked round the room. 'And a press release brimming with the sympathy and concern that she clearly doesn't feel.'

'He did beat her up, Jonesy,' Portia said.

'The world does not *know* that,' he retorted. 'She's got to *appear* devastated. I mean for fuck's sake, Lawrence Wall may never play again. He's got a punctured lung, broken ribs, two cracked vertebrae and a severed Achilles tendon. This wasn't some playground fight, it was nasty. There will already be a sea of floral tributes at the entrance to the club, a candlelit vigil outside the hospital and, PFU alert: if she wants even a chance at the Suressence contract, she is going to have to visit him. With flowers.'

'Okay Jonesy, good catch. I'll get Kelly onto it,' Thad said.

'What about the launch party for the film on Saturday?' Virgil asked. 'She has been looking forward to it, but there are some red carpet meet-the-public moments, which could be a risk.'

'Fuck, I'd forgotten that,' Jonesy sucked the arm of his spectacles ruminatively.

'She really should go if possible,' Portia said. 'It's a unique shop window overseas.'

'Can you keep her safe there?' Thad asked Virgil.

'Yes. I've already done a lot of work on it,' Virgil said, leafing through his documents. 'There will be a big security detail anyway. The stars arrive at the back of the hotel, via a private entrance off Park Lane, and there is only one five minute promenade at the front, with the press in an enclosure, and the public either side of them, also behind barriers. However, because it's a public road, there are no security checks or patdowns for the public. If we were talking about LA or New York, and were worried about firearms, I'd say cancel. Here I think on balance it'll be okay. I'll just make sure she doesn't do any autographs or get too close to the barrier.'

* * *

TWENTY DAYS

The next few days were mayhem. The press went crazy over the attack, and Jonesy Tolling's phone rang off the hook. Mira's social media following went through the roof. Every news bulletin gave more detail about the state of Lawrence Wall, particularly his Achilles tendon. Footage showed pubs full of nervous fans watching the footage of the attack. There were even assaults, with soccer fans laying into Qaeggan in pubs in Stevenage, Reading and Hull. Interviewees from Manchester to Leeds, Liverpool to London were quick to wheel out their pet theories for the benefit of the cameras. Blame for the attack was spread between rival clubs, rival players in Wall's own club and in the England camp, plus the England manager who had such difficulty in controlling Wall's on-pitch temperament. But a fair proportion trotted out the personal angle: 'Aye, it's obviously the ex,' said one elderly man, interviewed while laying flowers in the car park where Wall was attacked. 'Stands to reason after he slagged her off on TV.'

Virgil flicked through channel after channel, newspaper after newspaper, scoured social media and the same depressing skirmishes broke out again and again. The juiciest theory was that which ran closest to Lawrence Wall's heart.

The film premiere party went fine. Though there were dozens of rowdy Qaeggan, with the full make-up, wigs and black contact lenses, they spent much more time booing the American actress Annemaria Claverhorn than trying to get close to Mira. Virgil and four hotel security guys in evening dress were between the actors and the crowd, and Mira's turn was brief. Journalists' questions were deliberately drowned out by broadcasting the film soundtrack over the PA system. Virgil, facing away from her to the audience, only knew the moment had come when the crowd gasped and the blizzard of photographers' flashes began. It must be the dress. Mira was wearing a Cinderella-style scarlet ballgown, see-through below the thigh and above the shoulders. Her hair was swept over to one side. He turned to assess her trajectory. There were whistles and cheers from the crowd, and the scrape of the barriers edging forward in the crush as the chant began: 'We want Mira, we want Mira.'

Just thirty seconds later, she was back in without a hitch, though Virgil later read that Claverhorn had privately expressed fury at being upstaged at her own premiere.

The visit to the private London hospital where Lawrence Wall had been transferred to recuperate seemed an easier prospect, but turned out worse. Virgil suggested going at nine in the morning, as soon as visiting hours began, hoping it wouldn't yet be busy. But it was. The press pack had been poorly managed, and there was no rear entrance to the clinic.

While sightseers were supposed to be kept on the other side of the busy Westminster street, they overflowed the limited crowd barriers, and there were too few police officers to control them. When Mira's chauffeured car arrived it was from the wrong direction, leaving Mira to cross the street to the clinic. Virgil jumped out of the passenger side, and immediately had to deal with two photographers blocking his path. Mira, who was under instruction to get out on Virgil's side facing the crowd, instead slid along and opened the other door. By the time Virgil had opened the door she was supposed to emerge from, she was already on her way towards the clinic, with the car between them. A PFU in the making, as Jonesy would have said. Virgil watched helplessly as a reporter blocked her path and shoved a microphone into her face.

'How are you feeling about what happened to your ex?'

'Awful, naturally,' she responded as she tried to make a way through a gathering pack of reporters. By the time Virgil reached her side Mira was hemmed in, and being jostled by cameramen, sound booms and photographers.

Another question was hurled from the back: 'Mira, some bloggers claim you were involved in arranging this attack. What do you have to say?'

'How can you say such a thing?' Mira said, showing the huge bunch of flowers Stardust had supplied her with. 'I don't believe in retaliation.' By this time Virgil was sliding his body between Mira and the press, easing her way to the door. But the dreaded follow-up question emerged: 'Mira, retaliation for what?'

The only reply was the bang of double doors as Mira stepped

into the safety of the clinic. Once Virgil was confident the hospital security staff had secured the door, he turned to watch her receding down the long corridor, accompanied by a nurse. Even in a conservative raincoat, Mira's walk was mesmerising: Unhurried, elegant, even arrogant. It was hard for him to turn away.

Five minutes later Mira phoned Virgil from inside the hospital. 'He won't speak to me. I'm coming out.'

Virgil hesitated before saying: 'Remember what Jonesy said. It might not look good, coming out immediately, with the press all over.'

Mira gave a piercing screech of frustration. 'All right,' she yelled, 'I'll walk the bloody corridor for twenty minutes. Jesus Christ, who's the victim here?' There was a sharp crack and the phone went dead. Virgil shook his head and thought about the question.

When Mira finally emerged half an hour later, she was tight-lipped, her face closed. Virgil steered her through the gaggle of reporters to the waiting car. Once inside and safely away from the scene, Virgil watched her face in the rearview mirror. She looked up and caught his eye. 'I broke my phone when I threw it,' she said, showing him the cracked screen. 'I got told off by a nurse for making a noise. Just like I was a child.'

'It happens,' Virgil said. 'Where to now?'

'Well,' she said, leaning forward with a mischievous look on her face. 'I need to go home and change out of this matronly garb. Then I want you to drive me into the City. I've got a lunch date.'

* * *

267

Virgil dropped Mira outside some anonymous office block near the Baltic Exchange in the City, and despite her promising to call him once she knew where she was having lunch, she had turned off her phone. He'd taken the car to an underground car park and walked out onto the street to be sure he could get a signal if she did call back. He called Thad and expressed his misgivings.

'I can't protect her if she won't let me know where she is,' Virgil said.

Thad laughed. 'You can't live her life for her. She's twenty-three and probably feels like she's trying to escape her parents all over again. So who is this guy she's seeing?'

'I don't know anything about him except his name is Ram Dipani. He's part of a billionaire family of Indian shipbreakers.'

'Okay, Virgil. Do your best.'

Virgil waited four agonising hours for Mira to ring. When she did it was from an address in the West End. She and Ram had taken a taxi to some quiet restaurant that he knew would be away from prying eyes. Virgil eventually found the Soho side street and as he double-parked outside, she and Ram emerged, sharing a large umbrella. The Indian was film-star handsome, with a stylish jacket and designer stubble. Virgil emerged to open the door, and they both slid inside. Ram insisted on shaking Virgil's hand. 'Take care of this precious lady,' he said.

'That's my job and I'm doing it as well as I can.'

'Virgil would like to be my rock, Princess Diana style, but he's more like my favourite patch of gravel,' laughed Mira. 'Do you know, when I first met him, I thought he'd been named after the Greek hero, but I was wrong, wasn't I Virgil?'

'Yes. My mum named me after a character in *Thunderbirds*,' Virgil said.

It meant nothing to Ram, and he and Mira had to explain what the cult science fiction series was all about. Ram asked to be dropped off at his office, and during the half hour journey Virgil couldn't help noticing the bubbling conversation and laughter in the back. Ram had missed a meeting, but he clearly couldn't have cared less.

'This is me,' Ram said, as Virgil drove along Leadenhall Street. Virgil pulled over, and his eyes couldn't help straying to the mirror, where he caught Ram's rather shy kiss on Mira's cheek. The joyful atmosphere was quite infectious and he felt very pleased for her, seeing her beaming with happiness.

'Seems like a nice guy,' Virgil ventured.

'Oh Virgil, he's wonderful,' Mira said. 'So gracious, so attentive and a great listener.'

'I did read somewhere that the last true English gentleman would be an Indian,' Virgil said.

Mira asked Virgil to drive her home to pick up some fresh clothes, and as soon as he crossed London Bridge, she was on the phone, gushing to her friends about her first date with Ram Dipani. Suddenly she stopped talking and gasped. 'What's that?' she said, pointing to a great spray of red paint along the parapet of the bridge: *Kill the Bitch*. In the centre of the stylised B were two almond-shaped green eyes.

'Don't take any notice,' said Virgil. 'Just some idiot with a spray can.'

Mira's mood deflated immediately, and when they saw

a second graffito, this time on the metal sides of a railway viaduct, she suddenly looked like she was about to cry. 'Virgil, don't they know? It wasn't me. It really wasn't me!'

'Yeah, I know,' Virgil said. 'The joys of celebrity, eh?'

For the first time for four days, there seemed to be no journalists hanging around Mira's apartment block. He drove into the underground secure car park, perhaps her greatest protection against being buttonholed, and went with her in the card-operated lift to her flat. She looked relieved to be back.

'Home at last, Virgil,' she said, smiling at him.

'Yeah,' said Virgil as the lift door opened onto her floor. 'I'll say goodbye now. Sweet dreams. See you tomorrow at...'

She turned to see what he was looking at. The door to her flat and the adjacent black marble panel had been sprayed in bright red, foot-high letters: *Be careful, Mira.*

Chapter Twenty

NINETEEN DAYS

Virgil was supposed to be cooking a meal for Kelly that evening to inaugurate his new expensive kitchen, but instead of shopping for food, he'd sat with Mira for two hours in the early evening while she faffed around in her apartment, spending half the time texting, and the rest trying to work out what clothes to take to Baroness Earl's apartment. Given that it was an open-ended stay, Virgil imagined there could be any amount of stuff required.

'Thad told me that you don't want to go to any of the service apartments Stardust has offered, or the hotels,' Virgil said.

'Virgil, I don't like anonymous places. You can only exist there, not live. Besides they get really spooky when you are on your own. After what happened in Copenhagen I don't trust hotels to keep my presence a secret. There's always someone in the pay of the newspapers. At least staying with friends there will be people I can trust. No one knows where I'll be except you, Thad and Natasha.'

Eventually, Virgil delivered Mira and her three bulging suitcases to a swanky address in St John's Wood, north of the river. Natasha came down to meet them outside the imposing mansion block, so after carrying the luggage in, he left them to it. His thoughts turned to what might now be a high-pressure test of his cooking skills. It was after six, and the Balham market stalls he'd wanted to visit were long closed, so he picked up some fresh penne, mushrooms and cream cheese from the deli. The route home was different from usual, and he noticed even more anti-Mira graffiti. *Kill the Bitch* was prominent on Balham railway bridge, and on the brick beneath, dozens of stencilled poster-size images had green eyes with a cross through them. A new inventive cruelty.

* * *

Kelly arrived half an hour late, a fat folder of work still in her arms as he opened the door. 'Sorry, running a bit behind, didn't get time to buy any wine.'

'You're here, that's all that matters.' Virgil pulled her into his arms, kicked the door shut and kissed her fiercely until her documents slid, sheet by surrendering sheet, from her arms and onto the floor. He lifted her further, and she squealed as her shoes dropped off. He carried her to the bedroom and laid her on the bed. 'We've got a bit of time before dinner,' Virgil murmured, and pulled his shirt over his head.

Two hours later, the pasta still uncooked, Virgil awoke in a sensuous haze at the loss of Kelly's warmth. He propped himself up on a pillow to watch her. Naked but for black and now laddered hold-ups she was leaning away from him over the desk, holding a sheaf of documents. Her copper hair, corkscrewing over her shoulders, was burnished to gold in the light of the single desk lamp.

'Hey, no work now,' Virgil said.

'It's yours, not mine,' she said, turning back to him, holding Wōdan's latest card. 'I love this drawing of Mira,' she said.

'It's fantastic, really,' Virgil said. The psychiatric patient had really captured something about her, the eyes which were both bewitching but inscrutable, giving no clue to what she was thinking.

'That newspaper she's holding, it's just perfect. He's even managed to include the latest news, kind of,' Kelly said. 'It says Lawrence Wall was murdered.'

'What?' Virgil leaped out of bed. 'Where does it say that?' He took the card and put it under the light.

'Here. You have to hold it edgeways on to read it, to foreshorten the letters.' Kelly held up the card, folded edge to her nose, then handed it to Virgil. It was true. Edgeways on, the almost microscopic text sprang to life:

Lawrence Wall murdered

Then the subheading:

Football ace knifed in Friday night Manchester nightclub attack.

Virgil's jaw dropped.

'That is so clever,' said Kelly. 'How did he write so incredibly small?'

'No idea. But think about it,' Virgil said. 'The envelope was postmarked, lets see, five days before Lawrence Wall was attacked. He wasn't reacting to the news, he was anticipating it. He expected it. The location and the time, everything except the result was right…'

'But he couldn't have done it. He's in Broadmoor.'

'Not personally. But he's obviously got friends.'

Kelly's hands clasped her face. 'He was boasting about it. To Mira. But why?'

* * *

Virgil knew that keeping Mira safe had to start with making the apartment fully secure. The graffito by her door had worried her enough to keep her away. Even though there was nothing to indicate it was more than a prank, the fact that someone had got so close was a concern. Virgil had asked to see the CCTV coverage for the corridor outside Mira's door, but was astounded to be told that there was none, it was merely a dummy housing. Stefan Kados was apologetic, but explained that this was normal. 'Most residents and owners are foreign nationals, and often very wealthy,' he said. 'They jealously guard their privacy and many don't want there to be any record of who their friends and associates are. We are confident that with cameras covering the lobby, the entryways to the lifts on the ground floor and the car park, we are fully secure.'

'Really? What about the intruder in the utility control room?'

'We don't really know there was anyone there, do we?' Kados replied. 'The police were happy with the arrangements we have put in place. That room is now kept locked.'

Virgil didn't respond for a moment, so Kados – still in apology mode – said: 'If you would like to review the lobby and entrance images for the night in question, we are happy to grant permission.'

'No thanks. I don't know who I'm looking for, or when they arrived. If they were staying in another apartment, or up in the utility room, it could be a different day.' Virgil then asked that a camera be installed in the dummy housing on Mira's floor, but was told it might take several weeks because it would need the permission of the owner of the neighbouring apartment, who lived in Singapore.

'Okay,' he said, 'I've got a better idea. Don't lock the utility control room door. Let me install a wireless camera up there. I can get one with a movement sensor, connected to my phone. If our intruder comes back, I'll know immediately.'

* * *

SEVENTEEN DAYS

It was a full five days after the attack on Lawrence before the police called to arrange an interview with Mira. They were happy to visit Stardust Brands' offices, so Jonesy had prepared the full works. The biggest conference room, with floor-to-ceiling images of Mira in place. They had been told that no lawyer would be required, but arranged for one anyway. Jazam

Shah was already sitting with Virgil Bliss and Jonesy on soft low seats around a small glass coffee table when reception buzzed to say that Detective Inspector Colin Croucher and Detective Sergeant Gordon Highfield of Greater Manchester Police had arrived, a good ten minutes early. Virgil went to fetch them, wondering just how much rivalry there had been to get this interview. They were like two boys in a sweetshop, eyes everywhere at the svelte young women of Stardust. Croucher had an accountant's bearing but a worse suit; grey, baggy and overlong in the sleeves. His face was crumpled in an avuncular middle-aged way, and his lips were thin but mobile. Highfield was more street smart. Stocky, with a trendy haircut, fashionably full beard and a couple of piercings. Croucher, like Virgil before him, couldn't get the hang of the reclined seat style, and perched on the edge like a schoolboy waiting to see the headmaster.

Virgil introduced himself as Mira's security chief, and brought them through. He sat them at the small table, and made the introductions. Kelly came in to get them coffee, and Virgil noticed how they both stared down the front of her blouse and lingered over her legs. *Just wait until you see Mira.*

'I take it Miss Roskova is here?' Croucher began.

'Of course,' Jonesy said. 'Here she is now.'

A door opened at the far end of the room, behind where Croucher and Highfield had been seated. They looked over their shoulders, and saw Mira call a welcome. She was wearing a saffron-coloured button-up dress and blue court shoes, and gave them the full glory of twenty feet of catwalk approach. Jonesy and Virgil stood up, leaving the detectives in an undignified scramble to match them. Virgil watched closely. They were transfixed. She shook hands with them, even grasping Croucher's wrist with her other hand as Jonesy had suggested. 'I'm so sorry to hear about this ghastly attack on Lawrence, so I'm really glad you came here to see if there is anything I can do.'

'Well, this is only a routine inquiry at the moment...'

'And you'd just like me to answer a few questions? Of course.'

Jonesy had earlier placed a high upright chair a few feet back from the coffee table, so the cops would be looking up to her. Mira sat down, crossed her legs and smoothed the dress.

'We hadn't intended to tape this interview,' Croucher said. 'But as I see Mr Shah is, then we will have too also.' He turned to Highfield, who laid on the table a much larger and more old-fashioned machine than Shah's.

'So can I ask you, Miss Roskova, how long you have known Lawrence Wall?'

'Not quite seven months.'

'And how did you meet?'

'A TV awards dinner at the Carlton...'

'Was that for the zombie programme?' Highfield asked.

'Yes. *Village of the Dead*. Did you see it?'

'Of course,' he smirked. 'Everyone's seen it. It was brill.' To Virgil, Highfield already looked smitten.

'And I believe you have now broken up, is that correct?'

'Yes,' Mira laughed. 'Unfortunately, I think everyone in the country has read about it. Even my personal letter to him.'

'Well, indeed,' Croucher said. 'But you can't take everything you read in the papers on face value.' He looked around the table for support.

'That's certainly true,' Jonesy said. 'It's half my job keeping on top of that nonsense.'

'Would you say your relationship with Mr Wall was harmonious?' Croucher asked.

Mira suppressed a laugh. 'No, Inspector. Lawrence Wall is an elemental force of nature, as anyone who watches him play can tell you. I admired him, and like many women I found him attractive. But Lawrence isn't a man who meets anyone halfway. Does that make sense?'

'Makes perfect sense to me,' Highfield said under his breath, until silenced by a look from his senior colleague.

'Now, we have spoken to Mr Wall about the attack, as you would expect, and he is firmly of the opinion that you might have had something to do with it.'

Mira's gaze hardened, and as she shifted position, the tip of her shoe firmly pointed towards the inspector. 'I'm really sorry that he seems to be so hurt by our break-up that he has to resort to false accusations.'

'So, to be clear you deny it?'

'Yes, I absolutely deny it.'

'Inspector,' Shah said, 'if you are accusing my client of any complicity in this affair, I will have to remind you that she should be formally arrested.'

'I'm not accusing her,' Croucher said. 'I'm asking her response to an accusation made by her ex-partner.'

'Look, he wasn't my partner,' Mira interjected. 'He was a boyfriend, and not a particularly serious one. Lawrence's trouble is that he judges people by his own standards. If he is slighted he gets even, whatever the cost. He assumes everyone does the same. I would never lower myself to that level.' A gentle hand movement tossed the idea aside. Virgil was impressed by the performance. Vulnerability, dignified outrage, the moral high ground. It was all there.

'So were you slighted by him?'

She paused. 'He didn't treat me very well, I think it's fair to say.'

'He manhandled you once, didn't he? He did say that might be a motive.'

Mira's eyes flashed across to Shah and Jonesy, who both nodded. 'Manhandled? He punched me half a dozen times, and then tried to strangle me. I don't know what he told you, but I thought he was going to kill me. I jumped fifteen feet out of a window and ran for my life in my pyjamas in the middle of storm to escape him!'

'Why didn't you ever report this?' Croucher said. 'We could have pressed charges.'

'Are you joking? Against England's favourite footballer? Even if I won I'd never work again.'

Highfield smirked. 'Well, they say there's no such thing as bad publicity...'

'Oh yes there is, mate,' Jonesy interjected. 'You stick to policing and leave the publicity management to us.'

'I am sorry for having to ask you,' Croucher asked. 'But have you seen the CCTV footage of the attack?'

'I saw some of it on TV. But I couldn't face seeing it all. I abhor violence, I absolutely hate it. It disgusts me.'

'Had you ever seen any of the assailants before?'

'I don't think so. If Lawrence didn't recognise them, I'm sure that I wouldn't.'

'He describes them as being dressed as zombies from the TV show you were in.'

Mira looked at him, gobsmacked. 'You think I have a private zombie army? Salaried and fully equipped with black wigs and eyeliner?'

'Of course not.'

'Inspector, can I remind you that the online phenomenon of the Qaeggan is under no one's control. They do what they like. They make claim to be my supporters, but I don't support them, and I don't approve of what they do. Half the time they are stalking me! Virgil, do you have the pictures?'

Virgil showed them pictures taken of the graffito on her door. 'We gave this to the Met police two days ago and we've heard nothing,' Virgil said.

'Well, that's clearly a matter for the Met,' said Croucher, a smug smile conveying a clear impression: *well, what can you expect from that lot*?

The interview came to an end, and as they were shown out, both detectives asked Mira to sign publicity pictures for them. Once they had the pictures, Virgil followed them to the lift. 'Excuse me,' he said. 'I didn't want to mention this in front of Mira, because she hasn't seen it, but we believe we have a clue as to who organised the attack on Lawrence Wall.'

Highfield stopped dead in his tracks, a quizzical look on his face. 'Tell me more.'

Virgil steered them off to a small, windowless meeting room at the far side of the building and showed them the three letters that had been sent from Broadmoor. 'The thing is,' Virgil explained, 'it says "Lydia, I'd like to grant your deepest wish." When we first got this, we thought the gift was the card itself. But it isn't. The gift is the attack on Wall.'

'That's quite a leap of imagination,' Croucher said.

'No it's not, look.' Virgil showed them how to look at the text from the edge of the card, which gave the time and place of the attack.

'Hmm,' said Croucher, looking up at Virgil. 'This is fascinating. But if the sender is as you say in a secure psychiatric unit he would have great difficulty arranging this, wouldn't he? I mean, my understanding is that Broadmoor has enormous restrictions on communications from patients.'

'Apparently not,' Virgil said. 'This was posted in Peterborough, it didn't emerge like the others from Broadmoor's own censorship procedure.'

'They're not signed, though, are they? There is no saying that they are all from the same person, nor indeed that the artist and the sender are the same person.'

'It would be highly unlikely that we have two people sending the same unusual messages with such similar artwork, surely,' Virgil said.

Croucher exchanged a shrug with Highfield. 'Leave it with me,' he said, holding out his hand. 'We'll assess it along with the other stuff.'

Virgil reluctantly passed the cards across. He'd photocopied them earlier, but felt that the police really didn't see the significance in them that he did. Having seen the calibre of these two, Virgil decided that he would pursue his own lines of inquiry about Wōdan. If his job was to keep Mira safe, he had to follow his own instincts.

* * *

Virgil was just sitting down for a late afternoon meeting at Stardust Brands when things started to happen. First, there was a call for Portia Casals. Thad and Jonesy looked up as she stepped away, her face becoming tight and severe, her voice quiet. When she hung up, her face suddenly lit up. 'The police have caught the thug who pushed me over in the café. The Crown Prosecution Service just want to know that I will give evidence against him.'

'Fabulous news,' said Thad.

'Let's get him to clean off the graffiti too,' said Jonesy.

Before she could sit down again, Virgil's phone trilled. He picked it up, and saw that the CCTV in Battersea Harbour had been triggered. He called up the live image. It wasn't great resolution on the iPhone screen, but it was good enough to capture a young woman with long hair and a baseball cap on the platform. He couldn't see her face, but she did appear to have glasses. And she was young, a teenager at most.

'Cops after you too?' Jonesy said.

'Hold on…' Virgil stood up and watched as the girl opened a small backpack and took out a book, a torch, an iPad and a sleeping bag. She then sat down.

'Are we going to have this effing meeting or not?' Jonesy asked.

'Sorry. I've caught one of Mira's stalkers. She's a young kid, somehow got into the building on the maintenance floor above Mira's apartment.'

Virgil immediately rang Stefan Kados and told him. 'Can you get up there straightaway? She looks harmless enough, but I want to know how she got in.' He passed on the description. Kados said he would go up with one of the female receptionists.

Virgil hung up, delighted. Setting up the wireless camera hadn't been quite as hassle-free as Virgil had hoped. In the first twenty-four hours he got a dozen alerts triggered by the numerous maintenance people who came and went during the day on the lower level walkways. He then had to return and reset the device so that the beams were only triggered by movement on the highest platform, where the telecoms cabinet leading to the radio mast was. The next three days there were no alerts, and he began to think the device wasn't working at all. Now he knew it was. If this was just a kid, than at least it was one thing less to worry about.

'Alright. Sorry about that,' Virgil said. 'Where were we?'

'Our strategy for separating Mira's brand from the *Village of the Dead*,' said Thad. 'There is the analysis Jonesy prepared.'

Virgil stared at the document on the table in front of him. 'Ah. I haven't had time…'

'Okay. In case you hadn't heard,' Jonesy chuckled, 'the Hollywood blockbuster version tanked. A hundred million dollars spent, and only took two million on its opening weekend. Critics hated it.'

'It shouldn't damage Mira too much,' Portia said. 'She's only connected with the TV version. But it's a good time to emphasise other aspects of her brand.'

'Okay,' Virgil said. 'What do you need from me…?'

'You've read the blogs and posts and seen them up close,' said Jonesy. 'What chance is there that these effing zombies are going to melt away?'

'The hardcore, probably not much,' Virgil said. His phone rang again and he stared at it. 'Sorry. I'll have to take this.' As he answered the call Virgil saw Jonesy toss his pen on the desk, and fold his arms. It was Stefan Kados at Battersea Harbour. 'I'm sorry Virgil. We've got a bit of a problem.'

'Like what?'

'The girl ran away, and onto one of the roof walkways. We lost sight of her. We just called the police.'

'Okay. I'll be right over.' He hung up. 'I'm sorry everyone, I've got to go.'

'What is it *now*?' Jonesy snorted.

'You want Mira to escape the zombie connection? Why don't you come with me and catch the one who's marauding around the roof of her apartment building?'

When Virgil left, he wasn't surprised to do so alone.

* * *

The police were already there when Virgil arrived at Battersea Harbour. There were two WPCs at the door, and after explaining who he was, one of them escorted him in the lift to the maintenance floor. Out in the dome, a uniformed police inspector, loud hailer at his waist, was talking to Kados. Beyond him, two officers were out on the roof, crouching on the walkway with both hands on the handrails as they advanced into a gusty wind. Virgil didn't rate their chances of catching a nimble twelve-year-old.

'Want me to go out there?' Virgil said by way of introduction.

The inspector looked up, moustache bristling. 'Thank you, but we can't have you creating dangers for yourself or her. The child was seen to leave the walkway and walk across the glass roof panels over the atrium. They're probably strong enough to take a man's weight, but they're slippery as hell and I'll not risk anyone crossing them. If Ms Roskova could come here, she might be able to talk the child down. Otherwise we'll get a negotiator.'

'I'll see what I can do,' said Virgil. Before that, he decided to let himself into Mira's apartment. The management company didn't have a key, and Virgil kept it to himself that he did. He went quietly down the emergency stairs onto her floor and surprised a young girl standing by the lift. She was wearing Qaeggan facepaint, glasses, and a backpack. When she saw him, she gave a little shout of alarm and frantically pressed the lift call button.

'It's alright, I'm not going to hurt you,' Virgil said. She tried to dart around him, but he blocked her. 'Come on, I've just a few questions to ask then I'll let you go.'

'You won't hand me to the cops?'

'No. And if you answer me honestly, I might give you a very quick tour of Mira's apartment.' He slid the electronic key into the lock and opened the door a crack.

'Cool!' she said, then looked up at him. 'I remember you. From the building where Mira works.'

Virgil stared at her. 'Ah! You…you wanted promotional pictures. I do remember. Steff and…'

'I'm Ellie,' she said.

Virgil ushered her into Mira's flat and closed the door behind them. 'So how did you find out she lives in this building?'

'It said so in a magazine last year.' She opened her backpack and pulled out a much-used iPad with a cracked screen and dirty case. She tapped and flicked the screen like a pro, then showed Virgil an article. It was from the May 2014 edition of the *Wandsworth and Fulham Property Gazette*. He started reading: '*Village of the Dead* beauty Mira Roskova has recently paid two point five million for a penthouse in the yet-to-be completed Battersea Harbour apartment complex, further buttressing the attractiveness of this exclusive development.' Virgil was horrified. If a kid could dig this obscure nugget up so easily, then she really wasn't safe from those with professional skills and worse intentions.

'The mag said a penthouse at Battersea Harbour, which is the top, right? But we didn't know which building. So Steff brought some flowers and kept asking the doormen at each building where she should leave them for Mira. In the end someone told her.'

'But how did you get in?'

'I walked in with a family who lives here, like I was their kid. I got in the lift and no one asked. Course, I wasn't qaegged up then. I put the make-up on later.'

'How long have you been staying here? Isn't your family worried?' Virgil asked.

'Nah. My Dad don't care, my mum's on drugs and my brother's in young offenders. I mostly come after school, couple of hours, stayed overnight three times I reckon. Got some good pictures of her too, wanna see?' She offered him the iPad.

'No thanks. So how did you get off the roof just now?'

'I slid down onto Mira's patio, then climbed over onto next door's. There's a window there which is slightly ajar. I was able to use this to slid it open.' She showed Virgil a retractable metal tape measure.

'You're quite the little burglar, aren't you?' Virgil asked. 'Is this all just to get close to her?'

The girl shrugged. 'I think she's brill. I've seen everything she's done. I even saw that shit film they just done. I just look around me, at home and school and the streets, then I look at her. What she's got an' that. They say anyone can be whatever they want, if they try hard enough. Well, I just want to be like her.'

Virgil gave Ellie a very cursory tour of the living room, and saw her eyeing a giant box of chocolates that someone had sent Mira a week or two ago, and which still lay untouched on the kitchen counter.

'Are you hungry?' Virgil asked.

Ellie shrugged. He went to the fridge and looked through. Four bottles of champagne, a limp baton of celery and some cream cheese.

Ellie looked under his arm. 'So that's princess food, is it? That keeps her skinny?'

'I guess it would,' Virgil said. 'Tell you what. Let's get out of here. I'll buy you a pizza if you tell me some more. I want to find out exactly how you Mira fans get your information. But you've got to promise not to come here again, okay?'

'Hmm. Extra toppings and a stuffed crust?'

'Okay.'

'Then it's a deal.' She offered him a small chilly hand for a high-five.

Chapter Twenty-One

SIXTEEN DAYS

Virgil was surprised that a journalist would choose to meet in a vegetarian café rather than a pub, but the falafel at the Kali Deli in Shoreditch was delicious, and perhaps journalism had moved on too. He had already finished a plateful when the *Telegraph's* home affairs editor Peter Childswicke walked in, almost an hour late.

'So sorry. Bloody editorial meetings expand to more than fill the time available,' he said. Childswicke was a rotund sixty-something of patrician demeanour, his florid jowls humid with the effort of hauling his bulk up three flights of stairs. He shrugged off a dark grimy mackintosh, and further loosened the tie which was clearly struggling to contain his fleshy neck.

'I hope you don't mind,' Virgil said, indicating the plate of crumbs. 'Once you'd texted me, I thought I'd use my time usefully.'

'No, not at all.' Childswicke ordered a vegetable lasagne. 'So, I understand you have some information about where this Wōdan fellow is?'

'I have, but I want to trade it for some insight into this piece which I'm told you wrote.' Virgil took out a printout of the *Telegraph* piece that he'd seen in Mira's flat. 'I want to discover if your "invisible monster" is actually Wōdan.'

Childswicke took off his spectacles, breathed on the lenses, and cleaned them briskly on a napkin. 'Well, that is an interesting speculation.' He replaced his glasses and looked carefully around the room, assessing each table of diners. 'Just checking for High Court judges,' he chuckled, before leaning forward on his elbows.

'Can you tell me about the crimes this guy committed?' Virgil asked.

'Well, here is what I have pieced together. In March 2005, you may recall, three British schoolgirls disappeared while on a trip to Venice. It was a massive case.'

'I recall it, but I was in Afghanistan at the time. Remind me of the details.'

'Keeley Corcoran, Amber Tompkins and Destiny Simpson. They were all from the same school, Halliday High, in Clitheroe, Lancashire, aged thirteen and fourteen, on a five-day school trip. You know the kind of thing: art, architecture and history. They failed to show up for dinner on day two. Huge search, local police, lah-di-dah. Nothing. Three days later, the rest of the schoolgirls go home, and for three months not a dicky bird from the Carabinieri. Press is going mad of course. Think of the papers we can sell! Lovely girls, are they alive or not? Amber was a champion swimmer with Olympic potential. So far so mysterious, right?'

'Right.'

'So then, after three months, the Italian police make an arrest. And that's that. No info, nothing for a long time. I sat on my arse outside the regional police headquarters for many sweaty days waiting for some detail, then finally. Bingo! They had charged a local man, one Guglielmo Russo, aged thirty-six. Tersest police statement I ever saw. No detail, nothing. But with the help of a friendly staffer in the local police, we managed to get a little inside information. The first shock was that there were no bodies recovered, nothing. She had heard there was some other evidence, and whatever the Italian cops knew, they weren't letting on.'

Childswicke looked sideways, and leaned further forward. 'Now, Italian courts don't use a jury, even for major crimes. They have the Corte d'Assise, with two professional judges and six lay judges. And these guys sat in secret in advance of a full trial, and considered some documents. One was a legal opinion by the senior Italian prosecutor, one was a representation from a foreign power, and one a psychiatric report. They then decided our suspect, Russo, was not mentally fit to stand trial. However, now it gets complicated. In Italy since this thing called Basaglia Law, they basically closed down all the secure psychiatric hospitals in favour of community treatment.'

'For everyone?'

'Ah,' Childswicke held up a finger. 'Not the really dangerous ones, like Russo. So he stayed in prison, but under a different statute. That meant the press wasn't allowed to know anything about him, privacy and all that, and there was legal wrangling over whether he would ever go to full trial.'

Virgil scratched his head. 'I don't get how this relates to anyone in Britain?'

'Bear with me,' Childswicke said, his smile exhibiting the pleasure of gradual revelation. 'We have a good source in the Home Office. And I mean very high. And this source said that Russo wasn't Italian at all. He's a Brit, name of Jonathan Pearson, who had been given at least two new identities and had his own handler within the department. That explains the representation by a foreign power. We made our own checks and discovered that someone in the Home Office, who has the ear of the Home Secretary, got him brought home from Italy. In theory it was to face trial here.'

'I don't get it,' Virgil said. 'Are you saying this guy was a spy?'

'Well, either that or a protected witness of a very high order. Of course you'd think: Italy, ah! The mafia. But if it was a witness protection case that would involve someone from the MOJ, and that wasn't the information I was getting. However, while all that is as clear as mud, we *did* secure a copy of some of the evidence against Russo, which the Italians sent to the Home Secretary.' Childswicke smiled, enjoying the suspense.

'Which was…?'

Childswicke leaned in and whispered: 'That these three girls weren't just murdered. They were *dissolved* in a tank of nitric acid. Presumably after some horrific sexual torture over a number of days.' He leaned back to enjoy the look of horror on Virgil's face. 'A single hair from one of the girls was found on the outside edge of a vat near Russo's studio on the island of Murano, just north of the city, and hair of one of the others was found in a suitcase.'

Virgil then asked: 'I take it you've not been able to publish any of this?'

Childswicke wheezed a great sigh of regret. 'No. Because soon after Russo-cum-Pearson was brought to Britain a secret judicial hearing was held under Lord Justice Kirby. Representatives of the press were allowed to hear his decision, but not to publish any details of it. We still cannot publish the name of the defendant, his victims, or any significant details about the case. It's completely unprecedented.'

'Why all the secrecy? What were the grounds?'

'That's particularly interesting,' Childswicke said. 'Our lawyers told us that the usual reason would be because of the interests of a child. Section thirty-nine of the Children and Young Person's Act 1933 allows a court the discretion to bar the press from identifying an individual if it would lead to the identification of a witness, victim or defendant under the age of 18.' Childswicke lifted a warning finger. 'But, in this case Lord Justice Kirby didn't cite the act, which makes me think that by default it must be national security.'

'You mentioned that Russo had a studio. So he was an artist?' Virgil asked.

'Presumably. Does this bolster your suspicion that he is Wōdan?'

'Well, possibly. Two artistically-talented murderers, one disappears on his way into Home Office protection and soon after another emerges miraculously into the justice system with no history. The ages given for Pearson and Wōdan seem to match too. As I mentioned on the phone, I work as a close protection officer for someone that Wōdan has been stalking, sending her letters and cards. From Broadmoor.'

'So Wōdan is in Broadmoor. That's useful in itself.' Childswicke smiled smugly, and dabbed his chin with a napkin. 'So I take it you work for our sexy peer Lady Earl?'

'Actually no, I don't,' Virgil said.

Childswicke's fat lips formed a moue of disappointment. 'Shame. Her being stalked by a psychopath would be so juicy. After that clever piece of exhibitionism, our editors love the little minx, despite her politics. So who is it?'

'I'm not here in an official capacity so I can't identify my client,' Virgil said.

Childswicke sat back and folded his arms across his chest. 'Now come on Mr Bliss, neither of us is here in an official capacity. And I have been exceedingly frank and open with you. I think you owe me equal candour.'

Virgil held up his hand in acknowledgment. 'Alright, my hands are tied to some extent because she doesn't know I'm here. My job, as you can imagine, is to protect her from worry as well as danger. But here's what I can do.' He took out the photocopies of the letters and placed them before Childswicke. 'They're in Latin, but I have the translation…'

'It's alright Virgil, I'm an old Wykehamist. I can read it. Hmm. Phenomenal artwork. So your client is called Lydia, eh?' Childswicke rubbed his jowls ruminatively.

'Her name must be left out of it,' Virgil said. 'But if you can focus your resources to narrow down if Wōdan is this acid murderer, then at least I'll know what we're dealing with.'

'Well, from my perspective, if Wōdan is the artist-formerly-known-as-Jonathan-Pearson, and they are even thinking of releasing him, then the leftie hand-wringing rehabilitation train really will have come off the rails,' Childswicke snorted, and got up to leave. He then scribbled something from his phone onto a napkin. 'Here. This may be useful. It's the mobile number of Lady Earl. She's met Wōdan face-to-face. If you are genuinely worried for your client, she might be able to put your mind at rest.' He pulled open the restaurant door but then turned back. 'Or not, as the case may be.'

* * *

That afternoon Virgil rang the number, which was answered first ring. 'This is Suzannah.'

'Hello, I'm Virgil Bliss, Mira's bodyguard. I've ferried Mira and Natasha to your place a couple of times.'

'Of course. Natasha told me. She told me how well you looked after her during that awful crush at Wembley Arena. I'm in your debt.'

Virgil laughed it off, then explained that the artist she had sat for in Broadmoor seemed to be sending letters to Mira. It was his job to assess how much danger Mira might be in, but he hadn't been able to get any information through official channels. The baroness listened carefully, then answered: 'It makes some sense to me. I've seen a dozen or more of Wōdan's drawings and sketches of Mira, but none of other celebrities.'

'Would you say he is dangerous?'

There was a long pause. 'Well, he's certainly one of the cleverest people I have ever met. He could be dangerous if he wanted to.' A phone rang in the background.

'Look. I'm a bit busy at the moment, and I'm sorry I don't have any time at all this week.' Shall we say a week on Thursday, two o'clock? You know where I live.'

Virgil agreed, and asked: 'One last thing, do you know his real name?'

There was a long pause, as the phone continued to ring in the background, and then clicked into an answer machine.

'Yes. But I'm sworn to secrecy,' she said. 'The hospital is terrified of the press finding out.'

'I give you my word that it will go no further.'

The phone rang again. 'I'll think about it,' she said. 'Look, I have to get this call. See you then.'

* * *

FOURTEEN DAYS

The irritating buzz of the phone pushed into his sleep. Virgil reluctantly eased himself away from the delightful warmth of Kelly's nakedness, and reached behind for his mobile. It was eleven o'clock on Sunday evening. They had shared a wonderful restful weekend while Mira was in New York for a much-delayed Max Factor photoshoot, and all he hoped for now was the chance to savour a few more moments. It wasn't to be. The moment he picked up Mira said: 'Virgil, it's me.'

'You're back?' he asked unnecessarily. He'd been expecting her tomorrow.

'Ten minutes ago. I got a taxi from Heathrow and there were bloody zombies here waiting for me.' She sounded out of breath.

'Here meaning where?'

'Outside the flat,' she breathed. 'Full Qaeggan regalia, five of them, three cars.'

'Okay calm down. Do you mean in the building?'

'No Virgil, in the street. I avoided them by going in through the lift from the underground car park.'

'They're probably just fans.'

'Can't they leave me alone? I've been away for four days, and the first night I get back, the first night in my own home since they beat up Lawrence and already they're stalking me. I think I'll stay somewhere else tomorrow. I mean, they've got binoculars, looking up at my windows!' The ragged slur in her voice betrayed not only anxiety but alcohol.

'Have you called reception?'

'Of course. The duty manager went out to talk to them. They said they weren't breaking the law. I could call the police, but then I'll get loads of hassle online.'

'Yeah, I see the point.'

'But how do they all seem to know where I live?'

'Well, the press know, and your flat purchase made headlines. Everything's so much easier for them in the days of Google. Look. If you're worried, I can be there in forty minutes.'

'Great, okay. Thank you!' she sounded relieved.

'Okay, now precautions, Mira, remember? Don't go down to them. Let the front desk handle anything, let them know of your concerns. Don't call the cops unless you really need to.'

'Roger-roger,' she said, with a giggle. Virgil heard a slurp of drink in the background.

When he hung up Kelly glared at him. 'What's the problem?'

'Zombies hanging around in the street outside.'

Kelly groaned. 'So you're going. She calls, you go round. Just like that.'

'Come on, I have to,' he said, as he pulled his T-shirt on.

'I knew you fancied her,' she muttered.

'What?'

Kelly turned and watched him with narrowed eyes, her chin resting in her hand. 'Go on, go serve your bloody mistress. What chance have I got trying to compete with the world's most desirable woman?'

Virgil sighed and then kneeled on the bed to embrace her. 'It's my job. But Kelly, to me you are the most desirable woman in the entire galaxy.'

She looked at him, her blue eyes scanning his, searching for truth in his words. 'Show me.' She gradually pushed his face down, arching herself so his warm mouth slid over her large freckled breasts, her smooth milky belly and then finally into her wisps of fiery down. 'Make me come, with your lying tongue.'

* * *

A sense of melancholy held Virgil as he drove across south London half an hour later. The south circular traffic as usual was slow, which gave him chance to notice a few changes. Someone had sprayed more *Kill the Bitch* graffiti on the rusting ironwork of two railway bridges in Clapham North, making seven he would pass on this journey. A minute later along a pedestrian underpass he saw a line of identical poster-sized stencils. Green eyes crossed out in red. He'd seen hundreds in the last week.

He arrived at the Battersea Harbour flats a few minutes later than planned. He drove slowly through the access and parking areas for all six blocks. One of the cars that Mira had described, a yellow Ford with a long aerial, was on its way out with two youngsters inside. It was only on his return pass on the service road that he spotted the others: three men dressed as Qaeggan leaning against a tatty black Vauxhall Nova, smoking. Virgil went past, parked around the corner and phoned in to Mira to check she was alright. He told her what he'd seen and was going to investigate before coming up.

Virgil emerged from the car in a tatty hoodie and paint-stained trainers, his standard incognito gear. He slipped around the base of Mira's block to approach the trio. When he got within thirty yards they visibly stiffened, faces betraying 'big black guy approaching' anxiety. Two were quite young, maybe twenty, one tall, one short, and there was an older man of perhaps fifty with binoculars around his neck, wearing a car coat. The two younger ones had wigs and smudged face paint.

'Always nice to meet a gang of zombies on a dark night,' Virgil said cheerfully as he walked up to them. 'Not seen you round here before.' They appeared to relax.

'Nah. We're up from Bromley,' the older one said. He had a notebook, and nodded towards the doorway. 'Mira lives in this building. Did you see her at all today?'

'Mira?' said Virgil quizzically.

'You know, Mira Roskova,' oldie said. Virgil shrugged ignorance.

'Bloody hell, man,' the tall youth blurted out. 'Didn't you see *Village of the Dead*?'

'Or any TV commercials, like, ever?' shorty said, smirking.

'Ah, is she that fit bird with the green eyes?' Virgil said.

'Beautiful eyes. I mean, she's the perfect woman,' purred shorty, his eyes half closed in contemplation.

'Are you hanging round here just to get a glimpse then?'

'These two are pure Mira worshippers,' oldie said, indicating the youths. 'Me, I doorstep all the top female celebrities. I got pictures of Rihanna and Beyoncé, and a selfie with Isabelle Adjani. I once got nearly knocked down by Madonna's chauffeured car. I'm still hoping to track down Taylor Swift when she comes over.'

'What happened to the other two guys who were here?' Virgil asked.

'Ian and Greg had to go home,' said shorty. 'But we're staying. We just want to make sure she's alright. With all the hassle and that.'

'So what kind of danger is she in, that she needs your protection?' Virgil asked.

'Well, every soccer fan seems to hate her after what happened to Lawrence Wall, which we think is really unfair,' said the tall one. 'And there is all this disgusting graffiti. It must be very hurtful to her.'

'I'd love to take her home and look after her,' said shorty. 'She'd be safe with me.' A smirk took ownership of his entire countenance.

Virgil could see that these guys were more annoying than dangerous. Yeah, they might bug Mira, but if she made it difficult for them they would just find other ways to follow her. In the great scheme of things, he decided, the Qaeggan weren't much to worry about. 'Okay lads. If I see her, I'll let you know,' he said. He started to walk away, and then turned around. 'In fact, can I take your phone numbers? I work around here a lot, and so I might see something.'

They swapped names and numbers with Virgil, and gave him a thumbs up as he walked away. Colin was the older guy, and Aaron and Jack the younger ones. They could be useful. A few pairs of eyes available for free. Virgil went back to his car, wriggled into more formal clothes and after checking himself in the wing mirror, drove down into the secure garage and took the lift to Mira's door.

Chapter Twenty-Two

TWELVE DAYS

It was just before eight in the morning. Suzannah Earl had been up for an hour checking through the latest version of the Punishment of Offenders Bill, which was due back in the Commons. The shadow Home Secretary had asked for her input by the end of the week, and she wrote rapidly in pencil in the margin. There was a slight noise behind her, and she turned to see a sleepy-looking Mira emerge from a guest bedroom and tiptoe to the loo. In the shadow of slumber, this young woman she'd known since she was sixteen still looked like an overgrown schoolgirl. Scruffy pyjamas and dressing gown, her hair like some windblown bush and her face pale and flat without make-up, yet still somehow full of natural grace. There was no sign of life yet from Natasha's room. Suzannah enjoyed having the company, even at such short notice, and dusting off her culinary skills for an appreciative audience. She was impressed when renewing her acquaintance with Mira a year or so ago that the girl had a healthy appetite and hadn't picked up those terrible self-destructive dieting habits that turned so many catwalk models into anorexic waifs.

At ten past, Suzannah put on the kettle for tea and made herself a breakfast of sugar-free muesli and fruit. She had wanted to do her exercises this morning, but the utility room was crammed with Mira's luggage and there wasn't the space. Three massive suitcases. It was as if the girl was intending to stay for six months, but Natasha had assured her that it was just a week, until the worst of the Lawrence Wall stuff had blown over. Having one of the world's most desired sex symbols stay in her apartment had the allure of status and sophistication, but the reality was that it was even more chaotic than the sleepovers that Natasha used to have as a teenager when they lived in Birmingham.

When the tea was brewed she filled three big mugs, and delivered two to the guest bedrooms. It took a further hour, enough to almost derail her schedule, before the two were up, dressed and ready to go. She was planning to drive Natasha to the tube station, and then drop Mira off at Stardust Brands on her way to the Lords, where she might find some peace to finish her notes.

But as the threesome emerged bleary-eyed into the street towards the residents' parking spaces Suzannah heard a scream. She looked up from her handbag where she had been digging for the car keys, to see Mira leaning distraught against Natasha, who was steadying her. 'Oh God, not again!' she wailed.

'What's the matter?' Suzannah asked.

'Mum,' wailed Natasha. 'Look.' She pointed towards the street. Suzannah followed her gaze and saw her own lovely red BMW X4. The vehicle had been completely trashed. There were scratches all over it, the tyres had been let down, and someone had spray-painted *Stuck-up bitch* in foot-high white letters across the bonnet and roof.

'Oh my God,' the baroness breathed.

'Look, look,' Mira squealed, pointing further along the road.

'What?' said Natasha.

'Did you see that car, the silver one?'

'No, I'm a bit busy looking at mine,' Suzannah retorted.

'The driver was dressed up as a Qaeggan!'

'What, really?' said Natasha.

'Yes, really!' shouted Mira. 'A fucking zombie, here! Tash, for God's sake, how can they know I was here?' Mira screeched. 'Am I not safe anywhere?

* * *

ELEVEN DAYS

Two days later, Thad Cobalt convened a Mira strategy meeting. The good news, he said, was that Suressence were still keen to press ahead with a five-year deal, but had cut the upfront fee and back-end loaded the payments over the last two years.

'Well at least they didn't cancel,' Jonesy said.

'But they have sent us a revised contract with a couple more break and indemnity clauses,' Thad replied. 'We're getting them lawyered now.'

'But we're still in multi-million euro territory I assume?' Jonesy asked.

'Yes, depending if the breaks get triggered. Maximum over five years is still seven million.'

'We can't do anything about it, can we?' said Portia.

'Nah, we can't really,' said Jonesy. 'Meanwhile we're running a big problem with overheads. I've got a PR agency pumping out positive material about Mira, trying to drown out the shitstorm on Twitter and Facebook, and we've employed a graffiti removal agency that knows who to speak to at London Underground, Network Rail and other places to get us a rapid result. They've promised they can get it scrubbed off within forty-eight hours of appearance. But Portia, Kelly and I are still run ragged dealing with the social media side.'

'Virgil, how is Mira feeling?'

'Under siege. The last occurrence really threw her.' Virgil explained about the vandalism on the car. 'I have no idea how they could have found her there so quickly.'

'What do the police say?'

'Well, there is some luck. The CCTV gives only partial coverage, but it was good enough to show a woman in light hooded top, puffa jacket and jeans vandalising the car at about 4am. A second camera shows her getting into a silver car, and when her hood goes down she is indeed wearing Qaeggan make-up. But there is no image of the registration number. Still, it does fit with Mira having claimed to see a zombie drive off.'

Jonesy suppressed a laugh, and shook his head. 'Can't hardly believe it. Night of the effing zombies.'

'Why would someone who vandalises a car in the dead of night wait around until the morning?' Portia asked.

'Maybe to see the reaction of the victim?' Thad said.

'The cops were puzzled how anyone would know that the car is linked to Mira,' Virgil said. 'The only identification mark in it is the Parliamentary Car Park pass, which potentially links it to the baroness.'

'Oh shit,' said Jonesy. 'That's all we need.' He was looking down at his phone.

'What's happened now?' Portia asked.

'That girl who drowned last week in Essex? Turned out she was copying Mira's scene in *Village of the Dead*.' He showed the BBC news story to Portia.

…The body of thirteen-year-old Danielle Stevens was found wearing a white nightdress a mile downstream from where she was last seen on the river Roding. Police said they were not looking for anyone else in connection with the incident. A police spokeswoman said that it appeared the girl and her younger sister might have been trying to recreate a scene from the TV series Village of the Dead. 'It seems to have been a tragic accident,' the spokeswoman said…

'Right,' said Jonesy. 'Portia, draft us a statement of sympathy from Mira. I want it good to go to the press in five minutes, ten lines max, including a one-sentence soundbite along the lines of "Mira Roskova was shocked and horrified to hear the news of the tragic death of whatever-her-name-was". I'll get flowers sent to the family privately in her name, and a big floral tribute to be sent to whatever public place they are laying them.'

'We also need a "don't do this at home kids" paragraph,' Thad said. 'The lawyers will insist upon it. As far as we can see, any public liability would sit with the programme makers, but we have to get our marker out there.'

'I'll ring Mira and let her know,' Portia said.

'What's on her schedule today?' Thad asked.

'Nothing until this evening,' Portia said. 'Oh, but then it's a charity gala. I'll check her diary to make sure we don't have anything that might seem insensitive.'

'Get her to wear a black armband,' Jonesy said. 'I'll let Virgil know. Let's hope she doesn't get invited to the funeral. It's hard to refuse, even if it is the wrong sort of publicity.'

* * *

TEN DAYS

Childswicke rang Virgil three days after their lunch. 'I've had a bit of a breakthrough about who Wōdan is.'

'That was quick,' said Virgil. 'I've been trying to get that sort of information out of the West London Mental Health Trust for weeks.'

'Ah, well. It wasn't from them, or from Broadmoor for that matter. Between you and me I know a rather talkative bishop who is interested in reform and rehabilitation. Anyway, I thought you'd like to know that Wōdan actually goes by the name of William Mordant. Which is interesting, isn't it?'

'Is it?' asked Virgil.

'Well, William as we know is Guglielmo in Italian, the Christian name the acid murderer was registered under in Italy. But the surname, well, that's really quite chilling. Mordant, I mean really.'

'Why?'

'It's a little archaic but mordant means caustic, from the French. Mordant wit, and all that. It's the same word used for the nitric acid that engravers use to etch metal. There was an engraving studio next to Mordant's place in Murano, which was where he sourced his acid.'

'A subtle boast by an acid murderer,' Virgil said. 'That's really twisted.'

'I've also got some other news, which you might fear is rather worse. He's going to tribunal in a couple of weeks.'

'Tribunal? What does that mean?' Virgil asked.

'It's a review of his continued detention under section whatever of the Mental Health Act. Basically, if he can persuade enough shrinks that all this marvellous art has made him sane and safe, they will let him out.'

'What!' Virgil said. 'Just like that?'

'Well, probably via a few months in some intermediate security hospital I suppose. But nothing he couldn't abscond from. In two weeks we could have an acid murderer wandering about the place. Lock up your daughters time, eh?'

* * *

NINE DAYS

Virgil was at Stardust Brands before nine the next morning. What Childswicke had told him was gnawing away at him. But as soon as he stepped into the foyer of MacMillan House, Nelson the security guard called him over, and handed him a package from the fan mail agency, marked urgent.

'This came in late last night, but I guess no one called you,' Nelson said.

Following Virgil's instructions last week, the agency was couriering him anything addressed to Mira franked with a mental health postmark, anything written in copperplate, and anything postmarked Peterborough.

Virgil opened the package and found three envelopes inside. Two turned out to be innocuous fan mail. The third was in very neat handwriting, postmarked Wokingham, Berkshire. Virgil opened it and found a plain postcard with a message in Latin, dated three days ago.

O Lydia et toto animo atque invito defectum promisisti mihi respondere velint neque eos.

Once in his office he logged on and typed the message into Google translate.

Dear Lydia, you promised me heart and soul and despite your failure to respond I do mean to get them.

Ten days. Once again a reaffirmation of the website counter. Saturday 25 April. Just over a week from today. It had to be the tribunal. It had to be.

Thad came in, still in his overcoat, hunting for coffee in Kelly's cupboard.

'Thad, I've got to talk to you,' Virgil said.

'Sure,' Thad said. 'About now will be the only time I'll have the bandwidth, I guess. We've got a helluva week coming up.'

'I know. I've seen the schedule. We've got to lighten it up and get her away. She's in imminent danger,' Virgil said.

'Well, I don't know what we can do.' Thad led Virgil into his room and logged onto the system. 'See, she's almost back-to-back for the next two weeks. There's no free play to speak of. What exactly are you concerned about?'

Virgil showed him the latest letter, and reminded Thad of the catalogue of graffiti and damage. 'I think the final straw was someone lying in wait outside the flat where she was staying with Baroness Earl. No one should have known she was there. It's beyond amateurs, Thad. I know budgets are tight, but she needs more security. I can't be with her 24/7.'

'What about the police?'

'It's all been logged, and we've got a sheaf of incident numbers,' Virgil said. 'But the trouble is none of these issues on their own has convinced the Met that there is an organised campaign against her. It's just vandalism, graffiti and vague threats, even when someone got to her own front door. The Met gave me a PCSO as a contact, that's how seriously they've taken it. A hobby bobby. Contrast that with the Manchester police who send two senior detectives down here to interview her over the Lawrence Wall issue.'

'Wall was nearly killed. You can see their point.' Thad stroked his chin. 'How much of this does she know about?' Thad asked, tapping the letter.

'I haven't shown her the last few. I agonised about it, but it didn't seem worth upsetting her unnecessarily. But if this guy is for real, then she has to be told soon. And well before next Monday.'

Thad steepled his hands in front of his mouth and sighed. 'Look. We took you on because we feared a physical attack by Lawrence Wall. Now, I've read that Wall is out of intensive care, but they are trying to sew his Achilles tendon back together. He's on crutches so we don't have anything to fear in that department. Everything else is kinda peripheral.'

'But it's like Jonesy said. Wall's supporters, Internet trolls, twisted fans amongst the Qaeggan, they are all a threat and seem to know where she is. I'd really like to get her abroad for a solid few weeks.'

'How can a guy in Britain's most secure mental hospital possibly get to her?'

Virgil explained about the tribunal. Even though he'd now had a letter from the health trust apologising for any lapses and promising that communication rights would be withdrawn, letters were still arriving with external postmarks. 'He's got allies on the outside. If they can post letters, they can maybe do other things.'

Thad blew a sigh. 'Virgil. Look, you can see the immovable commitments in the next week: Monday 7.30pm, Royal Albert Hall, the Charity Gala for PlanetThirst, where she's the UN water envoy. Tuesday 12.30pm for the Art with Conviction auction at Christie's. A five minute introductory speech, for which I might add she is being paid a fortune, followed by a lunch with Ulan Kulchuk and the Bishop of Uxbridge. Then a 3pm helicopter trip to Kulchuk's estate in Bedfordshire to see new exhibition rooms followed by dinner. Wednesday, lunch with software entrepreneur Erik Hing. Friday 2.30pm funeral of Danielle Stevens, which the family pleaded for her to attend. Oh yes, and on Saturday at three a visit to wounded veterans rehabilitation facility with HRH Prince Harry. Next Monday as you know, we've got a meeting with the CEO of Suressence. He's asked to meet her, apparently there's no deal without his personal approval, so it's critically important that she focuses on this. Look, Virgil, you'll be with her on most of these, and most of them are private with very little public access.'

'There is at the funeral, Thad, that's the most worrying.'

'Okay, funeral aside. I mean, it really would seem a monstrous admission of defeat to just shut up shop and hide her, don't you think?'

'Alright, then let's get in extra security.'

Thad spread his arms. 'Virgil, the budget's shot to pieces in light of the cut in the contract value, you know that. I really think you are unnecessarily concerned. Now if you'll excuse me.' He started to pick up the phone. As Virgil left Thad called him. 'Virgil,' he said, hand over the phone mouthpiece, 'we need her to concentrate in the next week, especially with the Suressence bigwigs. Don't tell her about the letters, okay?'

Chapter Twenty-Three

SIX DAYS

It was the day of the PlanetThirst fundraiser at the Albert Hall. Virgil had been so busy on the phone to the organisers, and getting his own walk-around security check booked in that he hadn't had chance to do what he really wanted to. Which was to dig into Mira's school days. Had she known any of the acid-death girls? Had she ever attended Halliday High School in Clitheroe? She would have been a similar age. The stuff on Stardust's own website was pretty thin, referring only to the fact she had lived in 'numerous towns and cities' across the Midlands and North during her teenage years.

He'd managed to squeeze in a ten-minute water cooler meeting with Kelly, who had made her own checks. Kelly said she'd been right back to the CV and other forms filled out when Mira had joined Stardust in 2012, but under secondary education all that had been entered was: 'various.' Stardust had been so keen to get the beauty from *Village of the Dead* signed up that no one much cared about her casual way with forms. Kelly had also googled the school, and found examination lists for GCSEs and A levels, on none of which did Mira's name figure.

'I rang up the school, but they wouldn't disclose past pupil lists under data protection,' Kelly said. 'I also searched the local Clitheroe Advertiser online, in case she'd been in a school orchestra or sports day or something like that. No luck.'

'Of course, she probably wouldn't show up anyway,' Virgil said. 'With her mother being chased by debt collectors, they would have registered under different names each time they moved. That would also preclude voters' register searches too. I guess we've just got to do it the simple way.'

'If you ask her, she'll want to know why. It will only alarm her if she discovers that this stalker in Broadmoor has some chance of getting out.'

'I've got a plan,' Virgil said, finishing up his coffee. All he had to do was wait.

* * *

It was seven o'clock, and reclining in black-tie in a limo gliding through the West End traffic towards the Royal Albert Hall, Virgil felt like a fraudulent version of Prince Charming. Mira was sitting next to him, checking her eye make-up in a hand mirror. She was decked out in a full-length strapless tulle ballgown, designed for her by Versace, whose iridescent kingfisher and aquamarine tints were designed to bring to mind flowing water. On anyone else it would have looked over the top, a fairytale confection, but not on Mira. Her hair, now platinum blonde, was swept up and curled in the style of a forties movie queen, and her swan neck and shoulders looked almost alabaster. Reclining in the corner of the limo's leather seats she conferred style, glamour and grace on everything around her. *My God you're beautiful.* Virgil had almost blurted it out as he showed her into the car, but she had looked into his face and smiled in appreciation to see the sentiment written there anyway.

PlanetThirst had sent a car to bring her to the event where she was due to give a short speech, written by someone else. Virgil realised these precious minutes alone with her in the car would be the only ones for days. He thought hard, and began obliquely.

'It's funny how things affect you when you are a kid. Shocking experiences that sort of change you, know what I mean?' His eyes slid across to her. She was dabbing at the corner of her eye with a mascara brush, and showed no signs of connection so far, so he continued. 'When I was twelve, there was this lad in the class who I used to hang around with. He got stabbed and died in the street just a hundred yards from my house.'

'Did you witness it?' she asked, still tickling the eye.

'No, but the blood stains on the pavement were there for months.'

'That's awful,' she said perfunctorily. The other eye was now getting the mascara treatment.

'Anything like that ever happen to you?' Virgil asked.

'Not really. Well, some girls at my school got murdered, on a trip in Venice.' It was said with such casualness. 'You probably heard of it. There was a big fuss in the papers.'

'What year was that?'

'I really don't remember. Maybe 2005 or 2006? Something like that.'

'Did you know them?'

There was a pause. 'Well, vaguely. They weren't friends, or anything.'

Virgil considered her answer, so casually spun out. 'Were they the ones dissolved in acid?'

Mira had her lipstick out now, reapplying it to her full lips, and then dabbing with a tissue. 'Sadly, yes.' She gave him a curious searching glance. 'This is a strange conversation, Virgil? What's up?' Finally Virgil plucked up the courage to lay his trump card. 'Does the name Jonathan Pearson mean anything to you?'

They locked eyes for what seemed like an age. Her huge dark-rimmed eyes glittered in the reflected shop fronts, impossible to read. 'No, it doesn't. And I'm getting a bit bored with all these questions. Let me tell you something, Virgil. My school days were dull. I was a plain, mediocre swot, who shuttled from one school to another. I don't like to think about those times, because I obviously much prefer my life now. I mean, can you see why?' She spread her arms. *Look at me, just look at me.* Virgil thought of the advice Colonel Forsyth had offered him: remember which way your eyes should face.

Virgil fled from the intensity of her gaze. 'I'm sorry.' But he wasn't. Not at all.

The evening itself went to plan. After giving the speech, which was received politely, Mira's job seemed to be standing around looking beautiful next to officials and philanthropists for the photographers. Virgil had learned that no cause exudes so much merit that adding a famous beauty to the picture won't treble the chance of getting it into a newspaper. The classical concert came next, with the London Philharmonic playing for free, and punters paying fifty pounds a head. At the reception afterwards, Virgil once again noted the portly figure of billionaire Ulan Kulchuk, who steered Mira into a conversation with a group of what looked like Chinese officials. He had to admit, Mira did an excellent job of neither looking bored with the platitudes translated for her, nor alarmed at the close-range ogling which needed no transliteration. It was nearly 11pm when Virgil summoned the car to take Mira on to Ram Dipani's Belgravia home, seemingly her new bolt-hole. The goodbyes were said, Mira was whisked away, and now he was finally free to take the tube to Kelly's place. She had promised him a late-night brandy and 'something to take his mind off the job'. He smiled in anticipation, turned on his phone and checked his messages. There was one from Telegraph journalist Peter Childswicke.

'Glad you got me tonight,' Childswicke said when Virgil called back. He sounded a little tipsy, his voice slurring. 'Bit of a breakthrough on Jonathan Pearson-cum-William Mordant.'

'That's great. What have you found out?'

'I don't know if you've heard of Sir Richard Burbage? Former British Ambassador to Moscow in the 1990s, and now writer of rather overlong spy thrillers. Had a somewhat bibulous evening with him tonight, in which he tried to get us to write a review of his latest plodding potboiler. So I said: quid pro quo, old chap. Told him our suspicions, and he said he did recall that during Yeltsin's time someone by the name of Jonathan Pearson was posted to the Moscow embassy. He had some vaguely junior role in intelligence.'

'It's not an uncommon name,' Virgil observed.

'Ah. But this fellow was a fine artist. Couple of sketches still on the embassy walls somewhere, he believes. Burbage recalls Pearson as a louche fellow, a womaniser, vain, lazy and rather supercilious. Indeed, that was the general opinion in Moscow, though someone back home must have thought highly of him to post him there to begin with. But then Burbage let on the main thing he recalled about Pearson, a phenomenal memory. Burbage once queried the guest list for a dinner which included a new official submitted by the Russian Trade Ministry whom none of them knew. Pearson interrupted, and quoted from memory the entire intelligence file on this former KGB officer, right down to the name of his children, mistresses and the address of his dacha.'

'Amazing. But that doesn't get us very far, I suppose.'

'Well, it does and it doesn't,' Childswicke slurred. 'Burbage reckons that Pearson may be the agent code-named Tarkus, who stole the Black Sea submarine codes in 1992.'

'Now you've lost me,' Virgil said.

'Okay. Recall that after the break-up of the Soviet Union, the Russians were desperate to retain control of the full nuclear deterrent from the Ukrainians who, geographically at least, were entitled to control many nuclear missile silos and most of the Black Sea fleet with its nuclear missile subs. In 1994, Ukraine did actually give up that right, not before a lot of internal struggle within the naval hierarchy. Now, Tarkus tried to get the mechanised codebooks, which generated fresh launch codes every day, and smuggle them out. But actually what he got was different. It was the abort codes, available to the Kremlin, to override launches, obviously essential to make sure that an independent Ukraine could never target their former masters. These weren't freshly generated, and Burbage believes it would have been quite possible for them to have been entirely memorised, potentially giving the UK an ability to abort any Russian missile launch. His belief is reinforced by the fact that Russian sources indicate a female Ukrainian officer was turned to gain access to the codes, and she worked in Moscow, not Odessa or Kiev. Pearson, the charming lothario, would have been an ideal candidate to turn the female officer, and significantly he was removed from Moscow by London by 1995.'

'So if Pearson retired as, what, a twenty-five year old what would have happened to him?'

'Most agents end up in the security industry as consultants. But those who are considered vulnerable to retribution are given a new identity and location. Something like a witness protection programme. Assuming that is they weren't considered suitable material for the espionage hierarchy. If Pearson was Tarkus, his life would certainly be in danger.'

'So it would be safe to say that Pearson wouldn't be a name he would be identified with in civvy street.'

'Indeed. We clearly don't have all the aliases.'

* * *

FIVE DAYS

Ram Dipani's family home in Belgravia was a four-storey end of terrace townhouse, with nine bedrooms, five reception rooms, a library, basement gym, wine cellar and a glass-ceilinged swimming pool on the rooftop. It was also the perfect place to keep Mira safe. Ram was away on business, but his mother enjoyed showing Virgil all the features.

'We bought this from a Russian oligarch in 2009, so it has a panic room with its own air-supply, infra-red cameras front and back and rooftop movement detectors. We don't have a dog, but anyone tampering with door or window locks generates an authentic-sounding dog bark from speakers inside,' said Mrs Dipani.

'That's very impressive,' Virgil said.

'We don't normally have all this stuff set-up, but considering what has happened, we'll get the man from the company to make it shipshape and show you how to operate everything. I think she'll be completely safe. Although I won't always be here myself, we have two members of staff here at all times.'

'That's very kind, Mrs Dipani,' Virgil said.

'So how long will she be staying, may I ask?'

'Only three days. She's got to attend a funeral on Friday for a little girl, and it would look awful to cancel that. Then she's meeting Prince Harry on Saturday to talk to some wounded veterans.'

'Ram is hoping to get her to Mumbai for a month soon after,' Mrs Dipani said.

'That's a great idea,' Virgil responded. 'I wish she could go today.'

* * *

A quarter to midday. Virgil was at Christie's in South Kensington, making a risk assessment ahead of the afternoon's *Art with Conviction* auction. Mira's involvement, as with PlanetThirst, was as an adornment. A brief introduction, then standing around being photographed, and a dinner with the ever-present oligarch Ulan Kulchuk, art collector and admirer. Security was going to be challenging. The ground-floor hall had seating for hundreds, and anyone could come along.

Virgil was accompanied by a bespectacled young man called Tristram Clatterby, who looked about twenty-five but dressed like someone twice his age. Clatterby, a specialist in the Post-War & Contemporary Art department, pointed out that Mira, along with auctioneers and other art officials, had a separate side entrance to the bidding room which buyers could not use. 'Security back here is pretty tight, for obvious reasons,' he breezed. 'Can't have someone wandering off with a hundred-million-pound Modigliani, can we?'

Virgil picked up the brochure and flipped through the list of artists whose work was being sold. 'So you do have some stuff by Wōdan. I was wondering about that.'

'Of course,' said Clatterby. 'He's really hot right now. The thing about him and some of the others is that there is such a clear experiential spice to the oeuvre, and being so recent of course the provenance is rock-solid. Collectors love the idea of a narrative behind the work. But of all the prisoner art I have seen, Wōdan is easily the most collectible.'

'I wonder what sort of man he is?' Virgil said.

Tristram took off his heavy-rimmed spectacles and gestured towards the auditorium. 'Well, you may get the chance to find out. Mr Kulchuk yesterday requested that we find him a seat among the Künzler Trust party.'

'You mean he'll be here, this afternoon?'

Tristram grinned broadly as he guided Virgil up towards the stage, at the back of which several large artworks were kept sheeted. 'Yes indeed, with appropriate security of course. It's all been rather kept under wraps, but Broadmoor has given its approval, we understand. Mr Wōdan is rather keen to see his work being auctioned.'

'But he's a convicted murderer, an evil psychopath!' Virgil exclaimed.

'No doubt, Mr Bliss, no doubt. But, sometimes from out of the darkest abyss a redemptive talent emerges that the world is entitled to see.' With a flourish, Clatterby whipped off a sheet from the nearest artwork, revealing Wōdan's crucifixion triptych.

'Now tell me, Mr Bliss. Don't you think that this is a genius which should be unshackled?'

Virgil was speechless. His eyes were drawn to the female centurion, embracing but impaling the Christ figure. The woman's face was absolutely obvious. It was Mira, definitely. And in just a few hours she was going to come face-to-face with the man who'd painted her.

* * *

322

Virgil's impassioned call to Thad was met by a blank refusal. 'Virgil, there is no way she is going to cry off from this auction. She's contractually obliged to be there. It's a big earner, cash upfront. If she doesn't show, there are break clauses that would cost us thousands.'

'What if we say she's sick?'

Thad took a couple of minutes to look up the small print. 'Nope, as I thought. Feigning sickness doesn't help. The clauses still apply, and the insurance company will only pick up the tab for the break clause if their panel of three independent doctors unanimously agree that she is ill. Virgil. Do *not* tell her. I don't want her getting nervous.'

'But what if she sees him?'

'Virgil. She doesn't *know* the guy, isn't that what she told you? So she won't even recognise him. I really think you are worried about nothing.'

But Virgil was ever more convinced. Mira did know Jonathan Pearson, or whatever his real name was.

* * *

Virgil Bliss was waiting with Tristram Clatterby when Ulan Kulchuk's midnight blue Rolls-Royce drew up, twenty minutes before the auction was due to start. Kulchuk's own bodyguard, a slender and saturnine Israeli called Nome, guided Mira out. She was dressed in figure-hugging black flared trousers with a bolero jacket over a white frilly blouse. Her hair, now back to its natural chestnut shade, was piled high to display five-inch long platinum earrings, encrusted with emeralds, matching a pendant around her neck. She and Kulchuk stopped for photographers on the steps, with him standing one step above in a vain attempt to cancel out the height difference.

'Nice earrings,' Virgil said, as he fell into step beside her.

'A present from Ulan,' she whispered.

Virgil wondered what Mira's new boyfriend Ram Dipani would make of this act of generosity. Kulchuk was supposedly going through a messy divorce but clearly had time and money enough for grand gestures in other directions. Tristram led them all to an anteroom, where Mira was offered coffee and cake while Kulchuk went off to make arrangements. Virgil left Mira there for a moment, and slipped past a curtain into the auction room. It was now quite full, not just of the well-dressed and well-to-do as Virgil had expected, but a much broader range of the public. There were plenty of press too. Those registered to bid could be identified by the numbered paddles on their laps. Along the front a bank of telephones were manned by suited young men and women, ready for bids from foreign buyers, and there was a screen above the auctioneer's podium which gave bid values in six different currencies. Virgil had earlier seen the Künzler Trust seats, towards the back on the left-hand side. Though he could see the Bishop of Uxbridge, obvious from the maroon shirt and dog collar, and a rather elderly man next to him, there were still three unclaimed seats in the row behind.

As he watched, three people walked in together from the back. A very big grey-haired man, bearded, in a shapeless suit, then a blond man in a sports jacket and white trousers, and finally a statuesque black woman in a trouser suit. As they crossed the aisle to sit, a good twenty rows from the front, Virgil glimpsed a circlet of black around the ankle of the man in the middle: perhaps an electronic tag. Yet he could easily have passed as a Christie's official or a wealthy buyer. He was poised and dapper, the clothes well-tailored, the shoes polished. Wōdan. William Mordant. Jonathan Pearson. Acid murderer and artist. A man seemingly obsessed with Mira.

The auction was due to start in five minutes. Virgil walked up the aisle towards the Künzler Trust group. The bishop was talking to the man to his left, and Virgil's eyes instead made contact with Mordant. He smiled at Virgil as if they were already acquainted.

'And how is Ms Roskova today?' he asked.

Mordant smiled at Virgil's hesitation. 'Oh, don't worry, I've seen your face in some of the newspaper coverage. On the way to visit that poor footballer, I've forgotten his name, in hospital. Then at the Albert Hall. My name is Wōdan.'

'So you are a keen follower of Mira?'

Mordant laughed. 'Metaphorically only. But tell me, do you enjoy protecting such an exquisite beauty? Do you not suffer... temptations?'

'I'm a professional,' Virgil said. 'And everything that comes with it.'

'So, it's hands off for you, eh?' Mordant chuckled.

Virgil ignored the question, and caught the eye of the black woman. 'Oh, this is my own security assistant, Hope Trenchtown', Mordant said, with a twinkle in his eye. 'And next to me is my head of security, Geoffrey Featherstone.'

'Virgil Bliss,' Virgil said, reaching out to shake the meaty arm Featherstone held out.

'I wouldn't listen to any of his nonsense,' Featherstone said, tipping his head towards Mordant. 'We're here to keep him in order. He doesn't get out much. But some of these are his paintings. We're hoping to break the million-quid barrier.' He gestured towards the front, where the auctioneer was now taking his place.

Virgil headed back to his allocated seat at the side, where he could keep an eye on the audience. A Christie's official made an introduction, then Mira emerged from behind the curtain and walked to the podium. After the strobe-storm of flash photography had finished, and the applause had died down, she read a speech. She welcomed the considerable interest generated in *Art with Conviction* among buyers, and stressed how important the money raised was to further the cause of rehabilitation and victim support. Throughout her delivery, Virgil saw no sign that she had spotted Wōdan, until near the end. 'Particular thanks are due to the Künzler Trust, the Bishop of Uxbridge and Mr Ulan Kulchuk for having made the event possible...' she said, gesturing towards the seats where they were sitting. She blinked, open-mouthed, and then froze. She jerked her head down to the papers in front of her, frowning. 'So ladies and gentlemen, I would just like to...just like to...um.'

For a moment, Mira seemed suspended in mid-air, her head adrift on that long neck, her eyes drifting up behind her eyelids. Even as the crowd gasped, Virgil was already off his seat, but not quickly enough to catch her. Mira banged her head on the wooden podium as she slid to the floor, knocking off microphone and papers. Virgil shouted for a doctor, then knelt by her side, slipped off his jacket and placed it underneath her head. A crowd gathered around him, and as the hubbub intensified Virgil felt he should move her somewhere safer. Her eyelids fluttered, and she murmured something.

'Mira, Mira, wake up,' Virgil said, kneeling by her side. Someone passed him a glass of water. He looked up and saw the faces of Tristram Clatterby and Ulan Kulchuk.

'You need to get everyone back, give her space,' Virgil said, scanning the faces above for the one he most feared to see. Mordant wasn't there, but his minder, Hope Trenchtown, was. 'I'm a nurse,' she said. She knelt down by Virgil's side and asked for his help getting Mira into the recovery position. Hope unbuckled the six-inch heeled Manolo Blahnik's from Mira's feet. 'Ridiculous shoes,' she muttered. They then shifted her gently, so she lay on her side, supported by one arm and one leg.

Over the PA, Christie's announced a half hour delay to proceedings, and many of the buyers began to drift away for refreshments.

Finally, Mira stirred. 'Oh, I'm so sorry. Did I faint?'

'Yes, honey, you did,' Hope said. 'Quite spectacular, a real *Swan Lake* job. But you're going to be just fine now,' she smiled.

Mira sat wonkily on the steps of the stage, giving Virgil the chance to stand and look for Mordant. Just a few yards away stood the bearded guard Geoff Featherstone, clearly doing exactly the same. He hurried past Virgil. 'Hope!' he shouted. 'Hope? Is he with you?'

Hope looked up, puzzled. 'I left him with you.'

Virgil grabbed Featherstone by the arm. 'You've not lost him, have you?'

Featherstone shook his arm free. 'Not yet I haven't.' He lurched off towards the entrance.

Mira was still woozy, so Virgil bent down and picked her up. She seemed to weigh nothing. He whirled around to Kulchuk. 'Can you get your car to the loading bay straightaway. We need to get her out of here.'

'To hospital? Is she still sick?' the Kazakh asked.

'We just need her away from here, right now. I'll explain later.'

Kulchuk nodded, looked up and clicked his fingers. The bodyguard Nome appeared as if from nowhere, and Kulchuk gave him rapid instructions. Tristram Clatterby led Virgil through a back corridor and into his office, a high-ceilinged den of books and artefacts. Virgil set Mira down on a large green leather wing chair.

'Mira, listen to me. William Mordant has escaped. He's here in the building, and may well try to get to you. I need you to be honest for once, and tell me what you know about this guy. I can't protect you if you don't cooperate with me.'

Mira buried her head in her hands as if about to cry, but made no sound. She stood, chewing her carefully manicured nails, her dark brows freighted with worry. To Virgil she seemed like a churlish teenager contemplating an exam for which she had done not a minute's revision. Nome walked in, and announced in a thick accent that the car was in the loading bay. Virgil thanked him, and hurried Mira out of the room, his arm supporting her. As Nome held the door open, Virgil noticed a bulge in his jacket under the armpit. A shoulder holster, it could be nothing else. Mira clearly wasn't the only person with enemies.

As they led her out to the loading bay, Clatterby took Virgil aside and asked him a question. 'I overheard that Wōdan has disappeared. Is that true?'

Virgil allowed himself a grim chuckle. 'Yes, and it's pretty serious. Wōdan is William Mordant, the acid vat murderer.'

Clatterby's face distended in horror.

'Yep,' Virgil said. 'He dissolved three schoolgirls in a vat of acid back in 2005. And he's desperate to get his hands on Mira. Perhaps some geniuses should never be unshackled.'

Clatterby's jaw hung open. No words emerged.

Chapter Twenty-Four

William Mordant was amazed it had been so easy. He'd feasted his eyes on the real-life Mira Roskova, so grown up now from all those years ago, and every bit as perfect in the flesh as he had hoped. But he'd had no idea she would faint when she saw him again, what a bonus. Perhaps she finally realised that her destiny was catching up with her. Slipping away in the chaos hadn't been hard. Hope, God bless her, had rushed to help. Featherstone had been distracted, standing up to get a better view, leaving his jacket hanging on the back of his chair. It had been the work of a moment to take the wallet from inside. Then to ease himself away, and out of the auction salon. But one could forgive them both their incompetence, their lack of preparedness. Who would expect the artist to abscond *before* the auction at which his life's work was to be sold? Especially a man who had never given a moment's trouble during his entire time in Broadmoor.

Mordant had slipped out of Christie's and taken a side street away from Old Brompton Road and its many CCTV cameras.

Five minutes brisk walk and he emerged on the Fulham Road, parallel but further south. It was raining. He went into a charity shop and using Featherstone's cash bought a battered raincoat, a threadbare deerstalker and a scarf, which he put on. He then found a hardware store, bought a pair of secateurs and ducked into a pub nearby to go into the toilet and snip off the plastic bracelet of the electronic tag. It took surprisingly little leverage. He knew that by now his absence would have been reported, and the monitoring centre would be tracking the tag's movements on GPS. Time for a little fun. He took a bus to Buckingham Palace Road, and at Victoria coach station saw a queue of people waiting to board a bus to Edinburgh. He engaged a pretty Chinese student in conversation, and then while pointing out some sights worth seeing on her map, slid the tag into her backpack. That would be good for a twelve-hour Scottish jig in the hunt to find him.

Now he had a few chores to sort out. The equipment he needed was in a lock-up garage in Stoke Newington, and would be no more than a couple of hours work. Still, it would certainly make them take him seriously.

He was already confounding their expectations. They would assume he would take the first opportunity to get close to Mira. That was to underestimate him. He was still sure they didn't have any idea of the insidious umbilical from all those years ago that linked Mira to him. He didn't need to go to her. When the time was right, Mira would come to him.

* * *

Mordant remembered so clearly the first day he saw her. It was 2005. He was on his second week of supply teaching in the art department at Halliday High School, Clitheroe. One of the better schools in the area, and one which took its art teaching seriously. He was still getting used to the new identity that had been given to him at the retirement debrief six months before. John Peirce was his name. It was similar enough to Jonathan Pearson, the name under which he'd been assigned to Moscow, and under which he'd lived for the previous four years. He was on break duty, a windy March day, invigorating gusts from the Irish sea with a hint of rain. A group of boys, hulking shambling creatures, uniforms ripped and collars awry, were loitering behind the communal bin shed with an air of purpose. That was something these fellows exhibited only during mischief. Mordant moved for a better view, and saw they were casually but methodically twisting the arm of a smaller fellow. From the moment of his first teaching post, a dismal East London comprehensive, he had seen many such scenes. The smaller boy, presumably the possessor of cigarettes, money or pornography, had his face twisted in exaggerated agony as he was parted from his property. How perfectly even the most stupid children ingest the DNA of gangsterism: extortion, threats, ritual and public punishment, obedience, and – most important of all – silence to authority.

Then there were the victims. Here was one now, a year-eight female, Lydia Roskova, even newer to the school than he. She was probably just thirteen, coltishly leggy, pretty beneath her cheap and grim spectacles, scurrying through the playground with an A3-size art exercise book gripped in her hands. At yesterday's assembly, three girls had been excoriated by the housemaster for scorching her rather lovely wavy chestnut hair with a lighter. She still had a bandage on her neck. The wrong accent, spots, being tall and studious as well as new, she hardly stood a chance. No wonder she was crying.

'Lydia Roskova. Come here.' He beckoned her over. Her shoulders slumped at the summons, and she slouched over, wiping her face with the back of her hand. The unfashionably conservative hemline of her blue uniform pinafore dress, the scuffed flat shoes and the droopy socks gave her a gangling clownish air.

'What's the matter, girl?'

'Nothing.' Lydia flushed scarlet, unable to meet his gaze.

'It can't be nothing. You're crying.' He smiled at her.

'It's nothing, Sir.' She was gripping the exercise book as if her life depended on it.

'Show me.' He put out his hand. Reluctantly she handed him the book. Past her indifferent homework attempts, on the first hitherto empty page, someone had scrawled a large cartoonish version of her face, daubed in spots with huge glasses and goofy teeth. It was labelled 'Hideous Lydia'. She started sobbing, her body wracked with shudders.

'Come along,' he said. He took her into the art block, and sat her on a chair in the classroom. The smell of floor polish, poster paint and Copydex glue wafted into his nostrils.

'Do you know who did it?'

Lydia swallowed her lips, as if they might otherwise speak of their own volition. She shook her head slowly.

'I think you do.'

Lydia shook her head, and tears slid slowly down her face.

'You're certainly not ugly, you must know that.'

She looked up at him, as if seeking confirmation. Her eyes were a startling pea green.

'Do you know the work of Botticelli?'

She shook her head.

'I don't suppose you've ever had the chance to go to the Uffizi Gallery in Florence.'

'No, Sir.' She looked distracted and uncomfortable. Keen to escape.

'Well, Botticelli was a renaissance master who managed to capture timeless female beauty in his work.' He went over to a chalk-covered cupboard, took out a bunch of keys and unlocked it. He pulled a thick and heavy book *The Florentine Masters* from underneath a pile of papers. 'Let's see.' He flicked through carefully. Finding what he was looking for, he carefully turned the book so that Mira could see it. 'This is La Primavera. What do you see in it?'

'It's a load of women under some trees, Sir.'

He sighed heavily.

'I think they're apple trees. And it's evening time,' she said brightly.

'But what does it *mean*?'

'Dunno, Sir.'

'It means Spring, and is full of meaning about fertility, beauty and potential.'

'Sir, I'm going to be late for music.'

'You can borrow this if you like.'

'Why?'

'Why? You ask why! Because you are there. In this painting, scattering petals of perfection before an unseeing world.'

'It's heavy, Sir.'

'I suppose it is.' He hefted the tome, and shrugged agreement. 'The burden of beauty was ever thus. Never mind, girl. On your way.'

She might be plain now, but he could see what she would become. It was there in her cheekbones, the symmetry and angle of her eyes, her neck. Small signs, which the rest of the world didn't yet see. This girl was destined for beauty. But even he never imagined the stellar trajectory that destiny would take.

Chapter Twenty-Five

It was ten to midnight, and the rain was lashing down in St John's Wood. Runnels crawling down the windows and bouncing up from the roads. Baroness Suzannah Earl was getting ready for bed when she heard the text tone vibrate on her phone.

Im here 4u. let me in.

It wasn't from a number she recognised. But she looked out of the window. Across the street, in the glare of a streetlamp, she recognised him. Despite the deerstalker, the rain-darkened macintosh, there was an unmistakeable poise. How could he be here? He wasn't even supposed to be out. Had he escaped? Or had he absconded from an escorted trip? Part of her thought: phone the police, now, quickly. For God's sake, this man *dissolves* girls in acid. But the fact he had come here, to her, showed trust. He was a man besieged by mistrust, yet he had come to her. How could she betray him? When the buzzer went, she pressed the outside door release. Two minutes later she went to the door of her flat and opened it. He was standing there, drenched. He pushed the door open and walked in without waiting for an invitation. Water ran down his face and his jacket was soaked.

'You can't stay here, Will. You can't. It's impossible.'

'Suzy, I need your help.' In a second he was enfolding her in his arms, kissing her neck. 'Suzy, they are never going to let me out. The tribunal will be a farce. I'll die in there. Despite all your efforts it isn't going to work.'

'Look, Will, I'll fight for you. God knows I have already laid myself body and soul on the line in the cause. But you can't stay here.'

'Just one night, Suzy. Just one night. I promise.'

'No Will, it would be the end of me. Think about it. I'm a politician acting from a principle, not some lovelorn girlfriend.'

He stared at her, those mesmerising eyes, almost violet in her hall light. 'Suzy, that is precisely why no one would think of looking for me here. I'll be gone by six tomorrow morning. That's a promise.'

She searched his eyes. 'Okay, Will, I'm trusting you. But they will track you down, you know. You can't escape in the end.'

'Perhaps. But even if they find me here, your reputation will not be hurt. You could say that I held you hostage. I'm supposedly a dangerous psychopath after all, for whom human life has no value. No one would disbelieve you. They would never guess that I was drawn to you by the trust, the kindness and the desire that you kindled in me....'

He held her fiercely and kissed her, his lips and tongue running up and down her neck. His wet face and clothes soaked into her blouse, water from his hair ran down between her breasts. As he leaned her against the wall she heard herself begin to moan his name. He's right, she thought. One unforgettable night, for which I have the perfect excuse. I am the one woman who means something to him. I have created his pathway to freedom. He whispered in her ear what he was going to do to her, and she thrilled to the idea. 'Do it to me. Now.'

She didn't know whether it was two hours later or ten. It was still dark outside. The lamp on the bedside table was on, and he was lying naked, on one elbow, looking at her as she caught her breath. She saw the faint slick of sweat on his chest, flexing in the slow rhythm of his breath. 'You're an amazing lover, Will. But you don't have to catch up on all those years of enforced abstinence in one night, do you?'

'Don't I?' He smiled, the kind of smile that said: I know I'm good, but I still enjoy being told. 'Let's have a bath,' he said.

He helped her out of bed, still floaty and tingling. The en-suite light was already on. He ran the water while she sat on the linen basket and watched his muscular form, firm buttocks, defined stomach muscles, his cock softened but still swollen, slick with her juices.

He put out his arms, and lowered her into the warm water. Standing at the side of the bath he soaped her body carefully, her breasts and neck and legs. Then he sat on the linen basket, leaning over the side of the bath as he rinsed her petite form.

Mordant squeezed some shampoo into his hand and worked it into her copper hair, sliding his fingers into the tresses. Then as he rinsed her gently, he noticed at the ivory scalp just a few millimetres of iron-grey roots showing. A wave of revulsion swept through him. *This won't do. Not at all.* He knew there was only so long that he could pretend, when the only real perfect beauty was still out there, beckoning him. He slid her head further up the slope of the bath until it crested on the rim. He supported her extended head with his right hand, gently lowering it so her long, slender throat was exposed. With his left hand he caressed the full length of her body, from groin via tummy, breasts and clavicle to her neck. Her eyelids were fluttering in pleasure. He closed his own eyes, trying to recollect exactly the instruction book from all those years ago. There it was, page 61, with the diagrams, the text, but it was the exact vertebra that he needed to know. Where to apply the pressure, C_1 or C_2? He speed-read the words in his cavernous mind, and when satisfied let a small smile escape. She murmured his name and her eyes opened, lazy with pleasure, and trust. With his fingers he counted her neck vertebra, and finding the second, eased her head just a shade lower.

He took a deep breath, removed his left hand from her body and held her jaw shut. The final movement took less than half a second, before the scream had time to form. A twist of the head sharply left towards him, produced a sharp 'pop' and a gasp from the baroness. Then he knelt on her chest with one knee, and with all his strength snapped her head back and down, using the edge of the bath as a fulcrum. The loud crack of the vertebra parting masked the shrill animal noise from her. Her eyes were open; shocked but lifeless.

Mordant laid her carefully in the bath, drained the water, then towelled himself dry as he walked into the kitchen. He took an apple from the fruit bowl and examined it. The skin was mottled a beautiful polished red with striations of green. A Braeburn? Or a Discovery? The refectory at Broadmoor had only ever stocked the insipid Golden Delicious, despite his requests. He bit into the apple. It was crisp and tasty. He chewed carefully, and hummed to himself as he walked around the flat. Now to get to work on Lady Earl's mobile phone and computer. As her daughter was apparently one of Mira's best friends, it shouldn't be hard to lure them here.

* * *

FOUR DAYS

Richard Lamb wasn't looking forward to what he had to do today, but it was inevitable. Dawn Evans came in, looking for all the world like a dog dragged to the vet to be put down. Professionally, he supposed, that was just what was going to happen. She had been a very promising and enthusiastic nursing assistant, only her lack of guile had let her down. But then who was equal to William Mordant? He offered her a seat and took off his glasses. She was rubbing the backs of her hands and looking in her lap, unable to make even the semblance of eye contact.

'Dawn, a very serious matter has come to my attention. As you will be aware, William Mordant has absconded. When searching his room yesterday evening, we found some items.'

She nodded, and reached for the handkerchief that was up her sleeve. A slow sniffing began.

Lamb opened a large manila envelope and fished out a card. It was a Valentine's Day card, wreathed in hearts. He decided not to read out what was written inside, to embarrass her with the gushing endearments. He pushed it across the desk towards her. 'Did you write this?'

Dawn Evan's eyes, brimming with tears, flicked briefly up to look at the card. Her head sagged as if her neck had suddenly failed. She nodded, and whispered an emotion-choked 'yes'.

'It seems from the…er…sentiments written inside that you have formed an emotional attachment to this patient. Is that true?'

She nodded again.

'Then there are all these.' Lamb upended the envelope, out of which slid dozens of cards, a tiny teddy bear, and finally a homemade embroidered silken heart with a few words neatly stitched across it: *Will. I'll love you forever.*

'All yours, yes?'

Dawn nodded.

'That is bad enough. But since this discovery I have taken the liberty of checking the camera footage outside Mordant's room, and discovered that you visited him alone at night, in contravention of all regulations, on at least five occasions in the last month.'

Her head jerked up, and she looked confused.

'Dawn, you seem surprised that we know this. Are you?'

She hesitated. 'He said that the C corridor cameras didn't work.'

'He, meaning Mordant?' Lamb steepled his hands.

She didn't reply.

'Dawn. How long has this been going on? Your affair with him.'

'Six months. Six months on Wednesday,' she said.

'I'm sorry to have to ask this, but did these trysts involve activity of a sexual nature.'

There was a long silence. 'We made love, if that's what you mean,' she murmured.

Lamb shook his head. 'Dawn, for goodness sake! You have been on the courses, the training for this. You know *exactly* the kind of manipulative and antisocial personality Mordant has.'

'I do know what he's really like, but actually *you* don't,' she said, suddenly fixing an intense gaze on him. 'Will is a good man, a kind man. He should never have been here at all. He has never killed anyone. He swore on his life.'

'Well,' Lamb said, leaning back and taking off his reading glasses. 'His ability to lie convincingly isn't really in doubt, is it?'

'He loves me.' She said it flatly, as if trumping the argument.

Lamb restrained the snort of derision that he wanted to express. 'I doubt it very much, Dawn. You were useful to him, that's all. Now in less than an hour the police will be here to question you in the light of your relationship with him.'

'Why?'

'Well, you might have helped him set up a life outside, ready for his absconding. If you have smuggled anything in or out for him, provided him with a place to stay, or any similar help it would be much better to volunteer it now to me, rather than wait to have the truth dragged out of you by the police.'

She said nothing.

Lamb sucked his teeth in exasperation, and looked out of the window, across the wire fences of his domain. 'Look, Dawn. I decided to do this informally, rather than go through the full formal procedure of a security inquiry. I think it will be a little easier for you, though no doubt it isn't going to be easy per se.'

'Thank you, Dr Lamb,' she murmured.

Lamb's voice was low but grave. 'I have two specific questions. One. Was Mordant to your knowledge involved in the assault on Leonard Lucifer Smith?'

She didn't reply, but nodded her head.

'As I suspected. And two. Did you ever allow him access to the security control room?'

No reply.

'If you did, that would constitute a very serious criminal offence.'

Her voice was almost inaudible. 'I didn't.'

'Hmm. I have my doubts about that answer.' He leaned back, and put his hands behind his head. 'I'm not an idiot, Dawn. I do understand the reality. William Mordant is a very attractive and extraordinarily clever man. You are not the first member of staff to fall for such a dangerously charismatic patient. I'm sure you won't be the last, despite all our precautions. There is much about him that remains to be discovered, which makes him all the more dangerous.'

'So I'm going to be sacked?' Dawn sobbed, suddenly losing the last shreds of control.

'Well, you can hardly continue to work here, can you? What you have done isn't just a breach of regulations, it's an act of sexual abuse against someone in your care.'

'Abuse? No, it wasn't like that...'

'Our patients are classified as vulnerable adults. You were the responsible party. And whatever it seemed to you, the rules are clear that it was you who abused the relationship of professionalism and trust which should exist between you and your patient. It's a criminal offence, and if found guilty you will be put on the sex offenders' register.'

Dawn Evans was in floods of tears now. 'No, no, that's not true,' she wailed.

'Well, did he assault you at any time, or force you?'

She considered for a moment, then shook her head. 'No.'

'Did he ever do anything to you that was not consensual?'

She thought for a moment. 'No.'

'Then you have no defence, have you?'

Dawn Evans hung her head so low that she looked like a broken doll. Mordant's plaything, used up and abandoned.

He turned to his papers. 'I'm afraid my hands are tied on this. We have to suspend you for gross misconduct, and once the police have finished you will be escorted from the premises today.'

Dawn Evans began to wail like a child.

Lamb handed her a paper handkerchief. 'Now, this isn't yet a dismissal. You are entitled to a later meeting to which you can bring along a representative either from the union or a lawyer, or a friend, before this is formalised as dismissal, if you think any part of this process has been unfair. Here are all the leaflets that detail your rights.' He handed her a sheaf of brightly coloured pamphlets. 'However, I would greatly appreciate it if we could do this in a circumspect manner. An employment tribunal would be a public event, and your name and that of Broadmoor would undoubtedly suffer the scouring of an unsympathetic press. If we could informally make that agreement, I will happily extend your notice period so you get paid two more months.'

There was no reply. He glanced up at her, a small, nervous and desperate figure. 'Do you have any questions?'

She nodded. 'Once he's recaptured, can I apply to visit him?'

Only then did Lamb understand the depth of the hold that Mordant had over her, how the loss of her job, the stigma, the shame, the criminal record were nothing compared to the realisation that she would never see him again.

'Dawn,' he said, 'I have tried to save your feelings, but you have to wake up. We found this with the other stuff. It's obviously nothing but a piece of fantasy. Nonetheless, Mordant doesn't care about you. His thoughts are elsewhere.'

He showed her a cream envelope, addressed to the director, and already opened. She slid out an invitation card, on whose reverse was a message written in Mordant's copperplate.

Richard. Sorry to have to rush off like this, but I'm getting married next week. I would love to have stayed for the tribunal, but needs must!

On the front of the envelope was embossed a title:

Wedding invitation

*Mr William Mordant and Miss Lydia Mira
Nikolayevna Roskova*

Saturday 25 April 2015

Midnight

Venue TBA

Dawn Evans picked up the card and her face darkened and hardened, changing shape before his eyes. 'The bastard!' She tore the card in two. And then put the pieces together and ripped them in two again, her jaw set. She stood up, glared at Lamb and said: 'I take it you have finished with me now?' She was about to throw the fragments of card into his face, then thought better of it. Instead she put them back in the envelope, stowed it in her bag, and stalked out, slamming the door.

The moment she left, Lamb picked up the phone to Geoff Featherstone. Someone should make sure she hadn't retained any keys.

* * *

Dawn Evans slammed every door in the corridor as she strode towards the staffroom. Muttering to herself she almost bowled over another nurse as she tore down the stairs. How *could* he spurn her love, her affection and all the risks and sacrifices she had made for his happiness? How could he be so deluded as to even imagine marrying some world famous model who hadn't even heard of him? She went to her desk, unlocked the drawers and dumped her possessions, her casework, the mug with its kitten on the side, and her spare shoes all into one cardboard box. She tried to log onto her computer, but it flashed a message: access denied. She rushed, because she now knew there was something important to do before the police arrived. She grabbed a jotter pad and wrote a short, anonymous but very informative note. She folded it, put it in the envelope with the pieces of Mordant's wedding invitation, and slid it into her trouser pocket. She then headed for Cavendish Ward. She passed through three security doors, relieved that the access combinations hadn't yet been changed. This took her into a corridor she hadn't visited since the night of the six-man unlock, all those weeks ago. She then slid the envelope under the door of Lunatic Lucy's room.

* * *

THREE DAYS

Leonard Lucifer Smith was sitting in a wheelchair in Broadmoor's staff car park, waiting to go to Frimley Park Hospital to assess progress since his operation. Two uniformed security staff, Roger and Phil, manoeuvred the chair onto the disabled lift at the back of the plain white van, and when it was up, secured him inside. Lucy scrutinised them. Roger, the driver, with a florid face and white beard, was like a tattooed

Santa. Phil with cropped dark hair and a broken nose, more like a bouncer. Hefty blokes gone to seed in middle age, the typical screw physique. Easy meat if he decided to kick off. But they were talking over him like he didn't exist. Anyone in a wheelchair, well, they can't be much trouble, can they? They probably thought he couldn't walk. Well, he could. It hurt a bit. But he could do it. If he needed to.

On the night of the razor wire, they had eight screws with him down at A&E. Now just two. A complete loss of respect, that's what it was, despite the handcuffs they still kept on him. Still, in the two months since, much had changed. The whispers in his head that GCHQ was monitoring his thoughts had gone quiet. He'd stopped nicking kitchen foil from the Broadmoor nosh-house to line his room against radio messages. The shrink, Kasovas, was delighted at the progress he was making and had complimented him on not refusing a single day's medication in the weeks since the attack. But it wasn't the drugs, it was something in his head. It was almost as if he knew that he was now going to get a mission in life. And then, just yesterday, like a message from God it had arrived.

Dear Lucy,

I would like you to know that your injury was inflicted on you by William Mordant. Now he's absconded I'm sure you have friends outside who can trace him, and perhaps this invitation will help.

an anonymous friend

The great thing about all this was that Lucy had a very good idea where Mordant would choose to get married. And, with any luck, he would be there waiting for him.

* * *

Virgil had arrived as arranged, and was kept waiting in the cold outside the baroness's apartment block. The buzzer wasn't being answered, and neither was her phone. He was just about to ring Natasha when he saw her walk around the corner towards him. She said that he could wait inside until her mother arrived. 'Where's Mira?' Natasha asked.

'She's safe. She's staying with Ram's family in Belgravia for a couple of nights. It's pretty secure there. I'll be staying there as well for the next few nights, but I had arranged to meet your mother to find out more about this mental patient who escaped.'

'Ah yes, William Mordant. Do you think he'll stalk her?'

'I don't doubt it,' Virgil said as they waited for the lift.

Once in the lift, Natasha started working her phone. 'I'm just texting mum to remind her that you're here. It's unlike her to be late.'

They exited on the third floor, and walked the short distance to the apartment. Natasha unlocked the front door, and called out as they walked in. No reply. She wandered into the kitchen to put coffee on, after showing Virgil into the large and comfortable lounge. Virgil absorbed the various art works, one of which seemed to be a large drawing of the baroness, nude, wet-haired and apparently asleep draped over a settee. In fact it looked very much like the settee he was sitting on. Come to think of it, the cushion where he was sitting did feel damp. He stood up, and felt his trousers. Natasha came in and saw him prodding the seat cushion.

'What's up?' she asked.

'The seat's wet.'

'Really?' She prodded the seat. It was quite damp. Then she turned around and stood still. 'Oh. She's got a new drawing. It's another Wōdan. Look.'

Virgil looked back at the drawing. 'It can't be one of his, can it?'

'It looks like his others. I know the style by now,' Natasha said, sipping her coffee.

'But she's posing on this settee,' Virgil said. 'It's got the pattern, and the coffee table.'

Virgil looked at her saw her eyes widen. He took the framed picture off the wall, rested it on the coffee table and tried to read the signature which was partially obscured by the large frame.

'He's been here,' Virgil said. 'In the last twenty-four hours, with her.'

Natasha looked again at the drawing, then picked up her phone and rang her mother's number. It went to voicemail. 'I'm really worried,' she said. Virgil watched the fears tumble down her face, fears that would inevitably lead to the conclusion that he had just come to. Asleep in the drawing? Or dead.

* * *

Five miles from Frimley, Lucy announced he needed a toilet, and no, it couldn't wait. They whinged and complained, but Roger eventually stopped at a petrol station, and reversed round the back of the payment kiosk, up to the toilet. He and Phil unloaded him, and wheeled him past the jet wash and tyre air bay into the large disabled cubicle.

'Right. There you are. You going to be alright then, mate?' Phil asked.

'Fine and dandy, assuming you're happy to wipe my arse for me,' Lucy said, holding up his handcuffed wrists.

'Bloody hell! I told you we should have brought the closeting chain,' Phil said, referring to the ten foot chain which allowed a secured patient to preserve their privacy inside a toilet cubicle. 'But, no, you said it's just a short journey, he won't need it.'

'Alright, smartarse. Unlock him,' Roger said. 'It'll be okay.'

Phil got the keys from his belt and unlocked the cuffs, then turned to go. 'You're going to have to lift me on,' Lucy said. 'And close the fucking door. I need some privacy.'

'Jesus Christ,' Roger said. He closed the door, shooting an exasperated glance at Phil. They wheeled him next to the toilet bowl, bent over to get a lift under his legs, while Lucy put one huge arm around the neck of each. Just as they were about to lift he smashed their heads together as hard as he could. Phil hit the floor, out cold, while Roger needed to have his face smacked hard into the floor a couple of times to still his cries. Kneeling on the floor, Lucy grabbed them by the throat, a thumb hard on each Adam's apple as they came round. 'Make a sound, fill a coffin. Understand?' Their terrified eyes signalled agreement. He stripped them of phones and radios, got them to undress to their underwear, made Roger spread-eagle face down, and got Phil to handcuff him, arms behind. Then he handcuffed Phil, back-to-back and upside down against Roger. He balled their socks, stuffed them into their mouths, holding them in place with shoelaces tied tight around their heads. He then took Roger's second set of cuffs, pushed Phil's bare feet either side of one armrest of the wheelchair, and cuffed them together, so he couldn't move without taking the chair with him. He gathered up all keys, wallets, coins, which he wrapped up in a shirt with the phones. He squeezed himself into Phil's jacket, and felt in the pocket.

'Look. I've got twenty pence!' Lucy said, holding up the coin. 'If I hear as much as a whisper out of you, I'm going to take the air pump and shove thirty-three PSI of compressed air up your arses till you explode!'

Lucy found a pen on a chain by the cleaning rota certificate, snapped it off and walked to the door. Before leaving he turned to them and pointed to his own legs. 'Behold, he can walk. Hallelujah! It's a fucking miracle!' he closed the door behind him, scrawled *out of order* on the outside, and then climbed gingerly into the driver's seat of the van. He rifled through the glove compartment, found a pair of scratched sunglasses and put them on. Then he found the van keys, started the engine and drove off.

* * *

While Natasha again tried to ring her mother, Virgil discreetly searched the flat. The bed in the master bedroom was dishevelled, and had clearly been used, while the main bathroom was draped with soggy towels. The other two bedrooms didn't look disturbed. There was no sign of a body. When he came back into the lounge, Natasha had prised off the back of the picture frame. The drawing was indeed signed by Wōdan, and had been made on the back of another picture, a watercolour of flowers.

'Natasha, we have to ring the police,' Virgil said gently. 'When was the last time you heard from your mother?'

'This morning,' said Natasha. 'She texted me asking for Mira's mobile number and home address, because she wanted to invite her to a party.'

'Did you give them to her?'

Natasha nodded slowly. 'Yes, of course. And Ram's home address and phone too.'

Virgil sank his face into his hands. 'Oh God, I don't think anywhere is going to be safe now.' He looked up. 'Do you know why it was I wanted to speak to your mother?'

'Something about Wōdan I suppose. He's a murderer, isn't he? Is that what you are going to tell me?'

Virgil nodded slowly. He knew he couldn't dare go into details while there was still some hope that Suzannah Earl may still be alive. And Natasha, watching him, knew as much. It is probably too late now for the baroness. But saving Mira's life was still possible. Virgil picked up his phone. He had a long list of calls to make. Mira first, then the police.

* * *

Virgil didn't normally attend the Thursday afternoon Team Mira meeting at Stardust Brands, but these weren't normal times, and after making his calls he hurried along. He'd been guarding Mira at Ram's home in Belgravia for several days, and now they were both needed for a very important decision. The newspapers were full of the missing baroness and the hunt for the multiple murderer William Mordant. His obsession with Mira appeared prominently in many of the newspapers, alongside a chronology of the turbulent few months of the world's most beautiful woman.

'It's down to this,' said Jonesy, tossing his spectacles onto the table and folding his arms behind his head. 'Mira, you could easily cancel this funeral tomorrow. Given what's happened no one would blame you. On the other hand, if you do go, you'd seem courageous and principled, and it might help to erase some of the stain over the Lawrence Wall issue. We'd definitely see some positive social media outcomes.'

'Come on, we've got to keep her safe. That's the number one priority, ' said Portia, slapping her hand on the table. 'We can't send her out there!'

Mira, dressed in black jeans and sweatshirt, sat with her legs pulled up onto a chair, resting her chin on her knees. She turned to look at Virgil. 'What do you think, would it be safe?'

'There is going to be a significant police presence. If Mordant shows up anywhere near that village, they'll have him. But having said that, it is still effectively a public event. The newspapers have written up that you are going to be there, so it could attract any type of trouble. It's your decision either way.'

'The trouble is,' Mira said, 'I spoke to Mrs Stevens for over an hour just last week. She was crying the whole time, telling me how much Danielle adored me. And I gave her my word that I'd be there.'

'Yes, but I guess she'd understand,' Thad said.

Mira laughed. 'I don't know that she would. Her daughter died trying to emulate what I did in *Village of the Dead*. It seems pretty selfish to give my word and then break it. I mean, you guys are always going on about my brand and everything, right?'

'Moi?' said Jonesy, smiling.

'Yeah. I mean, I'm supposed to be pure, trustworthy, and dependable. Isn't that what you told Suressence?'

Thad shrugged. 'I guess I did.'

'I think you should go,' said Kelly. 'You're showing you are bigger than this. Virgil will look after you.'

Portia turned and glared at Kelly, as if she'd only just realised she was sitting there. 'Don't you have some of the post still to handle? The fan mail agency has really struggled in the last few weeks and could probably do with your oversight.'

Kelly looked outraged and turned to Thad, who nodded in agreement with Portia and said. 'Yeah. We've got a decision anyway, Mira's going. And perhaps we could get some coffee when you're done, Kelly. Thanks.'

Kelly stood up and stalked out, leaving an atmosphere.

'So Thad, are we going to get a press release together about it?' Jonesy asked. 'To emphasise her principled stand. Or do we leave them to draw their own conclusion?'

'It's a tricky one,' Thad said. 'We could offer some interviews just after the funeral, that would seem less self-serving. Just a few, maybe BBC, ITN and Sky. How's that sound?'

The next moment there was a huge bang, and the sound of breaking glass. The door to the next office flew open and a huge cloud of black smoke and dust blew in. They were showered in glass fragments from the transom panels above. Everyone sat stunned for a second and then a horrible screaming started from the next room, followed by the deafening sound of the fire alarm.

Kelly!

Virgil was on his feet in a second. He clicked his fingers at Mira and pointed: *under the table.* She was just staring into her lap so he yelled 'Mira, now! Everyone else lie on the floor. Don't anyone move until I get back. Mordant could be here.'

Virgil did a double take. A low keening wail from Mira was adding to the high-pitched shrieks from next door. On Mira's lap was a human hand, blackened, smoking and covered in blood. It wasn't hers.

Virgil jumped through the gap into what was left of Kelly's office. 'Kelly!' Her desk had been blown to pieces, the windows shattered, the ceiling completely gone, and charred ceiling panels smouldering all over. But her typist chair, though scorched round the edges, was barely damaged. It seemed to have a Kelly-shaped shadow of unburned material on it. 'Kelly, where the hell are you?' His siren-deafened and blast-fizzed ears could just detect her whimpering, but for a second he couldn't see her. Then he spotted her on the floor by the window, under a layer of blackened ceiling tiles. The moment he saw her he could see she was terribly injured. Her face was blackened and bloody, her torso a mess and most of her clothes shredded.

'Kelly, Kelly. It's Virgil. You are going to be okay,' he lied.

'My hand! Virgil, my hand's gone. I need it, I need it…'

Her arm ended in a wrist that looked like a chunk of seared steak. Virgil immediately realised what must have happened. A parcel bomb! She had opened a parcel bomb. Realising that she could die of shock, Virgil did his best to reassure her. 'We've got the hand, Kelly. And we'll put it on ice for you. I'm going for help, but I'll be back in a minute.'

He stepped back into the meeting room. Mira was under a table, whimpering, but everybody else seemed to be frozen, looking up at him. 'Portia, Kelly's severely injured. Call an ambulance, and the cops. Mordant may be in the building. Jonesy, make sure your phone is on, find a secure room or even a cupboard and stay there with Mira until I call to let you know it's safe. There may be other devices. Thad, find the control point for the sprinklers, they haven't been triggered and I'm worried the place could go up. There may be other bombs. Don't touch anything you don't recognise.'

Virgil grabbed some coats from a stand, and ran back to Kelly. As he lay a large coat over her, he saw that other staff were beginning to emerge now, confused or crying. Art director Jarvis McTear was staring around him in incredulity, his quiff blown to one side.

'What happened?'

'A parcel bomb. We've one critically injured. Now get everyone out, organise a roll-call in the street outside. Who are the fire wardens?'

McTear shrugged. 'I've no idea.'

'Find out. I want one here, and one outside to liaise with the emergency services.'

'Okay,' he said, seeming not to do anything.

'Move!' bellowed Virgil. 'Now.'

Suddenly the alarm stopped, and Virgil could hear himself think. He looked down and saw Kelly staring up at him, her blue eyes intense in a mask of soot.

'Virgil, listen. You've got to be careful. The parcel...'

'What about the parcel...'

'Not addressed to Mira,' she gasped.

'Then who?'

'You...'

Virgil blinked.

'Virgil, do you love me?'

Before he had the chance to answer, Kelly Hopkins shuddered, her throat rattling an unearthly sound. Then she went limp.

'Kelly. I do love you,' Virgil whispered, pulling her up into his arms. 'I really do. And I am so, so sorry.'

Chapter Twenty-Six

It was midnight before Virgil was finished at the office. The police and fire brigade had been and gone, the small fires caused by the explosion had never got going once the sprinklers finally began, but the whole floor was a crime scene and Stardust Brands as a business was essentially out of action. No one but Kelly had been hurt. The parcel had been delivered by a cycle courier that morning. Virgil's security guard friend Nelson remembered him because the courier seemed a little older than usual, but the sun visor and helmet made it hard to get a good description beyond the fact the guy was every bit as fit looking as the youngsters. The police had been pretty quick to pull up the CCTV records, but it seemed that he had emerged from a narrow alleyway just a few streets away.

Thad and Jonesy had taken Mira back to Ram's home, and were staying with her. Mira's hysteria over finding Kelly's hand in her lap hadn't changed her determination to go to the funeral of Danielle Stevens.

Virgil had gone to his own neglected flat, and after a long

shower and a change of clothes had scooped up the bag of overnight clothing that Kelly had left there. The change of underwear, the cosmetics, a novel she had been reading. On his mantelpiece was a card she had given him after the first meal he had cooked for her.

Lovely mushroom risotto. I thought a chanterelle was a light fitting until I met you!
XX Kelly.

As he re-read it, the poignancy of those carefree words pierced him and he felt his eyes prickle. Poor Kelly. He sat down, feeling quite sorry for himself.

The buzz of his mobile pulled him out of his reverie. He answered, and a smooth well-educated male voice said. 'Oh Virgil. Look at the mess you've made. You should really open your own post. Like I said: when it comes to Mira, it's hands off.' Then he hung up. Virgil looked at the number. It was Baroness Earl's phone. Mordant.

* * *

TWO DAYS

Virgil and Mira sat in a brooding silence all the way to Essex, their chauffeured Volvo saloon shadowed by an unmarked police car. Mira had gone for the full femme fatale look. Heavy eye make-up, a huge knee-length jet-black astrakhan coat and matching hat with veil, and lipstick in the darkest maroon. Her long legs were encased in sheer nylons, seamed at the back, and ended in black stilettos. Black leather gloves and patent leather handbag finished the ensemble. She stared out of the window at the grey sky, the hard east wind and the endless new housing estates, huddled grimly in treeless rows.

Virgil, lost in his own thoughts about Kelly, could no longer find the energy to try to squeeze out of Mira whatever it was that linked her to William Mordant. The whole story was much bigger than her now, with a full-scale police manhunt. One woman was dead and a peer of the realm missing, presumed murdered. The Met Police liaison officer, WPC Karen Thomas, had told him that Mordant's last phone call to Virgil from Baroness Earl's phone had been traced. By triangulating the phone masts that carried the call, the police had worked out that Mordant had been travelling eastwards on the M25 near the M11 junction. They would now examine the motorway camera footage in the area to see if they could identify the car. They were pretty sure they knew what to look for. Suzannah Earl had hired a red Renault Kadjar while her own vandalised vehicle was being repaired, and this Renault had been missing from the resident's parking area when the police checked. Its keys had not been found in her flat.

'Whether we find it or not, Mordant seems to be heading towards the funeral, so we warn you to be on the lookout,' the WPC had said.

They arrived at the village of Aythorpe Green, between Harlow and Chelmsford, three hours before the funeral was to start. The car dropped Mira at a secluded hotel twenty miles away, where a couple of her old colleagues from *Village of the*

Dead were staying. The death of Danielle Stevens had affected many of them profoundly, and they too had arranged to attend the funeral. Virgil left them there with the officers from the escorting car while he drove off to inspect the arrangements.

There was a small knot of people already at the tiny church. Virgil was introduced to Danielle's auntie Jenny, a formidable former hospital matron, who was organising the funeral. Virgil learned that there was only room for thirty-five friends and family in the church, of which Mira would be one, but the service would be relayed outside by speakers to those who could not get in. They were expecting at least a couple of hundred to attend. Virgil noticed immediately that there were only two parking spaces close to the church, with no others nearby in the village's narrow lanes. He asked for one to be reserved for Mira, to minimise the walk she would have to make past members of the public. This was agreed. The local police had already advised them to use crowd-control barriers, and these were already in place.

* * *

An hour before the funeral there were already over two hundred people there waiting, locals outnumbered by visitors about three-to-one. A mini-media scrum had formed too, encroaching on the wheelchair section by the church doors that Virgil had helped Jenny set up. Virgil scanned the gathering crowd, spotting three anoraked lads and four teenage girls, some dressed as Qaeggan. A uniformed policeman was chatting amiably to them. The make-up and tear stains doubled quite well for a funeral. To Virgil they looked like typical Mira fans, though he was less sure about the tall well-dressed man in sunglasses at the back. Virgil was wearing sunglasses to disguise the direction of his gaze, but as it was overcast he didn't expect anyone else to be in them. CID perhaps? It certainly wasn't Mordant.

Most of the guests had already arrived when Mira's car slid into view. Her elegant coat and veiled hat brought out gasps of admiration. A few called out her name, and one or two shouted out for autographs, which she at Virgil's advice ignored. It was only when a little girl of perhaps eight yelled out 'You are so pretty!' that Mira turned and gave a small smile.

The arrival of the hearse caused an immense hush. Four black-suited pallbearers bore up a tiny white coffin, seemingly too small for a girl of thirteen. A huge wreath of white roses swamped the casket, and at its centre sat a tiny Mira doll, one of those *Village of the Dead* merchandise cheapos that Jonesy so hated. Here, though, on the coffin of a girl who died trying to emulate her heroine it caused even Virgil to well up a little. Certainly, he could hear no end of sobbing among the crowd.

Virgil remained at the church door for the service, which was simple and moving. If only things had stayed that way. After the service Mira lingered in the church, talking to the family, but when she emerged she did go over to someone who called from behind the crowd barrier. A shortish woman, dressed in a black broad-brimmed hat, was holding a huge bunch of lilies. Virgil, five feet behind Mira, looked briefly left, where the tall man had been just a moment ago. He didn't see him now.

'I heard a report you are getting married tomorrow, is that right?' asked the lady with the flowers.

Virgil didn't quite hear the reply, he was too busy looking for the tall man. He still couldn't see him.

'Well that's what I heard,' the woman said, a sarcastic tone in her voice. Suddenly she had Virgil's attention. 'So have these from me,' she said, pushing the flowers towards her.

Virgil lurched towards the woman. His mind was fixated on something he recalled from training. Back in 1990 a woman had stabbed the German politician Oskar Lafontaine in the throat with a knife concealed in a bunch of flowers. Lafontaine's carotid artery had been slashed, and he almost died.

Mira was reaching for the flowers but Virgil cut in, pushing his arm between her and the woman. 'I'm sorry,' he said. 'No gifts.' The woman pulled the flowers back, scowled at him, then thrust them higher as if trying to get past his shoulder towards Mira. He interposed himself again, looking for the knife. But it wasn't a knife that came out of the flowers. A jet of fluid hit him in the face and neck, and spattered across the crowd. Screams erupted, and suddenly, agonisingly they were his too. *Acid, it's acid!* The thought tore through his mind. A burning agony crackled across his eyes and he stumbled. 'Mira get back!' he shouted, as he fell, his fingers tearing at his face. Helping hands turned him face-up, and he saw through his working eye, the tear-smeared image of a male Qaeggan above him, pouring liquid. Instinctively he put his hands up to protect himself.

'Keep still, mate' the voice said. 'This is water, we're trying to get it off.'

And then there was a scream, a deafening bang, and a long crackle through the sky. A gasp ran through the crowd, and an explosion of crows fled the trees.

'Look after Mira!' Virgil screamed.

'She's okay,' said a voice. 'She's right here.'

'Virgil?' It was Mira's voice, soft and comforting. 'I'm fine. I got a few spatters on my neck. But what about you?'

* * *

Three hours later, Virgil emerged unsteadily into the waiting room at Harlow Hospital A&E with a dressing over one eye, and his face shiny with skin cream. His eyesight had been saved by that Qaeggan, a trainee nurse it transpired. He'd used a water bottle to douse his eye and then inverted the eyelid to wash the inside while the ambulance was called. Mira had waited for him with police liaison officer Karen Thomas, and now rushed up to hug him.

'Thank you Virgil,' Mira said, giving him a kiss, which earned a wolf-whistle from a young man with a cast on his leg who had been admiring her from afar. 'You really put your life on the line for me.'

'It's my job,' he said. 'And it's not over yet. Did they catch the woman?'

'Not yet,' said the WPC. 'One of our plain-clothes officers gave chase but encountered a shot from a firearm. Fortunately she missed, but it allowed her to escape in a vehicle. We've got the registration. She won't get far.'

'The doctor told me it wasn't acid but household bleach,' Virgil said. 'It could have been much worse.'

'I've been so worried,' said Mira. 'First Kelly, now you.'

'We've got the weapon. A squeezy-type detergent bottle. Pretty amateur really,' the WPC said. 'Unlike the gun.'

'What about Mordant?' Virgil asked.

'We saw no sign of him,' WPC Thomas said. 'The man with the sunglasses you mentioned was our DC Martin Preece, the man who gave chase. We reckon Mordant didn't come here. That's despite him being on the M11 when he rang you.'

'That's really strange,' Virgil said. 'So who is this woman? And is she the same one who vandalised Baroness Earl's car?'

'We've got a name for the vehicle owner,' Karen Thomas said. She showed Virgil and Mira a DVLA printout. 'Dawn Evans. She's got no criminal record. Does she mean anything to either of you?'

Virgil and Mira each shook their heads. 'Means nothing to me,' said Virgil. 'Not on the list of known stalkers. But she mentioned something about you getting married tomorrow, didn't she? What was that about?' Virgil said to Mira.

'Really? I didn't hear that,' said Mira, her face blank. 'She said, "Have some flowers from me." I don't recall anything else.'

Virgil stared at Mira, her exquisite face, dark lips slightly parted. That she could look him in the eye and lie so brazenly. 'Come on,' Virgil said, laughing. 'She said it sarcastically. If I could hear her where I was, you certainly must have.'

Mira shrugged. 'There were a lot of people speaking to me.'

'Have a think,' said the WPC. 'If there is anything else you remember, you can add it to the statement.'

Mira nodded at Virgil. 'Let's get out of here. The press are beginning to gather outside. And I need a drink.'

* * *

Dawn Evans sat in her grey Renault Clio with the engine running and the heater on full. She was parked behind a disused barn near a farm track a few miles east of Harlow. There were geese honking in the distance and the sound of a far-off tractor. She didn't know exactly where she was, but once she'd left the funeral her options had narrowed down, as she knew they would.

On the passenger seat was her briefcase, containing all her precious things. The exquisite poetry Will had written for her. The sketches, the watercolours. Probably already valuable. She picked up and admired her photograph of Will. Taken in the Broadmoor studio on the sly, she'd sneaked it out on a data stick, then had it blown up and framed, and kept in a bedroom drawer at home to look at every morning and every night. So handsome, so wonderful. All the possibilities they had considered together, all spoilt by his wandering eyes and absurd ambition. First that tart of a baroness, flaunting herself naked for the nation to see. Warning her off was easy. Her home address was on the social worker's report, the one the baroness had to agree to before she was approved to have contact with Will. Dawn hadn't the courage to break into the flat, but smashing up the car was fun. Very cathartic.

Now this model. Mira Roskova. Dawn had only once asked Will why he had her picture all over the place, and he had replied: 'Because she is absolute perfection in female form. A muse fit for a God.' Not any more, was what she had wanted to tell him. At least not if that bodyguard hadn't got in the way.

Dawn had never been jealous in her life until she met Will. But having got hold of him, experienced him, she was never going to let go. Ever. There were no second chances for her. She wondered, with all the tablets she had taken and rather enjoyed, and this strange haze in her mind, whether she was now a candidate for the very institution she had worked in. A crazy woman, as obsessed as any of them. But that is what happens when you feel destiny in your hands and then have it snatched away. Nothing else is ever going to seem right again. Over the noise of the geese she heard sirens back on the motorway. She could just see the lights on the M11 embankment, maybe a mile away. Then she saw a car, blue lights flashing but no siren, easing its way slowly down the track behind her, splashing through the puddles. There was no way out.

She reached over the back of the seat and felt for the revolver. It had been in the heavy holdall given to her in Grimsby. Everything else she'd stowed for Will weeks ago in the London lock-up garage, along with some other stuff including the *Anarchist's Cookbook*, and various other guides to explosives. The gun was her get-out, and her original idea was to shoot the baroness. But she soon realised she could never do that.

She now placed the gun in her lap, hoping there were bullets left in it. She reclined the seat, and then thought how someone would afterwards have to clean up all the mess. She felt guilty for that, but not enough to stop her. She put the snub nose of the gun in her mouth, an alien sensation of cold metal, which tasted somehow like a nosebleed, against her teeth. She had both thumbs through the trigger guard. All she had to do was squeeze. A severe case of self-harm. Richard Lamb would recognise the syndrome immediately.

At the sound of the car doors, she looked in the mirror. Two policemen with flat caps and high vis jackets had emerged from the patrol car and were walking along the road towards her. All she had to do was squeeze.

She squeezed.

Chapter Twenty-Seven

DAY ZERO

Virgil was invited to stay that night with Ram Dipani's family. He was given his own luxurious room, while Mira and Ram, who was just back from New York, were allocated separate rooms under the watchful eye of Mrs Dipani. The family matriarch was also a qualified doctor and insisted on overseeing the application of more cream on Virgil's face and neck and an inspection of the dressing. 'At least you can afford to relax a bit now,' she told him. 'You've done your job very well.'

Certainly the hardest part was over. At the suggestion of the police, Mira had agreed to drop out of tomorrow's planned trip to visit injured servicemen with Prince Harry. The required security would have just been too onerous, and it was increasingly clear that Mira herself was exhausted. Instead, Ram had suggested to Mira that they bring forward their flight to Mumbai by a week. They would leave in the morning, for the month's rest and relaxation that she desperately needed. Virgil wasn't going, but he was confident they would be safe. After a few days in Mumbai they would head off by train to a country estate in the hills owned by Ram's uncle. No one outside the immediate family knew exactly where they were going and when they returned, Mordant would almost certainly have been caught and locked up again.

Virgil just had to get Mira safely through one more night. On their return from Essex at eight o'clock he had familiarised himself with all the door alarms, had gone up to the roof terrace and had the intruder detection systems there explained to him by Ram. There were two uniformed Special Branch officers outside the front door, and an armed response vehicle stationed in the square. Two officers would remain overnight. Mira was about as secure as she could be. From behind net curtains Virgil scrutinised the twenty or so journalists and the dozens of onlookers who had gathered outside. There were a few familiar faces from TV, but no sign of Mordant.

It was Mira's state of mind that concerned Virgil most. In the car back from the hospital she had spent most of the time on her phone, or just staring out of the window and looking self-indulgently miserable. Perhaps he was being a little unfair to her. She had been so stoical through all the stalking, the bleach-throwing and the death of Kelly. But she wasn't now. She looked thin and tired, a normal look for many washed-out catwalk models, but never for her. Her face was her fortune, and she had always exuded vitality.

After rechecking the doors and windows, Virgil turned in just after eleven, his own face sensitive and throbbing. He awoke shortly after midnight, when he heard a door bang and then some sobbing. Mira's voice. He was already halfway out of bed and reaching for his tracksuit before he heard the voices of Ram Dipani and his mother attempting to calm her. A little later there was more noise, and what sounded like an argument between Mira and Ram. Finally Virgil managed to get back to sleep, though the dressing on his eye was uncomfortable. In his dreams he roamed through Helmand. It was night, a cold, still, starry night, and there was an ugly cinderblock town in the distance. Grey smoke billowed from behind a building half a mile away, flame-flushed orange from below. He could see the remains of a vehicle beyond. In his heart he knew it was the blazing personnel carrier with his oppos in. He had to get there. Then he realised he had no boots and the ground was covered in broken glass. A click near his head made him start. Taliban, behind him! He murmured something, and then awoke.

'Shhh.' There was someone in the room. For a moment he was unsure where he was. 'Shhh. Don't make a sound.' The voice was familiar. There was a gradual weight on the double bed. It was Mira.

'What's up?' Virgil whispered. 'Has something happened?' She didn't reply, but eased the duvet up and slid in next to him. The bed gave an ominous low squeak.

'I'm frightened,' she whispered. She was wearing pyjamas, and he could feel her warmth as she brought her mouth up to his ear. His body, clad only in a pair of boxers, started to awaken very rapidly and he caught his own sharp intake of breath.

'I hope you don't mind me snuggling up.' Her breath was warm and minty.

God, how could I mind? 'Is it Mordant you are frightened about?' Virgil asked.

He felt her head nod against his neck in the darkness. 'I had a nightmare about him. I can't go to Ram's room because his bloody mother is on patrol.' She laughed, gently. 'So I've come to yours.'

'I'll always protect you, you know that. It's my job and I take it very seriously.'

She kissed him on the cheek. 'You're very sweet, but I don't think you can save me.

Did you know Ram's got a gun now?' she said. 'He says we'd better have one in case Mordant gets in.'

'He's not going to get in, believe me,' Virgil said. 'And I'd be a bit concerned if Ram's got himself an illegal weapon and hasn't had any training.'

'That's not what I'm worried about, Virgil. I'm worried about me. I've made mistakes that are coming back to haunt me,' she whispered. She ran her hand across his chest. Her body was hot against his side.

'What things have you done?' Virgil had a lump in his throat almost as hard as the one between his thighs.

'I'm so selfish. I wanted Lawrence to be hurt, and I didn't care about Kelly.' There was a catch in her throat, as if she was about to cry. 'I let her run around after me, and ignored her, and let her open my post. She *died* opening my post. And the whole time I just thought about myself.'

'That parcel wasn't addressed to you,' Virgil whispered. 'It was addressed to me. Kelly told me. Mordant wanted me out of the way. So if anyone should feel guilty, it's me.'

Mira sobbed. 'I've no time left, Virgil. No one can help me.'

'I can help you. But you have to be honest with me. The website, you know what it is, don't you? Countdown to a wedding. Why else would he send you a dress? And this woman, Dawn Evans, knew about it. It all adds up.'

'Virgil. I've been meaning to tell you something. It's awful, but I have to confess to someone. It's eating me alive.'

'I'll do whatever I can, so long as you tell me the truth.'

'It's an absolute secret. You cannot ever tell anyone,' she whispered, caressing his face.

'Okay. I promise.'

'I know William Mordant. From years ago. He was called Mr Peirce, and he turned up one day as an art teacher at my school in Clitheroe. He was absolutely gorgeous. Even though I was only thirteen, and very shy, secretly I fancied him as much as all the other girls did. I was plain, spotty and a bit goofy until I had my teeth fixed. I was also being bullied by these three girls; hateful, mean bitches. He reassured me, he nurtured me. He saw something in me that no one else did, and I sat for him for a couple of drawings. I loved it!'

She ran her hand gently down Virgil's hairless chest.

'He gave me a couple of the drawings but made me promise not to show them to anyone. I still have one at home, and you saw the other in Mum's room. He only stayed at the school a few weeks, I think he must have been a supply teacher. But one of the books he gave me had an address, a studio on an island in Venice. I asked him about it, and he said that he had been going to Murano every April for years. A few months after he left, our school had an educational trip to Venice, in April. It was expensive, but I begged my mother to let me go. Unfortunately the girls that hated me also went. They gave me a terrible time. I wagged off a museum visit and went to see him. I didn't really expect him to be there, but he was. He was very sympathetic and I poured out my heart to him.'

Mira laughed, a curious ironic tone. 'This wonderful man is the same one who was convicted of dissolving those three girls with acid.'

'I'd guessed something along those lines,' Virgil whispered.

Mira closed her mouth over his ear. 'But he didn't kill them,' she whispered. 'They were already dead. It was a terrible accident.' Then she breathed three more words in his ear.

'I killed them.'

Chapter Twenty-Eight

DAY ZERO

There was movement in the corridor outside Virgil's room, and they both fell silent. A moment later they heard Mrs Dipani's slippered feet padding away. They lay still for two more minutes, until they were convinced the coast was clear. Mira seemed to have second thoughts about her confession. She refused to answer Virgil's urgently whispered questions, and did not elaborate on her disclosure. She just slid out of bed and slipped quietly back to her room. Virgil lay awake half the night, wondering what to do. It hardly seemed credible that she could have been involved in such an awful event, yet she seemed utterly convincing.

When he finally did sleep it was for a long time. It was after nine when he awoke. There was a tapping on the door, and Mrs Dipani came in with a cup of tea. 'Our own blend of orange pekoe and Darjeeling,' she said. 'I think you'll like it.' She asked how his burns were feeling, and as he raised himself in bed, he realised they were quite sore.

'You're the only one I'm bothering to make it for. Ram is snoring away with jet lag, while Mira's just gone out.'

'Mira? Where to?'

'She didn't say.'

As soon as Mrs Dipani left, Virgil leapt out of bed and got dressed. He rang Mira's mobile but it went to voicemail. He left a message, knowing she wouldn't call back. He now suspected what Mira was doing, and he was already too late to stop it. He knew he really should put some more burn cream on his face and neck, and should certainly have a shower, but he didn't have time. He went to the lounge and peered out of one of the grand windows onto the beautiful square with its mature plane trees, just coming into bud. He saw the two policemen by the door, and a TV crew packing up their gear into a van. There was no sign of Mordant, but Virgil recognised Aaron and Jack, two young Mira fans. They were dressed as Qaeggan and hanging around by the railings on the square. The battered black Vauxhall Nova parked nearby confirmed they were the two who had been near Mira's apartment in Battersea nearly two weeks ago. Besotted but harmless. Virgil descended the stairs to the front door, opened it and called to the two young uniformed policemen who were standing on the pavement.

'Did you see Mira leave the house in the last few minutes?' he asked.

'Yes, sir, just a couple of minutes ago. She left the underground car park driving a black Toyota people carrier.'

'Aren't you supposed to go with her?'

'We offered, but she just said she was moving it to a less obvious location, and would be back in a few minutes,' the other PC answered. His face betrayed the smear of boyish glee that a few words from Mira wiped on the countenance of any male.

Virgil thanked them, went back into the house and rang Mira again. Voicemail. Ram emerged from his room in a silk dressing gown, looking every inch the Indian playboy. He saw Virgil's agitated state and asked him where Mira was.

'She's driven off somewhere.'

'But we're going to Mumbai in two hours!'

'I wouldn't be surprised if she has other plans,' said Virgil.

'What plans, Mr Bliss?'

'Did she mention a stalker?'

'The footballer?'

'No, someone a bit cleverer than Lawrence Wall.' Virgil could see from Ram's expression that Mira had kept him completely in the dark about William Mordant. The Indian sat down on an enormous damask-covered sofa, one of a pair that dominated the lounge. 'You know, I thought it was odd that she asked for the underground car park keycard last night when we've already got a car booked to take us to the airport. Maybe she had some luggage to move...'

'She didn't take her Porsche. It was a people carrier.'

'A black Toyota?' asked Mrs Dipani, overhearing. 'That's mine. The cheeky little cat! Why didn't she take her own car?'

'A turquoise Porsche convertible is a lot more noticeable than yours,' Virgil said, getting up and shrugging on his jacket.

'And she doesn't want to be followed. But I've got an idea. Ram, keep calling her phone. Ring me if you hear anything. And Mrs Dipani, why don't you call the police and report your car stolen. We need all the help finding her we can get, and the Met might at least alert other forces.'

'Tell her to be careful with my car,' Mrs Dipani called after him, but he was already out of the door. She turned to her son: 'See? I told you that nice girl from Hyderabad would suit you better, but did you listen to your own mummagee? No. You always know best, don't you?'

Ram shrugged, and turned the TV on, hoping to find some cricket.

Virgil walked out into the square and up to the two Qaeggan. 'Hi, remember me?'

'Yeah, what happened to your face?' said Aaron, the taller one, looking at the dressing over Virgil's eye. He was wearing a food-stained *Village of the Dead* sweatshirt.

'I had an argument with a bottle of bleach,' Virgil said. 'I'm actually Mira Roskova's head of security...'

'We guessed that,' said Aaron.

'...And now you've lost her, aintcha?' said Jack, smirking. 'She drove off a little while ago. In that direction.' He pointed towards Buckingham Palace Road, and looked a little smug. 'You won't catch her now.'

'Have you updated Qaegglog with it?'

They looked suspiciously at him, and then at each other.

'Look, I know you Qaeggan fans all share sightings of Mira,' Virgil said, taking out his phone. He keyed in a website address, logged in and then read from the screen. "'7.37pm. Mira arrives at home of Indian boyfriend in Belgravia." That's from your friend Colin. "8.03am. Mira leaves in black Toyota Land Cruiser, alone, destination unknown. Aaron." That is you, right?'

'Yeah, that is me,' Aaron said. 'It's not illegal. We only watch her in public places.'

'I don't approve, obviously, but I've got bigger worries, and I would really appreciate your help.'

'How did you find out about it? And how did you get a password?' Jack asked.

'Let's just say I've got a friendly little zombie mole.' Virgil smiled as he thought of young Ellie, who for the price of a stuffed crust pizza had shown him exactly how to access Qaegglog, the shared private blogging platform of Mira's hardcore fans. He was just thinking that it might not be a bad idea to ring her, when the phone screen updated.

9.16am. Mira passes Hyde Park Corner. Car loaded with bags. LE.

LE? Ellie! Was that her? Virgil showed the screen to Aaron. 'Do you know Ellie McAllister? Is this her?'

'Yeah. That's probably her,' said Jack. 'She's a real little fanatic.'

Virgil wondered why she would be up at Hyde Park Corner on the off chance Mira would pass. It seemed a little unlikely. He dug up her details on his phone and texted her.

Saw yr mira msg. whr ru?

The reply took a few minutes.

In her car under bags (lol!)

Virgil was gobsmacked. Somehow, Ellie had smuggled herself into the very vehicle that Mira was driving. Getting into the underground car park in the square would have been easy enough, but slipping into the vehicle itself? Virgil guessed that Ellie had her phone on silent mode, so risked another text.

Amazing! How u mng tht?

The reply came.

easy. slipd in whn she went to get last bag frm porsh. Hid undr blnkt. Bit puky. Eek!

Can u c out wndow?

No, but gogl maps on fone. Now in edgwr rd

Ok. If u c mira with blond man William Mordant text me

It looked like Mira might be heading out of London. Virgil was willing to take a chance on that. He went back into the house and found Ram watching Sri Lanka playing India in Colombo, and absent-mindedly checking his phone.

'Ram, I really don't think Mira is coming back. That's why she isn't returning your calls.'

He blinked at Virgil uncomprehendingly. 'But we're off to Mumbai. She wouldn't want to miss that, surely?'

'Do you have the keys to Mira's Porsche?'

'No. But I have my own car if you need to go somewhere.'

'Ram, we have to rescue her. She's heading into disaster. She's got half an hour's head start…'

'Then let's get a chopper. London Heliport's in Battersea, and we can be there in twenty minutes,' Ram said, suddenly galvanised. He picked up his phone, made a quick call, speaking rapidly to someone in another language. When he'd finished, he called down the stairs. 'Mummagee, just going out. We'll call, okay?'

Half an hour later, Virgil and Ram were in a Bell Jet Ranger rented by Ram's company, lifting off over a partially cloudy London skyline. The thudding two-bladed rotor blasted gunmetal crests on the sludge-coloured Thames as they began to climb high above Battersea. The Houses of Parliament and the London Eye were to the right, and the glinting pinnacles of the City's skyscrapers beyond, away to the east. The pilot swung sharply to the north, over Fulham, then Hammersmith and Wembley. Ahead was the great loop of the M25, flecked with myriad crawling vehicles, and beyond that the M1, gateway to the Midlands and the North of England.

* * *

Leonard Lucifer Smith was feeling quite smug. He was on the M1 heading north towards home territory. Manchester. Grey, wet streets, friendly pubs, real people, his people, his family. He'd risked one call to the family on the stolen phone yesterday, as soon as he'd snatched it from the screws, then chucked it. His brother George had then set everything up in two hours flat: a safe house in Hounslow, West London, ready for him to switch wheels and get some shut-eye, a new phone, some overalls, a pair of scissors and a wet razor to get rid of the beard. Early next morning the rest had arrived: a plain white Ford Transit, fully legit, a pair of sunglasses to cover those frightening black eyes, and a big woolly hat that he could pull down over most of his tattooed face. After the best part of twenty years banged up, the temptation was to use the screws' cash to buy himself a hot woman and some good beer. That, though, would have to wait. If Mordant had somehow kidnapped Mira Roskova, he owed it to Lawrence, who was still laid up in hospital, to nail the bastard before he got his wicked way.

Len had lain down on the mattress in Hounslow, with jets thundering overhead into Heathrow and thought yet again about what slow pain he was going to inflict on that scum Mordant. It had been coming for a lifetime. He could still remember as a nineteen-year-old scaffolder back in the eighties, doing a job at some crumbling manor called Hooksworth Hall in the Forest of Bowland. There he was, fifty feet up, at chimney level on a boiling hot summer's day, and hearing the crunch of tyres on gravel. Looking down he had seen some sixteen-year-old toff of a kid wearing a purple blazer getting out of mummy's flash car. The kid looked up, all carefully-brushed hair and butter-soft privileged face. Someone whispered an idea in Len's ear, a voice from the sky he had never heard before, but one that was later to become insistent, whining, and finally the bane of his life. Len did as it suggested. He plucked a loose tile from the roof and threw it down at the boy. It missed but shattered on the drive at his feet. The boy didn't jump, but stared insolently up at him, his hand shielding his eyes against the sun.

'Sorry lad,' Len had called, when faced with that stare, but he wasn't sorry. He had wanted to pulverise that gilded head. He wasn't even sorry later in the day when the boy's mother, having given the foreman half an hour's earache about the incident, demanded a proper apology from Len himself. He had walked up to the snooty bitch, done a little curtsey and then told her to fuck off. He was fired on the spot, nutted the foreman, then hitched back into Manchester where he spent every penny he could find in his mum's purse on tattoos. Wrap yourself in the Book of Revelations, that's what the voice had told him. Next week he marched in to see Uncle Jimmy, head of the firm. 'I'm fucking finished with legit jobs. I'm ready to crack heads for you,' he said.

That boy's conceited, arrogant face had stuck in his mind, but he'd never expected to set eyes on him again. Especially nearly twenty years later in HMP Wakefield. It was definitely him. They'd give him some other name, it wasn't Mordant then, and not Hooksworth neither. And he was segregated with the nonces, so it was hard to get at him. Nonce crime, little boys, that's what they had all reckoned, but no one knew for a fact, which was unusual because the prison grapevine was normally spot on. Then Len had snared a chance when he was being escorted to a court hearing. The corridor to the van bay went past the nonce breakfast sitting. Len had broken away from the screws and smacked Mordant a good clump, two-hander of course, with handcuffs on. Thought he'd done alright, as there was plenty of blood, but things changed. On the way back later in the day he'd passed under the nonce landing and someone had chucked prison napalm on him: boiling water with a pound of sugar dissolved. That stuck and burned and hurt like nothing he'd ever known. Still had scars on his neck.

Then Mordant had been shipped out, and it was years before Len had run into him again. Who'd have thought it? In Broadmoor of all places. Well, finally time to settle the score. Tonight's the night.

* * *

Ellie McAllister was feeling quite pukey now, and was really having second thoughts about what she'd done. The only space she had was a sportsbag-sized slot between two hefty suitcases in the back. Above her in a plastic carrier was a white wedding dress so long that the voluminous hem was spilling out of the bottom, rustling as the car juddered and the luggage jostled. Ellie's legs were folded right up and she had pins and needles in her backside. This was easily the closest Ellie had ever been to her heroine, but it wasn't turning out like she had expected. The plan had been at some point to pop up and make an apology, and then sit and talk with the world's most beautiful woman before she got dropped off at the nearest tube station, with enough stories about Mira's life to last forever. But now she was too afraid to let Mira know she was there. The woman drove like a lunatic, revving, braking sharply, stopping and starting, and all the time muttering angrily to herself. Mira always looked so cool and serene on TV, her hair like ocean waves of silky chestnut as she shook it in the shampoo commercial. Yet here she was raving like Ellie's own mother did when she was trying to find her drugs, banging the horn and swearing at the traffic.

Just when Ellie thought she was going to throw up, it all became a bit smoother. She looked down at the Google map which showed they were on the M1 in Hertfordshire, not far from Scratchwood Services. Oh God. How would she get back home from here?

There was a phone noise and Mira answered. 'Hello. Yes. Where are you now? Alright, I'll be there. No, alone. I gave Virgil the slip this morning. No, and I feel bad about it, he's done his best for me, poor sod. And you blew his girlfriend to pieces. Yes, well, what can I do? You're going to ruin my life, one way or another aren't you? That's the only reason I'm going through with this ridiculous ceremony. Will, I'm trusting you here,' she pleaded. 'You have to promise to stop the countdown.' There was a long pause. 'Yes. I know you were there to help me when I needed it, you never let me forget do you? But that was ten years ago, Will. I was a child.'

Ellie could not believe what she was hearing. Could the Will she was talking to be the William Mordant that Virgil had warned her about? She risked lifting the dress carrier above her a little and sneaking a look through a small gap. Mira had a mobile clamped to her ear as she drove. She was now wearing a cloth cap, like a glamorous version of what old men wear, and the same sunglasses she'd worn at the start. With the tweed jacket and white trousers she looked kind of horsey. Only Mira could still look great dressed like that.

Mira was still on the call. 'Of course I'm terrified of you. Who wouldn't be? You admit you casually and deliberately killed my best friend's mother just a few minutes after making love to her. Then you tell me you love me. And you expect me to believe you? I mean, you don't even know me. Yes I know I promised. I was thirteen! Thirteen, and you were a god. Back then I'd have married you on the spot if I could have. But this is 2015 and I'm a grown woman, and believe you me I've had better offers of marriage than yours. Billionaires, world famous sportsmen, and a very nice Indian man whom I hope to God you never get near. Oh, I will enjoy it, will I? How very male of you, to reduce it to that. I've heard enough and I'm hanging up. There's a police car on the hard shoulder. Wouldn't do to be stopped for using a mobile while driving would it?' She hung up, switched off the phone, and angrily tossed it on the passenger seat.

Forty minutes later the car slowed down, turned off the motorway and then stopped. She heard Mira get out. The door was slammed, and the remote locking clunked. Ellie risked a peek and saw they were in the middle of a huge car park. Google maps showed they were at Toddington Services. She texted the location to Virgil. There was almost no juice on her phone, so she turned it off. What was left she'd have to conserve for a final text, when they finally stopped. Two minutes later, she heard a man's voice. The rear passenger door opened and a large heavy suitcase and some plastic bags were dumped onto the back seat. The man took the driver's seat and Mira slid in on the passenger side.

'Are you sure you weren't followed?' he asked. Ellie thought he was very handsome, with wavy blonde hair and a lovely storyteller's voice. Ah, this was *the* man. William Mordant. If only she could let Virgil know.

'I drove twice around the car park before stopping, Will. No one followed.'

'Good. We'll get off at the next junction and take minor roads. This car may already be reported stolen, and I would really prefer not to have to kill anyone else for a while.' Mordant laughed in a way that Ellie thought was really creepy. It didn't sound like a joke at all. Now very scared indeed, she snuggled down as deeply into the crevice between the luggage as she could, letting the heavy dress carrier settle over her. She didn't think she could sleep, but she would try.

* * *

Virgil and Ram had been on the ground at Milton Keynes Heliport kicking their heels for hours. The chopper was so much faster than a car, but there was no point chasing around by air until they had a final destination. Ellie McAllister hadn't replied to any of his texts since confirming that they were at Toddington Services on the M1 at midday. The chopper couldn't land there legally, and if they had tried, Mira would surely have simply driven off. Instead Virgil had spent ages on the phone to the liaison officer WPC Karen Thomas, trying to get the Met Police to trace Mira from her phone. Eventually he was patched through to Detective Chief Superintendent Alan Middleford who was in charge of the search for Mordant. He agreed that the Met considered the taking of Ram's mother's car a crime. 'But we need some evidence that Mira herself is in immediate danger, before providing the resources needed to track her down in real time.'

'But she is in danger, she's going to meet Mordant,' Virgil said.

'I'm sorry, but based on what you told us, that really isn't credible. Why would she go to meet a man who is likely to kill her?'

'I can't give you a clear rationale, but I think she is being blackmailed,' Virgil said.

'Look, we were happy to provide Special Branch protection to the given address, but a celebrity leading us a merry dance across the country isn't the highest priority when we are investigating the possible murder of a member of the House of Lords as well as your colleague Kelly Hopkins. We've already posted the registration number of Mrs Dipani's vehicle to other forces, and that will be sufficient for now. Besides, it would take an hour or two to get the cell site analysis, by which time she could be a hundred miles away. I'll review that decision later in the day,' he said, then hung up.

'That's crazy,' Virgil said to Ram. 'Follow her, and you will get to Mordant, I'm certain of it.'

'Well,' Ram said slowly. 'I had no idea what I was getting mixed up in when I saved Mira's umbrella that day on Hungerford Bridge. Such a beauty, mixed up in all this ugliness.'

Chapter Twenty-Nine

Ellie awoke what felt like hours later. Her watch said three-fifteen. The car was being driven slowly on a bumpy road with lots of turns, and the suitcases and bags were bumping and wobbling around her. Ellie hadn't eaten since the morning, and hunger and thirst were chewing at her mind. She risked putting her phone on, and after waiting for an eternity, finally got a signal. Only nine per cent battery life left. Google maps showed just a few minor roads on a blank map, and she had to zoom out to discover they were in the middle of nowhere, rural Lancashire, way north of Manchester.

'We're nearly there, my darling,' Mordant said to Mira. 'Lovely Hooksworth Hall.'

'I nearly sought refuge in the hall myself,' Mira told him. 'After Lawrence had beaten me up. I crossed this very lane just wearing pyjamas. I've never been so cold or wet. Or scared.'

He laughed. 'Well, there wouldn't have been anyone here. The inheritance tax bill after my mother's death meant it had to be given up. My uncle passed it on to the National Trust over twenty years ago, but they only recently started work on repair. The paintings are in the National Gallery, the furniture in storage and the tapestries being restored. But the Great Ballroom is finished, and I have a key.' The car finally stopped and he said. 'Right, now to deal with the luggage.'

Terrified out of her wits, Ellie pressed the button on a text to Virgil. It could be the last one she ever sent.

@ hookswth hall lancs w mordant. help!

She then turned the phone off and squeezed it into a gap between the cushions of the rear seats in front of her, where she hoped it would not be found. Mira and Will were talking at the back of the car. The boot door opened and someone lifted the dress carrier.

'Oh my God, we've got a stowaway!' Mira shrieked.

Ellie looked up straight into Mira's face. 'Hi. I'm Ellie.'

Strong male arms seized Ellie and pulled her out. 'Now what have we got here, eh?' Mordant said.

'I'm just a fan,' Ellie pleaded. 'I didn't mean any harm.' The man had one hand around her neck and, for God's sake, he was *smiling* at her as he started to squeeze. She was struggling to breathe.

'Will, no, no, please don't kill her,' Mira said, her hands pulling at his arm. 'Please Will, please. I couldn't bear it, not another one.'

'Mira, you are a fool,' he hissed. 'Why didn't you take more care? Am I marrying a complete idiot?'

'I was in a hurry,' Mira said, tears coursing down her face, making her eye make-up run. 'Will, I had to drag all the bags on my own thirty yards from one car to the other because you wouldn't let me take the Porsche. I have no idea who she is, but please don't kill her.'

Mordant knelt down to put himself at Ellie's level, his hand still tight at her throat. 'You have a phone, don't you, little girl? All kids your age do. Where is it?'

'I lost it climbing in the car,' Ellie croaked.

'Don't fib to me,' he hissed, then put his lips to her ear and mouthed: 'I like dissolving little girls in acid. Just think. You could be my fourth victim!'

'I've got no phone, honest.' Ellie shook her head, and fought hard to stop the tears coming.

'Please don't, Will, please,' Mira pleaded again.

'Well, what the hell do you think I should do with her then?' he snarled.

'A bridesmaid,' Ellie managed to squeak out. 'Could I please be a bridesmaid?'

Mordant laughed uproariously. 'Of course! A bridesmaid, perfect.' He released the grip on her throat a little.

'Yes, we could do it,' Mira said, a tearful smile at the girl. 'We could.'

'Okay then. Go and fix your make up. I want to marry a beauty, not some tear-streaked Qaeggan. You look like one of your own zombies.' Mordant then turned and shot Ellie a dark glance which even a child could understand: *your death is merely postponed.*

* * *

Traffic on the M6 was heavy, but Leonard Lucifer Smith didn't care. He'd already picked up the shooter in Oldham, and was going to be at Hooksworth Hall well before seven, giving plenty of time to disrupt that midnight wedding. Lucy didn't give a flying fuck for history, but he was bright enough to know that others did. On the first day scaffolding at the hall, the day before the voices in his head, he was on tea break when he had overheard Mordant's mother. She was telling the foreman that every Hooksworth since the eighteenth century had got married in the Great Ballroom, and that's what her boy would do one day. So if Mordant had really abducted Mira Roskova, it was a no-brainer that he was going to impress her by getting her to the family seat for the ceremony. Stands to reason.

Well, he would put the mockers on that. It was time to break the good news to Lawrence that he was well on the way. He picked up his new mobile and rang the hospital.

* * *

The final text from Ellie McAllister galvanised Virgil. Mordant was there, in the car with her and Mira. And Virgil was still hundreds of miles away.

Virgil spent a frantic five minutes online trying to find out where exactly Hooksworth Hall was, then scooped up Ram from a seat in the heliport lounge in front of the cricket, and tugged him along at a run to the helicopter. Five minutes later they were in the air, destination Thewick, a village ten miles northwest of Clitheroe, Lancashire.

* * *

Ellie hadn't been to many weddings, but this still seemed peculiar. The Great Ballroom at Hooksworth was a fifty-yard long first-floor room with an extraordinary rococo ceiling. Plaster angels and cherubs surrounded panels painted with hunting scenes. The wood-panelled walls were pale where dozens of paintings had been removed. There was very little furniture apart from an incongruously tatty decorators' trestle table and half a dozen paint-stained chairs. It smelled of old dust and polish, and there were big cobwebs at most of the windows. The floorboards were marked by thousands of small dark dents, where in past centuries fine ladies had danced in high heels. And it was cold. Cold, damp and musty. From the biggest mullioned windows at one end she could see a large ornamental lake, flecked with noisy geese and ducks.

Mordant asked Ellie to help bring in the luggage. She went down, and had found the huge red plastic suitcase that he had placed on the back seat. If she moved it she might be able to retrieve her phone and toss it in the lake. She was terrified Mordant might find it. Ellie tugged at the case, but it was incredibly heavy and she could hardly shift it. It had a flowery but rather battered paper label on it that said 'S. Earl' and gave an address in London.

'No, no, I'll take that.' Mordant was standing right behind her. Ellie was unnerved that she hadn't heard him approach. Mordant lifted the case like it weighed nothing, and took it to a set of steps which led down to a basement door. He unlocked the door, put the case inside and after locking the door came back up to Ellie. He looked her up and down as if she was a full-grown woman and said: 'You really are a pretty little thing. You rather remind me of Mira at your age,' he whispered, bringing his lips closer to her ear. 'Now Ellie I know you probably want to try to escape but I just want you to know that if you try, I *will* catch you and then those terrible, terrible things I did to others will happen to you. You felt how heavy that case was? That's because it has a dead body in it. I have another case upstairs, just about your size. Do you understand what I'm saying?'

Ellie looked into those cold blue eyes, and she believed. She nodded her head slowly and he smiled. 'Good girl. You are four miles from the nearest main road, there is no telephone here, so best just do your job as bridesmaid. I am sorry we have no suitable dress, or flowers. Take these small cases to Mira.' He pointed out a pink vanity case and a metal make-up box. When Ellie got upstairs Mira called her into a room just off the ballroom.

It was a grand but dusty place with a dark wood canopy bed, lit only by a single hanging bulb. There was a huge wood-framed mirror on the far wall, and the image she saw reflected in it took her breath away. It was Mira, wearing the gorgeous white wedding dress. She had pins in her mouth, and was putting her hair up in a French twist. She had huge long earrings glittering with diamonds, and a necklace to match. She looked to Ellie like a princess. 'You are *so* beautiful,' she said. Mira smiled briefly then beckoned for her to come in, so she could shut the door.

'Listen to me very carefully, Ellie. I have a gun. It's in my jacket. Don't be frightened when you see it. I don't want to use it, but I'm going to save both of us.'

Ellie nodded. 'I texted where we are to Virgil. Was that the right thing to do?'

'You *know* Virgil?' Mira seemed gobsmacked.

'Yes. He caught me hanging round your flat. Sorry.'

'That was you?' Mira said, then sighed. 'I had thought I could fix this on my own without anyone knowing, but I have doubts. So, yes, you did the right thing. But it's hopeless. He'll never get here in time.'

Ellie stared at Mira and then blurted out. 'Do you really love this guy?'

Mira laughed, a short harsh sound pitted with bitter knowledge. 'I used to, when I was your age. But this man is not the man I adored.'

'So why are you marrying him?'

Mira put her finger to her lips at the sound of footsteps. 'Look, I've found you a white skirt and bodice that might fit,' she said brightly, but then looked at the girl's scuffed pink trainers. 'We can't do anything about the shoes though.'

Ellie whispered in Mira's ear: 'He says he's got a dead body in the red case. And a spare case just my size.' She began to cry hot quiet tears, and Mira wept with her, holding her close as her body shuddered in terror.

'It won't happen, Ellie, trust me,' Mira whispered.

A few minutes later Mordant knocked on the door and summoned them for a dress rehearsal. Ellie came out, wearing the new clothes, and saw that he had prepared a buffet of supermarket sandwiches and cake, and a bottle of champagne with two fluted glasses. Mordant himself was dressed in a formal tailcoat with a white bow tie, a crisp white shirt and shiny black shoes. He looked so like a prince that it was impossible for Ellie to believe he could enjoy killing, and travel about with suitcases full of bodies. Mordant ushered them past a camera and tripod, for a formal pose in front of the fireplace. 'That's where a portrait of my great grandfather Sir William Hooksworth hung. It's very sad that it's not here. My late mother would have been very proud.' He pressed a remote control and took a picture, then went back to adjust the camera.

Mira reached into her bodice and pulled out a small black pistol. 'Okay Will,' she said. 'I'm here and as you can see I'm ready to marry you. It's time you kept your side of the bargain. First, take the website down, then give me the car keys. Now.'

He stared at her. 'Mira, please put that ridiculous thing away.'

'I'll shoot!' Mira yelled, her jaw set hard. 'Don't think I'll hesitate.' She stretched her arms and aimed for the middle of his chest.

Mordant simply ignored her, took a slice of cake and fed it into his mouth. 'Hm, not bad,' he said, tipping his head approvingly.

'Mira, don't shoot him,' Ellie pleaded.

'It's alright, Ellie,' Mordant said finishing a mouthful of cake. 'It looks like a nice little Beretta 9mm, but actually it's a replica. There's no firing pin.'

Mira squeezed the trigger and the gun simply clicked. She looked in disbelief at the object in her hands which had let her down. 'Ram said he'd protect me.'

'Well, he did. It looks good enough to fool a casual observer. He probably wouldn't have the connections to get the real thing. You weren't too clever about it either. I saw from the sag of your jacket that you had something heavy in the external pocket. I'd merely suspected a phone. I had a good look when you were in the loo.' He brushed the crumbs off his hands. 'Nice try though. Spirited.'

Mira began to cry, crumpling onto a chair. 'What do you want from me?'

The sound of some kind of aircraft intruded. Mordant turned and ran to the window. There was nothing visible but the rhythmic thudding of rotors pulsed through the building.

'Right,' Mordant said, seizing Mira's arm. 'We've even less time than I thought, so we're bringing the wedding forward.' He took a handkerchief from his pocket, extracted a gold ring and turned to Mira. 'Do you Lydia Mira Nikolayevna Roskova, take me...'

'Where's the vicar?' Ellie interrupted. 'It can't be real if you don't have one.'

Mira laughed. 'Ellie, my darling, the whole bloody thing is a charade. It really doesn't mean anything anyway. It only exists in his head.'

The look that Mordant then gave Mira made Ellie feel very fearful for her. 'You gave me a solemn undertaking,' he growled. He pushed his face close to hers but she didn't give ground. 'You called me in desperation and I saved you. I cleaned up the mess, wrapped the bodies in plastic and wheeled each in turn back to my studio in my largest suitcase. That was six consecutive trips on the vaporetto trying not to look suspicious. I was even good enough to dispose of them…'

'In acid!' Mira yelled.

'Yes, because it *works*. And because the engraving studio had gallons of it. I took all the blame that should have fallen on you, and for ten years I have said not a word. I had never killed anyone, yet they thought *me* the monster. *You* of course, are as pure as a saint.' His face twisted. 'Mira, the embodiment of innocence. If they only knew what I know.'

Mira said nothing, but stared at him, her face grim and obstinate.

'Come on, my dear,' he hissed. 'Think of the website, ready to fire the pictures of you and those dead girls into the inboxes of a dozen newspaper editors. So, once again: Do you Lydia Mira Nikolayevna Roskova, take me William Mordant to be your lawful wedded husband?'

'I do,' Mira breathed.

'And I William Mordant,' he gabbled. 'Take you Lydia Mira Nikolayevna Roskova to be my lawful wedded wife. Yes I do,' He pushed the ring on her finger, and then seized her face, kissing her passionately. Mira's arms hung limp at her sides, and she looked as if she might faint if he released her. He broke away from the kiss and then said: 'So I pronounce us man and wife. Now, sadly, we have to leave.'

Ellie, having edged to the window, could see that the helicopter had landed on pasture at the far side of the lake, sending a flock of waterfowl into the air. Two people jumped out and were running, ducking low beneath the spinning rotor, towards the hall. They had a quarter mile or so to cover. Mordant followed Ellie's gaze, and ran to the window. 'Virgil Bliss. Well, well. That side gate is locked, he'll have to climb the wall. Come on, Mrs Mordant. We're going to the car.'

'I'm going nowhere until you kill that website,' Mira said.

'You'll do what I damn well tell you,' Mordant said, bundling her up effortlessly and carrying her struggling form over one shoulder down the stairs. They were nearly at the car when they heard a noise coming from the old stables away to the right. Someone was climbing the flint wall. Virgil's shaven head could just be seen edging over the top.

'Virgil, Mira's here!' yelled Ellie.

Mordant opened the boot of the Toyota, tossed the screaming Mira inside as if she was luggage, and slammed it shut. He climbed into the driver's seat, started the engine and sped away down the drive in a spray of gravel. Ellie immediately ran to the large wooden side gate next to the stable and slid the rusty bolt back. 'They've just driven off,' Ellie said as Virgil eased the gate open.

'Fancy a trip in a helicopter then?' he asked. Her face lit up. 'You'll have to run fast,' he said, as he and Ram raced her back to the chopper.

Chapter Thirty

Leonard Lucifer Smith had left Clitheroe a few minutes ago, and was hammering the Transit along the B6478 in the Forest of Bowland as he phoned his son.

'So where are you now?' Lawrence Wall asked.

'Just turning off to Hooksworth Hall. You were up here just a few months ago, weren't you?' he said.

'Yeah, fucking awful weekend,' Wall said. 'I tell you Dad, that woman drove me crazy, but I can't get her out of my head. Do you know what she said to me?'

'What?'

'That when she was thirteen she had promised to marry her old art teacher. So I says "Well, you've got me now so you'd better forget him," and you know what she says then?'

'Surprise me.'

'She says: "Sorry Lawrence, he still owns me heart and soul. You'll never be in his league." '

'So you lamped her one, right?' Lucy said, with enthusiasm.

'Yeah, and how. But it's nothing compared to what I'd like to do to him.'

'Get in the fucking queue, my son,' Lucy chuckled, throwing the van round a tight corner on the rutted track, which was now passing between high drystone walls. He only saw the Toyota at the last moment. It was coming head on, and there was no room to pass. Both vehicles skidded to a halt with inches to spare. 'It's him!' Lucy bellowed. 'I'm gonna fucking 'ave 'im.' He dropped the phone, and taking a deep breath to fight the agony he expected, leaned carefully down into the passenger footwell. He grasped the bag in which the Browning was stowed. By the time he'd eased himself upright, gun in hand, the Toyota was reversing back down the lane. Lucy took a few seconds with his eyes shut to fight a wave of nausea. A reminder of what Mordant had done to him. But he had a minute or two. If he remembered right from all those years ago, there was no other way out for Mordant's car but past him. He grabbed a packet from his pocket, popped out and swallowed another six ibuprofen and washed it down with a swig of Red Bull. Then he banged the Transit into gear and set off after his enemy.

* * *

The helicopter rose sharply over the lake and north towards the forbidding towers of Hooksworth Hall. Virgil could see that a good three quarters of the hall, including the chapel and belvedere, were covered in scaffolding. Beyond the formal garden, much overgrown, the lane went east towards Easington Fell and the main road into Thewick and Clitheroe. Virgil had watched as the Toyota, after almost colliding with the Transit, had reversed back a good half mile then turned right down a narrow walled lane. This southern track was rough, muddy and ran beside tumbledown farm buildings to an ancient stone bridge over the river that provided the estate's southern boundary. Mordant probably didn't know it yet, but the long drover's bridge was damaged. Most of the third arch of the four had fallen into the river, leaving a ten-foot long section of parapet on the right hand, with just a thin margin of stone walkway connected to it.

There was an adjacent hilly sheep pasture beyond the lane that the chopper could land in, so he directed the pilot there. The one unknown was the other vehicle, the Transit van now following Mordant. Virgil thought it was unlikely to be workmen on a Saturday, but too soon to be the police who were just leaving Clitheroe. If they were Mordant's friends, that would make life even tougher.

As the helicopter touched down Virgil, Ram and Ellie leapt out into the field. To their left the river was in spate, caramel swirls topping iron-dark waters laden with branches and other debris. They ran down across the rough boggy tussocks, struggling towards the drystone wall which separated them from the lane. There was a metal gate at the far corner next to the Toyota. They could see Mordant had pulled Mira from the car, and was dragging her towards the bridge. She was struggling with her long white dress in the muddy lane. The Transit had stopped right behind the Toyota. The enormous figure of Leonard Lucifer Smith, who Virgil recognised from the newspaper coverage of his escape, began to emerge, bellowing at Mordant.

Virgil needed to get Mira away from this confrontation, so put on an extra spurt of speed. He vaulted the gate easily, and sprinted past the Toyota onto the bridge. Mordant had already reached the third arch, and was dangling a screaming, struggling Mira over the edge, both her slender wrists grasped in one hand. Virgil recognised a huge strength in that grip.

Mordant faced him now. 'Any closer and I'm going to let her drop.'

Virgil paused, his eye drawn to the drop, twenty feet onto a damaged and jagged stone pier, and then another ten into the dark racing waters. Mira was yelling and kicking out desperately trying to get some kind of foothold on the edge of the bridge, but the tangled train on her mud-spattered dress stopped her feet getting any purchase.

The gigantic figure of Lucy walked slowly level on Virgil's right. In his peripheral vision he saw the gun, raised and pointed at Mordant. 'Don't be an idiot!' Virgil yelled and leapt for the weapon. But Lucy's massive left forearm blocked him, and swept back into his throat like a falling tree, flinging him against the left-hand parapet as if he weighed nothing.

Virgil got to his feet just in time to see Lucy open fire. Blood flowered like a rose across Mordant's shoulder. He let go of Mira, who screamed as she fell, kicking sideways against the stone pier. She just cleared the jagged stonework and tumbled into the water. Virgil ditched his jacket, leapt onto the parapet and dived thirty feet into the turbulent river. The cold impact of the water was like a hammer blow, and as he surfaced he saw the billow of Mira's dress ten yards ahead of him, meshed with twigs and heading downstream, like the plumage of some twisted swan. He ducked a snagging branch, then drove out hard with a fluid front crawl towards her. The gurgling water sucked on them both greedily, a thousand insistent fingers interwoven with Mira's voluminous dress, tugging powerfully. She reached out for him, and cried his name, as the water turned them both over, dragging them downstream. Finally he caught her arm, and as they were drawn past a riverside willow, grabbed overhead at a low branch.

Of the next five minutes of icy struggle Virgil had little memory until strong hands pulled him ashore and wrapped him in an exposure blanket. His bleach burns were throbbing, and his vision fuzzy, but he was still aware of blue lights, high visibility jackets, and the sound of radios. 'Where's Mira?' was his first question.

Male voices reassured him that she was fine, thanks to him, and in an ambulance. 'She wants to see you.'

Virgil was helped to his feet, and the first person he recognised was Ellie, who rushed up to hug him. 'Oh, you're so wet and cold!' she said. 'Come on, get in the warm.'

He was led to an ambulance, inside which Mira was sitting wrapped in a blanket, with a muddy face, cut lip and scarecrow hair. She was holding a hot drink. 'I was an idiot, Virgil, for thinking I could do it alone.' She smiled, and passed him the mug. 'Have some soup.'

The back door of the ambulance opened and Ram poked his head in. 'How are you doing?' he asked Virgil. 'And thank you for saving her.' The pulsing clatter of a second helicopter arriving drowned out the rest of his gratitude, but it showed clearly on his face.

Ellie joined them, bringing a fresh flask of soup, courtesy of the Fire Brigade. 'The cops have recaptured that huge bloke now,' she said. 'Whoa, he's very scary.'

'Ah, that's Lucy,' Virgil said. 'But what about Mordant? I saw he got shot.'

'He still managed to kick the Lucy guy somewhere low and nasty which made him fall over,' Ellie said. 'But Lucy still had the gun so Mordant ran away, trying to balance on the parapet. He'd nearly made it, but he got shot again, and fell onto the stones and smashed his head. The air ambulance is here, but I heard one of the policemen say he'll be lucky to survive.'

'I have to go to him,' Mira said, getting up. Two female paramedics outside the ambulance seemed surprised to see her stride out, bare feet on the track, dressed only in a blanket, but she brushed off their requests to return to the warm. Virgil followed, squelching along in his socks. Ellie went with them, completing what looked like a muddy refugee family. They passed through a gate into the paddock where the air ambulance had landed, a hundred yards away. Beside it was a yellow spinal board with someone on it, being tended by three paramedics.

'I want to say goodbye,' Mira said as she ran up. Mordant's face was flecked with blood, a huge bruise showing from beneath a dressing on his temple.

'He's barely conscious,' said a helmeted paramedic. 'We have to get him off quickly to have any chance.' Another member of the crew helped lift up the spinal board into the chopper.

'Will, it's me,' she said, reaching for his hand. His eyes flickered open for a moment, and he smiled and said something, inaudible in the roar of the rotors. Mira pressed her ear to his face, and Virgil saw her nod and smile. Eased away from him by the crew, Mira stood back and then shouted into the gathering roar of the engines, as the doors were closed and the crew climbed in: 'Will, I won't forget what you did for me all those years ago.'

* * *

After the helicopter became a dot in the sky Ellie walked up to her. 'Mira? You know he said you killed some girls. You didn't, did you?'

'I caused their deaths, but it was all a terrible accident. I didn't really mean to.'

'Why, what happened?

'I was bullied, Ellie. Bullied mercilessly and horribly because I was new at the school, and had the wrong accent. Sometimes I wanted to kill myself.'

'What did you do to them?'

'It was on a school trip to Venice. There were three of them. I'll never forget them. The leader was Amber Tompkins. She was blonde, sporty and popular, and had a seventeen-year-old boyfriend with a car. Her number two was Keeley Corcoran. She was pale, skinny, and lived in a caravan with her mum and three tough brothers. She used to delight in inflicting agonising Chinese burns, which she did on my first day at the school. But the worst was Destiny Simpson. She was clever and sly, and thought up all their cruellest ideas. On the first day in Venice, Keeley emptied my suitcase down the stairs of the hotel. But it was Destiny who stole my phone and texted a declaration of love to the best-looking boy in the class. The first I knew about it was when his girlfriend, the captain of the netball team, slagged me off in front of everyone while all the boys laughed. It was horrible. I begged Destiny to give me my phone back, but she said I had to buy it back with a bottle of Bacardi.

I went to see Mr Peirce, the only ally I could rely on. I wagged off a trip to the Doge's Palace, having made myself sick earlier, and instead took the vaporetto to Murano and found his studio. Fortunately he was there, all scruffy, and flecked with paint. I poured my heart out to him about everything that had happened to me and then: "They're so horrible, I'd just like to shoot them all." He laughed, and then said it wasn't a great idea, "But you could scare them into giving your phone back." He went to a drawer and pulled out a small gun.

"Is it real?" I asked. He nodded. "But why have you got it?" I asked.

"I have enemies. That's why you must never tell anyone I'm here, or mention my name." He waved away all my other questions. "Look, let's concentrate on those annoying girls. They won't believe you have a real weapon, so I'm going to load it with blanks." He slid some bits on the pistol, emptied out the real bullets and stuffed them in his pocket, and then dug out a

408

cardboard box from a locked drawer, picked out a handful of cartridges from it and loaded the gun. "These sound just like the real thing. They are very loud, and there is a flash and the smell of smoke. It's convincing but quite harmless. Fire it in the air, only once otherwise you might attract attention." He showed me how to hold and aim the weapon.'

'So you pretended you would shoot the girls?' asked Ellie. Virgil listened silently, realising that the young girl's innocent questions were managing to tease out the detailed truth from Mira where he had failed.

'That was the idea. Mr Peirce said I needed to lure them to a quiet place where no one would see or hear what I was doing. He came back with me on the boat, and showed me a series of derelict boatsheds on a rotting wharf at Calle de la Beccarrie near the railway bridge. It wasn't far from our grotty hotel, but no tourist ever went there. He had given me a half-full bottle of some local liquor called Strega, which was the lure to get them there. When he'd finished showing me what to do, I knew that I'd never have any trouble from them again. I saw Keeley at dinner time, and told her to get them all to meet me at the boatshed at ten o'clock. I told her how to get there, and said I had three bottles of Bacardi.'

'But you lied!' Ellie said, seemingly shocked.

'They came along early, and I waited inside in the darkness as Mr Peirce had suggested. I had a hurricane lamp he had lent me, and left it by the bottle of Strega. I stepped out of the shadows and closed the door behind them, as Amber lifted the bottle. "What's this shit? Where's the Bacardi?" Keeley opened the bottle, took a swig and spat it out. "It's disgusting, just like you. You can forget getting your phone back."

Destiny waved the phone tauntingly. Only then did I pull the gun out. For a second they just stared, until I fired. Even though I knew it would be loud, I was amazed by the noise and the recoil. Destiny dropped the phone, and they all screamed and ran from me further into the boat yard. There was a doorway into an outdoor inspection dock, and they ran through. It was a dead end, surrounded by a high fence with barbed wire on top, but that wasn't obvious. They ran along a wooden inspection walkway which ran around the inner edge of the dock, but it was only a few greasy planks suspended by ropes and they overbalanced it. They all fell into the water. I laughed at first, but then realised the inspection dock was deep, and the water was covered with a thick layer of oil and rubbish. They begged for help, so I tried to get them out with a metal pole.'

'Didn't it work?'

'No, they were coated with oil and grease they couldn't get a grip, and I wasn't strong enough to help them out without falling in myself. I could see that they were drowning, but didn't know what to do, so I rang Mr Peirce at his studio. By the time he arrived they had stopped moving.'

'Couldn't he help?' Ellie asked.

'No. It was too late. He asked me who knew that I was coming here, and I said no one. Then he persuaded me of something that I regret to this day. He said I should just go back and pretend to know nothing about it. He gave me some tablets to keep me calm. Then he said he would retrieve the bodies, and get rid of all the phones including mine, to stop them being traced. He promised to do his damnedest to make sure the story never got out. He said he didn't want me to ruin my life with this.'

'That was nice of him,' Ellie said.

Virgil grunted his disagreement and looked away.

Mira continued. 'It was, Ellie, but he really thought that if the bodies disappeared completely no one would ever know. He was wrong, but it seemed he never said a word about my involvement in all the years in prison and then Broadmoor. In fact he said nothing at all, through all the interrogations. When I asked him, just a few days ago, he said that it was obvious that blaming me wouldn't help him. He supplied the gun. He would be seen as responsible for the panic which led to their deaths, even though only blanks were fired.'

'He must have really loved you,' Ellie said.

'In his own way, yes. But he wanted a possession, not a relationship. I was the prize in the contract we made that night, and sealed in blood. In exactly ten years time, I was to go back to him. We were destined to be together, he said: "and by then you will be beautiful." I was happy to agree. I would have married him there and then if I could, I was so smitten.'

'But you're not now, are you,' Ellie asked. 'So why go through with it?'

'When he got tired of waiting to hear from me, he began with persuasion, then blackmail. He wrote to the fan mail address at Stardust. I didn't get most of the messages, but in one I did he said he had incriminating videos of me on my old phone, which he had hidden but never thrown out. They included them taunting me on my own phone, and the video of the shot fired in the warehouse. He gave me a website address with a countdown on it, which he said would release the videos to the press and police, proving I was involved in their deaths and had lied about not being there. I had no idea how bad they might be, but didn't see that I had a choice.'

'Why didn't you tell me any of this?' Virgil asked. 'I could have helped.'

Mira shrugged. 'I'd mentally buried the whole episode. I couldn't bear to dig it up.'

Mira and Virgil checked into a local hotel to warm up, and the police took statements. Ellie was taken in hand by a child support officer and a social worker, but Virgil made sure the police knew how helpful she had been. It was nine o'clock when Virgil asked what it was that Mordant had whispered to Mira as he was being put in the helicopter.

'He told me that he'd already stopped the website, and deleted the videos. He'd done it as soon as he saw me arrive at Toddington Services, once he'd seen that I was ready to fulfil my side of the bargain.'

* * *

The near death of Mira Roskova at the hands of a notorious psychopath was the story of the year for Britain's tabloid press. It had everything from espionage to murder, a sporting hero and a femme fatale. The Crown Prosecution Service after a long delay declined to reopen the cases of the deaths of Amber Tompkins, Keeley Corcoran and Destiny Simpson. Whether Mira had been there at the time or not, she was only a child. Mordant's overall culpability didn't seem in doubt in view of his subsequent murders of Kelly Hopkins and Baroness Earl. For the authorities it tied everything up neatly, and left no questions over the justice of having incarcerated Mordant to begin with. The only charge against Mira was taking a motor vehicle, for which she was given a caution.

The full story of Mordant, one of Britain's most successful post-Cold War spies, was finally told in the broadsheets. Even up until six months ago, he had been visited regularly by Godfrey Allen, who was a senior MI6 official, rather than the psychiatrist he claimed to be. Allen was always keen to run new information received from agents in Russia and Ukraine against the facts Mordant had long ago memorised about their aged nuclear missile systems. They were never sure he had disclosed quite everything. After the exposure, Allen quickly took retirement. He is expected to resurface in the House of Lords within a year or two.

For Virgil Bliss, personal protection work came to an end. He now works for a bank security company, and finds the anonymity reassuring after his public role with Mira. He visits Kelly Hopkins' grave in North London on the anniversary of her death each year, and has become good friends with her parents and brother. He always wondered about what might have been. For him, the idea of beauty is forever tarnished.

Leonard Lucifer Smith has recently been moved to a low secure unit, and may well be released within a year. He no longer hears voices, and always takes his medication. He walks with a stick, and has expressed interest in opening a dog rescue centre.

Lawrence Wall recovered, but never quite made up his fitness. No one was ever brought to book for the attempted hit on him, but the police assumed Mordant had arranged it. This was reinforced when a former patient at Broadmoor, too terrified of Mordant to speak out until after his death, anonymously told the *Guardian* that it was he who had been bribed by Mordant to spike Lucifer Smith's drink with Rohypnol. He had then led the stupefied patient back to the room where Mordant was waiting. Mordant injected Lucy with the potent sedative Dipravan, stolen for him by Dawn Evans, but not before Lucy had blurted out that his son was an England footballer, and would one day get him out of Broadmoor. Lucy had claimed Lawrence as his son before, and was never believed because no one ever visited him. So when Mordant laughed, Lucy retrieved a letter from under his mattress that proved it, and even gave Wall's home address.

Wall ended up as a manager running a so-so League Two side in the north. The world now knows that he is the son of a notorious psychiatric patient. After all the years in which he hadn't dare visit his own father in Broadmoor, the media reaction to the news has been surprisingly sympathetic. Even after everything he heard about Mira, he still regrets his quick temper and lack of finesse, letting the world's most beautiful woman slip through his fingers.

Ram Dipani has fewer regrets. At the insistence of his mother, he married the woman from Hyderabad. He never spoke to Mira again.

Ulan Kulchuk quickly bought up most of Mordant's artwork, knowing that it would increase rapidly in value now the supply had dried up. But something even scarcer eluded him. His marriage proposal to Mira was quickly but politely rejected.

Dr Richard Lamb retired from his job at Broadmoor Hospital in the wake of a critical report by the Care Quality Commission. He bitterly regrets his own failings, particularly in the training and supervision of Dawn Evans. He feels partially responsible for her suicide.

Bishop Harry Fielding too is full of regrets. For being taken in by Mordant, for believing that Ulan Kulchuk was interested in the cause of mental health reform when in fact he just wanted Mordant's paintings, and most of all for making the Broadmoor connection that would lead to the death of his friend and confidante Baroness Suzannah Earl.

Ellie McAllister has signed up as a catalogue model for an online retailer. But she hopes to eventually work for Diane Glassman at Pinnacle.

Stardust Brands managed to finesse Mira's new notoriety. The Suressence contract fell through, but thanks to Jonesy Tolling's hard work she secured an equally lucrative one producing her own range of cosmetics and fashions for a luxury brand in Milan under the name Mira Mira. She has moved to New York, and now sports a much more vampish image, with raven hair and dark clothes. She has released a few songs to absolutely no critical acclaim, and is talked about as a future Bond girl. Producers have now been forced to reconsider the opinion they once had that she couldn't act.

Epilogue

It was almost a year later when Virgil got a call from Mira's old friend Natasha. Once he heard what she'd discovered, he drove straight over to see her. There in the flat of her late mother, Natasha showed Virgil a mobile phone that had finally been returned to her by the police. It had been found amongst Mordant's luggage at Hooksworth Hall, and the accompanying police letter said it was her mother's. Natasha knew it wasn't. Someone had screwed up. It was an old Nokia, and had 'Lydia' scratched faintly into the plastic. Because there had been no prosecution in the end, and no reason to examine the phones, Virgil wasn't surprised the police had mixed up the ownership.

'Look at this,' said Natasha. She tapped the screen and showed it to Virgil.

There was a five-second video selfie of three giggling teenage girls, with their faces pressed together. 'Hello hideous Lydia, everyone hates you,' said the middle one, blonde and pretty. They all stuck their tongues out.

The next video briefly showed Lydia turning the camera on herself against a dark echoing warehouse-type background. Here was the thirteen-year-old that Virgil had never quite been able to picture. The roots of Mira's beauty were already there: the high cheekbones, that slender neck, those huge eyes. The braces on her teeth, the cheap spectacles, even the pimples, which were only partially covered by makeup, were just a temporary mask.

'I just have to record this, my moment of triumph,' she said, waving a black pistol in front of the lens. She turned the phone at two girls, bound and gagged with silvery duct tape and lying face down on the floor. A third, gagged and with tied ankles, was kneeling behind them. 'Right Amber, more tape around Destiny's ankles, and then put a loop or two around her eyes,' Lydia commanded. 'Quickly now, or you'll get a bullet from this.' She pressed the gun to the back of the girl's trembling head as she shrieked out another length of tape, and leant over Destiny's immobile form. The video ended with Lydia saying: 'Back soon!'

The final video panned slowly along a standing row of three bound, gagged and blindfolded girls. Amber was in the centre a head taller than the others. The barrel of the gun was just visible at the bottom of the image. 'Now come with me,' Lydia said, as if to an imaginary viewer, taking the phone forward beyond the girls and pointing it towards the floor. There, in the phone's harsh light was the edge of the concrete flooring and beyond the lip a two metre drop to oily, rubbish-strewn water. 'Nice down there, isn't it?' she giggled.

Lydia walked back, behind the girls, and made her way to the skinny figure on the far left. 'Goodbye Keeley!' she said, and shoved the girl over the edge. Even as she hit the water with a splash, Lydia yelled 'Goodbye Destiny, you bitch,' and threw the second girl over. Amber dropped to the floor, and attempted to roll away from the edge. At this point Lydia dropped the phone, and the only view was of a broken skylight. But there were sounds of struggle, and finally a loud splash, followed by the rhythmic slap of water on wood.

'Oh come on Amber, you can do better than that! I thought you were the best swimmer in the school.' A few moments later a breathless Lydia picked up the phone and continued her monologue. 'Thank you all for watching today this episode in the justified punishment of bullies.' Lydia giggled. 'I'd like to thank this Venice boatyard for leaving behind plenty of gaffer tape, and my favourite man for the loan of a gun. That's all for tonight!'

The video ended, and Natasha looked up at Virgil. There were no more on the phone. 'I can't believe it. I thought I knew her, but I hadn't a clue.'

'So much for it being an accident,' Virgil said. 'She lied to me, she lied to you, to everyone. Even to little Ellie. No wonder she couldn't risk letting these videos get out.'

'What should we do?' Natasha asked.

Virgil took the phone, and once again absorbed the graphic images of a young murderess, now a famous woman whom millions adored. He mulled over the efforts of Jonesy, Thad and Portia to build a pristine and innocent brand on such foundations. 'Mirror, Mirror on the wall,' he murmured. 'Who is the fairest of them all?'

He offered the phone to Natasha, and said: 'She's your friend.'

Natasha recoiled, shaking her head, as if the phone was poisoned.

Virgil shrugged, scrutinised the screen, and the video list on it. He weighed up justice and loyalty, both important to who he was.

Then he hit delete.

Delete.

Delete.

Crocodile Tears

I hope you have enjoyed *Mirror Mirror*. If you would like to visit my website **www.nicklouth.com** you can also download a free, previously unpublished short story called *Crocodile Tears*:

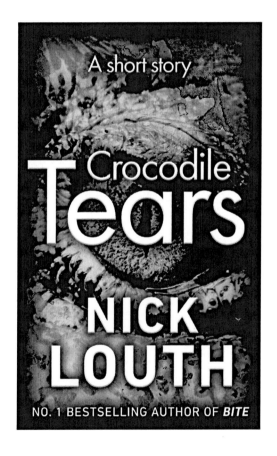

Acknowledgements

This book would not have been possible without the help of a number of experts. Gail Dymoke gave me invaluable insight into the workings of the secure psychiatric hospital system, and was very generous in her time correcting my many misunderstandings in this complex area. I'd like to thank Leon Hamilton of branding group SMC Europe for his help navigating the world of celebrity and endorsements. Simon Chambers, Paula Karaiskos and their colleagues at Storm Model Agency were kind enough to give me an insight into their world. Kim Booth ably helped with police procedural aspects. Any mistakes remaining are mine alone. I'd particularly like to thank the team at Harriman House, whose unflappable professionalism is unmatched. My reader's panel, particularly Sara Wescott, Cheryl Cullingford, Tracey Ruddock and Kate Mitchell, were very helpful in giving me an early reaction to the broad scope of the book. Above all, my wife Louise, always my first reader, provided invaluable insight, and to her this book is once again dedicated.

I would also like to thank readers of my previous books who have made detailed comments on Amazon, Goodreads and elsewhere. Please keep doing it! Feedback is enormously important to authors – we need to know if we have too many characters, if plotlines are confusing or there are too many flashbacks, just as much as we enjoy the praise. I read every single review of my work, and I do take notice of every detail you mention. So please, please, now you have finished this book take just a few moments to leave a review.

Lightning Source UK Ltd.
Milton Keynes UK
UKOW02f1201120816

280563UK00001B/3/P